Mattias Berg

THE CARRIER

Translated from the Swedish by
George Goulding

MACLEHOSE PRESS
QUERCUS · LONDON

First published in the Swedish language as *Dödens triumf*
by Natur & Kultur, Stockholm, in 2016
First published in Great Britain in 2019 by

MacLehose Press
an imprint of Quercus Publishing Ltd
Carmelite House
50 Victoria Embankment
London EC4Y 0DZ

An Hachette UK Company

A CIP catalogue record for this book is available
from the British Library.

ISBN (HB) 9780857057907
ISBN (TPB) 9780857057891
ISBN (Ebook) 9780857057884

10 9 8 7 6 5 4 3 2 1

Designed and typeset in Minion by Libanus Press, Marlborough
Printed and bound in Great Britain by Clays Ltd, Elcograf S.p.A.

"The end of war is peace or victory. But to the question, what is the end of peace, there is no answer."

HANNAH ARENDT, *On Violence*

FOR
LINDA, VERA
and GRETA

April 2013:

In an unprecedented move, a U.S. Air Force commander stripped 17 of his officers of their authority to control and launch nuclear missiles.

The officers, based in Minot, North Dakota, did poorly in an inspection. They were ordered to undergo 60 to 90 days of intensive refresher training.

August 2013:

A missile unit at Malmstrom Air Force Base failed a safety and security inspection "after making tactical-level errors—not related to command and control of nuclear weapons," the Air Force Global Strike Command said.

The 341st Missile Wing operates about 150 of the 450 Minuteman III nuclear-tipped intercontinental ballistic missiles in the U.S. forces, according to an Air Force statement.

October 2013:

A military officer with high-level responsibility for the country's nuclear arsenal lost his job.

He was formally relieved of his duties as deputy chief of U.S. Strategic Command. A military official said his demotion was connected to allegations that he used counterfeit gambling chips at a casino.

October 2013:

Just days later, a U.S. general who oversaw nuclear weapons was relieved of his duties after he boozed, fraternized with "hot women" and disrespected his hosts during an official visit to Russia, Air Force officials said.

The General led the 20th Air Force, responsible for three nuclear wings.

According to an Air Force Inspector General report, he bragged loudly about his position as commander of a nuclear force during a layover in Switzerland, saying he "saves the world from war every day."

January 2014:

At the Montana base, 34 Air Force officers entrusted with maintaining nuclear missiles are accused of cheating or turning a blind eye to cheating on a competency test.

From C.N.N.'s "Nuclear Scandals Timeline", January 2014

KANSAS CITY, M.O.—A sprawling new plant here in a former soybean field makes the mechanical guts of America's atomic warheads. Bigger than the Pentagon, full of futuristic gear and thousands of workers, the plant, inaugurated last month, modernizes the ageing weapons that the United States can fire from missiles, bombers and submarines.

It is part of a nationwide wave of atomic revitalization that includes plans for a new generation of weapon carriers. A recent federal study put the collective price tag, over the next three decades, at up to a trillion dollars.

This expansion comes under a president who campaigned for 'a nuclear-free world' and made disarmament a main goal of American defense policy.

From the New York Times, *September 2014*

1

SNAP

September 2013
Stockholm

1.01

I had been so very close to the President. Never more than a few feet away during official duties, always with my briefcase prepared. Even when he accepted the Nobel Peace Prize. When he gave that damned speech about a world without nuclear weapons.

You must understand. But you won't.

How we had been consumed, taken in, seduced yet again by the fire. Not so much through our guilt as our innocence. My own diabolical innocence.

We called it "The Nuclear Football", as if it was some kind of game. And talked about "Pressing the Button", but there was neither a button nor anyone who did any actual pressing. To me it was more like an occult ceremony, a magical-technological transformation trick. Carrying out a series of procedures in the correct sequence, with the help of the codes, to render insecure the one thing in our entire civilization that should be the most secure of all.

The contents of the briefcase had been so highly classified that few apart from us knew about them. From the start there were only four primitive objects there. The Black Book with every possible operational option for retaliation or attack; a folder listing the underground bases to which the President could be taken at times of maximum alert; a note summarizing the structure of our nuclear weapons system. And then the square plastic counter with the codes the President was to use when identifying himself to Centcom. We called it "the biscuit".

During the Cold War, it was more or less understandable. As soon as the briefcase was opened a signal was transmitted to Centcom. After the President had used "the biscuit" to confirm his identity, he and the Carrier of the briefcase faced a number of choices according to the war plan then in place. The last step was for Centcom to follow the President's order and carry out the launch itself.

But things had become complicated with the developing wizardry of digital technology, as well as our own much-altered war plan. We were assured that the guiding principle was still "Always-Never". The nuclear weapons should *always* be ready for launch within half an hour, but *never* capable of being dispatched in error.

Yet over the last decade the boundaries had been extended with each new technological advance. Once both circuits and micro-processors had become small enough, it was possible to integrate parts of the detonation mechanism into the briefcase itself. Centcom now seemed more or less superfluous. Everything merged into a single whole. The difference between "always" and "never" began to dissolve. In the end it became impossible, even for me, to distinguish between safety measures and launch procedures.

That is when the thought of escape came to me.

1.02

Our gigantic sortie took off into a clear blue morning sky, like a lumbering bumblebee defying gravity. As usual, our first leg was to Andrews Air Force Base—and from there we went on over the Atlantic. We were more than seven hundred people, an entourage worthy of the Sun King himself three centuries ago. Air Force One, five other more or less identical Boeings, twenty-nine cargo planes, forty cars, 250 security staff, three hundred advisors and members of the White House press corps, two more Cadillacs.

And the Nurse was sitting so close. Monitoring my every movement.

I was saddled with her from the start of our journey, after I had collapsed in the culverts under the air base as our aircraft was being refueled. Which was the only way I could interpret the last message from Alpha: "CREATE MORE TIME. PLAY SICK!" It was naïve to imagine that my own little moment of weakness would have any effect whatsoever on our vast convoy. That it would be able to hold up the immense machinery involved in a state visit.

Yet in my overheated imagination, right there and then, I believed it. So I let myself fall headlong into the cement tunnel leading out to the helipad. Screwed my eyes shut, while some of the medical orderlies carried me into the examination room.

It is easy to believe that one is irreplaceable. If anyone, then me, the Carrier of the briefcase, the man with the world's most critical assignment. Before my little collapse, I had no idea about our backup plan either. But as the doctor was talking to our logistics people, I found out that even I would be swapped for a substitute.

From the outside, nobody is meant to be able to tell whether the helicopter is, in fact, Marine One, with the President and myself on board, or just another of all our look-alike helicopters. If the airplane is Air Force One out of the many in our armada. From whichever airport we touch down at, we are always transported behind smoked glass in Cadillac One, also known as "The Beast", with a five-inch-thick floor of reinforced armor. With another limousine, identical from the outside, traveling just in front or just behind.

But in these times of sweeping cosmetic change, of doubles and false identities, no-one is irreplaceable.

And because I suddenly became aware that somebody else in the Team would take my place, I had to blame it on a passing fever. When my preliminary readings turned out to be in perfect order, I was given clearance to travel with the Team. I had no earlier mark on my record, no contrary indication, not from all those years. But I was forced to accept the Nurse as a personal escort. For safety's sake, as they put it.

As she sat down next to me in the helicopter, in the row behind the President and the First Lady, I could not help feeling that this was meant to be. That the Nurse, in one way or another, was part of the plan.

The state visit to Stockholm was mysterious, written into the President's calendar at the last moment. In strict terms, it could only be referred to as an "official visit", since there had been no invitation from Sweden's head of state. The only plausible reason for traveling to this particular corner of the world was that our government wanted to make a diplomatic point to Russia, the country we were scheduled to visit. If Edward Snowden had not just been granted asylum there.

Our security people had not been happy about these late changes. Priority in Stockholm would be given to external security and would tick all the right boxes despite the short notice. The advance party had been sent out as soon as the date was fixed. But what was called "internal security" was an altogether more complex matter.

In the weeks before our departure, we were warned to increase our vigilance. There were rumors about moles within the organization. In the Team we kept a close eye on each other, watched every move. And on this occasion we were not given our final instructions until on board Air Force One—and only after we had taken off and could no longer communicate with anybody who did not have clearance.

Our team consisted of four special security agents, not counting Edelweiss. He was our operational boss and the one giving our daily briefings. He was the one the rest of us followed, admired, respected—but above all feared. His body was monumental. Like an entire foreign planet with folds and pockets, craters, deep secrets. He would stroke his chins as he pondered one of our questions. Then deliver the answer with his surprisingly soft, clear voice: often saying things that no-one else would even think of Still less say out loud.

We were told that it was Edelweiss who had hand-picked each of us on the basis of our specialist skills, in the desperate days following 9/11, when all other available structures had failed.

We also gathered that he had been given a free hand. That often requires a filter, a layer which both empowers and conceals, relieves the decision-makers of responsibility for their decisions. Sometimes numerous, almost invisible sheets: like a vast millefeuille in which the bottom level always protects the upper one, complex sequences of knowledge and not knowing, none of which can do without the other.

In our own cases, camouflage was the beginning and the end. It was referred to as a "military approach to precautionary security measures". After our training in the sealed wing at West Point—which continued in parallel with our university education, allowing us to practice our abilities to lead double lives and to deceive—we started putting our new-found skills to use. For the most part, I was sent out on short solo missions of increasing ardor. At first small, and then bigger sabotage operations, designed to ensure that our country should not be exposed to the same thing, resolving or setting off almost invisible conflicts in countries which many people had never heard of, unleashing domestic political turmoil elsewhere in the world.

In my other life, I completed my doctoral thesis in moral philosophy. Interminable sessions with my mesmerizing supervisor went on throughout the remainder of the 1980s and all through the 1990s, in parallel with my special duties in the security world. I took my doctorate in September 2001, five days before the attacks on the World Trade Center.

Some weeks after that, on November 4, we were brought together in a windowless lecture hall two stories below ground. Like silhouettes, shadows, ghosts from earlier times: some of us maybe even on the same special forces training course at West Point. But we had all been through cosmetic surgery at least once since then. I did not recognize anyone in this select group.

And not one of us understood the implications of our having been brought together. We had answered the encrypted summons, from which could be gleaned that the formation of the Team would be the beginning of our new life and the end of the old. An invitation which we had felt unable to resist.

There were more of us than I would have expected for what had to be a very special assignment. That meant that the core would be smaller—and everything around it much bigger. The Team itself might not consist of more than eight to ten people, and the rest would make up the support functions.

It became apparent that the Team—Edelweiss called us "NUCLEUS", as in the center of a cell or atom—would consist of six chosen ones, including himself and someone unknown, who went by the name Alpha.

And after more than a day's wait without food or drink, no doubt intended to make us more malleable from the start, Edelweiss appeared. That enigmatic figure with his enormous silhouette. Floating and formless, like an apparition in the ill-lit room. He who had been my main teacher at West Point, maybe for the others too, and who would be in charge of our lives.

20

Edelweiss began with the official version. The vague formulation that defined the Team's place in our new war plan, transformed by the shock-waves from 9/11: "A small, mobile unit acting as a separate protection squad in times of peace, side by side with the President's own command, and which in case of crisis and war can operate with full autonomy."

Then the unofficial version. Edelweiss had been given a free hand to create something new. A phoenix from the ashes of the World Trade Center, from the ruins of our old security system, from what in every way was a "Ground Zero". Now that all our existing structures—the security services, the surveillance system, our counter-terrorism efforts—had proved to be inadequate.

His idea was that our team should be the spider in the web. Or rather, both web and spider. An amorphous structure binding together all the existing functions: the C.I.A., the F.B.I., the N.S.A., the Secret Service . . . But which could also operate in the gaps between them.

Edelweiss told us that he had no idea who had given him the task. He only knew that someone using the pseudonym Alpha had written him credible e-mails, with sufficient encryption in place to have convinced him that the orders came from the very top. There was no doubt one more layer or filter between Alpha and the President, but perhaps no more than one. And that layer, in turn, must have been given a free hand by the President.

Our goal seemed simple. Edelweiss' orders were expressed in broad terms, and the person who had given them did not want to know the details of their execution. Everything had one focus: stop something like this from happening again, anything like a hostile airplane flying into the World Trade Center in broad daylight. The idea was for us to take all necessary preventive measures outside the scope of conventional intelligence work. The end would justify the means.

What he described in the ensuing three or four hours—with Edelweiss, time in some way acquired another consistency—was at first sight a defensive assignment. Our team should stay close to the President and his own security detail during state visits and other official public duties. Should become a sort of floating security layer, flexible and adaptable, ready for *any conceivable situation*.

In short, it was meant to be what one now calls "hybrid warfare". To combat hidden sabotage, digital attacks, advanced psychological warfare, political destabilization, ever more ingenious assaults on our infrastructure. And be able to strike back—using the same weapons.

In the case of serious crisis, the strategy was turned on its head. The Team could then be transformed into a raw strike force, focused on the enemy's weakest points, with methods at least as unthinkable as their own. Its nature could be altered, as Edelweiss expressed it in one of his elaborate yet precise metaphors, in the same way that an amphibious vehicle operates both on land and water.

When the global security threat stood at its highest level—LILAC—reserved for the one thing that could destroy the world at a few minutes notice: a nuclear threat from another state or from terrorists—the President himself should be placed under protection. Until the threat was neutralized, the Team would take over covert command of the whole military apparatus. Including the nuclear weapons system.

"You have to be ready for every conceivable attack on the country's security. And more than that—for every inconceivable one too," Edelweiss said.

"First and foremost, this requires our imaginations to be greater than the enemy's. Which is what we will have to work on, our creative ability, our impulsive intelligence. Each one of you is an exceptional agent already. But once we've been through this together, you should see yourselves more as artists."

He ran his hand over his chins.

"But what distinguishes our assignment is that it's to do with nuclear weapons. Things which you can't compare with anything else throughout military or even human history, because by their nature they were so far outside our experience. The only meaningful difference between them and other fantasies, say the lightsabers in 'Star Wars' or Superman's X-ray vision, is that nuclear weapons became reality."

Another pause for effect, as Edelweiss peered around him in the half darkness.

"There has never yet been a full-scale war using battlefield nuclear weapons. Nobody knows how that might affect us, how we would all turn out in a situation like that. That's also what we are going to explore together, my little lambs, under more or less controlled conditions."

The extent of our authority under those conditions seemed astonishing, even to me. The briefcase would of course be the jewel in the piece. Our innermost and outermost secret, our last resort, the chained beast. First, the thing we were most of all tasked to protect, then our ultimate offensive weapon.

"The most important object in the world," Edelweiss called it— before handing it to me at the end of that first meeting. With this small gesture turning me into both savior and destroyer. The center not just of the Team, his NUCLEUS, but of the universe.

From that point on he called me the Carrier. As if it were some sort of virus.

Around me were the few others: at a respectful yet inquisitive distance. Zafirah, who tried to persuade me of the blessings of ultra-violence. Her interest in everything that had sufficient striking power, as she put it, was pathological. According to her own account, it had started with heavyweight boxing, the never-ending shows night after night with her father in Bahrain, and had then just escalated. Martial arts, M.M.A., military close combat. She was the one whom Edelweiss always sent into the thick of things during training. Often alone and unarmed against a number of opponents.

To see her at a distance, that compact little woman with her shimmering headscarves, one could never guess what Zafirah was capable of. What she and I had done together to the Taliban in Afghanistan and Iraq, deep inside hostile territory. That is how it is with genuine specialist skills. There is no need to advertise them—until there is no alternative.

Apart from us two, the Team's operational core consisted only of two identical security guards, whom we alternately called Kurt and John. They looked after everything to do with personal protection, both in theory and in practice, as well as most of our technical equipment. Always surrounding me, of course, bedding in the Carrier with their mighty bodies, exuding latent violence. Committed to laying down their lives for me at any moment. Or rather for the briefcase.

Behind the scenes, however, the apparatus was larger. All of those we never or seldom got to see: strategists, observers, technicians, psychologists, medical staff and other support functions. And in addition doubles, decoys and substitutes. These strange functionaries who together make up the security world's extras.

We were not permitted to mix with any others in NUCLEUS outside work. We were instead encouraged to refine our civilian identities, to lead a full double life, the preference was for a family. Edelweiss spoke about having been inspired by none other than Kim Philby. He said we would increase our operative capability, keep on our toes, be ever ready, by forever manipulating our surroundings in that way. Besides, not being stationed together would reduce our exposure to elimination at a single stroke.

So after almost twelve years I still knew nothing about the others in their civilian lives: had no knowledge of their "real" or "alternate" existences, no idea who they were, these camouflaged people handpicked for our camouflaged assignments. Not Edelweiss, nor Zafirah, John or Kurt.

And least of all Alpha.

None of us knew who or what that was, even whether man

or machine, some sort of digital function. Edelweiss himself after all these years claimed that he had no idea. That he got his orders from this mysterious signature in the form of double-encrypted messages on his screen: protection assignments, transfers, the scope for our next training scenario. Nothing had persuaded him that Alpha was a living individual. Many of our training maneuvers also seemed so haphazard, in terms of both objective and significance, that they might as well have been generated at random.

Yet it was the training which tested and hardened our team, fused us together like glass in the heat of the moment, transformed us into artists. Early on in our history we took part in two regular military invasions. Afghanistan was first—November 13, 2001, nine days after we had met in that windowless headquarters below ground—and then came Iraq, on March 20, 2003.

But it was in situations during training that we could be confronted with the most extreme challenges. The sorts of thing that we had been created for.

Not least a simulated full-scale nuclear attack based on our strategy document "Global Strike and Deterrence". The gravest threat to the survival not only of the nation but of the whole world, the extinction of mankind, Ragnarök. The sort of moment in history which a paleontologist alone can grasp.

And so now we were sitting there at the walnut table in the conference room inside Air Force One, going through the routines for the official visit to Stockholm from September 4–5, 2013. After all our years in the Team, the challenges posed by our assignments were still a paradox. Building the same state of high alert, being prepared for anything to happen, at any time, required us to act with extreme precision, to follow our training without deviation. Every little routine had to stand out like some sort of prelude to Doomsday.

Edelweiss had his way of going about it, always getting us to pay full attention, to sit bolt upright in our chairs. Just his way of opening with "Good morning, my little lambs" chilled us to the core. After his first few lectures in West Point's sealed wing, I had nightmares for weeks. So when he now opened his eyes and fixed his look at the projection screen in the conference room, we all did the same, as if spellbound.

The decisive difference between this official visit and earlier ones was that something would now be happening. An incident at least as grave as those we had faced during the most serious of our maneuvers—and this time, what is more, for real. The run-through carried much more significance than all of our earlier rehearsals.

And no-one other than me knew anything about it.

As usual, the three-dimensional animation began with our intended escape route in the most critical situation. Alert level LILAC, when the President was to be taken under protection and our team would assume command of the whole military apparatus. It showed POTUS and FLOTUS surrounded by our fast-paced escort, in which our Team had been mixed up with the President's own handpicked security detail. With me never more than fifteen feet away from him, the briefcase in my grasp, ready to use.

Now I saw all the strictly classified information I had never been able to get at during my research: details of the path we were to follow. If the need arose, our escape route would run from our quarters at the Grand Hotel to the assembly point at the helipad in Stockholm's Gamla Stan. The secret emergency exit on this occasion turned out to be a narrow little hatch to the left of the last set of stairs, down toward the goods entrance of the hotel on Stallgatan 4.

But from then on the escape route became less narrow, in the form of a gigantic tunnel system deep in the bed-rock, stretching under the whole of central Stockholm and its outer edges.

This system was unknown to the public, according to Edelweiss. I tried to find the best place to split off from the Team—but the number of possibilities seemed almost endless. On the sketches, the system looked like an enormous *terra incognita*, in which our escape route was marked in red and most of the rest was a morass of dotted lines and shaded areas: like a map of the world before it was known to be round. According to the observers in our advance party, we would also have to depend on headlamps down there, because none of the tunnels had light sources.

The escape route started off heading northward, through passages running under the Blasieholmen peninsula. Once we were level with the platforms of Kungsträdgården Tunnelbana station, we would turn sharp west and then immediately south, passing through underwater tunnels. Then we would continue further south, deep under the Parliament, the Royal Palace and the oldest parts of the city, rising to the surface again at the helipad at the edge of the water on Riddarfjärden. From there, the airborne forces would take over, leading POTUS and FLOTUS to safety escorted by an alternate non-NUCLEUS Carrier of the briefcase while the Team would muster for a counter-attack.

Edelweiss froze the animation at an immense verdigrised copper gate. It originated, he said, from the ruins of the seventeenth-century Makalös palace, according to him one of the most beautiful and talked-about buildings of the time, and had been installed in the walls of the underground system as a part of its artistic decoration. He made a point of saying that the gate had not been opened since it was put there in 1983, and that it could likely not be budged so much as a fraction of an inch without the greatest difficulty.

Yet the observers in our advance party had felt uncomfortable with even that minimal risk: of somebody making their way in from the passages of the blue Tunnelbana line directly beneath the President's quarters. The whole Kungsträdgården station had therefore been sealed off in preparation for our visit.

Every time Edelweiss played the animation through again, so we could learn the escape route by heart, my first impression became clearer. Next to the copper gate you could see something set in the rock wall, more regular than the rough pattern of the stone: a paler, small square. The similarity to the control panel outside our own secure facilities—reminiscent of an ordinary, innocent electrical box—could not have been a coincidence.

So having no idea how I might be able to realize my crazy dream, I determined that the copper gate from the Makalös castle would be the invisible crack in the wall.

The starting point of my and Alpha's impossible escape out of the Team. "We two against the world."

1.03

A natural cloud can weigh five hundred tons. A mushroom cloud so much more.

Before I was given my assignment, I used to wonder how all that weight would affect a person. How it would feel to exercise control and power over the nuclear weapons system, to be the finger on the Doomsday button. The man with the briefcase. The Carrier.

When I came to the Team in November 2001, I had for some time harbored doubts. My doctoral thesis had in essence been one long questioning of the justification for nuclear weapons I tested the limits, challenged, pushed and tugged at the issues. At first I had even thought of calling it "The Atom: A Moral Dilemma", but I was persuaded by my supervisor to change the title to "Lise Meitner's Secret".

My home life revolved around a family who knew nothing about my other existence. I played the roles of researcher and family man—with a well-educated wife, two girls and a boy aged eleven, nine and seven, a house in the suburbs and drinks on a Friday with our middle-class neighbors—in the same faithful way as that of "The Man with the Briefcase". Everything had been false and true in equal measure.

And there's nothing to say that one's feelings become weaker while leading a double life. Rather the opposite: this intense heat, the intricate interplay within a life which all the time had to be *manipulated*, just made everything more intense. Even though I was play-acting on all fronts, for many years I was able to be both passionate and professional across the board. Until the briefcase's inherent weight, the absurd load of my assignment, began to be too much for me to handle.

But I still went along with it for a few years more, while doubt and hesitation grew. I was like a Hamlet within the nuclear weapons system. Then, out of the blue, I was contacted by Alpha. I came to realize that I had an unusual ally.

And the time had now come. Tense, I waited for the signal, even though I still had no idea what it might look like. Peered through the tinted windows as we sped through empty streets into Stockholm.

Over the years we had got used to never seeing city centers other than just like this. The same the world over, wherever we came. The most vibrant and sprawling cities, empty and sealed off, devoid of natural life. The buildings intact, the people gone. As in the aftermath of the big bang, the detonation of a "neutron bomb".

The briefcase was on the floor between my legs, in accordance with the regulations which governed movement by transport, the security strap fastened over my left wrist. The President and the First Lady exchanged small talk on the rear seats of our car, speaking softly so that none of the rest of us could make out what they were saying.

I unclenched my right fist, squinted at the print-out and recited under my breath the allocated sleep times for myself. Zafirah 00.00—02.13, Edelweiss 02.13—04.55, Erasmus 04.55—06.00. Kurt and John never slept at night during our shorter state visits, but still seemed to get enough rest while we crossed the Atlantic, when they shared guard duty equally.

Yet again, Zafirah had drawn the winning lot. Edelweiss assured us that the sleep times were allocated at random—but once again I had ended up with the last and shortest slot. They must have had suspicions about me for such a long time.

Now my allocated sleep time would only let me have sixty-five minutes, with a marginally reduced level of internal surveillance, before Kurt or John came to wake me. And the Nurse would no doubt follow me all the way into the bedroom, ready to sound the alarm at the slightest unnatural movement, even though she did not figure anywhere on the roster.

She was slumbering beside me in the car, to all intents

disengaged, even though we had almost reached the hotel. I ran my eyes over the Nurse's face, her heavy make-up, the dyed-blond hair, the short, compact figure. Tried to get a feeling for who she was. To understand why just this person had been allowed to accompany me here, been given this assignment.

A dull day then passed, as if in slow motion. The spare itinerary showed the extent to which this official visit had been thrown together in haste. Our reception at the Kungliga Tekniska Högskolan was a disappointment. There was no sense of history at all, no experimental reactor R.1, no glimpse of the rooms in which Lise Meitner might have worked. Only the dull exhibition halls and a number of sterile display cases with a variety of "environmental innovations".

The First Couple had played their roles, as usual, nodded and said this and that, asked all the right questions. They had even had a short time to rest before the dinner while we installed ourselves in the temporary surveillance center, a grandiose two-storey high corner room on the upper floors, with bracket lamps fixed to the walls and a thick blue carpet covered with small yellow crowns.

From this vantage point we could keep watch over all of the entrances to the hotel, as well as large parts of the surrounding terrain facing three points of the compass. On the other side of our wall, with connecting doors, was the Presidential couple's lavish seven-room suite, laid out over four floors, including the luxurious little bedroom on the top level of a cupola which had been added to the building. But since the observers in our advance party had failed in their efforts to have the hotel install bullet-proof glass in the room's panoramic windows, it could be used now only as a relaxation room for the bodyguards.

As usual it would not take me many seconds to reach the President's side if the alarm was sounded. Or, in this case, leave his side.

The Winter Garden banqueting hall also lay but a few doors from our space. It was there that the dinner was going to be held, starting in about an hour and continuing until just before midnight, when official events always ended. Protocol dictated that the President's own detail was in charge of physical personal security, but Kurt and John began to set up our own portable monitors along the longest wall of our corner room. In the meantime, I made myself comfortable in the heavy marble window frame, from where I had the best vantage point.

The view was like a fake. A piece of theatrical scenery, a picture postcard, as artlessly idyllic as the whole of this neutral little country. I stared out at the sun, the light, the sky, a whole illuminated world which I would soon have to leave. When Alpha gave the signal, it would at the same time be the starting gun for a new existence for us both. Forever on the run, like some quarry, prey, rats underground. Yet I had no idea what I was waiting for. What kind of sign.

I let my gaze sweep on, across the throng of people outside the hotel not just hoping for a glimpse of the President—they were after the scent of some accident, maybe even a terrorist attack: people, just like sharks, are attracted to blood. As the time passed, the light from the setting sun started to filter through the houses along Skeppsbron, on the opposite side of the water. The scene darkened with the light, the baroque facades lost their earthen colors, ocher and umber, and the sun sailed behind the stately but lifeless buildings like an enormous red balloon.

My watch showed 19.31. Ten minutes till sundown. So often it had been the secret signal to launch an attack, with our superior night-combat technology. Operation Desert Storm, Operation Iraqi Freedom, or full-scale nuclear weapons training. The aim was often to start at the very moment when the sun dropped like a mysterious piece of space rock straight down into the sand and the desert night fell in an instant.

During the last minute of daylight I stared as much at my watch as at the view outside the window, counting down to myself. At 19.41, exactly on time according to the calendar, the fiery globe's last contour dipped below the horizon: as if swallowed up by the enormous tunnel system under the platforms of Kungsträdgården station.

But still no sign of Alpha. No signal from the one person who could help me.

Time passed. Just before midnight, Zafirah also disappeared, the first one on our roster heading up the stairs to the bedroom floor. Every half hour throughout the night the Nurse laid two warm—almost sweaty—fingers against my wrist, checking my pulse. She had taken up position next to me in the window frame. Stroked my forehead, making sure that my body temperature had not started to race away again.

I myself peered ever more often at my watch, soon at intervals of only a few minutes. The briefcase seemed to burn at my feet.

At 04.50, a few minutes before it was my turn to sleep, Zafirah pushed herself between me and the Nurse. With a serious look she told us that she had received new orders, now that the results of my medical tests taken just before departure were available. That she should also take her rest with me and the Nurse, for safety's sake.

So when Edelweiss came down from the bedroom level, still drowsy and with the many folds in his face creased from sleep, Zafirah got to her feet and led me up the stairs while the Nurse fell in at the rear of our little column.

I was allowed first into the bathroom. Through the walls I could hear Zafirah moving her sofa-bed until it blocked the bedroom door from the inside. With her almost inhuman ability to master her small, muscular form, to focus her whole force onto one tiny point.

For the benefit of the Nurse, Zafirah said that she very much wanted to be able to look out through the window on the opposite side of the room, "to lose myself in the pale northern darkness". I never heard any answer. Maybe the Nurse had fallen asleep.

I put the briefcase—never once out of reach—down next to the toilet and relieved myself while standing up, with the black security strap still around my left wrist. I splashed outside the bowl as much as I could, marking the gold mosaic which must have cost hundreds of dollars per square foot. When I emerged, the Nurse was lying snoring on the outer side of our double bed, a dark sound with some lighter overtones. I eased myself over her and pressed myself hard against the wall.

The trick of course is never to let yourself sink below the surface, either mentally or physically. Beneath me, the sheet creased, like wrinkles blown by the wind on the ocean surface or the desert sand. But time raced on, as it does when it is running out. First 5.11 a.m., then 5.23 a.m., barely before I had time to blink. Light started to leak up over the facades of the city, from below the horizon, ocher and umber returning from the earth's core. The screeching of gulls sounded like vultures through the triple-glazed windows.

And then there was no more than half an hour left for me to get some sort of indication of how I was going to get myself out, to solve the classic riddle of the locked room, find the invisible crack in the wall.

I slid myself backward in the bed, tried to find a position from which I could observe as much as possible, both inside and outside the bedroom, find a lead. My wrist-watch showed 05.57. Three minutes left until Kurt or John would come to wake us up.

At that moment, the alarm went off. The howling sirens drowned out the cries of the seagulls, cut right into my brain.

At last: the signal from Alpha.

1.04

The field cell phone showed the highest possible alert level, LILAC. *Large-scale nuclear attack with critical consequences for global security.*

Without thinking, I tried to turn on the bedside light, but nothing happened: the power must have been cut. Yet the light of dawn shining through the windows was strong enough—it hardly made any difference when we turned on our headlamps, leaving our hands free. Our movements were lightning quick and yet dreamlike, despite the deafening shrieks of the alarm, making it impossible for me to communicate with either Zafirah or the Nurse.

We went at top speed down the stairs from the bedroom level to join the rest of the Team. Touching base with the President's own security detail, checking our combat packs and the briefcase, taking up our positions, out through the doors of the surveillance suite. In my case, at most five feet from the President. Apart from the alarm, everything was calmer than usual. Quietly counting our steps, as if choreographed, while we made our way toward the emergency stairs at the far end of the corridor.

I kept a firm grip on the briefcase in my left hand. With the alert level at RED or above, the security strap could no longer be attached to my wrist, so as not to delay any possible use of the Doomsday weapon. We could hear the chaos of the mêlée of people behind the safety doors in the stairwell, the panic of the hotel guests, desperate cries, a baby's piercing yells. Fear ran like a bass tone underpinning the alarm.

Some of the President's own security detail were in the lead, just as in the animations, with the First Couple immediately behind. I fell in between them on the way down the stairs. Zafirah pushed her way in just ahead of me, with Kurt or John behind. The

Nurse was right beside me and all of a sudden stuck her small but surprisingly strong left hand in my right one. So I would have to shake it off to be able to draw my weapon.

Once I had squeezed through the little hatch in the wall by the last set of stairs and was standing close to the hotel goods entrance on Stallgatan 4, one foot on the first step of a long and rusty spiral staircase, I glanced back at the Nurse. Even with her bulky medical backpack she followed me nimbly through the small opening. She too must have been hand-picked and specially trained.

After forty-three rotations in the narrow spiral stairway—never losing control, always keeping a close eye on the situation, the First Couple and our lines of retreat—we reached ground, as in the animations, the even floor of the mystifying tunnel system.

But not one lamp could be seen along the rough rock walls, no cabling, not a trace of anything which would make it easier for those needing to move around inside the immense tunnel system at normal times. For those who had built it. For whatever reason anyone might even have thought of devoting so much effort to something like this, here—in this neutral country, at peace for more than two hundred years.

The Nurse squeezed my hand so tightly that it was impossible to tell if she was wanting to protect me or to be protected. In fact I had not much more information than she did. From level RED and up, all technical details were classified at least one layer above me. All I knew was that I, or rather the briefcase, was regarded even in those situations as both the ultimate counter-strike weapon and the most important thing to be protected—after the President.

And that Alpha had to be somewhere in the vicinity. Had to be the one pulling the strings, letting the whole plan unfold, step by step. Our escape together from the Team.

In contrast to the appalling din up in the hotel—the alarm, the rippling panic of the guests—the sudden silence here within the bed-rock was unreal. We were breathing in short bursts through our noses, to reduce the noise coming from the group.

Although our speed was equivalent to high-intensity short interval training, I had a dream-like feeling that we were standing still while the enormous tunnel system was rushing back past us, like a tsunami of stone. It seemed as if there were constant new passages on either side of our path, appearing in the circular gleam cast by our headlamps: a myriad of alternate tracks leading out into the darkness.

The President now passed me to the left to be next to the First Lady, so that only Zafirah was between the First Couple and me. The President had never devoted much attention to any of us in the Team. To the country's Commander-in-chief, we were for the most part faceless figures, functions rather than human beings, pretty much seamlessly mixed up with his own security people. Even I was probably no more than "The Man with the Briefcase". The unknown person who would always be close.

Our formation hurried forward. The Nurse was right behind me, holding my hand in a grip which tightened for every turn in the labyrinth, with an astonishing strength for somebody so small. My pulse increased, I could now feel it clearly in my chest, not because of the exertion—I had never been fitter but with the insight that I would have to take the next step all on my own. Alpha had given the signal, fired the starting pistol. The rest was up to me.

Yet I had no idea how it was going to happen. I knew nothing beyond the short encrypted messages sent to the cell phone at the playground, and beyond the fact that I would only have a few seconds to act. Not enough for me both to get out of the Nurse's grip and to draw my weapon, however fast I did it.

I saw Edelweiss's animations before me. The verdigrised copper gate would soon come into view on our right-hand side. I heard something beating. There was an intensive ticking, like a timepiece, a clock-work mechanism. My eyes passed over the rock walls, looking for some form of detonation device—before I realized that it was my own racing pulse.

So I improvised.

Just before the last bend I gripped the Nurse's left hand even harder. I could have bent it right back and broken it, snapped her wrist like a biscuit. She cannot have weighed more than 110 pounds, but that ought to be enough.

When I caught sight of the small symmetrical installation in the rock wall—it was a control box, no question about it—the Nurse suddenly gave my hand a squeeze back. It must have been a signal. But I still followed my instincts and improvised: I braced myself against my left leg and swung her around my left shoulder with my right hand.

Kurt-or-John fell headlong, not only because of the force behind the human sledgehammer but also from sheer surprise. Blood and glass splinters from the headlamp spattered across the rock.

The Nurse let out a shrill sound as I swung her around again—this time aiming in front of me. Zafirah hardly had a second in which to turn before the Nurse's head, sticky with blood and covered in razor-sharp shards, hit her straight in the face.

Still there was an unreal silence, as if everything was muffled. Only a weak whimpering from the Nurse, not a sound from Zafirah or Kurt-or-John. With blood running over their faces, they were all fumbling for their weapons, which the impact of the Nurse had knocked away from them, trying hard to understand what had happened. What had got into me. The First Couple had already been bundled away among their own security detail and continued at full speed, while a few others separated themselves from them.

That was how they were going to try to solve the impossible puzzle: to be able to protect the President and at the same time neutralize the Mole. And also take care of my briefcase.

But my thoughts were already several steps ahead. Before any of the President's men had got back to Kurt-or-John, still less passed by his enormous figure blocking the narrow tunnel, I had flipped open the lid to the control box and uncovered the buttons on the panel under it.

I did not need to think, my fingers moved automatically as I keyed in the only thinkable code. The first message which Alpha had sent to me, artfully encrypted, the start of our whole elaborate communication over the course of twelve long years. The long sequence was 102 115 101 922 G52 0N6 161 512 211 019 R2D. It became, once deciphered: WE TWO AGAINST THE WORLD.

There was an audible click from the lock. The mighty copper gate swung open with a piercing screech.

I tightened my grip on the Nurse's wrist—she was now almost unconscious—and stepped through, dragging her in just before the gate closed again. The salvo of gunshots from the Team and the President's men smattered like muffled keystrokes on a computer console as they hit the surface of the thick metal. We were alone, in the sealed-off underground station.

I wish I could say this was a sign that I was still capable of empathy. To show how it had survived all these years, my entire transformation; that something of the real me remained deep inside. But even the decision to take the Nurse with me was purely a tactical one.

I would be forced to go significantly more slowly, since I would be carrying a full combat pack and also the Nurse like a broken doll by one hand, the briefcase by the other. Besides which she would leave a trail of blood along the floor, which our pursuers could not possibly miss. Before I tested the elevator which led down to the platforms I therefore considered leaving the Nurse there. Like wounded prey, for the others to pick up or not, perhaps delaying them for critical moments.

But I did not do it. The Nurse's hand had given a squeeze in the tunnel just before we reached the control box, clearly some sort of signal. And since I still knew nothing at all about Alpha's wider plans, I did not dare to rule out the possibilities: that maybe the Nurse would turn out to be useful. Or the Nurse might even be Alpha. So I laid her across my shoulder and started to run down the first escalator.

The elevators from the station's next level had been shut down. There were also man-high barriers at the ticket gates, like a wall of toughened glass, but I managed to get over them with all of my load by shifting the briefcase, the Nurse, my combat pack and myself one at a time. Then I ran on as fast as the weight would allow, down the dizzyingly steep second escalator leading to the platforms. It was heavy, but no worse than on one of our desert training maneuvers with two simulated wounded men to carry in at least forty degrees of heat.

In my intense research before our departure—when I still had no idea what use this was all going to be, if any—I had read that the escalator was one of the longest in all of Stockholm. The sound of rubber soles against metal, my rhythmic and controlled breathing even at top speed, were the only sounds penetrating the silence of the bed-rock. I counted my footsteps . . . 148, 149, 150, 151.

Then I was down there: in the cabinet of horrors on the way to the platforms, the artistic and historical installation in the station which I had studied during my days and nights of research. But I was still not prepared for it. The lighting was spare and theatrical, as in a museum, the emergency illumination seemed not to be working all the way down here. The sealed-off station was only lit up in places by the old-fashioned street lamps, with their flickering ice-blue neon spirals and the weak sheen from the gargoyles built into the rock walls. With the help of my headlamp I was still able to hurry on through this weird underworld. It seemed to me as if I were already dead.

I also saw that there were black and white radiation symbols in the naïve paintings on the ceiling. I had not noticed them during my research, maybe none of the photographs had been taken at the right angle. For a moment I felt myself sway. The briefcase seemed to be sending out its spell, but I kept going, crossing the checkered floor in hard, short bursts on my way to the platforms.

I looked at my watch. Almost five minutes since we passed through the copper gate, and no sound of our pursuers.

The load over my left shoulder must have weighed at least 165 pounds, including the Nurse's bulky medical backpack. With my own combat pack, the total must have come to more than two hundred pounds. Sweat ran from every pore, mixing with the Nurse's blood to form sticky trickles down my back. Just as I was making my way to the platforms, I was at last forced to stand and catch my breath, gasp for oxygen. My mind needed it, as much as anything. And I had an idea, a hypothesis. Not much more.

The gold-colored cross on the rock wall looked exactly as it had in the photographs. To the left of it stood the God of War with the dead wolf over his arm, everything was as it should be. As I put down the briefcase and carefully laid the Nurse next to it on the checkered terrazzo floor, I could clearly hear the dull thump all the way down here. Our pursuers—parts of the Team, maybe some of the President's own men, those who were not needed to lead the First Couple through the tunnel system away to the helipad—must have forced the copper gate with a powerful and probably excessive explosive charge. They would not have had time to make an exact calculation.

The alarm immediately went off. The underground platform was bathed in a yellow, rhythmically flashing light. My pulse fell rather than increased. What had felt impossible during the early part of my training, to achieve anything at all with such a powerful adrenaline rush, quickly became addictive.

My watch showed 06.03. Eight minutes since the alarm sounded at the hotel, my escape seeming both lightning quick and endlessly drawn out. It should take at least two minutes before they managed to make their way through the remains of the gate, which would probably be obstructed by rockfall from the explosion, and to get down the two escalators. Then it would be about fifteen seconds before they had us within range of their guns—and a few moments more for them to assess the situation. To weigh the alternatives.

I began to run my fingers around the base of the statue of the God of War, methodically searching. The decrypted message to the cell phone at the playground had read "AROUND MARS". At first it had meant nothing to me—until I studied the photographs from the underground platforms. Then my eye lit upon the statue. The God of War, Mars.

Liquid was slowly seeping out along a vaulted niche behind the statue, like a tiny artificial waterfall. Close up like this, one could even see the thin yellow runnels in a narrow gap between the rock wall and the floor. Maybe it was part of the statue's design, maybe not. Just to the left of the statue there was something on the ground that could have been taken for the cover of a well, about three feet in diameter, and it too went in under the base of the statue. So there must be something under it.

Only when I could feel the small control box on the back of the God of War, did I glance at the watch: already 06.05. The pursuers must now be on the lower of the escalators, on the way down to the cabinet of horrors.

It was not easy to key in the twenty-nine numbers and four letters from that position, lying half-curled around the statue. Even to be able to fit one's arm between its base and the uneven rock wall by the platform was hard, not least to move one's fingers nimbly enough to press the correct buttons in the right order. But on the other hand: it was not meant to be easy.

When I had managed to register the same sequence as at the copper gate, the cover of the well shifted reluctantly. It was weightier than I had thought, reinforced with lead or steel. The mechanism juddered and rattled. Soon a small staircase could be seen, swinging down to the right, in under the statue itself, into the darkness.

I drew the Nurse close to me and thought that I could see her mouth move a little through the grimace on her face, but I could not hear anything against the piercing noise of the alarm. I lifted off my combat pack and took out the rescue harness—and after wrestling for a few seconds with the semi-lifeless form, I managed to secure the Nurse to me with her face buried in my chest. During the struggle she seemed to come to life a little and began to wave her arms weakly. When she realized that I was going to carry her off, maybe even deeper underground, her helpless flailing increased.

Out of the corner of my eyes I thought I could see our pursuers some tens of feet away, one or more of them with drawn weapons. But it could just as well have been the magnified silhouettes of my own movements in the light of my lamp: an illusion playing against the rock wall.

The cover of the well started to close. Time seemed to be up. I put my foot in the gap and hoped for the best—and after an eternity the cover did after all stop, half-shut. Despite the Nurse being harnessed to me, the briefcase and my full combat pack, I was able to push my way through the opening and start down the spiral staircase, with the cover of the well closing above us.

Then we plunged headlong. Deep down into the bed-rock.

1.05

We managed a more or less controlled landing. I landed first on my back, then the Nurse, harnessed to me, her face on my chest. We had trained jumps and landings so many times, for so many years, with every sort of complication, finally from considerable heights both with and without parachute. Learned to roll on pretty much every kind of material. The ground down here felt as even as in the tunnel system we had fled through, maybe here too it had been covered with spray cement. If we had fallen on untreated, sharp points of the bed-rock instead, we would have been much worse off.

Everywhere was pitch-dark with an ominous quiet. I checked my watch: 08.11, still September 5, 2013. The impact must have knocked me unconscious for a time. Then I switched the watch into altimeter mode. Negative 252 feet, almost to the measure that Alpha's encrypted messages had indicated.

I tossed my beret out into the darkness and carefully drew my hand over my shaved head. I expected blood and splinters, maybe even brain tissue—but it stayed dry. I felt raw and bruised, but not cut. My left hand locked onto the briefcase. I traced the lamp with the fingers of my free hand. The glass was intact, despite everything. I tried pressing the on/off button—and my immediate surroundings were bathed in light again. The impact of the fall had switched it off.

I let the beam illuminate first the briefcase, which remained intact, undamaged, then the Nurse, and I examined her head to toe as I had been trained. No external signs of damage, apart from the bloody mess on her head. Her pulse was low but stable. As I leaned over, I could feel a weak, warm flow of air coming from her mouth and nose.

Then I looked up and let the glow from the lamp play over the area around me, trying to orientate myself, understand what had happened. We were in the middle of an enormous chamber detonated out of the bed-rock, perhaps some sort of rest area for the users of the tunnel system. The rough ceiling must have been at least sixty-five feet above me, and the metal spiral staircase stopped about fifteen feet up. In the light of my lamp I could now see the rusty ladder we should have taken to lower ourselves the rest of the way—if I had not assumed that the staircase continued all the way down.

My whole body gave a sudden shudder. During my research I had read that the tunnels at Kungsträdgården Tunnelbana station were home to the dwarf spider, *Lessertia dentichelis*, whose habitat was otherwise in mines and deep caves. It had appeared as an uninvited guest at the inauguration of the northern entrance of the station in the late '70s. Now one of its kind was crawling over my left hand, over the security strap of the briefcase. I closed my eyes. Looked away. Breathed deeply. Although I had a horror of spiders, this one was tiny, not much larger than a tick.

I shook myself until I could no longer feel it and resumed my search along the walls. Somewhere there had to be a concealed lighting system, something that would also give me an idea of what awaited us further inside. I could not believe that a tunnel network as advanced as this would have been built without one.

As if working inside a diver's bell, I moved my head to examine section after section of wall, without seeing any sign of wiring or lamps. Not even when I got to my feet—my battered body swaying, my black, tactical combat uniform ripped—for a closer study of the rock walls, could I see anything which stood out from their natural contours.

In each of the lower corners of the vast rock chamber there were cavities, small caves which were even darker. I shone my lamp into them, one after the other. But the light reached only a few short feet before the darkness took over.

So, for the moment I left the unconscious Nurse and the two

packs behind, to make a closer inspection of the tunnels and try to gain some sense of where they might lead. The first one was so narrow that right from the opening I had to crawl. And then it just got narrower. Everything vanished into darkness behind me, since my body soon blocked the beam from my forehead lamp. The briefcase remained in my left hand, my drawn weapon in my right hand, while I wriggled forward on my elbows.

Soon both of my shoulders scraped against the tunnel walls, even though I was moving pretty much in a straight line. Just a few feet into the tunnel I could no longer turn around—the only way to get out would be to crawl backward, scrabbling like some sort of crustacean. Without warning my left elbow hung free and I lost my grip on the briefcase as it fell. The security strap alone stopped it from plummeting into the void. When I looked down to shine the light into the darkness, I could see no bottom.

Reversing out took more than twice as long as it had done to crawl in. The next tunnel too, working clockwise around the chamber, turned out to be the same sort of dead end. After perhaps sixty feet into an increasingly narrow passage, my lamp revealed an even darker oblivion. A different sort of structure than the level spray cement on the floor of the tunnel system suggested that this too would drop down into the underworld. With effort, I once again backed out. The palms of my hands became boiling hot in the attempt and blood appeared in the cracks of my knuckles. I was drenched in sweat, even though my watch showed that the temperature down here was only a few degrees above freezing.

The whole tunnel system seemed like a labyrinth of dead ends and hidden chutes. These were not natural geological hollows: the same people who had constructed the passages had also built in an intricate web to block anyone who did not know the correct route through them.

But two openings remained. Just as I had lain on my belly, my legs stretched behind me to start making my way in again, this time into the third tunnel, I felt something cold and smooth against the front of my right thigh. I crawled back out with caution and angled my light down.

At first I saw nothing—except that it was not blood, as I had at first thought and feared. Then I spotted the line, flush with the surface of the spray cement. A straight line of extinguished light diodes ran along the floor and disappeared into the tunnel. I ran my fingers over the glass I had felt through a tear in my combat pants.

Once again I lay prone and followed the line with my fingers. After just a few feet the diodes swung off in a semi-circle, around yet another abyss, before the tunnel continued on. I could not help nodding to myself in satisfaction. I had never before seen the problem of underground lighting solved in this way, high-tech and yet so old-fashioned at the same time.

I'd had no idea who or what I would find inside the tunnel, but certainly not this.

When I had wormed my way some hundred feet into the cavity, and carefully made my way around the abyss, the first bright red door appeared like a mirage in the gleam from my headlamp. Unlike the other cavities, this one gradually broadened out until I could stand up by the time I reached the control box, perfectly concealed inside one of the folds of the rock wall.

I opened the lid of the box—another replica of those outside our own underground facilities—and punched in the same code as before: twenty-nine numbers and four letters. One by one, the massive protective doors opened.

I made a quick tactical calculation. Tried to evaluate alternatives in a situation where most of the variables could not be quantified. I had to work with "the unknown", as Edelweiss had taught us.

A tunnel remained to be explored, one which could lead us further. But for now the code had worked. Had let me into the fallout shelter: as good a signal as any. On the other hand, the idea of shutting myself up in here, inside a minuscule dug-out deep down inside the bed-rock, was not easy to accept.

In the end, the thought of threats from outside—from the rest of the Team, from the President's own men, or even from the people who had once built this enormous system—decided things for me. With difficulty I first dragged the Nurse and then the packs in through the tunnel. When I had pulled shut the last of the security doors, a normal gas-lock door with a pressure seal, I tried again to enter the code on the control panel just to the right, inside the entrance. The five diodes spun around for an eternity before stopping on "ERROR". However much I tried pressing the buttons, tearing at the handle of the security door, heaving and yelling.

That was when, for the first time, I vomited, into a drain on the floor. In part because of the extreme violence, using the Nurse as weapon; after all my years of service, nausea often washed over me at times like these. In part from physical exhaustion, from the exertion of fleeing with such a heavy load for such a long time. But also because of the predicament I found myself in: locked behind monstrously thick doors in this tiny fallout shelter.

I had been all alone above ground. Now I found myself alone again, except for the unconscious Nurse—but this time precisely 253.3 feet down in the bed-rock.

1.06

So I just sat there and waited for Alpha, hoping against hope that this place was where we were to meet, at the exact depth given in the encrypted message. I had no choice but to believe.

After a while I took a notebook from my pack and started to scribble, to sketch out my story for you to read in posterity, the chronicle which you now have in your hands, which you must have stumbled on or managed to track down. My account of how it started, and perhaps how it ended.

When it was past 18.00, and I had managed to get some way into my record, the Nurse was still lying there, more or less unconscious. I tried to coax some water into her—at the same time I myself drank as much as I dared, without having the slightest idea how long we would be stuck down here, and ate the first of the crunch crackers from my pack. Most of the water I tried to feed the Nurse ran off her closed lips. When I tried with care to prize open her mouth, to get at least something down her throat, she had a violent coughing fit, although she remained unconscious. Maybe I would have to open the Nurse's own medical pack and put a drip in her, although I was not sure it was worth the trouble.

Everything felt shut off, as if already part of history. The briefcase stood next to me, never more than two feet away, but now seemed more than anything like a dead weight. All this advanced technology had lost its meaning in this long-abandoned shelter, where it would be impossible to have it connect.

Nevertheless I decided to give it a try. Seen from the outside, the briefcase was not much to look at. The shell was made from tough aluminum encased in black leather and its spacious interior was surprising. But it was human nature to draw comparisons between things, to use metaphors whenever possible. So the briefcase was to this day still known as the nuclear football, even though the war plan codenamed "Dropkick", from which the nickname came, had been scrapped decades earlier.

The first step, just to be able to open the briefcase, had its own ritual. Not only the correct biometric information, but the correct way of handling the thing. You were supposed to apply simultaneous pressure, firm but light, with eight fingers plus a thumb to the invisible points on the front of the briefcase, splay your hands as unnaturally as a concert pianist. The classic combination lock was a dummy. Designed to tempt unauthorized persons to put their fingers in the wrong place, which would send the briefcase into lockdown mode at once. In other words: impossible to open even for me. After each time we practiced dealing with enemy attempts to take the briefcase, it always reset itself with different codes and pressure points.

There must after all have been some sort of network in the fallout shelter, something which allowed the briefcase to connect with the database—because the briefcase now opened with its usual soft whining sound.

With reverence I stared into the briefcase, for the first time since my escape from the Team. The world's most important object: torn from its habitual surroundings.

Everything was in its place despite my heavy fall down into the chamber. The four analog documents in their cut-to-measure foam-rubber compartments. Sacred, surrounded by myth, but hopelessly dated even decades ago. The book with the wax-cloth cover containing the out-of-date operational options for use in case of extreme crisis, thumbed by ten Presidents before the current one. The plastic-covered folder with the typewritten list of underground bases to which our Commander-in-chief could be taken when the alert level was at RED or LILAC. The faded note of information from 1965 describing the structure of the nuclear weapons system. The plastic counter with the secret codes the President was to use when he identified himself to Centcom— "the biscuit".

The thinking was that they would only be used if he lost the chip with the codes which he was meant to always carry on his person. But since every one of our heads of state had managed to mislay that object on some occasion, even as one sock always vanishes in the washing machine, we had had to keep "the biscuit" until the present day.

According to our current war plan, this digital technology side-by-side with fading paper and a plastic counter would make the briefcase even harder for an enemy to understand, if seized.

Much of the hidden lower level of the briefcase consisted of the matte-black metal keyboard. Not even that was particularly noteworthy: a classic standard model conforming to M.I.L-S.T.D.-810 G tests including Explosive Atmosphere, Pyroshock and Freezing Rain.

What distinguished the keyboard was its inside, its functionality and capacity. Everything it was able to control.

To get at the keyboard, I folded up the hooks in each of the four corners of the foam-rubber layer and with care lifted it and our analog information out. You could not see anything underneath, just a leather covering, as if the briefcase ended there.

And few parts of our body are as hard for us to control as our little fingers—which was why it was only thanks to them that I managed the next step. It had taken years to control them in the same way as index fingers, to make that evolutionary leap. It needed months of effort to work up my strength there, in an exercise as demeaning as it was refined; Edelweiss called it "The Waltz of the Little Fingers".

So I now pressed eleven three-digit sequences, using both little fingers at the same time with measured movements on the nodes on what appeared to be the bottom of the briefcase. The protective panel slid to the sides and revealed the keyboard. Once I had keyed in the rest of the initial codes, the metal screen on the inside of the lid also slid to the right, with a vivid red circle appearing on the screen. I looked straight into it. The iris recognition system was the last step in the security procedures: they had become more elaborate with time, as the briefcase became a kind of autonomous command module.

When the text "READY FOR COMMAND" appeared on the screen, I went no further with the ritual. Instead, I began closing the briefcase down again, each step in reverse, so that it would not go into lockdown.

All the functions were in order, it seemed. But without Alpha, whoever or whatever it was that controlled the whole chain, I would not be able to get further. So I stayed there and waited, in what was both shelter and prison, locked in behind ten-inch-thick ramparts of welded sheet metal.

I let my eyes scan around me. Everything in here followed the regulations to the letter. The floor, the walls and the ceiling were covered with the same metal. The edges of the outer doors sealed with copper plate, so as to minimize the electro-magnetic pulses. The whole room was also mounted on springs, so that it would sway rather than be crushed when the big bang came.

It looked just like any one of our top secret shelters under the bases in the endless plains of the Mid West. Yet I had never seen anything like it. Here, of all places: a doll's house-like hideaway built to withstand a direct hit of the strength of the Hiroshima bomb. In this insignificant country, midway between Moscow and Brussels.

Even the color-coding of the different small sections followed the international standard. The section of the wall behind the control panel with the light-emitting diodes had been painted purple for "Command/communication". The border of the wall around the inset cupboard was pale yellow, indicating "Stores". Continuing clockwise, facing the doors, the wall was first orange for "Passageway" and then blue for "Restroom/hygiene".

This last consisted of two parts. First there was the decontamination area, not much bigger than ten square feet: you were meant to screen yourself off with a lead-lined plastic curtain and rinse

52

away what you could of the radioactive fallout using a hand-held shower. Behind the same curtain there was also a sort of electric waste grinder sunk into the floor, surrounded by the same welded steel plate and copper plate. But this state-of-the-art toilet seemed to have stopped working.

The fallout shelter had already become an unbearable place. The drain in the floor near the hand-held shower was blocked by the last of the vomit which I had spewed out after the extreme violence of our escape. There were more bodily fluids some hours later. The usual reaction to an extreme adrenaline rush, however much you train, try to prepare. The stench made me catch my breath, inhale as little as possible through my nose, inside this strange little space.

The rest of the shelter was brilliant red, the color for "Emergency Exit", which was ironic given that I was locked in with little chance of escape. Only the lower part of the wall, directly opposite the entrance, had been painted green for "Sleeping Quarters".

On the floor the Nurse drew my attention again, the sound of her occasional whimpers. She must have been one of the "support functions" behind the scenes. I had seen her for the first time only a few days ago, I could not recall having so much as heard her voice. Yet I had inflicted severe injuries on her. The scent of her perfume—cloying, penetrating—was overwhelmed by the stench of blood and urine. Her uniform was also now more red than green, her garish, dyed-blond hair a mess of blood and dirt and glass splinters from the headlamps, the shards looking like a crown of thorns. Her whimpering grew a little louder, she almost seemed to be coming to, before falling back into her darkness. Once I had my own strength back, I would be her nurse, carrying out the emergency surgery which we had been taught in the sealed wing at West Point.

For now, exhaustion began to wash over me. It was two days since I had had even a brief sleep, in addition to lying mostly awake during the period just before our departure. Another dwarf spider came creeping along my left arm, in the direction of my wrist, climbing over the security strap of the briefcase. It moved with science-fiction-like speed given how small it was. As it reached the skin over my artery, I killed it with my pencil. Felt my skin freeze, shivered, as if I had a fever.

But I had to get a grip on myself, not let panic carry me away. The complete lack of activity in here became harder to bear with each passing hour. I had no information. I checked the depth meter on my service watch once more: it was a normal altimeter, but our technicians had adapted it to provide underground readings. And it did say 253.3 feet, just as in the encrypted message Alpha had sent to the cell phone at the playground. Twelve hours had now passed since I broke away from the Team and took the Nurse with me—and I still had no idea where everyone else was. All of our pursuers. Or rather: the chosen few.

According to instructions, no search bulletin would have been sent out, no digital message about my escape, not even in the most encrypted form. A very small circle would have been kept informed, and that would be it. Apart from the Team, I guessed only the President himself—unless Edelweiss had decided just to inform him that the alarm had turned out to be false, a minor technical hitch, as with so many other supposed nuclear weapons attacks in the course of the decades, and that the situation was now back to normal. Plus, a couple of our most senior military commanders. Probably not even the First Lady—and certainly not my own family.

So if Alpha did not come for me, fetch me from this escape-proof underground prison, nobody would ever know what had happened.

Tiredness continued to creep through me, like a drug. I shook my head and stood up to take a look at the Nurse. She felt chill, as if already dead, even though her pulse was ticking weakly in her wrist. I huddled up close to her, my pistol in my right hand

and the briefcase in my left, the security strap on my wrist. I had to get a few minutes of rest.

Over the years, it had become increasingly difficult to distinguish dream from reality, step by step they had slid into and out of each other. So I did not really know if I slept at all, or if I was still doing so when the diodes in the control panel by the door started to whirr. I noticed no difference when I pinched myself in the arm. The message on the panel really did say "OPEN".

I got to my knees, using the Nurse's more or less lifeless form as a shield, and tried to steady my weapon. I pointed it at the height of the heart. The mean height of men in the U.S. is five feet ten, here in Scandinavia presumably a bit more. The door handle began to be pressed down. There was a mechanical click. I undid the safety on the gun.

I heard the voice before I saw the face, that melodic intonation which had made me sweat through sleepless nights. It was also the voice that caused me to release my index finger from the trigger.

The surprise made me recoil against the green wall. That it should have been her, of all people. Through all those years.

1.07

She had wanted us to call her "Ingrid", but among her students she was only ever referred to as "Ingrid Bergman". Even though she did her best to hide her beauty—with her long straggling hair, even then graying, falling to her shoulders—the Swedish movie star's classic looks were etched into her face. At night we used to watch the movies over and over. Always in the same order, from light to dark: "The Bells of St Mary's". "Notorious". "Spellbound". "Dr Jekyll and Mr Hyde".

You must understand. But you won't.

That even I had once been an ordinary young person with no clear direction, pretty much the same as anyone else, with deep but not yet incurable wounds from my childhood. That I became obsessed with mathematics and physics at an early age, ciphers, numbers theory. But that I then, for one reason or another, felt that I needed an overview of the history of ideas, of mankind's thinking throughout the ages, and some optional courses in moral philosophy. Constructive thought as some sort of compass, a map out into the world, maybe even as therapy.

Instead, I met Ingrid Bergman.

After her first lecture I had a blinding headache. And then it got worse. She challenged everything we had thought or believed in, the uncertainty spread far beyond the lecture hall, the slightest detail sometimes meant life or death for me. How long I brushed my teeth. The interval between red light for cars and green man for pedestrians. The choice between taking the steps up to the university library one or two at a time.

I counted seconds, interpreted signs. Everything stood on edge. Absolutely nothing was settled or fixed any longer.

Just then, I also received my first "approach", as we called it. By that stage, they could have got me to do just about anything.

We knew that other students had already fallen for the recruiters' spiraling promises: they were said to come back at least once with guarantees of even bigger scholarships and increasingly adapted courses. Assurances that in future even the world of business would be crying out for our specialization.

At first I supposed that they had confused me with someone else, or that somebody in my corridor had given them my name as a joke. That I would be recruited by them did not seem likely. A fundamentally useless young man, pacifist since his teen years, unable even to decide which way to walk over the campus lawn, at this stage with unruly brown curls and apparently good-looking in a melancholy sort of a way. A lost, contrary student who could as easily have prepared a massacre at the university as study its moral consequences.

But the recruiters would not give up. Ran down the list of names with their index finger and found my name. Checked the spelling and date of birth. After they paid me a second visit I decided to try out after all, went along as if sleep-walking, counted the steps up the spiral staircase in the unused part of the university building leading to the helipad. Interpreted random parts of graffiti as signals addressed to me.

West Point was an hour away. I stared down at the shadow of our helicopter as it raced above the surface of the Hudson, but the military academy could as well have lain in another galaxy. On arrival there I vomited my entire former life out into a waste paper basket and then started, to my own great surprise and probably theirs too, to score top in the tests, one after the next. After only the third session I was selected for special training.

The requirements were clear from the start. Those of us in the special training group should at all costs continue our studies, in parallel with our course at West Point, and finish them in style, as if nothing had happened. We were to start working up our first alternate identity. The double life was demanding but manageable. I was furiously driven, a fire in my belly, wanting, it seemed, to take some sort of revenge: on existence in general, the meaninglessness of life, my father.

Since we did not have supervised studies more than three days a week, and the training at West Point mostly took place outside office hours—often late, sometimes in the form of repellent interrogation training sessions long into the night—the logistics were possible. No-one was waiting for me in my dorm. The corridor lay desolate and dark when I returned, and in the mornings I would spin the latest yarn about my fictitious girlfriend Sarah, with whom I said I was more or less living. The smoke-screens soon became an integral part of my existence.

Everything ran through my mind more or less in the same way, slid into and out of my being. Military life and moral philosophy, lectures, the Middle Ages, the violence, the ideas.

On the flight to West Point I would sit there, minutes after we had streamed out of the auditorium and I had taken one of my alternate routes to the helipad, trying to absorb what Ingrid Bergman had been telling us.

I turned my notebook this way and that without understanding in which direction I should be reading the letters. The insights which very recently had seemed so fantastic, were now little more than foreign symbols. Something which had cooled and solidified. In vain I tried to recall the heat of an hour before, the memory not only of Ingrid Bergman's thoughts but her entire being. All that was left were random bullet points. Capitalized phrases, a rash of exclamation marks, the occasional question.

Slowly I read them out loud to myself, the pilot next to me enclosed in his headphones. "CLIQUES!", "MIRRORS!?", "VISCOSITY!", "DUALISM!", "THE TRIUMPH OF DEATH!". Usually she wrote from left to right, but sometimes also from top to bottom. Before the end of the lecture she would join up the bullet points on the blackboard, like an intricate crossword or a Scrabble board.

Everything taken together seemed to form a gigantic cipher, full of hidden meanings, secret connections she called them, *correspondences*. Buried links between the history of art and weapons technology, eternal truths and the geopolitics of the day.

To begin with, we students had sat together and tried to interpret all this, help each other to understand what she was hoping to get across. We speculated over where her intriguing accent might have come from. Was she German or Dutch? I thought she was Swedish, like the real-life Ingrid Bergman. But as time passed, our relationship to her world became something much more personal and private for each of us. We all thought that our understanding was the correct one—and did not want to disclose this to anyone other than to Ingrid Bergman herself.

Nobody dared to contact her directly. The more that Ingrid Bergman drew us into the world of her thoughts, the more she seemed also to need to keep us at a distance. The most that she would do was to nod at those students she ran into on campus: she seemed to put all of herself into the lectures, emptying herself entirely.

I had been the exception. Although she must have been at least ten to fifteen years older than us—a time in her life when she should have had a firm base, a nuclear family according to the norm—she cast long looks back at me when we happened to run into each other in the library or on the lawns. It might have been my imagination, my heated dreams. But the other students confirmed it. Made comments.

In due course it was she who became my academic supervisor. After I had completed the basic course, with top grades in each subject, the idea was that I would write a dissertation and that they would arrange everything for the benefit of my double life.

I still sometimes wonder how they could have let me go so far, choosing the particular subject that I did. I can only speculate that even then Edelweiss saw me as a possible candidate for the world's most important assignment. And that somebody who so intensively called the whole nuclear weapons system into question, could never be suspected of serving the ends of that system: that my research, in the standard way of such paradoxes, would be for him the optimal camouflage.

The working title of my dissertation was "The Atom: a Moral Dilemma". At first, Ingrid Bergman suggested that it should center on Giordano Bruno, the sixteenth-century philosopher who was accused of heresy and burned at the stake. From him, threads also ran back to antiquity and the so-called "atomists" in southern Italy.

Bruno was a typical Ingrid Bergman figure—somebody who could get her animated, play a sufficient role in her own dramatization of world history: always lit up and theatrical.

But I wanted to go further. Right up to the fire. My first thought had been that the dissertation should center on Robert Oppenheimer, the "Father of the Atomic Bomb", who after Hiroshima and Nagasaki pleaded for nuclear weapons never to be used again. But Ingrid Bergman dismissed that as conventional, even banal.

I next tried Andrei Sakharov. The Russian nuclear physicist who was one of the leaders of the Soviet hydrogen bomb project, the step after the atom bomb, and then became the world's best-known dissident and pacifist. But think about the language, was Ingrid Bergman's only response. By the time you've learned enough Russian, your scholarship funds will have run out.

I could not tell her that I had long since mastered that language too, after both Russian and Arabic courses at West Point. Or that I had inherited my linguistic skills—as well as my German—from my mother.

So then I suggested Lise Meitner. During my advanced course in the theory of science, Ingrid Bergman had described her as the greatest female scientist ever. Einstein had apparently called her "our Madame Curie". An Austrian Jewish physicist, she had fled to Sweden immediately before the war, and there she was the first to comprehend the principle of nuclear fission—before being hidden away behind an obscure research post at Stockholm's Kungliga Tekniska Högskolan.

Meitner turned down all the increasingly persuasive requests to move to Los Alamos and to join in the Manhattan Project's work, refusing to get involved in any sort of military research. Despite that, the over-excited reports in the newspapers after Hiroshima and Nagasaki referred to her as none other than the "Mother of the Atomic Bomb". The world's press lined up outside the boarding house in Dalarna province where she was on holiday at this historic moment. Hollywood wanted to produce a movie about her with the title "The Beginning of the End". She was incredibly well known at the time—and now was almost forgotten.

It was even said that Meitner had before the war worked out how one could build an atom bomb. While she was still in Germany, she had smuggled out the secret and passed it to the Americans. In the movie script, she was supposed to have fled with the bomb itself in her handbag. That was what decided her to turn down the proposal.

When I mentioned the name, Ingrid Bergman was more or less lost for words. "That's a fantastic idea," she said at last, "absolutely brilliant."

Quite soon the idea appeared to be better on paper than in reality. The problem was not the German, which both Ingrid Bergman and I were able to understand more than adequately. Nor the fact that I, because of my other life as a special agent, could never get clearance for private travel overseas—and most of what was interesting about Meitner's story seemed to be in the Swedish archives. All I had to do was to tell Ingrid Bergman that I had a pathological fear of flying, which did not appear to surprise her at all: sensitive and talented young man that I was.

That problem resolved itself easily enough because Ingrid Bergman traveled to Sweden regularly to research in the Swedish archives—sometimes she was away for the whole summer—and she copied for me Meitner's letters to friends and scientific colleagues the world over. It was then that she told me she came from a small town in the far north of Sweden, but that she had when young mostly worked as a boss' secretary in Stockholm. Before she happened to fall head over heels in love and follow the object of her affections to the U.S., where eventually she began her studies.

The real problem was that there was so little information about Meitner that one could get one's hands on. Almost nothing about what she had been doing in Sweden during the war, at a time when the academic world was buzzing with rumors about extensive research within nuclear physics, and both sides thought that the other already had a finished bomb. Or what she had been involved in for all those years after the war. Who she really was. Meitner seemed to have wrapped herself in secrecy.

Even the correspondence with her nearest and dearest turned out to be ambiguous and hard to fathom. At the same time as members of her Swedish circle were giving accounts of magnificent parties at her home, she herself was sending out stifled cries for help in German or English to her friends overseas.

So hardly a week went by without my trying to abandon my project. And hardly a week went by without Ingrid Bergman, equally frenziedly, dragging me along, pushing, urging, enticing. At times it almost seemed as if she were ghost-writing my dissertation. During our supervision sessions, which I recall like dreams, she must have persuaded me to keep going more or less against my will. The while calling me "my treasure", as if we were in a relationship.

When I had completed all the theoretical courses for my doctorate, Ingrid Bergman gave me a present, a portrait to put on my desk in the office which I was then assured. It was a photograph of Lise Meitner in the laboratory at the Kaiser Wilhelm Institute in Berlin. She is looking straight into the camera, wearing strangely formal clothing for somebody who is carrying out experiments.

But the striking thing about it was her face. Meitner's mouth appeared a little crooked, as if she had had a stroke, which was hardly likely. She could not have been more than forty in the picture—and she was twice that age before her first stroke occurred. Yet there was something additional, a hidden membrane, which disturbed the picture. The answer to the riddle came if you covered up one side or the other. The right half was sad, undecided, almost sickly. The left one determined and open, with an audacious little smile.

That photograph provided both the title—"The Two Faces of Lise Meitner"—and the direction of my dissertation. That it should deal with the idea of having more than one side to oneself. And be-neath the surface it would be as much about myself, my double life.

But Ingrid Bergman refused to accept the idea. What she wanted and it was impossible to resist her: after our sessions I felt drained—was for the title instead to be "Lise Meitner's Secret".

I could at no time bring myself to tell her that I never really understood what Meitner's secret was, or whether there was one. Yet in the end I managed to describe it in a general enough way, to satisfy Ingrid Bergman. So the development of nuclear physics and mankind's inability to withstand its own scientific and military potential, how the whole impossibility became the only thing that was possible, the sweeping theoretical basis for my dissertation.

Against all the odds—and even though the style was closer to that of a literary essay than it was soberly scientific, since I was always finding myself carried away by the momentum of the thing—the dissertation survived its examination by an introspective and humorless exiled Bulgarian.

Immediately after that came the attacks of September 11, 2001. And then the summons to join the newly created team which was to save the world.

They also arranged my new double life in a very elegant way. At the same time as I took my place in Edelweiss' team, they stowed the other me away in a research post with minimal teaching responsibilities at The Catholic University of America in Washington D.C. A gloomy early-nineteenth-century castle with pinnacles and towers, no more than a couple of thousand students and some surprisingly interesting manuscripts in a dark archive called Sister Helen's Library.

Those who thought they knew me well—a few fellow researchers from university, the odd friend I dared have and had managed to hang on to—were told that I was more or less burned out after my work on the dissertation and needed to get away on a long journey, alone. I was given a new name, a new identity and a new appearance. Two operations in little more than a month, followed by a long and painful convalescence, in the gap between my dissertation and the new job.

During the year that followed, before I met my future wife at a party and the same evening went back to her place with her, I had also tried on a few occasions to contact Ingrid Bergman. Anonymously, obviously, from telephone boxes outside abandoned training grounds or somewhere in the desert. I had not caught so much as a glimpse of her since I had defended my dissertation. Nor re-read my thesis, hardly given it a thought. But I could not forget her, however hard I tried. The faculty and the university switchboard had both given the same answer. "Ingrid" had handed in her notice and moved on. No, unfortunately, no forwarding details.

To the official visit to Stockholm and the escape, I had nevertheless brought my—or perhaps I should say our—dissertation. I was after all going to Lise Meitner's involuntary home. The place of her long, puzzling exile.

And now we were meeting again. After twelve long years it was Ingrid Bergman—"Ingrid"—who walked into the fallout shelter. Pulled the protective doors shut, one after the other.

I tried in vain to make sense of what I was in fact seeing: my former lecturer and supervisor, in full combat gear. Ingrid Bergman seemed to be carrying exactly the same equipment as I was. A uniform with understated insignia, backpack, headlamp, her weapon drawn. In all respects her equipment was the same as my own, apart from the briefcase.

Her hair was short and jet-black, a higher forehead than when I last saw her, her nose bigger. Colored lenses and heavy camouflage completed the job for which the cosmetic surgery had prepared the way. She was changed yet not erased. Someone who knew her would still sense an Ingrid Bergman underneath it all. That quick little smile, the look.

There was so much that I would have liked to ask her. Where she had disappeared to, what had happened, why.

"What are you doing here?" I managed to say.

"I could ask you the same, Erasmus. If I didn't already know."

She went to the Nurse, crouched down and muttered "Jesús María . . . Jesús María . . ." over and over again, like a prayer. Fingered the glass splinters in the Nurse's forehead with a troubled look.

And suddenly the Nurse did give a tiny start. There were some weak reflexes in the cheek muscles and the eyelids, a small movement in the left leg. Like a cat moving while dreaming.

"She'll surface soon," Ingrid Bergman said.

"I can carry her with me now. We've got to get away from here," I said.

She stared at me.

"Erasmus, my treasure, for the moment we're lost to the world. Yes, we have to regroup, but not right now. Nobody's going to find us here. Hardly anyone knows that the system's intact, that it even exists."

"But you do?"

"Sure. Too well, probably."

I looked at her, searching for words. My mind seemed sluggish and helpless in the face of her verbal pirouettes.

"So is it you who is our Alpha?"

"Well, was. Until this morning, when I set off the alarm."

"Where were you during my escape, in that case, before you got here?"

"Oh, here and there, the usual thing."

I waited out her artificial pause, hanging on for her confirmation—until it finally came:

"And now it's *we two against the world*, Erasmus."

With her hair cut short she no longer had to fight it, no brushing the fringe out of her eyes as she used to. I could not take my eyes off her.

"You still look like Ingrid Bergman," I said.

"You think? I'm not sure that was the idea. But here's the person you'll soon be able to ask."

Then she huddled up to the Nurse and immediately fell fast asleep, just like a child.

1.08

I was fumbling far back into my childhood for memories. Scratching away in my notebook while the two women lay there, very close, sharing the same languor. Little by little the picture cleared: like a half-remembered scene out of an old movie.

It was my thirteenth birthday. I was sitting at the kitchen table with my mother. Cryptography already captivated me. I was trying to teach her the basis of book ciphers, even though she was a humanist through and through. To share with her my obsession.

The key to the disclosure of the top secret principles of the atomic bomb, which the Russian spy Theodore Hall had smuggled out of the Manhattan Project, was contained in one of our most famous collections of poetry, which I thought might interest her. Operating at a distance from each other, Hall and his courier Sax had used the same edition of Walt Whitman's *Leaves of Grass* for their cipher. The numerical codes indicated which pages, rows and letters of the book should be used to decipher a message.

It was a simple method, which both appealed to and could be understood by someone just into his teenage years—and also, so I supposed, by my mother. Yet it was a significant help in allowing the Soviet Union to detonate their own nuclear test charges much earlier than we had thought possible. Only four years after the bombs that fell on Hiroshima and Nagasaki.

So I picked out an old paid—or maybe it was unpaid—bill from one of Mom's chaotic piles of paper, turned it over and started to work away in my neat handwriting, explaining as I went along. First we choose a key sentence, I said, for example: "I love you". Then we give a number to the first letter in each of the three words in the sentence. So 1 stands for I as in "I", 2 for L as in "Love" and 3 for Y from "You", right?

But the drawback in using such a short sentence as key, the

lost and prematurely middle-aged youth in me continued, is that it gives you so very few numbers and therefore so few possibilities. Because if I write 123 in a cipher which has *I love you* as its key sentence, that only leaves us with "ILY" in clear. And you can't encrypt any proper words with such a short key sentence. The code 213 gives you "LIY", 132 "IYL", 231 "LYI", 312 "YIL" and 321 "YLI".

And it does not have to be some sentence from a book, I said. So long as both sender and recipient—and ideally nobody else in the whole world—know which key sentence they are using.

My mother was staring at the paper, seemed absorbed by it.

"But let's say that I keep writing," I said with enthusiasm, "adding to that sentence a little bit at random while we're sitting here at the kitchen table anyway, for example like this: *I love you . . . just as senselessly as my pretty weird and hellish father, for the time being and onward into eternity, Amen.* Then the number of possibilities becomes so much greater. Besides, there's only you and me who know that this sentence even exists: it can become our own little secret which we'll never reveal to anybody, can't it?"

Her faint smile encouraged me to keep going.

"Let's use that key sentence to decrypt the cipher 122129, for instance. Do you want to have a go, Mom?"

She nodded and put her spectacles on while I gave numbers to all the words in the new sentence, as neatly as before on the back of the bill.

"So let's begin", I said, "by taking the easiest interpretation. Let's read it as 1-2-2-1-2-9. That gives us the first letter in the first word of the key sentence: which is *I*. Then we have the first letter of the second word, which is *L* from '*love*'. Then another *L*, another *I*, another *L* and finally the first letter in the ninth word: *P* from '*pretty*'. But that doesn't make up a real word—only 'ILLILP'."

"But if you read some of the numbers as two-digit numbers, like this: 12-21-2-9, we get something different. The first letter in the twelfth word in the key sentence is *H* from '*hellish*'. Then you take the first letter from the twenty-first word, which is *E* from '*eternity*', the first of the second word which is 'L' from '*love*' and then the first letter of the ninth word: 'P'. Do you want to read it out for me, Mom?"

She shook her head. So I read out loud, in my clear little voice: "The book cipher 122129 with this key sentence gives you the clear text HELP."

I looked proudly at my mother—until I saw her twisted grimace. Then she shut her eyes and put her hands over her ears. Scrunched up the paper. Started to rock back and forth.

That was the moment when I realized that she was sliding into her own world, far beyond my reach or that of others. That key sentence, concocted at random, also became my own dark mantra. *I love you just as senselessly as my pretty weird and hellish father, for the time being and onward into eternity, Amen.*

For nights on end I rattled off the words as I tried not to fall asleep, since the dreams were worse than reality. Used the sentence as a key in my own restless search for hidden signs. I applied it to everything, from car license plates and telephone numbers to stock market figures and sports results: even though the clear text hardly ever produced a single comprehensible word.

My mother had been in an institution ever since, so I was convinced that I alone could possibly know our key sentence. Until the day when the packages started to arrive.

The first brown envelope was lying in the mailbox outside my office on December 22, 2001, just before the Christmas break. It was a month after I had joined the Team, a few weeks after our return from Afghanistan: what I had pretended both at home and to my colleagues to be a guest lecture tour in the Mid West followed by a fictional week's backcountry skiing to explain away my cuts and bruises.

At the very top it said "MERRY CHRISTMAS!" in green ink. Then my name and workplace, in the same anonymous capital letters.

ASSISTANT PROFESSOR ERASMUS LEVINE
SCHOOL OF PHILOSOPHY
THE CATHOLIC UNIVERSITY OF AMERICA
WASHINGTON D.C.

The envelope bore neither stamps nor a zip code, somebody must have delivered it by hand. Which might have meant that it came from one of my colleagues, though envelopes like that could be left at the ground-floor reception. Security at the university, even after 9/11, was not impressive.

I followed the routines with care before opening the envelope. Felt it with my fingertips for irregularities, smelled it for any trace of chemicals.

Inside were a dozen articles cut out of newspapers and magazines. They all dealt with the fact that the nuclear disarmament talks between ourselves and Russia were on the point of collapse, an historic moment at which the media was more taken up by global terrorism, the Muslim threat, in fact. I had read all these articles and columns. Their common theme was that we in the U.S. were on the point of unilaterally withdrawing from the Anti-Ballistic Missile Treaty, which had been one of the cornerstones in the balance of terror since 1972. This was a development that would lead to a dramatic worsening in the climate for nuclear weapons negotiations.

The clippings had underscores in green ink, in some cases of long passages, sometimes the odd sentence in which a few words had also been circled. At first sight they conveyed no clear meaning. Presumably there was more to them than met the eye.

Having without success tried the most obvious methods—from assembling the underscored words into functioning sentences, to combining the first letters of the words in different ways, or the last ones, those with an even number, those with an odd number, following the Fibonacci sequence, every imaginable series of numbers, forward and backward—I finally had a go at different variations of dates. A classic yet long-forgotten means of teasing out a hidden message.

I started with the day's date: December 22, 2001. Shuffled the twelfth, twenty-second and first circled words in every possible way—but without the smallest sense coming from it. Then I took the next most obvious date. My birthday was February 14, 1963. So I put together the second, fourteenth and sixty-third circled words in different combinations.

Suddenly the sequence of words "against the world" appeared. And if instead I wrote out the year of my birth, 1963, in full, taking it as indicating the first, ninth, sixth and third circled words—There it was: "WE TWO AGAINST THE WORLD". *Against,* not *on the side of.*

That preposition could have been the difference between a lunatic and a pacifist. Yet all I did was pile the articles up in my broad marble window bay, on top of one of the piles which was spilling out in all directions. In that way, whoever had left me the articles would be able to see through the window and know that I had read them. A small signal that I had engaged with them. That I was willing to join in, test the boundaries, until things started to go too far or get out of hand.

The cleaners seemed not much interested in the papers, perhaps because they did not stand out from the rest of the piles. My office was one entire analog mess.

What had started out as a number of unsorted heaps had over time come to resemble a rolling tide of paper with no beginning and no end, no visible boundary between insignificant and meaningful, dog-eared newspapers and books filled with underscores in red ink or neon-green highlights, classic volumes of scientific history treated any which way, reports from inspections of nuclear weapons bases, dissertations in the field of natural sciences of which I did not at first understand one iota, D.V.D.s and old broken V.H.S. cartridges, drafts of some earlier ideas of mine—some significant, some less so—incomplete lines of reasoning, papers which had got stuck in the printer and just been laid in the mess by a colleague, cutaway diagrams of submarine

designs, designations of different missiles, cassette tapes of interviews with researchers which I had never got around to listening
to, table after table listing the efficacy of thermonuclear weapons,
unsorted minutes of disarmament talks going back more than
sixty years, ever since the invention of nuclear weapons, strident
pamphlets, counter-arguments.

The entire shapeless research project which I called "The long
chain reaction" staggered on, under and across my own desk.

Which is why the envelopes could keep coming, once a month
or more often, with none of those around me seeming to notice or
care. Jammed together with everything else in the mailbox—with
my persistent ordering of new research material I took advantage
of my curiously unlimited budget—the evidence could then lie
in the window bay for all the world to see.

And so it went on for a decade, while my doubts about everything that I was doing in my military guise increased. When the
articles arrived—even though I had often already read them—
these feelings grew. The absurdity of the nuclear weapons system
became ever clearer to me. The rhetoric was being peeled away,
the arguments crushed.

From 2010 on, the articles also began to confirm what the
Team, the inner circle, had known for years. For example, a Russian
military analyst expressed the view that the risk of nuclear conflict
had not been so great since the height of the Cold War thirty
years earlier. But, he argued, the global disarmament mechanism
had no time to deal with the issue.

An American peace researcher pointed out that the top-level
meetings about nuclear safety which were still taking place were
chiefly dealing with political instability in the smaller nuclear
nations, and the risk of the spread to other states like Iran and
North Korea. But nothing at all about the arsenals of the two nations
who dominated the scene—Russia and us, the United States.

As one famous peace researcher put it in an article which
arrived in my office in March 2011: "The world's most powerful

leaders have now met three times in the last eight years to discuss 17 per cent of the global stock of nuclear weapons. The remaining 83 per cent have not been discussed at all."

In the same way that the articles were a theme with variations, the cipher system also changed each time, while adhering to the same core principles. Each time the key to decryption required the arrangement of a number of words which had been circled in accordance with a certain system. Each time the message in clear was "We two against the world".

And then it was February 2013.

I was going to celebrate my birthday, in peace and quiet as usual, with a simple dinner at home with my family. On the morning of that day yet another brown envelope was in my mailbox. But this time the outer appearance was different because the envelope creased around the contours of a hard, flat object within and it had been carefully taped.

At the top I read "HAPPY 50TH BIRTHDAY!" in the same neat hand as ever. Under it was the usual address. I sat there for a long time before I pushed the D.V.D. into my computer, fingering it, inspecting the plastic, trying to weigh the risk, judging whether our little game was going to end like this—with a banal explosion in an office in D.C.'s Catholic University. But I ran it through my own private anti-virus program, obviously not the university's inadequate one, and started to play the movie.

I had seen "Mata Hari" once before, at the university's film club during my student years. But it had not left much of a mark. Seeing it now, I was surprised by how powerful the movie was. From the first scene—the firing squads executing the spies, its sudden brutality—all the way to the dark ending. When Greta Garbo as Mata Hari is led away to her end, head held high, her back to the camera: the spy who was said to have bewitched the whole of France.

After the end of the movie I felt extremely unwell. I went out, drank a few mouthfuls of water from the fountain, took some deep breaths in the dead end of the corridor where I had my room. Nothing helped.

So I lowered my head between my knees and small symbols seemed to start spinning inside my closed eyelids. I opened my eyes, shut them again and sat down at my desk with a pen in my hand. Tried to wait out my twitching muscles, the interplay between my brain and my reflexes, but without success.

I pushed the disc in again, did my best to relax, make myself as receptive as possible. A little more than half-way through I again felt my sub-conscious being stirred in that peculiar way. Now I was convinced.

In the Team we had tried out steganography. The old art of concealing the fact that a secret message exists at all, as distinct from cryptography which only hides the message itself. The classic example was Histaios, the tyrant of Miletus in the late sixth century B.C., who had his slave's head shaved and inscribed on the bald scalp an important dispatch about an impending war. He waited for the slave to grow his hair back before sending him off.

Even that technique had its shortcomings. To begin with, the one thing that is rarely described in the story: how to convey to the recipient what needs to be done to get at the message, for example shave the messenger's head. If you make that too clear—in the old days by writing, more recently with a telephone call or yet another dispatch using a different technique—the information becomes too vulnerable and easy to crack. And if not clear enough, how would one know that there was even something being transmitted?

I ran the movie from the start a second time, and waited for that strange feeling to grow again. This message would presumably be double-encrypted. Partly with steganography—some kind of message hidden within the file, being the movie—and partly with some subliminal technique. The hidden message can only have been shown for a tenth of a second or so, at the most a few frames, something which our normal perception would not pick up.

That is why I had felt so ill. When my conscious was trying to catch at something which by its nature was out of reach.

After watching the movie again, its symbols remaining insufficiently clear, I downloaded the steganography programs which we had tested in the Team. SteganPEG, Secret Layer and QuickStego, which could both hide intelligence and crack the codes.

Digital steganography, the art of hiding secret messages within apparently innocent data files such as family photographs or YouTube clips, had become fashionable some years earlier. But in the endless race between the code setters and the code breakers, even this technique started to be hauled in. One of its drawbacks was the change in file size, noticeable however small the message.

But none of the programs helped me to uncover the information I was looking for. I sat through the entire afternoon, watching the movie over and over, without getting any further than identifying the frame in which the message must have been planted. In the scene in which Mata Hari starts to tug at General Shubin's arm—to stop him from revealing her adored Rosanoff as a spy—that feeling in my brain started assert itself. And then it reached its climax at the precise moment when Mata Hari shoots Shubin.

Darkness had fallen outside the tall windows of my office when my right hand started to move the pen over the notebook, as if of its own accord. There were thirteen numbers and two letters there now: 161 221 192 D12 U15.

As if straight from my sub-conscious, written out automatically.

Then there was only one thing left to do, whether I wanted it to or not. The words rolled out from the back of my head. *I love you just as senselessly as my pretty weird and hellish father, for the time being and onward into eternity, Amen.* There was no doubt. Reading the sequence of numbers as 16, 12, 21, 19, 2, D, 12, U and 15 and using my key sentence resulted in something that simply could not be a coincidence.

The clear text was "THE OLD HUT". And the unfathomable implication was not only that somebody other than my mother and I knew the key sentence—but also that the same person was aware of the boys' and my favorite hiding place in the abandoned playground.

Now that I knew what I knew, I literally had no idea where to turn. I went out into the deserted corridor, but the automatic neon lights had little time to come on before I went back into my room again. Threw up into the sink. Sat on the floor with my head again between my knees, while the nausea rose and fell.

Eventually I got to my feet and walked all the way to the abandoned playground. My watch showed 19.04. If I was quick I could still get home in time for the birthday dinner.

There was nobody to be seen. I pushed my way into the dark bushes where the hut had once been. Pulled on my gloves, felt under the last of the rotting bits of plank—and immediately found the cell phone.

There was a grayish envelope symbol in the primitive display. The message was encrypted using the same key sentence. I ran my eyes over the thirty-five characters, as a musician would read a score: 615 19C K12 192 814 20V 216 219 162 181 721 R/1.

In clear, "STOCKHOLM FIVE SEPTEMBER".

Suddenly I had a direction, a place, a goal—as well as a dispatcher. The last number was a signature as clear as anything could be in the world of cryptology. Because it was the position for the letter "alpha" in the Greek alphabet.

I no longer had the slightest shadow of a doubt. The message could only have been signed by one person—or machine.

1.09

Unblessed are the believers, Edelweiss used to say. Blessed are those who know.

So I did not speculate how Alpha could have known my greatest secret, the key sentence, the scene with Mom at the kitchen table thirty-seven years ago. Could have cracked the code to my whole life. Not then—when all I did was to delete the simple message and reply 19K, "O.K.", before I put the cell phone back in the same place. Nor after that time, either.

Partly because I could never be sure if I was communicating with man or machine. And partly because it was all overshadowed by the realization that I had somehow managed to acquire an ally, a confidant.

I had been wondering about escape for so long, been looking for the opportunity, indeed ever since my basic training at West Point. And when I became part of the Team, that temptation had only grown. After I got involved in the nuclear weapons administration and was given my assignment, became one of the carriers. Saw how far-reaching the issue was.

The simple thought had been to just vanish, never again to reappear. Some quick changes of identity during my escape, the way we normally would, and then lower myself into the eternal ice with the briefcase.

Yet I knew that it would make no difference. Other than to me personally: that I alone would be spared my moral dilemma. But the rest of it would stay intact. They said the briefcase became unusable as soon as the system was broken. After they had altered the codes, and the whole security structure down to the minutest detail, somebody else would take my place and the whole caboodle would go back to what they called normal.

But now—with each new message to the cell phone at the

abandoned playground, always synchronized with another brown envelope in the mailbox—everything became as much possible as impossible. To leave my family and my whole double life. In some way break out of the Team together with Alpha. Escape with the briefcase still fully functional, my finger on the launch button. We two against the world.

I had no idea what the plan could be, beyond the rudimentary instructions which came to the cell phone during the seven months between February and September 2013, until two days before the official visit to Stockholm. But I took it for granted that Alpha knew exactly.

And I had for so long been straining at the leash, testing the limits of my civilian identity, been stirred by the mysterious envelopes with the articles. My presence in the School of Philosophy coffee room had long since become a trial for most people. I would kick off with a simple assertion, already at the time when we withdrew from the A.B.M. Treaty in 2002: that the nuclear weapons issue was troubling me. How strange it was that so few people talked about the biggest issue of all. That here we were, as close to extinction as we had been during the Cold War.

Most of my idealistic, left-leaning colleagues gave the same answer: that there was surely no longer any nuclear threat worth talking about. Weapons of that kind had after all been taken off the apocalyptic daily agenda after the Wall fell. I had begun to argue back, with quiet determination, confining myself of course to public sources yet still getting ever closer to the line.

For more than a decade I had held forth in the coffee room, pointing out that there were still upward of twenty thousand nuclear warheads distributed across the world's surface. That the Doomsday Clock, which a group of committed natural scientists set periodically based on their judgment of how close the world is to man-made catastrophe, had been moved to just two minutes to midnight to reflect the nuclear threat. That, according to the U.N., mankind could end world starvation by giving only one third of the global expenditure on nuclear weapons to the poorest countries. That the cost of the world's stock of nuclear weapons had been calculated at close to a trillion dollars per decade. Yes, I clarified for these godforsaken humanists, that's a one followed by twelve zeros.

Later, I could only recall all this as if through a haze. How I had ground on that in the U.S. alone we had produced more than seventy thousand nuclear warheads between 1945 and 1996, more than all other countries put together. In recent years, compared to those before 9/11, we had at the same time increased our defense budget by more than 50 per cent—while our national debt was greater than our G.N.P. Now we were spending five times more than China, ten times more than Russia, on our military apparatus.

Then I would go on to lecture them about the renewal. The "Revitalization", as it was called: the coming generation of nuclear weapons. I stressed that this was what really caught the eye—and was yet rarely commented on. That the whole of our nuclear arsenal was in other words going to be renewed, at a cost of at least a trillion dollars during the coming thirty years. Once again: a one and twelve zeros.

Many commentators, I would go on, claimed those figures were way too low. That to replace the twelve Ohio-class atomic submarines would cost at least 110 billion dollars. And that renewing the B.61 atomic bomb, our faithful servant from the Cold War days which was still loaded onto F.16 aircraft at our bases all over Europe and elsewhere in the world, would cost five billion dollars per year for the next decade.

Somewhere around there, the majority of my colleagues would have taken themselves back to their offices with many a sigh. Only the most radical stayed and chimed in.

Sooner or later one of them would also take up the internal aspect. For example, say that they had seen a documentary about the fabled "nuclear code" and learned that for a long time it had consisted of just eight zeros, 00000000—because it should be as easy as possible to send off the missiles in a crisis.

I used to say that I had seen the very same documentary.

And that the lead times, according to what I had read, were still at least as short as during the Cold War. The Russians' intercontinental missiles could reach us in half an hour—and in the continental U.S. we needed two minutes before the corresponding rockets, and twelve before the nuclear weapons on our U-boats, were airborne and counter-attacking. That would give the President between eighteen and twenty-eight minutes to reach a critical decision. Under the greatest possible pressure, dealing with all of the controls needed to ensure that the alarm was not a technical glitch, which was by no means a rare occurrence.

I could have told them that the internal scenario was more rapid. By the time it would come to light that a handful of people with the necessary level of authority had gone to pieces, or had consciously and resolutely decided to take matters into their own hands, not much time at all would be left to arrest the process.

But I never did tell them. That is where I drew the line.

I had, however, begun to refer to the books written by Bruce Blair, a former missile operator, which were published in the 1990s. According to him, during the Cold War it would have required at the most four moles to set off a full-scale nuclear attack, including two personnel at the operational level to confirm each other's breaches of orders, thereby rendering the whole so-called "No Lone Zone" rule meaningless. Our fail-safe regulations prescribed that no one person could be alone with the critical controls and were still cited by our authorities as a guarantee that nothing unforeseen could happen within the system. Furthermore, a maximum of two personnel would be needed at a sufficiently high strategic level.

It was also Blair who had disclosed that, a long way into the '70s, the security codes had been no more advanced than those eight zeros, so as not to slow down launch procedures. After he had lectured at one of our highly classified internal security conferences,

Zafirah asked him how many moles it would take these days. How many do you yourself think, he had answered, bearing in mind digital vulnerability, mobility, the deliberate nature of our decentralized war plan? Twenty? Ten? Two?

If some of my very few Republican colleagues stayed on in the coffee room, they would be capable of defending our security routines with a strange fervor. Insist, for example, that the briefcase was always within reach of the President—according to what they had read in magazines without any "alarmist agenda".

I could have answered that there was indeed in theory a close proximity between the President and the briefcase; also a complicated structure of bodyguards, competing security teams, the chance of lightning-fast and unpredictable things happening. *The human factor.* That the physical distance between the President and the briefcase could in practice change—but that it never was short enough to stop one worrying about it.

And that it had been me, and none other, who was the main Carrier of the briefcase.

1.10

Now the briefcase was lying beside me in the fallout shelter: torn from its complex context, just like me. It was now more than twenty-four hours since I had broken out, taking the Nurse with me. Half a day since Alpha had joined us in here. After I had been communicating with her for more than half a year before my escape, using nothing more than one-way messages to a cell phone at the abandoned playground, without having the least idea who she was.

I had done my uttermost to interpret the encrypted messages, whose clear text rarely became any clearer: "SIGNAL", "AROUND MARS", "NEGATIVE TWO FIFTY-THREE POINT THREE", "THE SHELTER", "CREATE MORE TIME. PLAY SICK!"

When Ingrid Bergman—Alpha—finally woke up, it was 8.13 a.m., Friday, September 6, 2013. I went straight to her, as soon as I saw her body start to move, and I asked her that question:

"How did you come across my key sentence?"

Ingrid Bergman did not answer. She just kept on stretching, seeming not to hear. I repeated the question, louder—and that woke up the Nurse. She opened her dark-brown eyes and stared right into mine. As much terrified as aggressive, like a wounded animal.

"You hate me," I said.

I was not sure if the Nurse was able to answer, and in that case if her ability to speak had suffered temporary or permanent damage. I took what was necessary out of my backpack: scalpel, suture thread, needles, anesthetic, syringes. Ingrid Bergman was now wide awake and moved away from the Nurse when she saw my equipment. Put herself by the inner door, to give me plenty of elbow-room for the stitching.

Then it all happened with lightning speed. The Nurse let out

82

a shrill screech, like a war cry, before throwing herself over me. I thought that the normal holds would be enough, but the Nurse matched me, move for move. Our nurses have obviously had military training: yet I parried her initial attacks without any great difficulty.

But it is all too easy, isn't it, to let your guard drop. Even when things are moving at lightning speed, to be so sure of victory that you lean back and take it all for granted.

The Nurse suddenly dived in under my guard. Grabbed my balls, tore and twisted at them, squeezed until they felt crushed: that indescribable pain shot all the way down to my knees. I was as shocked as the Nurse had been when used as a sledgehammer on Kurt-or-John. Without letting go of my testicles, she managed to get hold of the syringe with her other hand—and plunged it deep into my chest.

It was not the strongest of drugs but very fast-acting, spreading throughout the arteries to my whole body. My legs softened at once. Slowly, I dropped to my knees, like an old elephant.

From that position I saw the Nurse pull the scalpel from my left hand. How she held it, ready to strike. Ingrid Bergman did not move from where she had retreated over by the inner door, she just sat there, observing the action.

The scalpel was raised—and then disappeared. Some of the glass shards fell onto the welded steel floor with clinking, crystal sounds. Blood flowed from the Nurse's forehead. With quick and practiced movements she sewed the incisions herself, without an anesthetic, before tearing off some toilet paper and wiping away the blood. Finally she took some bandaging from her own pack and nonchalantly wound it around her head.

Then I heard her dark voice for the first time.

"Stay between me and him, Ingrid, every fucking inch of the way. If he tries anything again, he's dead."

2

TIMEOUT

September–October 2013
Ursvik, Sweden

2.01

We moved through the labyrinth of the tunnel system as fast as we could, Ingrid and the Nurse in the lead while I fell further and further behind, like a dead weight. The anesthesia flowed through my body, heavy as mercury, contributing to my nausea, at best dulling the pain. The Nurse had all but ruptured my scrotum, though she had left me able to walk. Feverish, I vomited in the darkness.

At regular intervals Ingrid Bergman paused to check that I was still in touch. Just a glance back so she would not lose contact with either me or the Nurse ahead of her, searching for a way through the passages like a tracker dog. All that energy, even though she had so recently been unconscious. Maybe she had just put on an act. She had certainly managed to absorb the impact with Zafirah and Kurt-or-John better than should have been possible.

In the glow from the light-emitting diodes in the floor—which Ingrid Bergman had lit from the control panel inside the fallout shelter, as effortlessly as she had then opened the doors—everything turned blood-red and dream-like. We were in a dark womb. The diodes showed us the way through the vast tunnel system: the one, the only right choice among all the false paths.

It must have taken years to carve out the bed-rock, maybe even decades. Large numbers of personnel and materials could have been moved around within the system without problems, entire units, medium-weight armaments.

I could feel in my stomach that we kept going deeper, and the altimeter reading on my wrist-watch registered 260 feet below. The tunnels were narrow and claustrophobic: my head was inches from the roof, but we had been trained to master the elements. Through air and fire, deep in the earth and under water, we had prepared ourselves for everything that was unnatural. Ultimately, for the end of the world.

The system was similar to our own—top secret links between strategic points tens of miles apart, *correspondences* far below ground. Whole cities growing downward, like stalactites, civilizations beneath the earth's surface, unknown to all but a tiny number of people with the highest security clearance. But this complex went deeper and wider than anything I had experienced before.

I breathed more heavily with each step. The anesthetic hung like a lump of fat around my heart, my entire musculature aching and cramping. Soon small dots seemed to appear along the tunnel walls. When exhaustion reaches the threshold of oxygen starvation, one simply begins to hallucinate, tries to escape reality in any way possible.

So I knew that the little dwarf spider—which was soon growing to the size of the walls, finally beginning to engulf the whole tunnel system, like a deluge from an invisible source—only existed in my imagination. Though that was not a great comfort.

I had no choice but to stop and get some liquid inside me and take one of our crunch crackers. From the start, Edelweiss had rejected the normal self-heating field rations and instead got our physiologists to develop a new type of nourishment, to a degree inspired by the space program. Highly concentrated, tasteless nutrition. Thin discs, grayish sacramental wafers, which took up no room and could be eaten whatever your condition. Except if unconscious or dead, as Edelweiss had said when he first presented them to the Team.

"When it's crunch time, all you need is a crunch cracker. And for you, my little lambs, it's always crunch time."

Time 09.41, depth negative 289.4 feet. Had we not been heading downward, I would hardly have made it much further. Ingrid Bergman turned and said, "not much further to go now". My hearing had also started to fade, with each step it became harder to take in the physical world around me. I had often to step sideways, as if my feet were skis and I were trying to clamber across the rough slope of the tunnel floor, just to stop myself from falling headlong. The reflexes from my years of training were all that enabled me, in my current state, to keep a hold on the briefcase.

Without warning, the two women came back up to me. Put themselves, as I was now, with their feet on either side of the steep tunnel. If anything, it was even harder to stand still like that: Ingrid Bergman had also planted herself next to me, lest my legs gave way. Muttered something overblown about needing to make arrangements for security, *to put us beyond the reach of angels.*

And in those circumstances it was not difficult to let them take the briefcase from me.

When Ingrid Bergman reached toward my left hand, I tried at first to put up some resistance. Then I gave in, put my blind trust in her: my lecturer, supervisor and mentor.

She took the briefcase in her left hand, slid down gently like a skier, until she found a position where she could put it on her knees. Used the combat pack on her back as a cushion against one rough wall, boots braced against the other. Then she reached over her right shoulder and took out a wrinkled piece of paper from one of her pack's outer pockets.

The light-emitting diodes on the tunnel wall cast a weak red sheen over the sketch. Yet even from this distance, about fifteen feet now that she had slithered down, I could see on the paper an outline of the inside of the briefcase—but covered in thin, penciled lines, arrows and strokes in different directions.

I wondered why she did not light her headlamp, but got my answer a moment later.

"It's easier to do this if the light's better. But I don't think we want to illuminate ourselves more than necessary," she said.

The Nurse and I positioned ourselves as Ingrid Bergman had, backs against one wall and legs against the other: my upper body throbbed with the effort. Then we both pushed forward from the walls to be able to see as much as possible. As close to her as we could—without coming too close to each other.

"I'm not sure that we need to be doing this already. Whether the Test Rooms remain connected to the outside world. But let's assume so in any case, as a hypothesis, which will force us once and for all to cut off contact with our old friends."

Ingrid Bergman held up the paper in the light from the diodes. Tilted it in my direction, away from the Nurse.

"Have you seen, Erasmus? Quite the piece of handicraft from hell!"

I began to make out what the lines and arrows on the sketch represented. The wiring itself inside the briefcase, the thing that would always allow them to know the briefcase's position. It had been kept secret even from me. I could never find it, however much I had, over long hours, fiddled about with the innermost parts of the briefcase.

I had supposed it to be a single point—most likely the usual G.P.S. transmitter, which our technicians forever managed to make smaller—rather than this elegantly constructed pattern. According to the sketch in Ingrid Bergman's hand, the wires ran into and out of the heart of the apparatus, resembling a medieval tapestry: there seemed to be no possibility of removing them without setting off both an alarm and a local explosion. Which would expose and obliterate whichever enemy had somehow managed to come by the briefcase and attempted to remove the tracking system. At the same time, it would destroy the briefcase, rendering it unusable. Just as they had assured us.

Now Ingrid Bergman put the sketch between her teeth and, leaning forward over the precipitous pathway of the tunnel, flipped open the briefcase. She seemed to have mastered the hand movements at least as reflexively as I had, the waltz of the little fingers, the ritual for revealing the keyboard. Then she held the drawing up in the dark red glow of the diodes.

"What do you reckon?" she said.

I could not find an answer, did not know what she wanted me to say. Then I heard the Nurse's dark voice.

"Like, impossible. Two optic fibers, twisted hard around themselves, so thin that you're meant to think they're a single fiber. I know there has to be a way. But do you really want me to try, Ingrid?"

90

"What happens if you don't succeed? Hell-fire?"

"Apart from the fact that alarms will instantly go off at Centcom and we'll be sending smoke signals for everybody who wants to know where we are? No fucking idea. I just followed the drawing the technicians gave me, like a sewing pattern. But those lunatics can think up pretty much anything."

Ingrid Bergman seemed to hesitate for a moment before nodding at the Nurse. There was so much we did not know. A cloud of secrets among us. Nobody wanted—or was allowed to have—the *whole picture*. Not even Alpha.

With great care, the Nurse lifted the open briefcase off Ingrid Bergman's lap and set it on her knees and then took three sizes of scalpel from her medical pack. I looked at my wrist-watch as she started: 10.24, September 6, 2013. Perhaps, I thought, this was as far as our escape and our lives would go.

The Nurse opened and closed the briefcase a few times, all the right hand movements, her little fingers each on the correct points. Kept feeling around the leather cover of the metal case. Leaned forward, listened, as we were trained to do: trying to catch the mechanism's own breathing.

I glanced at Ingrid Bergman. She was following developments with as much apprehension as I was, her nervousness seemed genuine. The Nurse picked up one of the scalpels and tested it on the outside of the briefcase—before she chose a second one with a thinner blade. Then, with infinite care, she slit open the leather from the outside never more than a hair's breadth at a time, her tongue in the corner of her mouth. The light from her headlamp revealed pearls of sweat strung across her upper lip.

In the end she slit the rest of the briefcase's lid in one long straight cut. Two ultra-thin optic fiber threads were now visible under the leather. She pulled the full length of them out, let them fall onto the ground with a casual flick of her left hand, like surgical thread.

"Shit, I hate working backward," she muttered, "trying to work out what the hell you were thinking."

Then she lifted open the top, felt with similar care inside the lid, in the foam rubber filling between the pockets and the different parts of the mechanism, parts which I had never myself thought of as being significant. I noticed all our futile bits of information proudly in their places. The Black Book, the list of our underground bases, the information folder, "the biscuit". Knew that the essential parts were still concealed: the keyboard that covered half of the lower part of the case. The screen inside the lid.

The Nurse made two straight vertical incisions into the underside of the lid, at the point where the screen ended. I felt my body cramp, the static electricity over my scalp, just waiting for the explosion. Shut my eyes, the evolutionary, albeit pointless, reflex that we all learn.

When I opened my eyes, I saw the Nurse picking out with extreme delicacy the thin optic fiber threads which had been wound around each other, separating them one by one, fraction of an inch by fraction of an inch, with the finest of her scalpels. Each moment lasted an eternity. I glanced at my watch: barely two minutes had passed since the Nurse started to take out the tracing mechanism.

The fiber threads in the underside of the case seemed if possible even more complicated. According to what I could make out from the sketch, they appeared to have been bound together with the threads in the lid to form one single intricate pattern, in which it was impossible to identify which was beginning and which was end. Yet the Nurse was still switching rapidly between outer covering and the insides. The next time I opened my eyes, more threads were discarded beside her—and the briefcase was back in my left hand.

I swallowed, blinked. Breathed. Let the air rush out of my lungs.

"Thanks," was all I could say.

But it was not the Nurse answering.

"Thanks to you too, my treasure. The secret is to find the right assistants," Ingrid Bergman said.

2.02

The dreams, through the chemical haze, came back more viciously than ever.

I had endured terrible nights for so many years. Ever since I started my research work in the '90s.

I thought it must be because of the stress. The endless threat of being unmasked. Not just academically, with a supervisor who demanded so much, but in my whole double—or maybe even triple—life. The apparently incompatible identities which in some way came to meld like an alloy: family man, moral philosopher and Carrier. All of that has to seep out in one way or another, even with a person like me.

From the start, the dreams were of violence. Flashes of hyper-realistic visions of me doing the most appalling things to friends or family, those I held most dear. First to my mother. Soon to Amba, even to the children.

As I began to study the history of atomic weapons, my academic work became woven into these brutal scenes. Images of burning buildings, cities crumbling, bubbling with cooking asphalt and human remains, as if out of a documentary: sleeping hallucinations rather than ordinary dreams.

I was always the one playing the main character—even though my identities in the dreams changed. The only thing they had in common was the savage acts which ended them, often carried out in similar fashion. I could not tell a single other person about this. Not my supervisor, Ingrid Bergman, not Amba. And never, ever, our team's psychologists.

The series of macabre images this particular night—the last dream, the one which woke me up: the only one you can ever remember with any sort of precision—ended with me once again being Robert Oppenheimer. In the most classic scene of them all.

93

The nuclear test went by the code name "Trinity". A small group of researchers gathered outside the little town of Alamogordo on July 16, 1945: for the first time able to see the effects of my creation, little more than three weeks before testing it for real over Hiroshima. The result of our combined efforts. In a little more than three years, more or less around the clock.

The setting was as high-tension as the experiment itself. Beethoven's 5th Symphony, the Destiny Symphony, boomed through the concrete bunker from an old-style portable gramophone, while the thunder outside rumbled along with the music. I waited, impatient, sulking, keeping myself apart from the other researchers and senior military until the storm had passed overhead. Kept scribbling until the last moments, noting down my speculations as to how strong the explosion was going to be—pure guess-work—on the little notepad with squared paper. When the time came, I walked slowly out of the bunker to observe the miracle in the desert with my own eyes.

And for an instant it seemed as if all my calculations inside the secret laboratory had been underestimates: as if the atmosphere itself had caught fire.

The landscape was bathed in a glowing light many times stronger than the midday summer sun. The color was at once and in some incomprehensible way both golden and purple. The reflection lit up every mountain top, each ridge, the smallest crack in the surrounding peaks, with a clarity and beauty which nobody could later capture in words. I reflected that this is the awe the poets have sought to describe throughout the millennia.

Thirty seconds later came the pressure wave and straight after it the indescribable roar, a resounding premonition of Doomsday. An event of extreme violence which only the Almighty could have created before. When the whole sequence of events began to ebb—even at my distance it felt as if some low-pressure area were sucking everything from us, like waves washing out from a beach—we started to pump each other's hands. Slapped each other on the back, laughed like children, giggled in relief, almost in a state of hysteria.

The mathematician with whom I had made a bet as to whether or not the experiment would ignite the universe asked for his ten dollars, a boyish smile on his lips. I smiled back, a little ashamed. In part because I never thought that anything of that sort would indeed occur—that I was the one chosen to cause the world to end: Ragnarök itself—but rather had assumed that his more or less playful bet had been some sort of incantation to protect us. And in part because I had no money on me.

So I asked if I could instead pay by giving him a quotation, which I had come to think of while all this was happening. He looked at me, skeptical, with his childish mathematician's face, not understanding. Then he slowly nodded.

The words are from *The Bhagavad Gita*, I told him, the Hindu scripture that as a spiritual seeker I always had close to my heart. They describe how the god Vishnu tried to frighten the Prince into doing his duty. I intoned them for the mathematician: *Now I am become death, the destroyer of worlds.*

He looked bewildered, as if he had expected more, but then seemed satisfied. Started to say that the quotation could well be worth ten dollars, as strange as that was!

But then he got no further—before I started to tear off his head, taking great pains in doing so, the same way one twists and pulls at a root to extract it from the soil. And only when I had got this close to him did I discover that the mathematician bore a striking resemblance to my youngest child.

Who, furthermore, had the same name as the prototype of the bomb. The one which an unfathomable chain of events had just detonated, without igniting the universe after all.

Trinity. The light of my life.

2.03

I could not stop fiddling with the bandages, despite the excruciating pain, trying to work out what she had done.

The whole area between the upper part of my cheeks and my hairline burned like the fires of hell. The Nurse had made what seemed to be her biggest intervention around the eyes, had no doubt changed both their size and shape. That tends to have the greatest impact. Changing the look, the expression, the whole personality with the help of the "mirror of the soul". Then continued up over the forehead. Made it bigger or maybe smaller, lifted, smoothed, put in wrinkles. Taken away or added a number of years.

For hours I had lain and waited for the woman in the bunk next to me to wake up, Ingrid Bergman, Alpha, so that she could tell me who I was. What I had become. I had the cannula in the back of my left hand, and over the same wrist the security strap of the briefcase which, thanks to the Nurse's first bravura performance, was without its tracking mechanism. Now, for sure, we were "lost to the world", as Ingrid Bergman had told us.

My watch indicated 19.52, September 9, 2013, depth negative 307.7 feet. I stuffed the notebook back into the very bottom of my combat pack. Put aside my chronicle for you in posterity, my account of everything that had happened since we left the fallout shelter three days ago. The night lights in the roof of the enormous rock chamber, sixty-five feet up, had been just enough for me to keep working on my chronicle as I peered through the minimal slits between the bandages covering my eyes.

I lay on my back in the stone-hard bunk. Tried to find a position in which I was comfortable. And, at that moment, Ingrid Bergman woke up.

Sat upright, cast her eyes around, ran her hands over her face.

Then looked straight at me. Even she was covered in bandages, all the way down over her throat. But her voice was intact—although her lips too must have been modified. The melody floated out through the narrow opening where the mouth was, seemed to fill the whole rock hall, all the way up to the roof.

"You don't make a very convincing mummy."

I waited for her to continue.

"Quite a few people are better dead than alive. But you're not one of them, Erasmus."

In the silence that followed I saw another dwarf spider move over the back of my hand. I pinched my arm hard in an attempt to work out if this too was a hallucination—but the only result was an uneven red patch on the skin, while the little creature clambered over my wrist-watch.

"Who are you?"

It was only with difficulty that I was able to form the question, moved my lips as little as I could. The stitches cut like barbed wire into the corners of my mouth and around my eyelids. My whole face flared, as if covered with hot wax under the bandages.

"As I said, my treasure: your Alpha."

"And before that?"

"The Carrier of the briefcase immediately before you. While I was your supervisor, working on your dissertation, before NUCLEUS was created."

I tried to keep my mouth steady, but it seemed to have a life of its own. My voice sounded slurred and frightening—even to me.

"And before then?"

"Your lecturer. She who taught you everything."

"And before then?"

Ingrid Bergman did not answer, brought the quiz to an end and turned to face into the rock chamber. I followed her look: the movements of the bandaged head. In addition to our two metal bunks and the moveable surgical lamps, I could make out a number of undefined bits of apparatus further away in the dark, like gigantic bugs now extinct. It seemed to be some kind of technical equipment which time had left behind. Manual microscopes, gauges with big displays, computers with mounted, open-reel tapes and light bulbs, all made of metal and covered with a thin, red-gray coating.

Turning my head, first to scan the shorter side of the rock chamber and then the longer one, I was able to get an idea of its size, despite my limited vision through the eyeholes in my bandages. I decided that it must be at least two hundred feet by two hundred, like two running tracks next to each other, with a total surface area of almost one and a half square miles. In other words, the size of a modest hangar. At most a quarter of it was illuminated by the emergency night lighting in the roof, a further quarter lay in semi-darkness—while at least half of the rock hall was plunged in darkness.

Nowhere was there a sign of the Nurse. I let my eyes search further around the visible quarter: past shelves fixed onto the rough bed-rock wall, fume cupboards with rows of flasks which looked as if they had never been touched, crystallization bowls and graduated glasses. Empty, aged climatic chambers. A man-sized X-ray spectrometer, which might have seemed miraculous in the mid-1960s. An M.S.E. centrifuge which was at least as bulky.

"Where the hell *are* we?"

Ingrid Bergman gave no answer to that either, still facing away from me, staring into the room.

"What do you know about the others... the Team, Edelweiss, the President himself?"

She started, turned her bandaged head with caution to me: as if I had woken her. Had to clear her throat before she could answer.

"So far as Kurt and John are concerned, I know where they are. And I would guess that all the others are in about the same place, back at the starting point. Sitting there on the other side of the Atlantic, trying to determine where we have vanished. How the bed-rock can have gobbled us up."

"How can you be so sure: how do you know they're not on our trail?"

"Because you can't search for something which doesn't exist. Which never has existed."

"And yet here we are."

"True, my treasure. Here we are."

Just as I had begun to get to my feet and to go off to investigate where we might be, Ingrid Bergman broke the silence. Started to tell the story. Feeling her way at first, then picking up pace.

It was a strange scene, a filmic moment. Two mummy-like figures in metal bunks in a vast rock hall, illuminated by a weak, bluish glow seeping from the night-light of the neon tubes. Some sort of melody flowing out of the hole cut into the bandages around the mouth of one of the mummies.

And it took an hour before she was done. Afterward I had no idea if any of it was true, even so much as a single word of it.

*   *   *

Her real name, she said, was Ingrid Oskarsson. I had continued to stare unblinking at the white of the bandaged head until a register in the voice—"so, call me Ingrid"—drew me back. She had been a promising science student, with peculiar side interests in cultural history, hand-picked fresh out of high school to work in the top secret Swedish nuclear weapons program, managed by the mighty Swedish National Defense Research Institute, the F.O.A. At the end of the 1950s, the project was divided into an "S." program and an "L." program, the names characterized by the genius for security policy euphemisms which were preferred by the young social democratic government of the time. "S." stood for "shelter"—and its primary function was to conceal what was being carried out by "L.", as in "loading".

The process was concealed under a similar, ponderous use of bureaucratic terminology. Aided by the expression "Extended security research", one could at a measured pace take all the steps necessary for making a finished atom bomb, while the general public was none the wiser.

According to Ingrid, "*Freedom Of Action*" was another of those coded expressions. The official meaning was that, in case of war, the country could change course and begin production of a Swedish atom bomb. But in fact a number of those weapons should have been finished by then, the work completed behind a veil of secrecy. Ingrid referred to it as dupery of the public and the politicians on a grand scale over a number of decades. Awareness of the Swedish atom bomb project was kept within a tight group of people.

"It was also during the first half of the '60s, that we began to build this sprawling tunnel system. It just kept growing—and soon we started to refer to the whole construction as the Inner Circle. I wasn't the person managing the project, not in practice, we had so many engineers, after all. People who loved dead ends, chutes, gizmos, hidden lighting systems, technological finesses. You know, Erasmus, *boys*. Like all the technicians behind the scenes of NUCLEUS."

I looked into the holes that were her eyes: could see that her eyelids were shut. As if she could picture it all whilst telling her story.

"And even before that, the whole of central Stockholm was riddled with holes, like a mature cheese. We could fit eight thousand civilians plus the entire government into the Klara air-raid shelter alone, and the atom bomb-proof one at Katarinaberget was the world's biggest when it was completed in 1957. Besides that, there were the years of what was referred to as "city transformation" and renovation of the center of town. The demolition of the old heart of Stockholm, the newspaper district, the destruction of cultural historical sites, the expansion of the district heating system after the war. Vast modernistic projects above and below ground— which at the same time served as a cover for all the construction which was going on deeper in the bed-rock. So we linked the existing facilities, creating nodes within our own navigation system: the new geography, in which we blasted out the most secret installations further below the district heating construction, so that nobody who was not authorized would have any business being down at that level. And spread out this underground landscape as far as we could. Wider than the city itself, in fact."

She opened her eyes again, behind the slits. I felt her looking straight at me.

"We took our inspiration from the building of the underground train system in Moscow, all that monumental energy. Even this took its time, of course, years, half a decade of day-to-day work for many secret bus-loads of explosives experts and mining engineers from Kiruna: the most skilled of workers. And the basis for it was already there. A number of world-class facilities deep in the Scandinavian bed-rock, perfect for secrets and protection, not even the angels could reach there. All that was missing was a person with the right kind of spirited imagination. Or rather, two."

Beyond her, I could make out parts of the apparatus, the out-of-date laboratory equipment. Everything seemed to be there as before, abandoned in a controlled flight, left neat and tidy. Or as if somebody had been there not long ago to clean up.

"But even all of this—years of tunnel construction, detonations every night, as far below the surface as a human being can bear to spend time without losing their senses—was just a means and not an end. The Inner Circle nothing more than a transportation system with a number of connected laboratories. As well as a way of making everything disappear, if that should prove necessary. Including ourselves and all our discoveries, the whole topography of secrets, the halls of mirrors. Into the same invisibility in which it had first been created."

She shivered in the chill of the rock chamber. I handed her my blanket, which she at once wrapped around her own one. A cloud of breath rose toward the roof, like smoke from a dragon, as she continued.

"You understand, Erasmus, we had come a long way. Much further than the rest of the world realized. Sweden as a territory had, after all, been asleep: it had kept itself off the battlefield for more than 150 years. But during and after the Second World War, we had acquired hidden strengths. Real superheroes. Prominent nuclear physicists. Not just Lise Meitner and Manne Siegbahn, our own Nobel Prize winner, but also Glenn Seaborg—who was of Swedish descent and who retained a deep love of this country. All civilized countries have had scientific golden ages. That inexplicable accumulation of knowledge and talent in some lucrative field during a specific historical period, whether it be navigation or the petroleum industry. And this field was very much ours. But you know all that, my treasure. At least in theory."

I thought I saw her playful eyes behind the bandages. It was the first hint since our unexpected reunion: that she and I had worked so closely, for so long, on my elusive dissertation. She acknowledged that I knew about the broader Swedish context. Nevertheless I did not react, let her lead on.

"I myself never really made the grade on the scientific side. But I had one god-sent gift: I could pull the wool over people's eyes, society as a whole and the politicians, public opinion, whoever. My specialty was in that *mental* side of things. So I suppose my biggest contribution lay in keeping the secret secret."

A sound came from the unlit part of the rock chamber, someone was moving in the darkness. My body tensed—but Ingrid kept going, regardless.

"For safety's sake, we kept the management of the project not just within the Inner Circle, but to its very core. So there weren't many who themselves knew the tunnels by heart. Had the entrance codes to the different sections, could follow the light-emitting diodes through the mass of the bed-rock, were aware of the structure of the whole labyrinth. Who didn't just have instructions to follow—but knew the full scope of the project, both the tunnel system and the secrets within."

Although a shape was emerging from the gloom, she wanted to finish what she was saying. And that needed just one more sentence.

"I should say there were two of us."

When the Nurse joined us in our dimly lit part of the hall, she too was heavily bandaged. Not in one series of dressings over the whole of her head, like us, but in three separate bits. On the forehead, where the glass splinters from the lamp had penetrated. Under the eyes and around the mouth. The three sections were distinct from each other—I assumed because she still needed to be able to work without having her head draped in bandages, to make a series of incisions on herself, always maintaining some freedom of movement. Or perhaps because this particular Nurse seemed to do everything her very own way.

"I know, you should have got more rest. But Ingrid says that we don't have the time. So this sure as hell isn't going to be much fun, unless of course you're funny that way."

She ran a quick check on pulse, temperature, oxygen supply. Then the Nurse asked us to hold up our drips ourselves while she wheeled our bunks across the rock chamber, toward an almost invisible door. When one came right up to it, a small line could be discerned in the rough rock wall. I didn't see the door handle at all until the Nurse pressed it down and I heard a muffled click. I gripped the briefcase harder, the cannula tight over the back of my hand. I felt my pulse quicken from that minimal exertion.

The chamber that we now came into was approximately fifteen feet by fifteen, and at least as high. I made out another metal bunk, X-ray equipment, an unwieldy defibrillator, needle destroyers, four portable spotlights, a hydraulic operating table, a full-length mirror and something that looked like an autopsy table made of tiles. Everything covered in the same red-gray coating as the equipment in the larger chamber. The atmosphere was heavy with the 1960s, the Cold War, the passage of time.

"What do you think, my treasure?"

I did not answer, didn't even turn toward Ingrid. Tried with my limited field of vision to observe the Nurse on my other side: what she was going to do with us this time. Saw her start to dig around in her gigantic medical pack, while Ingrid picked up her story again.

"In these two laboratories, at the deepest point in the bed-rock, negative 308 feet, we studied the effects. On the dead and the living, humans and animals, short-term and long. The instant and eternity. Everything was so new for us, you see—and for the rest of the world. That's the sole mitigating factor in our defense. We called them 'Test Rooms'. What we thought of as military humor, Erasmus. You know: keeping things at arm's length. Keeping them relative."

Our psychologists always stressed how important it was, after our operations, to be as few as possible when the bandages were removed. Not to do the rounds, not to have unauthorized people about. In an ideal scenario only the doctor and the patient. To get over the shock of being confronted with someone different staring back at you from the mirror. And the whole monstrous side of it. The stitches like rails across your face, the seeping wounds, large bluish areas.

But now I was lying here in the bunk in front of the mirror, together with someone I knew nothing about, even what she was doing here, and wondering what she had made of my face. And with another person who could just as easily have been telling me fairy tales as telling me the truth.

She—Ingrid Bergman, or maybe Oskarsson, Ingrid—was the first one out. The Nurse maneuvered her higher against the bed-head, so she could see herself in the mirror. Undid the bandages, like a Christmas present, from the bottom up: chin, mouth, nose, eyes, forehead. I was already gaping far too much when the lower part of her face was uncovered. Felt the tear in the corners of my mouth as my stitches came undone under the dressings, one by one.

104

At least twenty years had been lifted from her. Under the grotesque bruising, there was little left of the mature Ingrid Bergman. No round face, no full mouth, nothing soft or spirited left at all. Instead she had acquired heavy eyelids and even higher cheekbones, thin lips, the mouth a straight line. The whole face had become younger, but also more severe.

I understood right away, of course, what the Nurse had been after: whom she had wanted to bring out. But I said nothing.

Then it was my turn—while Ingrid lay there and stared straight into the mirror, saying not a word, trying to piece together herself and her new face. I laid the briefcase on the bunk. Braced myself against both sides with my knees, prepared for all eventualities. When the Nurse removed the bandages, loop by loop, it felt as if she were pulling pieces of barbed wire out of my skin.

You can never be prepared for the unguessable. However much you train to do just that.

So I had to put one foot on the floor, and try to fend off the feeling that I was falling not just forward but inward, even though I was propped against the bedhead of the metal bunk. Took a succession of deep breaths when I saw *myself*, or whatever I was supposed to call it, in the mirror. Transformed beyond recognition.

My nose was the most striking thing. A large meaty lump in the middle of my face, still swollen, blue-red. Even my mouth had become thicker, coarser, because my lips had been made much fuller. But the totality of the change was most noticeable. Not just in certain parts of my face—but in everything that had been me to this point. It was the work of a master.

The Nurse, the master herself, stood between my bunk and Ingrid's. Put her hands on my shoulders and looked, with me, in the mirror.

"Lionel Barrymore. Don't you think?" she said with a meaningful smile.

I made no reply, did not even know if it was a question or an answer. Some sort of code.

"You know, Erasmo: 'Malaya', 'You Can't Take It With You', 'Mata Hari', 'Grand Hotel', 'Sadie Thompson'."

The list of movie titles sounded like a badly encrypted message. I combined them in my mind to make a conceivable yet incomprehensible message. *Mata Hari in the Grand Hotel in Malaysia tells Sadie Thompson: 'You can't take it with you'.*

"'Mata Hari' is probably the only one I've seen . . . But that one I've seen a great many times."

She said nothing, just wheeled me and Ingrid away from the mirror, the drip stands along with us. When we had got back to our places in the larger rock chamber, the Nurse changed our drips and tucked us in—so tight that we would, in our current state, not be able to get out.

"O.K., sweet dreams. And fucking keep still for the next few days. Anything beyond breathing and blinking is at your own risk."

2.04

After precisely thirty minutes, Ingrid wobbled ahead of me toward the door opposite the one leading into the operating theater, where I imagined the Nurse was. Long enough for her to have fallen asleep.

My whole body felt like jelly, pain was burning all over my face. I heaved my weight after her through the darkness, up to the concealed entrance. Just as Ingrid opened the door—it sounded like the exact code that she had used to get us both out of the shelter and into the Test Rooms: eight beeps, in the same rhythm—all of a sudden my legs folded under me. I keeled over to the side. Fell straight onto the razor-sharp edge of the last fume cupboard along the rock wall.

Ingrid helped me into the tunnel system, now coal-black. Carrying her headlamp, she switched it on and directed the beam at my hip. A large patch on the uniform jacket, about four inches by six, was red-brown with blood. I stopped myself from checking in on my body: knew that adrenaline can suppress the pain of even the worst injuries.

"It's O.K., I can hardly feel anything. We can stitch it later. Just take us where we're meant to be going," I said.

"Absolutely, my treasure. We'll soon be in a safe haven."

She switched off her headlamp again and went down the spiral staircase at astonishing speed. That woman—whoever she might be—must have phenomenal basic fitness. I clung to the handrail, concentrated on keeping up through the pitch-black, not losing the feeling of her proximity.

"Besides, you don't even have a scratch."

I heard her voice from somewhere down the stairs, stopped and waited. Knew that the follow-up was on its way, after the artificial pause; just held on for that melodic voice. Her seductive little tales.

"What you've got on your jacket isn't blood, Erasmus, but a compound of gunpowder and rust—which has covered most of the metals in there for decades. Gunpowder accelerates corrosion, as you probably remember: not even stainless steel remains rust-free when enough test charges have been detonated, small proto-types for bigger things. So there were a number of reasons why we called that place the Test Rooms."

Proceeding down the spiral staircase, I tried to recall Edelweiss' lectures on this very topic, check whether any of it might be true. Still I said nothing. As soon as my feet touched level ground, the L.E.D.s in the tunnel floor came on. Ingrid was standing a few feet ahead in the middle of the passageway; as far as I could see, without having contact with any controls along the wall.

"How did you do that?" I managed to say before running out of breath.

Without replying, she set off again at an even faster pace—all but breaking into a run—along the shining red line which extended as far as the eye could see. And even though I could not remember the last bit to the Test Rooms at all well, with the anesthetic still humming through my body, I was almost certain that the diodes were showing us a different route to the one before.

I breathed in as deeply as I could, trying to oxygenate myself down here in the close and humid tunnel system, and set off after her. For some reason Ingrid seemed to have recovered better than I had, even though I had devoted the whole of my adult life to preparing myself physically for just this sort of challenge. Maybe it was the paradoxical effect of her age: the twenty years which separated us had given her much more time to train.

Whatever the reason, there was nothing to suggest that the woman who was half running ahead of me was close to seventy years old. No evidence, other than scant biographical details which as students we had found in the university's registers—after taking bets as to her real age.

Her backpack—a combat pack which seemed a replica of my

own—was my navigational beacon: the only thing I had to steer by, that I needed to keep in my sight. Underneath it one could also see something smaller, flatter. It looked like a normal case for a normal laptop. But it couldn't be.

After half a mile or so heading straight, the L.E.D.s along the tunnel walls began to show the path leading up a steep gradient. Here again we placed our feet on either side of the steep passage, crosswise to the fall line, braced ourselves against the walls, allowing us to keep going, albeit at a slow pace. I kept an ever tighter hold on the briefcase as we climbed. Wound the security strap around my wrist, until my fingers began to grow numb and my knuckles bled from scraping against the rock walls.

Ingrid was now panting. As she turned regularly to check where I was, the blue of her bruised face appeared even stranger in the red glow of the diodes.

My wrist-watch showed how fast the tunnel passage was rising to surface level. At 22.54 the depth was 247 feet; at 23.08, 167.7 feet; at 23.21, 107.9 feet—and at 23.46, 26.9 feet. Then, on a small ledge at the foot of yet another winding spiral staircase, Ingrid drew up. Looked at her watch and turned around.

"Fourteen minutes left. That's more than enough."

She reached toward my combat pack, and took something out of an outside pocket before I had time to react. Then, leaving her own backpack on the tunnel floor, she disappeared into one of the system's passages.

I had nothing else to do but remain standing there in the light from the diodes, peering into the tunnel where I had last seen her. Had no other place to go: abandoned in this strange underground landscape. I wasted no energy trying to guess where she had gone, why, or for how long. A few moments or an eternity. I just counted the seconds and then the minutes for myself.

At 23.51—after the five longest minutes of my life—she came back into the red glow with a quiet little smile.

"I sank them, Erasmus. We're not going to have any more use

for our field cell phones, neither yours nor mine. Quite the opposite. The telephones are their only live link to us, spreading fairy dust throughout the universe, even though we've taken the batteries out. So they had to vanish into the chasm of hell. Take this one instead."

Ingrid put something plastic in my right hand, folded my fingers round it, as if it were a surprise. But of course I knew in an instant what it was. Had so often weighed it in my hand. I had felt how heavy yet light it was, the seeming impossibility of our possible flight—until the old-fashioned cell phone had one day disappeared from the bushes by the hut. After the last encrypted message from Alpha, which read "CREATE MORE TIME. PLAY SICK!"

"I bought them in a small store off the beaten track many years ago, while this type was still available. They're not connected to the net and there's no built-in tracking system. I got them when people could still rely on technology and each other. Three for the price of two, the exact number we need."

Ingrid looked at her watch—and I did the same. It was 23.55. She put her combat pack down and took out four crunch crackers and a bottle of water. With a certain formality she gave me two of the crackers even though I still had rations of my own and, after taking a few big mouthfuls herself, handed me the bottle.

"From now on everything that's mine is yours, Erasmus. Food and water. The flight and the plan. We share the divine solitude of the savior."

2.05

At exactly midnight we were helped through the hatch, Ingrid first, by a man's powerful hand. From my worm's-eye view, lying on the white clinker floor looking up into the glare of the ceiling spotlight, I could barely distinguish his outline. He looked to be six and a half feet tall. Almost eight inches more than Ingrid, and as upright, slim, showing the signs of hard training. Military through and through.

Their relationship was evident at once. I observed the ease of brothers-in-arms, and from the intensity of their first embrace, it was clear that they shared more.

Although I could not pick up enough of what they were saying— it was now more than ten years since Ingrid had taught me the basics of Swedish—the scene was almost too clear: the reunion left neither of them unmoved. In spite of all their years of practice, they could not hide the weight of the moment. Nor their efforts to conceal it.

Perhaps it was because I was lying there, silently observing them. Or maybe, more likely, because one other person was standing a few feet away in the tiled room. A woman who, to judge from their gentle choreography, was likely his wife. How tenderly he brought her forward—so she too could give Ingrid a long, loving hug.

As my eyes adjusted to the blinding white light of the room, the details became clearer. At first I assumed this was yet another sort of laboratory from the old days, but then I saw that it was a laundry room. The tall man pushed the dryer back over the opening through which we had come, without obvious effort and using only one hand, while picking up Ingrid's backpack in the other.

I tried to memorize the face. His eyes were at least as ice blue as Ingrid's, hair cut to less than an inch, and he was going gray at the temples. A fine-looking if anonymous Scandinavian that could have played the hero in a B-movie. The woman was shorter, well below average height. She looked almost small beside her husband and Ingrid. Her hair had a tinge of gray and had been put up in a tight chignon.

The woman stumbled over me in the shadows, but caught herself. Only then did they seem to realize I was there on the floor. Ingrid made a sweeping gesture in my direction and the tall man reached down to me. It was a degrading position to be put in, as if to disarm me.

"So this is Erasmus," he said in perfect English, giving my hand a hard and determined shake. "Sixten Lundberg. Good to meet you at last. I've heard a lot about you."

"Erasmus Levine, sir," I said, as distinctly as I could given my flabby new lips.

"And this is my wonderful wife," he said, executing an elegant side-step in the narrow laundry room—like a dancer—to allow her to shake my hand.

"Aina Lundberg. It's a miracle that you've managed to make it here!"

Her thick accent made me think again of Ingrid Bergman, the actress. Images from the past telescoped forward to the present. When Sixten had pulled me to my feet, again with one hand, treating my loose-limbed body like a child's, his look flicked from my swollen face to the briefcase lying on the floor next to me.

"So, the man with the briefcase . . . Imagine, that such a thing still exists."

As he led us out of the laundry room, Aina behind us, his words rang in my ears, *that such a thing still exists.*

As we went up the white-glazed pine half-flight of stairs into the hallway, I tried to get some sort of grip on the situation— although my strength was ebbing after the surgery and then the journey here to Sixten and Aina, when I should have had a few days at least to recover. I looked around for surveillance equipment, places where people could break in or attack from the outside, possible escape routes.

I saw no trace of concealed microphones, cameras, hidden alarms. In fact no distinguishing features at all: the whole of the newly built house seemed to have been standardized to the point of extinguishing all character.

Only someone with something to hide lives as impersonally as this.

The one break in all of the white was a pale-blue rag mat, and a natural-pine key-cupboard with a small red heart painted on the front. When we got to the kitchen—where the cupboard doors and shelves were also white—Sixten swung around and said we should go ahead. He would bring drinks right away.

The living room was colorful, almost strident, in comparison. Ingrid took a seat on the mustard-yellow sofa. I more or less fell into the matching armchair opposite and looked around to get a sense of who these people might be. Ingrid met my eyes with a soft smile.

But the room betrayed nothing special. The curtains and the deep-pile rug were in exactly the same shade of yellow as the sofa and armchair. Three marine watercolors hung on the walls in white plastic frames: sea and sun in a mildly naïve style. An illuminated display case contained rows of the best glasses, apart from those which had been set out on the glass sofa table—large ones for beer, small for spirits. I swallowed heavily. The smell of honey from the scented candles on the serving trolley made it hard to breathe.

I looked at my watch. It was perhaps significant that the curtains had been drawn, shutting out life outside on a Monday around midnight. And that they were lined with heavy black cloth on the inside. I got to my feet, legs unsteady, and went to touch the fabric.

"Like our blackout curtains, Erasmus?"

I could not hide my surprise, or rather consternation, at how close Sixten had come to me without my noticing. He was barely

113

two feet behind me, carrying three Bloody Marys on a tin tray. He must have had the same training as Ingrid. They had no doubt made a fantastic couple—for those who were on their side.

"This weight probably vanished from our military stock decades ago: it was designed for use during war and in times of peace. I picked up a few bolts when I had the chance, thought that they might come in handy. And when Ingrid contacted me after all these years, they found a natural home here. From a distance, if by chance anyone should have the idea of spying on us, it looks as if we've already turned out the lights and gone to bed. Gives the full illusion, I'd say."

"Nice."

Since I knew absolutely nothing about either the man or his wife—even whether they were indeed called Sixten and Aina—I had to keep him at a distance. But it was not easy. With each passing minute he put me more at my ease, with his natural manner, his old-fashioned, almost boyish charm. Before he placed the glasses down on the table in front of us, he twirled the tray on his fingertips, as if it were a basketball, spilling not a drop.

"Aina will be ready in just a moment. But try her patented Bloody Mary in the meantime, it's got a kick in it, I can tell you. My wife doesn't drink a drop herself—she has her principles, that woman—but she doses up both the tabasco and the alcohol like there's no tomorrow. I don't think you'll find a better painkiller this side of the medicine chest."

Ingrid nodded, closed her eyes and raised her glass. Muttered a "*skål*". I followed her lead. In my fragile state, the alcohol went straight to my head and I lost focus rather than regained it. Yet a sense of gentle well-being settled across what had been, only moments ago, my very sore face. Almost from a distance I heard Sixten's voice as he raised his own glass—"There's only me left then, so, *skål* to you all!"—and he too knocked it back.

When Sixten led us out to the kitchen, to the table which Aina had laid for us, she said "only Swedish specialties" to me in her

114

endearing accent. With the first course, toast with fresh shrimp, she filled our glasses with aquavit and beer. Meatballs and mashed potato came next. The meal closed with "Ambrosia cake", its white icing bright against the brandy and coffee she served with it.

I managed to stay sober, thanks to Sixten on my right. He showed himself to be an excellent conversationalist. Managed to keep my feet on the ground, always finding new things to engage me with—even in this situation, after our escape, with the briefcase settled between my legs under the kitchen table. Nothing which could in any way put our position at risk. Just enough easy and entertaining differences between Swedish and American culture, food here and there, the particularly difficult "sje-" and "tje-" sounds in the Swedish language. In other words: everything except what we should have been talking about.

The alcohol was a diversion, an evasion, flight as maneuver. Something which made things easier and harder in one and the same mouthful.

Because what I was witnessing was a high-drama reunion, celebrated with liquor and conversation. Not that Sixteen and Ingrid were impolite or had eyes only for each other. Strictly speaking it was Aina and Ingrid who were more absorbed in one another. They sat there holding hands, exchanged long, wandering sentences in Swedish which I had no possibility of deciphering because Sixten was keeping me fully occupied.

Nevertheless Ingrid and Sixten kept watch over each other with small stolen glances. Things that would never normally be noticed—except by someone whose life-long job has been to observe.

If I had kept drinking the alcohol, instead of pouring most of it into a bushy weeping fig next to where I was sitting, I'm sure I could have asked them myself, let all inhibition go. Even in Aina's presence, I could have wondered about Ingrid and Sixten's common history. What exactly they had together.

But I did not ask it. Not even when Aina stayed in the kitchen to take care of the dishes, she said, and the rest of us went back to the living room, shut the door and sat down next to each other on the mustard-yellow sofa; Sixten still with a brandy balloon in his hand. I in the armchair opposite.

While Ingrid took her "computer"—the same sort of portable command terminal that I had only seen Edelweiss use before—out of its small case and started it up, Sixten began his questioning. It became increasingly tough, like some sort of lie detector test without the detector.

"Tell me, Erasmus . . . you had a family, right? And left them, just like that. Because of *the cause*?"

His gaze was like veiled hypnosis: gentle and yet razor-sharp. I tried to catch Ingrid's attention—she hardly looked up from the screen before answering my implied question.

"He's snow white, Erasmus. Had the highest security clearance of us all. Including me. Only the Lord himself was more blessed."

Ingrid continued to stare into the screen. I sensed the static in her gaze, she was on edge, like a hand grenade with the pin pulled, capable of saying anything.

I sat and said very little, hesitant. Then I went for it. Since I now had nothing else to cling to, nothing whatsoever in the entire universe—and since this man invited trust. It felt like a confession. I spoke as slowly as I could without becoming incomprehensible.

"Yes, a wife and kids. Two girls and a boy between seven and eleven. My wife gave them slightly unusual names: Unity, the boy Duality, Trinity."

"And you've been deceiving that woman for all these years? Kept her in the dark as to what you were doing, even that you were in the military, living a double life? Used your research post at university—moral philosophy, wasn't it—as your cover?"

"Yes, sir. Fully in line with regulations."

"Of course, of course . . . But still, what a thing to have to deal with."

Sixten looked at me again, I felt the heat of his proximity on my face. I was not sure if he meant me or Amba—but did not want to ask. In the silence, all you could hear was Ingrid clicking away at her keyboard. After what must have been a minute, Sixten poured brandy into Ingrid's balloon and then into his own. Slowly he took a sip.

"But then you left all that behind? Wife, children, the Team, your job as Carrier of the briefcase? In the middle of this official visit to Sweden?"

"That is correct."

"And what is your plan now?"

That was as far as I could go. Partly because I did not know how far our trust in Sixten should stretch in the present context. Partly because I had no idea myself.

Apart from the summons to meet Alpha in a fallout shelter 253.3 feet down in the bed-rock in the course of our trip to Stockholm, I had not received one single concrete detail. The rest had been an unresolved puzzle. Circumstantial evidence, some leads, more or less educated guesses.

In the end I had placed my life in Alpha's hands. Maybe everybody's lives, the whole of mankind's. *We two against the world.*

I began to formulate an answer for Sixten. Something which would be vague enough, and not betray the fact that I knew no more than he did himself. There was a taste of blood in my mouth. Without thinking I raised my glass to my wounded lips, only to discover it was empty. Sixten poured a generous measure of brandy into his balloon and pushed it over to my side of the table. I drained it in one, felt the warmth spread through my chest, and was ready to break the silence.

If Ingrid had not got in ahead of me.

"He knows as little as you do, Sixten. I hadn't wanted to lead any of you into temptation. Until now."

She made a small gesture to me—and I squeezed next to her on the sofa. There was just enough room there for the three

117

of us. She smelled of skin, and something else, maybe disinfectant following the operation. We all stared into the screen.

"This is our most satanic work of art. The only thing created by man which is a constant threat to all of his other creations. No-one can imagine its possible uses, the full consequences. Not the military. Not the politicians, the general public, not the individual. Not even me."

Ingrid squinted at Sixten on her left, then at me, and then she looked straight ahead.

"And that is the only reason this work of art still exists. You can't fathom its proportions: neither calculate its effects in any understandable way, nor present it to the public—without seeming alarmist or unseemly. That nobody really knows anything about the real effects of the present-day nuclear weapons system. Whether mankind could survive a world war using those means. Now that not only we, but the enemy too, have access to them."

I blinked, my eyes tearing up from the bright light of Ingrid's portable command terminal, and I searched my memory. The image was well-known and at the same time totally strange, as if from another era. *Before the escape.*

I had seen it so many times in those days, as part of Edelweiss' repellent scenarios, the simulated nuclear weapons attacks designed to eradicate mankind; had them welded into my consciousness for more than a decade now. The warheads neatly distributed all over the globe—every one of them more powerful than the one that fell on Hiroshima. No longer just fission, splitting the atom, but now fusion too: atomic nuclei molten together in what were called "hydrogen bombs" or "thermonuclear weapons".

And behind these neutral-sounding scientific expressions was the same process as in the sun's incessant internal explosions. With immeasurably high temperatures and very real Doomsday potential.

Not even we in NUCLEUS had been allowed to know the exact number of our own nuclear weapons. The official figure was 7,700 of those separate, apocalyptic suns. It was reckoned the Russians had 9,500, but in our training we counted on them having significantly more. Roughly two thousand of the world's warheads were thought to be at the highest state of alert, ready to be connected and co-ordinated in one way or another, with or against each other.

For us the real number made no difference. It was in any case far more than we needed to simulate absolutely anything.

When Ingrid pressed the keys on the terminal, red lines appeared one by one between the yellow triangles covering the world map. They showed the over-arching structure: how connections ran from or to our nuclear weapons bases, which nodes should be protected and where, and how. I tried to recall the details. It felt like a lesson from an earlier life. My head was bursting with alcohol, pain and exhaustion. Soon the whole surface of the world was covered in red lines and yellow triangles—in some places so thickly that the countries under them could hardly be seen.

Then Ingrid zoomed in on the U.S. All places I knew in my sleep, every foot both above and beneath the surface. The tunnels we had run, crept and wormed our way through. Trained all day long to prepare for what was called "Unauthorized nuclear weapons launch". First to protect, and then to counter-attack, with our own Doomsday tools.

There were now no longer any names on the screen, but they were not necessary: just a number of angry yellow warning triangles. During our first week in West Point's sealed wing we had to learn by heart everything about our seven nuclear weapons bases. Rattle off their geographical locations, mark them on a skeleton map, learn everything about manning and threats and alarm systems, so we would be able to recite it all, as Edelweiss put it, even when unconscious.

So the letters popped up automatically in my mind. It tended to arrange everything in sequences of three, just like the nuclear weapons codes or the sets of genes in living organisms. From east to west the initials of the active bases' names and states produced SJN CWM BLM NDW WMM KW—standing for the air force bases Seymour Johnson in North Carolina, Whiteman in Missouri and Barksdale in Louisiana, the missile bases Minot in North Dakota, Warren in Wyoming and Malmstrom in Montana and the Kitsap submarine base up in the north-west corner of Washington State. From north to south the sequence was MND KWM MWW WMS JNC BL.

Then Ingrid zoomed out from the map, followed the red lines from one continent to the next. When she zoomed in again, on Europe, the names of our active nuclear weapons bases there came to my mind as readily.

Running from the south, the initials of the bases and countries hosting nuclear weapons for us read ITG TIA IRG BGK BBV HLU K. In other words Incirlik in Turkey, Ghedi Torre in Italy, Aviano in Italy, Ramstein in Germany, Büchel in Germany, Kleine Brogel in Belgium, Volkel in Holland and Lakenheath in the United Kingdom. From the west, LUK KBB VHB GRG GTI AII T.

When Ingrid had zoomed in far enough, I could see that some of the lines on her map were dotted. Two of them ran from Kleine Brogel in Belgium to each of Volkel in Holland and Büchel in Germany.

The rest of these lines went to two places which I did not know of as nuclear weapons bases—altogether different locations, marked on the map with black crosses. One in the southernmost part of Europe, on the tip of Italy, in this resolution perhaps Calabria, possibly Sicily. The other in the far north of Norway, possibly in Sweden: in any event, a long way inside the Arctic Circle. From each cross, a thin dotted blue line connected to the yellow triangles all over the world, all of our nuclear weapons bases.

I had never seen that link—and had absolutely no idea what it could represent. To judge from Sixten's reaction, he too was in the dark. At last she started to explain:

"So, I've been tampering with our own global system. Pushing the nodes around. Reprogramming the system of connections. Day and night, over many years, whole decades. Baudelaire would probably have called them *correspondences*, all these secret underground linkages. I prefer to call it all the Nuclear Family. In any case, it's now impossible for those back home, on the other side of the Atlantic, to tinker with the structure. There's quite simply no longer any living being who can work out what will happen when one goes into the nuclear weapons system at any particular point: for example, tries to disconnect your briefcase, Erasmus. Not those who are pursuing us, not the President, not you, scarcely even me. But the risks of trying it are far greater than the upside. That's the only thing I can guarantee."

In the silence, I could hear Aina bustling about in the kitchen, the gentle clatter of dishes, the dishwasher being started up. Doors in modern houses are rarely well sound-proofed—although these ones might have been reinforced. Ingrid lowered her voice further.

"But I didn't manage to finish all the preparations before we were forced to leave. So you see that some of the lines are still dashed or dotted. What we now need is some peace and quiet, here in our safe haven, plus a few field trips sooner or later. Then with Erasmus I can conclude the work."

I turned to her. Saw how she licked the corners of her mouth: her stitches too must have broken open.

"The idea therefore," she said, "is first to link up each of these points and lines, our hellish charges across the globe, to complete the circle—and then to disconnect them all at one and the same time. To short-circuit the whole damned Nuclear Family in one blessed moment."

I closed my eyes, could clearly hear Aina humming. Unless it was my imagination.

"And that will be the end of the system. Every single circuit burned out from the inside. Can you imagine how complicated it would be to reconstruct? No politician would be able to push anything like that through, given what it would cost, given the ethical complications. For nearly half a century now this has been like a secret little movement. A number of people in the know have been involved from the ground up, contributed their little bit to ensure that the system appears watertight from the outside, but with significant cracks within. Waiting for someone to have the technology one day to bring all these invisible weaknesses together: to come as a savior. Or as several saviors."

Sixten gave a little cough. Poured the last of the brandy into his balloon glass. Took a swallow before putting his question.

"But doesn't that sort of . . . linkage exist? Isn't it possible now to fire off America's nuclear weapons all over the world? I reckon that quite a few of us were under that impression. But we've been imagining it?"

"No—and yes. Never before have the connections been put together in this way: fully mobile-driven. Beyond their control, without any of the networks passing through Centcom."

"And the other briefcases? The Vice President's, the Secretary of Defense's?"

"Already disconnected, Sixten. The moment Air Force One became airborne on the way here, to your and my little promised land. Only the angels on high were watching it happening."

Ingrid turned from the screen and gave each of us a triumphant look, as if expecting applause.

"That will bring to an end the era of nuclear weapons. The first epoch in mankind's cultural history in which it could have destroyed its own species unopposed."

Sixten seemed as dumbfounded as I was. He emptied his brandy glass before asking the obvious question.

"But what did you have in mind for the rest of the world, Ingrid? Russia? North Korea? Iran? It seems to me that America would be a lame duck if your plan really were carried through. Open goal for the first long-range ballistic missile that comes along, if I understand you."

"We'll deal with that as soon as we're done with the U.S. and its European allies: the rest of the global contact net has already been rigged. The future has to begin somewhere, after all. In any case, everything's going to look perfectly normal on the screens, like a magic mirror—we've spent decades building up a parallel fictitious system. Not even the most realistic training exercises will reveal anything out of the ordinary. Not until we're about to fire off nuclear weapons for real, in a crisis, for the first time since Hiroshima and Nagasaki. And at that point it won't be possible."

I swallowed, with some difficulty. Ingrid's plan was insane, of course. Grandiose, deadly dangerous for us all, for the whole of mankind. I had known nothing about what lay ahead, what sort of plan Alpha had made for us following the escape. Yet I did not believe even her about all this. I could feel how she was looking at me from the side, scrutinizing me, trying to read me.

"And then we'll all have to say our very best prayers that no-one manages to capture our souls. To make us do the exact opposite in that lonely little moment when everything is to be unplugged— and fire off the whole system instead. Because all of the weapons have to be put online for them to be short-circuited, all of our thousands of warheads across Europe and the U.S. The weight of all creation will be on our shoulders alone. Do you think you can cope with that, Erasmus?"

She could sense my doubt even though I said nothing. The smell of adrenaline, fear, which people say dogs can sniff through thick walls.

"I know, my treasure. It's a high-risk plan. The most dangerous since the dawn of time. But to get rid of the nuclear weapons system you unfortunately need the same conceptual madness as for its introduction. Banish pain with pain."

Again silence, thick as the velvet in the blackout curtains, these reinforced doors. I looked furtively at my watch: the time was close to zero four hundred. It had taken so long, or so little time, to understand who was leading this operation. The wide reach of just one person. Ingrid's unimaginable impact.

Sixten cleared his throat, seemed to be having trouble keeping his voice steady.

"And what role had you envisaged for me, Ingrid? Beyond being your safe haven, as you described it?"

"That's more than enough, Sixten. The gods are already singing your praises. There's nowhere else in the world where we can vanish like this, as if swallowed up by the bed-rock."

"And you know that I don't want to become any more involved than that, Ingrid: I've done my bit. This is critical for me. And it's even more important for my wife."

"You don't need to say that, dear friend."

The silence which followed was even denser, if that was possible. The noise coming from Aina out in the kitchen had stopped as well. I tried to say something, if only to break the mood—but could not find any words. In the end, Sixten continued with his questions.

"But you had somebody else with you, didn't you? A nurse, who you nevertheless chose not to bring with you here tonight?"

"Correct. She's very good to have along, gets things done in her own unique way. But not everybody has to know everything."

"You've referred to her as just 'J.M.' in our contacts, Ingrid. Is there anything in the way of a real name?"

"Possibly. They say she was originally called Jesús María, a promising textile artist from some nowhere town in Mexico. But she's been with us for ever, behind the scenes. Can transform whomever into whatever, heal and cut, likes working with human skin, but she also produces miracles out of other materials. I tend to think that textile warfare is her specialty. Mostly she tries things out on herself, is the undeclared U.S. champion of body modification. I managed to get her to come along. It wasn't easy: Erasmus had to put on a bit of amateur theatricals on departure, simulate a sudden, momentary collapse—and you're not exactly the most talented actor, my treasure, if you don't mind me saying so. But in the heat of the moment, just on the way out to the

124

helicopters, the security people did after all follow my orders that Jesús María needed to come along too, to keep Erasmus under close observation. So she got foreign travel permission. For the first time ever."

"So she doesn't have clearance, you mean?"

"Are you kidding me? Jesús María is like a wounded animal, lives on old injustices, which is the only reason I managed to get her along here. But she's never let us down in action. And if it hadn't been for her, I wouldn't be sitting here today. She and I are blood sisters. Literally so."

I turned to face Sixten, since I could not bear to keep looking at the world map, all the lines, triangles and crosses: Ingrid's whole crazy plan. He was practically upright now. Seemed to be taking on more and more of his old military persona, I thought, despite the alcohol. He had to be a seasoned drinker, may have spent decades as a fringe alcoholic.

"And do you know the current locations of the others? Have you got any co-ordinates for them?"

Ingrid tapped away at the keyboard. A blue ring appeared on the Eastern Seaboard, level with D.C., the White House, our own headquarters. Remained there motionless.

"That is?"

"Kurt, no less. One of the Team's two, nowadays totally identical, bodyguards. Jesús María put a chip in his neck during surgery—as you do to a cat—many years ago, when the technique was brand new. So she would always know where he was. Only Jesús María and I knew about it. Now it's very useful, pure gold."

"Looks like he's back at the starting point."

Sixten knew more than he had let on. Ingrid must have given sufficient information for him to accept his role in what was going on, be willing to take the risk of hiding us away from the world's most advanced surveillance apparatus.

"Is your thinking that the rest of the Team must be close to . . .

Kurt? That they're working in that kind of tight formation?" he asked.

"Edelweiss gives the impression of being predictable: he's usually parked at the other of our two portable command terminals, except when we're on official duty. He prefers not to move more than a few feet from headquarters. Rarely does. But it's impossible to foresee where the power of his imagination will take him, even for me. Zafirah's probably at the sharp end of things now, she's always the one to throw herself into the thick of things, together with Kurt or John. But right now they won't have the least idea where we've got to."

"And the other outfits? The administration, Secret Service, C.I.A., special forces? The global search that must be under way for such high priority targets as you two?"

For the first time Ingrid turned directly to me.

"Hardly anyone knows that we even exist. Isn't that right, my treasure?"

I felt the strength of her glare, so I turned back to the screen. Still without being able to get out a single word.

"Hardly anyone has an idea who we are, or where, you see. Or of the Team's existence. And the few who do will keep on doing whatever they can to stop anybody from finding out—now more than ever. Finding out that we've had this type of experimental crack unit, contrary to all procedures, even at certain times with full operational responsibility for the most dangerous weapon in the history of mankind. So their goal will be to envelop us in the same silence from which we first emerged. Melt us back into hellfire, like a pack of tin soldiers."

"And how many would you say know the whole story, Ingrid?"

"If you mean that we ever existed, then the innermost circle which Edelweiss called NUCLEUS, and I would say about twenty or so in addition to us. If you mean that I and Erasmus have broken away with both his briefcase and my portable command terminal still in hair-trigger alert, you'd have to reckon half that number. The President, inevitably, as well as the rest of the Team and a very small number of our most senior commanders. All the others who were here with us in Stockholm will probably have been told that we were taken down some days ago. Rendered harmless, in terms both of existence and function."

A last little pause for effect.

"But as we always used to say, Sixten: 'What is essential is invisible to the eye.'"

2.06

I could only blame what happened next on my exhaustion.

The fact that it was closer to 5.00 a.m. by the time we came back to the Test Rooms. My having been knocked off course by Ingrid's plan. My lack of physical training for nearly four days—while at the same time having been on the receiving end of a number of anesthetic injections. My body's reaction following the surgery.

But it was purely a beginner's mistake. The sort of error I had not made in decades, hardly at all after beginning my special forces training at West Point as a new cadet, little more than twenty years old.

We could not find Jesús María, not in the large rock chamber where Ingrid and I had our bunks or in the smaller one, where she had carried out the surgery and then gone to lie down for a rest. We searched frenetically, splitting up so that we could cover a larger area, searching with the help of our headlamps far beyond the circle of light thrown by the night lights. Maybe Ingrid really was anxious that something might have happened to her "blood sister". As for me, I was worried about where she might pop up next: like the time in my youth when a gigantic hairy spider had simply disappeared among the sleeping bags during a scout trip.

The darkness, the bed-rock, the plan, everything being so unreal—all of it probably increased the tension. And also the feeling from the two largest display cases furthest in toward the western long wall, which I had not studied closely before. I shone my headlamp into them, one at a time—with rising fascination and alarm.

In the right-hand case were a number of stuffed animals, packed tightly together, in lamentable condition. A zebra on which most of the beautiful coat along one side seemed to have moldered away. A tiger in an attacking pose with its head laid bare: only a thin white membrane protected the cranium. A mighty rhinoceros, with parts around the eyes and the horn which were white. A troop of monkeys of different sizes and in varying states of decay.

The left-hand display case was even more nightmarish—with a number of skeletons neatly lined up. First humans, everything from tall adults to very small children, after that animals by turn, based on what seemed to be their genetic proximity to mankind. More monkeys and apes, and in addition pigs, dogs and many smaller skeletons which I could not identify.

Here too everything was in a terrible condition. The skulls on several of the humans had crumbled, as if eaten away, all the monkeys and apes were missing body parts and each of the skeletons had some marked damage.

My own condition still being fragile, I had difficulty in bringing down my pulse. So I became amateurishly keen when I suddenly sensed something inside the man-high glass display case with the stuffed animals. A tiny suggestion of movement between the chimpanzees and the gorillas, right in front of the tiger. So lightning quick that you could hardly register it: just a fraction of a second.

When I took a couple of steps into the unlocked case, shone around with my headlamp among the crumbling animals, I felt the chill of some sort of silk around my throat. Twisted many times to make it as thin as possible. To cut properly into my larynx.

"Where the hell have you been?"

With her free hand, Jesús María pulled the door of the display case shut again—and switched off my lamp. As I gasped for air a sickly sweet smell streamed in through my nostrils. I tried to work out if it was moth-proofing for the stuffed animals, or some sort of knock-out drug. In the end I decided it must be something for Jesús María's private needs. Something she was heavily dependent on.

Jesús María relaxed the pressure around my throat for a brief moment before tightening again. That was the usual strategy. Let the victim think he might escape—only then to make him lose hope again. Psychological destabilization as well as physiological. I began to cough. Partly because I had to, partly to play for time.

"Checking things out. Where our pursuers might be," I finally said.

She kept up the pressure with the noose around my throat. Possibly pulled it a fraction tighter.

"I don't take prisoners, Erasmo, I promise you that. You've got exactly three seconds. What the hell are we doing here?"

Torture training is just theory, however realistic the exercises are said to be. It is always harder to hold out in actual practice. The spirit is willing, but the flesh is weak.

"We were up with someone who calls himself Sixten. He seems to have worked with Ingrid in the Swedish program, in the old days."

"That much I know . . . that guy. *More.*"

Yet again Jesús María relaxed the noose, maybe half an inch—before she pulled it tight again. Soon I would be able to hold out no longer. I could see small dots in the air: the first sign of serious oxygen starvation.

"His wife is called Aina."

Jesús María loosened the noose, half an inch, three quarters, an inch. Probably realized that I would not be giving her any more information, would follow regulations by giving her details which were correct but without significance. I heaved for breath, tried to get in as much air as possible—and just then she tightened up again. Harder than before.

"Now you've got one second, Erasmo. For real."

I did not have enough oxygen for more than a few words at a time. The syllables crept like fat caterpillars over my swollen lips.

"They had blackout . . . curtains in the . . . living . . . room."

"Half a second!"

The blood was draining away from above my throat, as if my whole head was being cut off. I tried shaking my body, to communicate that I knew nothing more of value, but could not move.

130

My legs started to fold. My grip on the briefcase loosened. It fell to the floor of the display case, the security strap starting to cut deeply into the flesh of my wrist.

Yet I made one last attempt. Nearly everybody wants to be admired, most of the time.

"She said . . . you had been . . . textile . . . designer . . . Mexico. You make . . . beautiful . . . thig . . . things."

Jesús María hesitated for a second, let go a little, tightened again—before finally releasing. But probably not thanks to my flattery. More likely because she had realized what so many torturers had before her: a dead informant loses all meaning. His value falls from one hundred to zero.

"True. You can check for yourself, Erasmo. Follow the pattern and even someone like you should be able to understand."

Some kind of fabric suddenly enveloped me, until I was covered closely in it from head to toe, like a body stocking. I could probably have freed myself, especially someone skilled like me. If Jesús María had not also tied me to both the gorilla and the chimpanzee.

So eventually Ingrid had to free me—once she had found me in the dark, among all the decaying stuffed animals. First she tried to undo the impossible knots. Then she cut them open, before putting the briefcase back in my hand and helping me out of the display case.

Long before that, Jesús María had given me a piece of advice. I only just heard it through the thick glass, her voice whispering as she closed the door of the display case on me, on her way back into the smaller of the rock chambers.

"But don't believe a single goddamn word that witch says, Erasmo. Take my word for it. She can pull the wool over anyone's eyes."

2.07

I had spent days and nights reading the reports. Tested myself again and again, against those who did suffer breakdowns. Edelweiss also insisted that we must have the essential parts of the report in our combat packs. That we should never forget those hidden risks. That we, or someone else in our immediate surroundings—even within NUCLEUS itself—could be the very one the report anticipated. The Chosen One. The Destroyer. The carrier of the disease.

The initials of the classic 1958 report, "On the Risk of an Accidental or Unauthorized Nuclear Detonation", seemed to be a play on the name of the research institute, the R.A.N.D. Corporation, and described at least one case of great importance. A heavily intoxicated officer managed to overpower the guards at a nuclear weapons base and started to make his way in among the rockets at the launch pad. The intruder was stopped in time, and no details of what had happened had leaked out.

The type of incident that went on all the time, and hardly anyone was aware of it. Our world of secrets, that strange little snow globe.

At that point, more than half a century ago, the American airforce alone had twenty thousand personnel who worked more or less directly with nuclear weapons. Not even a medical diagnosis of "occasional psychosis" was a bar to recruitment. Each year a few hundred were transferred to other duties on the grounds that they had exactly those symptoms—and according to the report an estimated ten to twenty people involved in managing nuclear weapons suffered psychological breakdowns every year.

The case notes were graphic, like literature, a horror movie. I still knew them by heart. One 23-year-old pilot, for example, was delusional. Some hours after speaking to a senior officer he was "overwhelmed with fantasies of tearing that person apart. He enjoyed the violence of the judo class. He felt like exploding when in crowded restaurants, though the feeling lessened when hostile fantasies of 'tearing the place apart' came to him."

Flying warplanes became the ultimate liberation for him. Having the potential to hold the necessary power in his hand.

I read these case studies again, in a new light, horror-struck after Ingrid had presented her delusional plan at Sixten and Aina's. Saw not only myself, but certainly her, in these psychological profiles.

Nor were the R.A.N.D. Corporation reports on "Deliberate Actions as a Cause of Unauthorized Detonation" comforting: "We are here concerned with unauthorized acts that are done more or less deliberately with an intent to bring about the detonation of a nuclear weapon. By and large, intentional acts will not be prevented by the safety measures that are effective against human error, such as the requirement for several independent steps in the arming process, safeguards which prevent inadvertent manipulation, and training personnel to maintain safe procedures.

"The borderline between an inadvertent mistake and a deliberate unauthorized action is vague. On the one hand, subconscious motivations may contribute to certain apparent errors; on the other hand, they may lead to actions that seem to be deliberate. An intent to cause destruction may be perfectly clear to the person who performs a certain act, or it may be concealed from him in his subconscious; it may be persistent and lead to a long-range plot, or it may arise as a fleeting impulse. For some seemingly deliberate acts, no motive at all can be discovered."

I read on, put the neutral leaflet that Edelweiss had made of the central pages of the report down on the blanket and then my notebook over it, hiding any sign of what I was reading. Trying not to glance at Ingrid in the bunk beside me.

"The most dangerous disorders are those of the paranoid group. Advance detection is often difficult because persons afflicted with

133

such disorders can act conventionally enough to avoid arousing suspicion. There are two delusional complexes frequently observed in people with paranoia or paranoid disorders which could bring forth the intent to cause an unauthorized nuclear detonation. One is the desire to seek fame—even by a purely negative act—and to immortalize one's name. The other complex is the idea of having a special mission in history.

"The interval between the hatching of the destructive idea and the actual attempt may last anywhere from a few weeks to several years, during which these madmen can sometimes plan shrewdly, watching for an opportunity to carry out their intentions. It is this kind of methodical plotting which is particularly serious for nuclear weapons safety."

I had a feeling that Ingrid gave me a look, as if wanting to ask me something. I sensed her warmth and intensity. But I went on reading:

"More frequent than these paranoid acts are senseless destructive acts committed as a result of impulse disorders or psychopathy. Usually they do not have the scope and magnitude of the paranoid group, but if they involve highly destructive tools they can also lead to catastrophe. But familiarity with nuclear weapons may also breed carelessness. Moreover, people with certain impulse disorders may even be tempted by the power of the weapon and its potential destructiveness, giving them the feeling of excitement, adventure, and drama. Pyromaniacs, for example, frequently desire to see tangible evidence of their personal power on a large scale and may plan for months to obtain jobs in hospitals or even in the fire department itself."

And then the conclusion in the psychiatric appendix, the last part Edelweiss had put in his extract of the report. The chilling fact that what was called "Unauthorized Nuclear Detonation" was the perfect fantasy for people with paranoid tendencies—and that they were often drawn to precisely this sector.

Just because nuclear weapons provided the possibility of

catastrophe "of a magnitude unknown to persons who might have been similarly tempted in the past. Nuclear weapons will not only make acts technically possible that could scarcely have been dreamed of before, but they may even constitute a specific attraction for those with paranoid potentialities. In fact, in certain paranoid delusions, a nuclear detonation may seem the ideal tool for translating the fantasies into reality."

So here I was: in the company of what seemed like at least two such lunatics, on the run, hidden from the rest of the world.

My watch showed 09.56, September 11, 2013. Twelve years since we got our blank check to do whatever we wanted, with the entire so-called international community on our side. And more than a day since Ingrid slipped into a rehabilitation-induced lethargy, after extricating me from the glass display case.

Eventually I gave up reading, had no choice but to linger in this uncertainty, and put the leaflet back in my combat pack. Instead— to distract myself—I took a closer look at Jesús María's strange piece of fabric. Tried to understand what it was that had enveloped me in the glass case. To follow the detailed instructions which Jesús María must have written on the black fabric while she was waiting for us the other night, with arrows and dashed lines in what looked like chalk.

Fold here. Pull the zipper up along edge "A" and bring it to opposing edge "C", then fold into "F". The briefcase goes in the pouch which this creates—and the combat pack in the compartment on the underside. If you do this right, the decals will appear on the outside of the upper pocket. And just be aware that I'm bored to death, Erasmo. You're taking forever!

But in spite of all my efforts, I could not bring together what Jesús María had called THE HYBRID. In enormous capital letters all the way across the long side "E". So when Ingrid finally woke up I was forced to ask her for help. It was immediately apparent that she was familiar with the way Jesús María thought, her twisted creativity, clearly on a level with her own. After an hour or so we

135

had managed to assemble the strange construction. A sort of combination of case and backpack—with the capacity not only to *hold* but also to *be* both.

"This is how Jesús María passes the time. The art of folding, like origami, or a traditional Japanese kimono. Clothes which can take a day to put on and which at the same time become some sort of ceremonial armament. Equipment which is indistinguishable from its structure, where surface and what lies beneath constantly change places."

She put the empty contraption on my back, tightened the straps, found the exact balance. It was both incredibly light and surprisingly heavy. Like silk with steel or lead woven into it, a mythical hero's armor. In some way the weight gradually spread across my back until I no longer noticed it.

Ingrid lifted in first the briefcase and then the combat pack, each in its designated compartment. Both of these bulky objects disappeared almost without trace, swallowed up by the shapeless and more or less organic hybrid. The difference between having zero and 110 pounds in there was bewilderingly small. Then she also took my weapon and put it in its dedicated place: a long narrow compartment at the side, hidden yet easily accessible.

I put the hybrid on the ground, walked around it with Ingrid to examine how it was constructed. The combat pack and my nuclear football had not exactly become one—but rather something new, a third something. There were compartments everywhere, zips, possibilities, alternatives. There was also a clever little hole for the security strap of the briefcase, so that I could still keep it over my wrist, even with the hybrid on my back.

But the decals were the cherry on top, Jesús María's ironic nod toward this whole business. Using satire to disarm history's heaviest weapon.

Because her experimental carrying equipment, which now held the "most important object in the world", was covered on top with bits of fabric from foreign cities in typical '60s and '70s style. The name of each place plus a kitschy little textile design image—of just the kind one had on backpacks and padded jackets in my childhood.

Rich kids could buy "St Moritz" or "Chamonix" on their ski trips with their parents. Soon they added "London", "Rome" and "Paris", perhaps, from their solo educational trips in Europe. I was given "Aspen" and "Niagara Falls" by some distant relatives.

Now Jesús María had recreated these very decals, together with some other less usual ones, and sewn them onto the hybrid. The camouflage was perfect. Even a trained eye would not see more than a gigantic travel backpack of the old sort, plucked out of the cellar after many years.

It was still hard to talk, my whole face was too tight. My lips felt grotesque. Only if I formed my words at the very front of my mouth could I manage a sentence—but that was enough to express my unconditional surrender.

"She's good."

"Isn't she just, Erasmus? The world lost out on a major artist."

"How did she get hold of the material?"

With a sweeping gesture, Ingrid indicated the rock chamber's south-east corner. Only when I let my headlamp light up the darkness could I see the broken office chairs which had been stacked there, higgledy-piggledy. As well as the mess next to them: tattered yellow rubber gloves for sun, torn blue hospital blankets for sea. The white stuffing from the chairs must have been the snow in the decals.

"Composite materials, you might say. Wrecked goods, like the woman herself."

"You mean that Jesús María made the decals with her own hands?"

"Mmm . . . Jesús María has the memory of an elephant. Way too much so for her own good."

I bent down and lifted the hybrid onto my back again.

"But it was I who asked her to make that for you, Erasmus, so you can disguise the briefcase and have both hands free from now on. I can guarantee you'll need them."

"She does what you tell her?"

"On odd days. On even ones she does different things."

"So which was it yesterday, when she shut me in with the apes?"

"Oh, don't take that too personally, my treasure. Jesús María gets confused between different men. She lives in her past."

2.08

Those who have not lived through it think that sabotage, military offensive, counter-attack, not to mention war, are explosive occurrences. That everything unfolds in rapid sequences of endlessly dramatic movement. In fact, there is mostly immobility.

Edelweiss used to preach that we had to anticipate *nothing* just as watchfully as *absolutely anything*. The nuclear weapons system is based on this. The mere fact that it is there creates a sort of existential half-way house, where one is constantly as close to war as one can be, even during times of peace: however low the alert level is. The wet-behind-the-ears recruits who are sitting there furthest down in the bed-rock—in the indescribable solitude of the missile silos—have to guard the Dragon with the same vigilance at the lowest level of military preparedness as at the highest, because the system itself is by far the greatest potential danger. All day long. The whole year. Decade after decade.

And it was in just such an existential no-man's-land, a gap in both time and space, where we now found ourselves. Ingrid said that we should take the chance to rehabilitate ourselves while we could. Before she was ready with her planning; before she gave us our marching orders.

So while she continued clicking away on the portable command terminal or practiced her yoga—the *asanas* which had names like "Warrior", "Destroyer of the Universe" or "Corpse Pose", defied description—I picked up my strength training again. Running was only a distant dream, really to be able to stretch out, lengthen my stride, push my body to the limit.

According to Ingrid, Jesús María did nothing physical: needed no training, since her fuel consisted only of dark matter. Pure vengeance. Unclouded hatred. We did not see much of her either, apart from when—once a day at most—she opened the protective doors to her inner rock chamber and came out to help herself to some of the masses of food that Sixten had put in our refrigerator. Like the rest of the machine park it seemed to have been left behind from the '60s.

After I had done my light training session—increasing each day the number of reps, even though my body might not be ready for the intensity to be raised—I went into the shower room. The space must have had a different function in the good old days. I did not ask Ingrid about it because her answers rarely made me any the wiser. I turned the tap counter-clockwise as far as it would go. At first I had been amazed that the water started to run after all these years, and then at how icily cold it could become in the Scandinavian bed-rock. In due course I wobbled back to the metal worktop where I had left my training gear, half-paralyzed with cold.

I decided every morning that I would ask Ingrid about the next phase, and every evening I fell asleep without having done so.

On Friday the 13th a week had gone by since our flight. The day which more or less all of the western world had chosen as a symbol of ill luck. Ingrid had spoken about what she considered to be the most likely origin of this during one of her mesmerising lectures: how a number of Knights Templar had been imprisoned by Philip IV on Friday, October 13, 1307 and then tortured and executed.

It was also the day on which the curse of inactivity and un-certainty—the creeping in my body, the slow increase in my pulse: phase two or perhaps even phase three already—was finally broken.

First I heard the eight beeps from the control panel by the door. Then in came Sixten, fired off his warm smile.

"Do you fancy doing a round, Erasmus? Giving your spirits a boost?"

His running gear seemed at least as high-tech as mine, as was the clever backpack with two water bottles in pouches on the front of each of the shoulder straps. They not only demonstrated that Sixten was a committed runner, but also that he was at least as much of a perfectionist about it as about everything else.

"Ingrid has told me that you like running. So I thought it would be nice to have some company—and at the same time show you something of the surroundings. It might interest you, Erasmus."

My watch showed 21.43. Late enough for us not to have to worry too much about bumping into anyone, early enough not to seem suspicious if we did so.

I looked at Ingrid. She met my eye, nodded.

"Have faith in your pretty new face, my treasure. You can hardly recognize yourself. So how would anyone else?"

2.09

Nevertheless, I pulled the thin, stretchy bobble hat down over my forehead further than was needed, just to deal with the temperature. The training clothes were a mandatory part of our combat pack. Edelweiss—who never himself walked more than a few feet—used to stress that keeping as mobile as possible counteracted the almost physical pain of inactivity.

The watch showed 16.1 degrees in the Test Rooms and now 7.3 up here on the earth's surface. The air was crisp and brittle as glass. Just to be outside was dizzying. Everything was familiar and yet so unfamiliar. The same sky and the same moon as when I was feverishly waiting for the signal, looking out from the suite at the Grand Hotel, waiting for first sunset and then sunrise, before I found out who Alpha actually was and anything at all about her insane plan. Before the world was turned upside down.

Sixten noticed that I was catching my breath. Stopped and gave me a worried look.

"How's it going, Erasmus? Is the backpack too heavy for you after your surgery? I'll take it if you want."

"Thank you, sir, but I can hardly feel it."

"Good. It's a bit out of the ordinary from the point of view of running gear. But even if we bump into someone unexpectedly tonight, or some time in the future, it'll be fine. I prepared the neighbors for the fact that relatives from America are coming to visit. I thought that you would have a lot of equipment, stuff to carry that might look odd—so I laid it on a bit thick. Said that you were semi-professional bird watchers, that you were going to study some unique Swedish biotopes."

Sixten took off his own voluminous backpack, large enough to conceal not just one but two telescopes. Without a word he handed over one of them, which I left protruding enough so that it could be seen clearly. The sign of a twitcher.

Then he took the lead again, running at a comfortable long-distance pace, in the range of ten minutes per mile. At that speed I could follow him relatively easily. It felt so strange to have both hands free and yet not be in civilian mode. The apparatus swayed softly inside Jesús María's hybrid, the world's most important object, contained within her thin and yet tough fabric, the magic she had wrought.

We left the houses and the glow of the streetlights. Steadily I lengthened my stride, felt the intoxication of freedom. As we passed the last windows before the wooded area I could not help having a quick look in. Small red lamps in the children's bedrooms, blue moons with gold stars, cuddly toys. I let the memories come, wash over me, like blood, before I erased the images from my mind.

Then the darkness took hold. Tall trees, roots and rocks on the ground. Sixten was obviously used to moving in unlit terrain. When we had got far enough in, he stopped and waited. Here we were surrounded by fir trees, as in a chamber in the forest, I could hardly see the sky through the dense branches.

I glanced at the weakly illuminated numbers on my wrist-watch: 22.49, September 13, 2013. I was now in Sixten's hands. This was a man it was easy to rely on. Yet I tried very hard to keep my focus—tensed all over when I heard through the darkness how he started to move in some way, the rustling of his windcheater, the situation changing. I readied myself to draw my weapon from the hybrid before he had time to get much further.

But Sixten was quicker than me. In the next moment I felt the cold of his bottle against the back of my left hand, just above the security strap. I raised it to my mouth and took a little of the sports drink, even though neither of us really needed it after running for such a short time at a light long distance speed. But he was not attacking, he was reaching out to me. Making a gesture.

"All the same it's odd, you know," he said.

I waited, watched, listened to the heavy silence. Until the pulse had subsided in my still delicate frame. Until Sixten at last said:

"How the lies just came. Almost by themselves, when I was going to talk to the neighbors about your arrival—and suddenly made up all that stuff about bird watching. That the machinery could start up again like that, with turbines and drive belts going full tilt, the whole business. After forty-five long years."

I had to fight to keep down the sticky sweet aftertaste of the drink. Could hardly have said anything, even if I'd wanted to.

"Can you imagine it was Aina who wanted to move out here? That she, who hated everything to do with nuclear weapons from the first day, had seen a brochure about this nice new area in Ursvik and suggested we come and have a look. As soon as we stepped off the bus she began to sob like a little girl over her memories. Couldn't stop telling me how fantastic the sense of solidarity had been during the so-called Ursvik March in 1961: the first large-scale protest against the Swedish nuclear weapons program. That it was this which got her into studying jurisprudence at Lund University, to choose a life in the law, this which was the starting pistol for the whole of her pretty formidable engagement."

Still no sound. Save for Sixten's gentle past tense and the soft hum of night-time motorway traffic.

"And you understand that I felt incredibly uncomfortable. Nya Ursvik was going to be built bang on top of our most secret installations from before. The Plutonium Laboratory, the Metallurgy Section, the Test Rooms. Even if they were impressively deep down I was worried that someone would stumble upon the network of the old system during the construction of the houses."

A shock, like a shivering fit, ran through me. Partly because the temperature had dropped to four below and I was dressed for movement. Partly because Sixten's intimate old man's voice got right to me.

"I hadn't been entirely honest with Aina either, saying only that I was involved in highly classified research out here. And as soon as the Swedish program was axed I was transferred to the disarmament section—which at first felt peculiar. But I was by no means alone. The fact is that Sweden's delegations at the international conferences included many other unofficial advisors, who had earlier been active in our own nuclear weapons efforts. I could even say that we became a power in disarmament because we never became one in rearmament. Because of our history at the time, circumstances, you know how it is, Erasmus. The power of destiny."

Sixten fell silent, seemed to hesitate. His outline had started to become visible through the darkness.

"So when Aina brought me along to some out-and-out activists' meetings, in the early '70s, I had not got around to telling her what I had been up to in the old days. And then after that the timing somehow never seemed right. A pathetic excuse, admittedly."

When a moped puttered along somewhere nearby, Sixten fell silent again. Even though it was far away, he did not go on with what he was saying until the rider had stopped and had ample time to get indoors.

"So it was impossible for me to agree with what she wanted. We had a spacious house with a proper yard, and we weren't in any need. Even though Aina pointed out the rather nice-looking small lawns which had been drawn in the brochure at the back of the houses here, as well as the wooded area close by—she even went so far as to find out that there were places nearby with relatively rare species of birds for me to study—I should say that I never got into serious negotiations over it. And that's how the situation remained for a quite a long time. A sort of ceasefire, so as not to let the battle over our future home crush our wonderful marriage, just when we had both retired. Until Ingrid called, forty years to the day after she and I had separated."

I recognized the sound now. The little swish when one sort of plastic brushes against another. I took the bottle from Sixten's hand and emptied it in one go. I suddenly felt overwhelmingly thirsty. His story seemed to consume as much energy as a proper long run.

"Ingrid said that she had discovered my wife's name in the record of some minor action. That your people had registered her presence among all the others, in what must clearly have been an extremely systematic mapping of your ideological opponents, all the way down to and including little Aina Lundberg in neutral little Sweden. That Ingrid had seen the first name and the family name and simply put two and two together. Just as she herself was beginning to plan your flight in earnest, and needed a safe haven to start out from. A whole succession of circumstances, I should say. The rather strange ironies of history."

Sixten took a swig from the other bottle.

"And after that the situation was the direct opposite. In other words impossible for me not to do what Aina wanted, to move out here to Ursvik. She would otherwise have interpreted my reservations as if I wanted to avoid memories of Ingrid—when she got in touch I had felt compelled, despite everything, to tell Aina—and of course this would be the most perfect hiding place on the globe. In my humble opinion the only underground tunnel system in the world which is so extensive and at the same time so unknown. Or what do you say, Erasmus? You who are much more up-to-date than me?"

I did not answer, glanced at my watch. Not long to go till midnight.

"It took about a year before we moved here. For that I will always be grateful to Ingrid: that she brought me and Aina together again in this way. To the end of time."

The hum from the motorway had as good as dried out. Silence crept in, you could feel it through your clothes.

"So how was it for you, Erasmus? Was it the double life, all the lies to your wife and kids, which eventually reached their natural limit? Or the *cause* itself? I know it's often a combination of different factors—but still, could you pick out any one thing that finally got you to take this rather grandiose decision?"

I had been expecting the question. Knew that even genuine

146

confidences are barter goods of sorts: you have to give in order to get. For a moment I was quite sure that I was about to say something decisive and irrevocable. About the long-faded sessions with Ingrid on my dissertation, about how the decision had grown imperceptibly, seemingly beyond my control.

Then the icy cold returned, the shivering through my whole body. He may have thought that I was only shrugging.

"It was no doubt as you say, Sixten: a combination of factors, hard to distinguish one from another. But I'm starting to get a bit cold. Can we move a little, do you think?"

2.10

I tightened the straps on the hybrid, looking for that weightlessness, and frequently had to adjust the balance as Sixten increased our pace. First to less than ten minutes per mile, then steadily nearer to eight. Maybe to test me, two runners competing with each other, to see what I was capable of, even in my current condition. Or perhaps to warm me up again.

But my body did not respond anywhere near as well as I would have liked. Even when the pressure was on, regulations prescribed at least fourteen days of rehabilitation after surgery or physical trauma, although in practice that was seldom possible.

The sentry box on the far side of the wooded area made me start, instinctively, feeling exposed. I glanced at Sixten. The area within the gates was bathed in a sharp yellow light.

"You can relax, Erasmus. The box has been unmanned for decades. The construction company puts up the spotlights, to scare away the kids who play here in the evenings—and the night watchman doesn't start his rounds for another hour."

I checked my watch again: just past midnight. Then we squatted to get under the bars and stopped in front of two low barrack buildings with peeling gray paint.

"So here it is: the scene of the crime. The facilities for all of those who worked on the nuclear weapons program at the National Defense Research Institute, the F.O.A., a maximum of two thousand people in the mid '60s. On your left you have the Women's Building and on your right the significantly bigger Men's Building. But most of us with high security clearance were stationed deep underground."

We walked a long curve through the area, with Sixten a step or two in front. Outside the half-collapsed fence behind the barracks there was a smaller section of forest. On the top of the slope above it one could make out a building covered in plastic sheeting. He nodded up at it.

"The Office. They're going to turn the whole site into an independent school. You've come in the nick of time to see anything at all."

Sixten ran ahead, ducked through a hole in the fence. After that the forest path became extremely steep, in fact almost too much for me to handle, more climbing than running. It cannot have been anyone's plan that people come this way.

Once we had got up onto the illuminated asphalt-covered space, which would probably be the schoolyard when the conversion was finished, Sixten led us into the gloom beyond the reach of the spotlights. Up to the electricity box next to some flat cables by the darkened building's emergency exit. After he had keyed in the code on the concealed set of buttons, again eight beeps, the double doors opened and the floor inside was bathed in light.

"Excuse the mess, Erasmus. They had to check the levels of radioactivity in here: how much was literally in the walls."

What we saw, squinting against the light, was demolished offices on either side of the corridor. Rooms lay ruined to the right and left, only the most basic elements remained, plaster was splitting from the ceiling, whole sheets of it fallen, holes smashed in the partitions with a sledgehammer.

Sixten made his way purposefully through the familiar corridor—and turned around with a little smile when we had emerged into a sort of wrecked light-well with at least fifteen feet of clearance up to the ceiling.

"But there's one thing the vandals haven't got at yet."

He clambered nimbly in behind a mound of debris to the enormous, white-painted wall and waved at me to follow.

"Do you see anything, Erasmus?"

I looked for the usual signs: developing cracks, uneven surfaces—or perhaps in this chaos, any sign at all of structure.

"Nothing. What are we looking for?"

149

Sixten took off his backpack and got out a multi-purpose tool—which he stuck straight into the bottom right-hand corner of the wall. As soon as he began to dig around in there, plaster flakes fell away in a puff of crumbs and dust.

"A trifle, of course, artistically speaking. Although Ingrid said that she had never seen anything more beautiful."

In what had now become visible of a naïve painting, one could see four people in green protective suits busy with a decontamination operation after a radiation accident, or possibly a nuclear weapons test. Sixten continued to uncover more and more of the fresco. Large pieces, sometimes a whole hand-sized section of plaster in one go.

"So far as I know, nobody else was aware of who painted this, although the signature should have been a clue, what with all the cryptological talent concentrated here. But it was only Ingrid and I who were up so late at the Office—and it didn't take me much more than a couple of weeks of intensive night-time work, while we still had some sort of free time. And then we disappeared down underground like mountain trolls. Lived pretty much furthest down on the laboratory levels for many years after that."

From the time Sixten managed to pull away the first piece of plasterboard, it took no more than a quarter of an hour before the whole enormous mural was uncovered. It was at least thirty feet by ten, a highly revealing witness to a highly classified activity. In the bottom right-hand corner, the four decontamination workers in their protective suits formed their own little gray-green square—and on the left-hand side was a chemical section with flasks, bottles and molecules.

But the center of the picture was devoted to the atom bomb project. Three soldiers with pocket torches were lined up alongside an imposing, stylized green missile. At the top, along most of the width of the painting, a white mushroom cloud spread out. And in the very middle of it all you could see a couple close together. He had crew-cut dark hair and brown loafers, she wore pink flat shoes and had a blond pageboy cut. The man was handing a small black box, with "F.O.A." written on it, to the woman.

So there was no doubt. The couple could only be Ingrid and Sixten themselves, back in the day—and it must have been a ring inside the box.

The signature in the left-hand corner was a small cryptological masterpiece. The allusion to the nuclear weapons system, the missiles in their underground cages, created simply by combining the couple's initials in the right way: "SILO 1962". Sixten, Ingrid, Lundberg, Oskarsson.

The artist observed me expectantly.

"What do you say, Erasmus? Not too bad?"

I kept quiet now, too: what could I say? Let my eyes continue to play across the mural.

"The new boss of the F.O.A., who came here when the program was to be buried at the start of the '70s, was not that amused, apparently. But the work of covering the traces had to be done in a hurry, so plasterboard would have to do."

Sixten stuffed the multi-purpose tool back into his backpack and took out a system camera.

"I've promised Ingrid to keep a record of the painting, before they destroy that too. We called it our 'engagement picture' because there was no other way for us to formalize it. Relationships of that sort were not allowed inside the organization, in theory, although we weren't the only ones in practice."

He walked right up to the lovers in the center of the painting, then changed to a wide-angle lens to be able to capture the whole subject and backed away as far as he could in the light-well. Then he put away the camera and took a spray canister out of the backpack. Quickly and in a matter-of-fact way, he covered up not just the lovers in the middle but also all faces in the painting as well as the signature with a thick layer of white. Then he looked at his watch.

"Right, job done. The night watchman will be starting his

rounds soon. Which means we've got about thirty minutes from now before we have to be off the site."

My watch showed 00.52. As best I could, since he took them two steps at a time, I followed Sixten all the way up six floors.

There was not the same scene of devastation at the top. The impression was more that it had been abandoned in great haste. The line of rusty metal desks along the right-hand wall seemed untouched since the heyday of the Swedish nuclear weapons program. Traces of the mainframe computer had been allowed to remain at the far end of the windowless corridor, beyond the two half-open, broken, electric sliding doors. Holes for the cables had been drilled into the walls.

"Well, Erasmus, here you can see the Liaison Center: the entire, rather impressive whole which we managed to put together. All of those underground laboratories with the tunnel system and then this office above ground."

Sixten pulled a chair out for me by one of the metal tables in front of the perforated short wall. Then sat beside me and again started to poke around in his backpack. Got out two small packets, one for each of us, and a thermos of coffee. I tried hard to undo the sandwiches with the same care which had obviously gone into wrapping them, to follow the same procedure in reverse, without really succeeding. It was perfectionism, down to the smallest detail. The slices of liver paté lay in the exact center of the rye bread, the pickled gherkin not a knife's edge out of line. And when he poured the still-steaming coffee into the plastic mugs, there was precisely the same level in both—as if he had used a pipette.

Then he went on with his account. Step by step, year for year, while we stared into the holes left behind by the mainframe computer.

"At first I mostly had to sit here and test initiation mechanisms, calculate implosion processes, long days and nights, not getting much sleep. But I was a wet-behind-the-ears engineer, don't forget, and found pretty much all of it extremely exciting."

152

I glanced at the time, tried to get him to hurry up. Fourteen minutes left until we had to be gone.

"Progress in the actual scientific work was quick, almost frictionless. The official designation of the S. program was "Research program for shelter and defense against atomic weapons". And who would be opposed to that? To find out how one protects oneself against something of that sort? But the significant thing for us was the L. program, where the loading wash constructed. Everything under cover of the S. program's smoke-screen."

Sixten poured the last of the coffee, again dividing it equally between the two cups, and said that public opinion began to get too hot for them, in spite of the camouflage. As early as 1956, Sweden's National Federation of Social Democratic Women had taken a stand against the country's nuclear weapons program, and opposition spread rapidly. When in a newspaper interview in 1957 the head of the F.O.A. openly claimed that Sweden could have its own atomic weapon in as few as six or seven years, he was promptly sacked. Popular writers, the minister of foreign affairs, all sorts of celebrities came out against the Bomb.

I nodded with impatience, already knowing enough about all this from my dissertation.

"But just then, in the program's darkest hour, along comes this young girl, straight from high school in Kiruna. You could say she was a godsend. The word was that she was a master cryptologist, a natural talent, at seventeen years old. Before long she proved to be not only exceptionally good at encryption—but also at pulling the wool over people's eyes. That applied to everybody: the most senior politicians as well as our immediate superiors. Formally she started as an assistant clerk, on salary grade F.2 if memory serves, and ended up as a departmental head. In practice, irreplaceable."

"Ingrid Oskarsson."

"Right. I should say that she could encrypt reality itself."

I stole another look at my watch: 01.14. Eight minutes until the time by when Sixten had said that we absolutely needed to be out of here. Yet no trace of urgency in his voice.

"And not a peep was heard for thirty-five years. Not a word about the program: that Sweden had once planned to have its own nuclear weapons. Not a word about secret tests or underground laboratories, the F.O.A.'s actual role, before a series of articles came out in 1985. I cannot say that I was innocent of the cover-up. But Ingrid was the architect behind all these magnificent smoke-screens and the shell organizations."

Then he looked at his watch. Perhaps now a touch of haste in the way Sixten gathered up the mugs, plates and thermos and put them in the backpack, even though he took time to fold up the sandwich paper. When we got to our feet, I had to ask about the strange pale rectangle on the wall to the left of where I had been sitting. It looked as if somebody had removed a painting from there too.

"Yes, that's where the control panel used to be. The one that regulated the lighting system, the diodes in the tunnels, the sliding doors up here, everything mechanical and hydraulic, all the electronics. That too disappeared without trace when the program was buried."

Then he pressed right there, in the very center of the empty square on the wall—which opened soundlessly. At that exact moment, when the lighting across the whole floor went out and before the wall closed behind us again, I could spot the night watchman's torch flickering in the staircase at the far end of the corridor.

"Cool," I said.

"Oh, that's no big deal. Just a toy. But it is amazing how much of this still works," Sixten replied.

He hurried on ahead through the pitch-black stairwell, his headlamp unlit. I had to keep a firm hold of the handrail so as not to lose my footing. Once on level ground—I reckoned it to be a floor below the one we had come in on—he keyed in something on another concealed control panel, to judge from the sound. A circle opened up in the floor. Underneath, the red L.E.D.s showed the way back down into the underworld. Sixten continued his secret history while we followed the path.

"The objective of the military authorities was that we in Sweden should produce at least ten nuclear charges annually by the end of the '60s. Each one of them was to have an explosive force equivalent to that of the Nagasaki bomb, that's to say ten to twelve kilotons, and rising a good deal higher than that. I assume you must be wondering how a small country like ours could have such economic muscle—and there I can say that only part of the funds came out of the government's published means, or out of coded transfers to the F.O.A. from other bodies within the defense department. The biggest part came from our top secret financier."

I did not ask any follow up questions, or did not want to reveal either my knowledge or my ignorance. At 155.5 feet below ground, the track of diodes came to an end at a massive protective steel door. Sixten pressed in the code on the control box and we passed through the shock-wave tunnel, the blast doors. Once we had passed the last lock, he gestured at the room and shook his head.

"The Plutonium Laboratory. It was in here that our First Tier nuclear weapons program foundered."

The rock chamber was significantly smaller than all the other corresponding laboratories I had seen. When Sixten pushed the black rubber-covered button, the neon lights came slowly on. There might have been nobody in here for decades. The laboratory looked as if it had been theatrically left to history: one clean mug; an unused notepad; a loose electric lead on a desk. A collection of props from Sweden's dreams of becoming a nuclear weapons nation. Its new era as a great power.

"And plutonium, especially Pu-239, is a gnarly little bastard, as you know, Erasmus. Not just the alpha particles and the impressive toxicity. Also pyrophoric to such a degree that it can ignite at any time, which at first made it troublesome for us even to handle the substance. Yet all of this was only a smokescreen."

Even now, I resisted my urge to ask questions. He rapidly opened and closed the protective doors to the different laboratories, sometimes with such speed that I hardly managed to see anything. From my dissertation research, I did of course recognize the terms on the signs, even in Swedish. CRITICALITY ROOM straight ahead of me, METALLURGY to the left, MECHANICAL INITIATION to the right and further along the same side NUCLEAR INITIATION. Beautiful capital letters in chrome, seemingly covered in the same red-gray gunpowder dust as in the Test Rooms. The march of history.

We passed the air locks at the far end of the laboratory and were suddenly out in the tunnel system again, on the far side of the Plutonium Laboratory. Sixten picked up his story, in the dreamlike glow of the diodes—as the history itself grew ever more unreal.

"And all the time we had to move ever deeper into the bed-rock. For Second and Third Tier development we needed highly specialized sites, with only the smallest number of the select few having any insight. That's when we had the Test Rooms blasted out. 325 feet down in the bed-rock of the Fenno-Scandinavian Shield. We chose an exclusive little team of researchers, highly qualified but also sufficiently old that they would probably not be alive when the secrets leaked out, as eventually they would. So that they could never be witnesses."

Sixten's voice became hoarse, almost a whisper.

"And our researchers did die, as planned, one after the other— but much quicker than expected. Partly due to age and partly the secondary effects, I would guess. At first I admit I saw it more as a curse: something along the lines of what happened after Tutankhamun's tomb was opened, and I just awaited my turn. But when nothing happened, I started to think about exposure times and realized that the researchers had spent far more time down there than Ingrid and I did. And when I then came down to the Test Rooms again, a year or two ago, for the first time in four decades, I got to see how dreadful the condition of the animals and humans

156

in the display cases was. Then it wasn't hard to imagine how the researchers had gone through the same process of systematic disintegration."

He stopped, turned to me. In spite of the weak light from the diodes on the tunnel floor I could clearly see Sixten's face twist into a grimace. How the stiff and correct mask lapsed—and suddenly he threw his arms around me.

"I'm sorry, Erasmus, but it's just so dreadful! What we did then, without really knowing anything about the effects, and what you are still doing . . . so desperately looking for the formula to exterminate ourselves. Isn't that utterly incomprehensible?"

I nodded. There was so much I wanted to ask, all these veiled remarks, stifled indications. But I knew that the mussel could snap forever shut if one was too eager to get at the pearl. That's what Edelweiss used to say.

So I let Sixten regain his composure, lead us further down, without my having the slightest idea where we were. He kept checking his watch. After another couple of control boxes we emerged into darkness: unprepared tunnels, without either light diodes or floors being covered with any sprayed concrete. Then he got his headlamp out of his backpack and led me over the raw bed-rock, holding me gently under my left elbow because I did not take my own lamp out of the hybrid. It was a way of showing confidence. Giving back something in the exchange game.

"Where are we now?" I said, not least to underscore his authority as pathfinder.

"In the furthest outer edge. The idea was to make the area impressive. In total, 215,000 square feet of ground, many miles of tunnels just to connect the living quarters with the different laboratories."

"But it didn't end up like that?"

"No."

A short pause for effect.

"It ended up many times larger. An almost exponential growth

157

in the original plan—and not at all how it was first intended. I should say that in the end it was only Ingrid and I who had an overview and could work out precisely where one thing began and the other ended. Over time at least half of Stockholm was burrowed out and tunneled through. A complex system in which inside and outside somehow began to swap places, like a logical paradox, an impossible picture by Escher. And even though we called it all the Inner Circle, nothing down here was really circular or symmetric."

After a few minutes of watchful walking—even Sixten stumbling every now and then despite his headlamp—he stopped and bent forward, mumbling:

"S.T.33, S.L.143 . . . just after the bend . . . I'm sure it was somewhere here . . ."

Then I saw it, maybe before he did. A red trap-door in the ground, blasted into the uneven bed-rock, with the same type of chrome capital letters as in the Plutonium Laboratory. I could read "F.E." in the light of Sixten's lamp.

"So what's under there?"

"Haven't got the faintest idea."

"You haven't looked? Seriously?"

"Dead serious, Erasmus."

His tone darkened. I stood, waited for him to continue.

"Aina isn't too happy about my digging in history—so I promised her never to find out. But eventually I came to think that you could do it, Erasmus. There isn't anyone better suited."

"And why don't we just open the hatch now, Sixten?"

"Because we don't have the key."

Once again: there is a time for follow-up questions, just as there is for answers. I continued to let Sixten dictate the pace.

"Besides which, we've got to get back up now, pretty quickly—so we'll have to take the shortest route. Don't let me out of your sight."

The time was 02.38, the depth 195. My whole body was

158

aching as we moved steeply through the dark, raw tunnels with Sixten's headlamp shining the way, our breath growing heavier. I was drained after the run and the sight-seeing tour. After Sixten's story.

By 03.13 we had come up to level negative 18.4 feet. Then I recognized where I was: this was the last spiral staircase up to Sixten and Aina's house. We must have taken some sort of dark short cut, one of a myriad alternatives through the tunnel system.

Sixten entered the code on the box in among the crevices in the rock wall—and the concealed trap-door hatch above the staircase slid aside. He crawled up first, then helped me through the hole with my enormous hybrid, and glanced at his watch.

"We'll have to get a bit of a move on."

He pushed the washing machine back over the trap-door and started to move the dryer, revealing what seemed like another ordinary but somewhat oversized drain. I thought it must be another way down into the tunnel system, possibly an emergency exit from the house in case the first one became blocked. He got this trap-door to open.

What this revealed was a metal panel with a muddle of tiny controls and abbreviations lying flat under the floor. Most of them began with "T", from 1 to 191 in symmetrical rows from left to right. There were also longer abbreviations such as "T.R.C.1", "T.R.F.C.6", "N.I3", "T.232" and "O.G.F.4".

"So here it is," he said with a satisfied little smile.

"Yes: the control panel from the Liaison Center up in the Office," I said.

"Spot on, Erasmus. I took it with me when everything was to be removed: thought it might come in handy. And I've worked for a long time, I'd like you to know. Prepared for your arrival down to the tiniest detail, even though Ingrid kept me waiting so long for an exact date.

"The hardest part was the initial work. To connect our house— we were still able to choose this very one, since it didn't have the best view but was perfect for my needs, logistically and geologically—to the system. I knew that the thickness of the surface layer out here varied between ten and fifty feet and that this part had the softest clay. Yet it took time to dig down the necessary thirty-six feet or more before striking one of our old tunnels. Then to break through into it, synchronizing with the construction company's night-time work so that no-one would notice the racket, and at the same time avoiding tunneling through into their own network.

"But I got to know the developer out here, decent guy, who was happy to show me all of the plans. Then there was a rather extensive bit of electronic installation. New control boxes along the whole system, new code, new network down in the Test Rooms."

While Sixten was telling me this, interesting as it was, I was studying the designations on the control panel. It offended the cryptologist in me that I did not understand. So in the end I had to ask for a clue.

"T.R.C.1, for example, Sixten? O.G.F.4? Or T.232? Just so I understand the idea."

"Yes, yes. The first ones are quite easy. The lighting in Test Rooms Case 1, furthest in on the eastern short wall. The Office Ground Floor Switch 4. But then it gets less straightforward. The 'T.' designations stand for the L.E.D.s in the floors of the relevant tunnels. Counting from the surface downward, in a rather complex cross-section system referring to the relative level where the particular connection ends: T.232, in other words, is tunnel number 232 from above, seen in cross-section, within the Inner Circle."

I just stared at him. All this elaboration. All these efforts to hide. Something.

"There is of course a lot more I could explain about this, but now's not the time. Using this control panel, however, we were able to turn the lights on and off at pretty much every point in our vast system. And you can imagine how I was amazed when the entirety of this machinery—the diodes in the ground, the

160

illumination in the laboratories, basically all of the hatches and doors except for the ones up in the Office—still functioned."

"The display case furthest in along the short eastern wall—the one with the stuffed animals, the gorilla and the zebra?"

"Correct. I'm illuminating it there now: a bit of night lighting for you and Ingrid."

He flipped up the switch marked T.R.C.1, gave a quick smile and looked at his watch. I did the same: almost 04.00.

"I don't have time to explain more. Eventually I'll tell you about it all, before our day of reckoning. But I can say that we needed to know more about the long-term effects of certain particular substances—so I managed to get hold of those animals and skeletons, which back then were in magnificent condition, and which would otherwise have ended up in some store room at the Natural History Museum. And when I returned to the Test Rooms after four decades, and was so shaken by their condition, my first intention was to get rid of them before your arrival. But then I thought they would be a kind of witness to all this horror, what the fight is actually all about. Hopefully be some kind of inspiration for your imminent mission."

Then Sixten pressed on the edge of the control panel, which hummed around in a half circle. What now appeared was a seemingly complete sketch of the Inner Circle. Not only all the connecting passages but also the chutes—marked with black blobs—and side passages shown as dashed lines through the bed-rock.

"We needed a detailed plan of this underground landscape: the cartographers produced a minor miracle. Don't you think, Erasmus?"

I nodded, waiting for more.

"But this wasn't actually what I wanted to show you."

Sixten began to search with his fingers behind the map, between the paper and the metal plate itself. Had to reach around the whole control panel before he managed to get the object out.

"It was this."

161

He put a key in my hand—it bore the same letters as on the red trap-door: "F.E." The double-sided sticky tape, which had been used to attach the key to the back of the map, stuck to the palm of my hand.

"It's as if it's been lying here, waiting for you. Erasmus Levine, of all people. What were the odds of that, do you think?"

I could have asked what sort of key it was, what there might be under the trap-door in the unlit tunnel, why I was the chosen one. But I did not—because everything about Sixten said that there was no time now. He looked at his watch and took a deep breath, before covering up the control panel with the dryer and pushing the washing machine aside again. I dropped the key into the zipped pocket of my waterproof pants and followed him through the hole leading back underground.

"Time to deliver you into Ingrid's care, so I can return here before Aina wakes up, always on the dot of five. As I said, she doesn't like me digging around in history. And certainly not at this time of night."

2.11

I had a hypothesis, but not much more.

As soon as Sixten had left me, closed the last protective door from the outside, I took my dissertation from the pocket of my combat pants. Ingrid was fast asleep: she did not seem to have woken up to register the fact that I had returned.

My watch showed 04.41. The display case with the crumbling apes was lit up thanks to Sixten's control panel. The gorilla seemed to fix its one good eye in the direction of my bunk. It would not be easy to get any sleep—but I was not even trying.

I had not leafed through my dissertation for more than a decade. Not since Ingrid had without warning left the university and I became a part of NUCLEUS, was moved to the little Catholic University and buried myself in Sister Jane's dark library, met Amba, started the family, had the children, one after the other, as if following a model set up by someone else. I could hardly recall anything of what I had written.

I turned the pages, intently examining the sentences in search of one particular thing—though I could no longer remember if I had mentioned it in the dissertation.

Introduction
It started with Einstein's discovery in 1905, as astonishing as it was fateful. Three letters, one digit, an equals sign. E=mc2. The formula for both the sun's life span and the end of the world.

In a dizzying and seemingly predetermined sequence of events, from Einstein's equation up to the end of the Second World War, his theory would become the most brutal fact. Radiation, decomposition and radioactivity became high scientific fashion during the first half of the twentieth century. The indivisible atom suddenly appeared anything but reliable. Each discovery came hard on the heels of the last: reality itself seemed literally to be collapsing before the very eyes of the researchers.

In due course the formula was proved in the most macabre mathematical experiment ever to be carried out, down to and including the very skin of the civilian population, all of those who were burned into black lumps, first in Hiroshima and then Nagasaki. The two atom bombs over Japan were and remain the only practical tests of Einstein's equation.

The Second World War was decisive for mankind in learning the riddle of the Bomb. There were so many apparently separate factors—but with the benefit of hindsight they cannot be viewed as anything other than linked, orchestrated, like a symphony of fate.

Not least in playing a crucial role were the stepped-up Jewish laws in many parts of Europe. The Italian Enrico Fermi was one example of all these intellectuals who were first dispersed and then united, in the service of the American government. Having received the Nobel Prize in Stockholm in 1938, Fermi did not return to his native country, the by now Fascist Italy, but instead immigrated with his Jewish wife to America and in due course joined the Manhattan Project in Los Alamos. Many brilliant nuclear physicists, who were themselves or whose close relatives were of Jewish heritage, took the same path. Leo Szilard from Hungary, the Dane Niels Bohr, and Einstein himself.

Yet according to available sources, Einstein never became directly involved in the creation of the atomic bomb. Rather he exploited the platform of his pacifism to try to persuade the President not to abuse the power he himself had foretold with his formula.

But the principal riddle remains Lise Meitner. At the outbreak of the Second World War, and following the death of Marie Curie in 1934, this Austrian researcher with Jewish heritage was the only really prominent woman within nuclear physics, and the one exception other than Einstein to the intellectual diaspora to Los Alamos. The accepted explanation is that she refused to work on the development of so terrible a weapon. Instead, she fled to Sweden in 1938 and after the war became a Swedish citizen.

The remarkable appellation "The Mother of the Atomic Bomb", for somebody who was said never to have worked on it, was given to her above all because of a mythical walk which she took over the ice in Kungälv on the Swedish west coast in 1939. It was said to have been on that very occasion that Meitner and her nephew Otto Robert Frisch realized how to understand the nature of nuclear fission. How, from one single uranium atom, one could derive two barium atoms.

That a single element could in this way be transformed into another was theoretically unthinkable and seemed to be nothing more than a transmutation, pure alchemy. Everything that mankind had dreamed of since antiquity and the time of the old magicians.

According to the myth, during their ardent conversation, Meitner and Frisch had sat down on a fallen tree in the forest. Brushed away the snow and taken out paper and pen.

What followed was a key moment in the history of science. On Meitner's piece of paper the picture grew of a balloon filled with liquid: how it slowly expanded before finally bursting. They called this process "fission", a term which until then had stood only for how a biological cell splits itself in a natural and organic way.

Six years later the world was to learn what this fission could bring about. That it was in practice not at all gentle and organic—it was unthinkably hard and violent. Only days after the detonation of the bomb over Hiroshima, the world's press was lining up outside Lise Meitner's boarding house in Leksand in the province of Dalarna, three hundred miles north of Stockholm, where she was taking her summer vacation. It was the beginning of August 1945. So it was Meitner who had to explain the theoretical principles of the new superweapon: Meitner who there and then was christened "The Mother of the Atomic Bomb" in the headlines.

But there is nothing even in these interviews from Leksand that says anything in more detail about what Meitner was doing in Sweden, what sort of trials she was conducting with the aid of experimental reactor R.1 in the massive rock chamber under Stockholm's Kungliga Tekniska Högskolan. Scarcely a trace remains of her research. After she received Swedish citizenship in 1949, there is more than a ten-year gap in the sources, before, in 1960, it is known that Meitner moved to live with relatives in Oxford and in due course died after a succession of strokes.

All of this—the vagueness, the absence of sources and records, the strange choice of a new homeland so far from the world's leading nuclear physicists in Los Alamos, her friends and colleagues—suggests the existence of what I have chosen to call "Lise Meitner's Secret". This is the subject of the dissertation which follows.

2.12

I got no further before I fell into a kind of stupor. The following night, once Ingrid had fallen asleep, I read on—and the night after that. Yet I found no trace of what I was looking for.

When I had gone through the whole dissertation, after two or three similar nights with the staring gorilla my only waking company, I was exhausted. Every night I fingered the key which Sixten had given me, locked myself in the shower room and weighed it reverentially in my hand. Felt all of its symbolic load. Carefully studied the engraving: "F.E." Following the third of those nights, I decided to ask Ingrid about it as soon as she woke up, to tell her all about Sixten's tour, the red trap-door in the tunnel floor with the same inscription. And then I never did.

Sixten gave me no lead either. He came down to fill the refrigerator a couple of times a week, greeted me warmly—in the same way as before our long talk. As if it had never taken place, with all the secret history he had shared with me, all this trust. As if he had never given me the key to a space few others could have ever seen, maybe no-one had.

One evening, just before he had finished filling up our supplies and while Ingrid was in the shower room after yet another yoga session, I confronted him. Started gently, so the mussel would not close.

"We couldn't go for another run, could we, Sixten? It was great to be able to stretch my legs, breathe fresh air."

He gave me a sympathetic look. Almost pitying.

"I wish we could. It must be hard work for you here in the bed-rock, I do see that."

Sixten stopped, seeming to concentrate on getting the last of the meatball sandwiches with beetroot salad and a slice of orange into the fridge next to the tubes of cod's roe paste, which Ingrid appeared to be emptying with regularity.

"But I've promised Aina not to head out like that again. She was beside herself with worry when I got back to our bedroom after our little tour. Poor thing had lain awake all night—and that hadn't happened since Ingrid made contact a few years ago. She had even started to imagine that I'd gone off with you lot."

He managed to fit the broad sandwich in beside the tubes, as precisely as he did everything else.

"So at least until Aina's jubilee, which will be trying enough for her as it is—not to be able to invite any guests apart from you, because we don't dare tempt fate at the moment—I don't want to disturb her more than I can help. But I can let you out to go running on your own, Erasmus. As long as Ingrid is happy with that."

As Sixten packed the empty containers into his backpack, I wondered whether I could ask about the key. In the end I held back. I suppose I did not want to trouble either Aina or him any further.

"That would be great, Sixten. I'll check with Ingrid."

It took time. Each initiative started to feel ever heavier, as if we were under water. Edelweiss would say we must now be in the fourth stage of the curse of tranquility. So I did what I could. Methodically built up the level in my strength training on the floor beside the bunk. Checked the briefcase, its contents, the mechanism, the functions, over and over again. Repeated the rituals. Mumbled the different steps for launch, as if they were prayers for myself. Kept writing in my notebook. Trained, showered, trained, in an unending wait for Ingrid to give us our orders.

Just after my return from the long tour with Sixten, she had said that we would be ready to regroup soon. Proceed to our first stop, one of the few places which had still to be connected up to the whole, before her plan could be set in motion. By the time she said "soon" to me again, a month had passed: we were deep into October.

There was now also a sweetish smell around the Nurse, whenever she momentarily abandoned whatever it was she was doing in her smaller rock chamber and passed by Ingrid's and my bunks on her way to or from the refrigerator. It was as if she did not have much to do with us.

Nor was there the slightest peep from across the Atlantic. Not from the Team, nor from Edelweiss, nobody was put forward to negotiate with us, not even the President himself. Nothing.

That too was entirely in accordance with the directives: our escape had to be concealed by them as by us. In some of our training exercises, public opinion had swung in favour of the terrorists. Even if they were threatening to blow up the world, having commandeered the means to do so, sooner or later the tide could turn against us. The fact that the U.S.'s proud system for mastering The Weapon—all these dual controls and double checking, piles of proclamations and international documents to stop it spreading to other nations—also involved something like our strange little team.

The silence, unlike in our training, was ghostly in the extreme. Finally I asked Ingrid if I could go for that run around the area on my own. Perhaps not so much for the sake of the exercise, the oxygen, the sky. But to see if the world above ground really was still there.

"Absolutely, my treasure. So long as Sixten is happy with it."

Once more her confidence—in both him and me. When Sixten next came down to fill up the refrigerator, he was aware of his other task: to follow me to the surface and let me out of the house at about the same late hour as the first time.

Aina had already gone to bed.

"I'll set the egg timer to one hour. After that I'll call the police," he said with a straight face.

With some ceremony, Sixten turned off the house alarm—they seemed to use it even when they were at home.

"And keep to the forest, Erasmus. The security company looks to have increased their patrols after the mysterious demolition of a wall up in the new school development."

Only then did he give his warm little smile. Looked at me with his deep-blue eyes and opened the door.

170

"Bye, my friend. Please take care."

Out on the sidewalk everything swam before my eyes for a moment. I took a few unsteady steps before I got into my stride. My whole compromised state. Solitude, freedom, captivity, all at once. The air felt fragile and ice-cold. It crackled in my nostrils as I lengthened my stride toward the wooded area, the thermometer on my watch showing below zero. Ingrid had said during our rare conversations that it was unusually cold for the time of year.

Naturally this was another test set by her. To let me run free, literally speaking, with the primitive cell phone my only lifeline. To see if I came back. The Nurse had certainly put some sort of tracer in the hybrid I took with me, no doubt as hard to find as the one that was in the briefcase.

And where was I supposed to go to? Back to my family, which I had been betraying for so long? The rest of the Team? To a court martial, a death sentence?

When I got to the place to which Sixten had taken me, the hollow of dense trees, I did not turn back again as I had said I would, but went further on the path which I had memorized since our tour together. Once I caught sight of the yellow surveillance light, I followed the fence around the area. The sense of being able to choose my own route, simply pull a little at my chains, was intoxicating.

Up by a massive white wooden building I stopped to drink, to breathe. My heart was pounding. The timer on my watch showed that I still had twenty minutes until Sixten's deadline: I must have run faster than I had calculated. Thoughts raced through my mind as I looked at the facade of the building. The sign seemed to be newly made from an old original: "Gunpowder Railway. Ursvik stop." The laminated images on the building showed train enthusiasts gathered around an electric engine which looked to be from before rather than after the Second World War.

Then I started to run again, as if by remote control, following the rusty rails. I found myself on a narrow path between the structures and the forested rock wall to my right. Five substantial metal doors appeared further along. Probably one of the upper entrances to the Inner Circle that I had seen on the plan in the laundry room.

That was when I saw them: outside the fifth and last metal door, counting from where I was standing. Instinctively, I tried to find somewhere to hide, before realizing that would only seem even more suspicious. Instead, I increased my speed to get past them as quickly as possible.

It would have been striking enough with any two adults standing in an embrace just there and then. But since the couple consisted of Sixten and an unknown woman, it was even more remarkable.

It was instead the couple who took cover when they saw me, stepping up toward the dark, wooded area with long strides, but I was able to catch a clear sight of the woman in the construction company's surveillance lights. Short blond hair, almost as tall as Sixten, certainly more than five feet nine. And at least twenty years younger.

After that I ran a long loop back to the house, so that he would have enough time to return before I knocked on the door. My timer—and his egg timer—buzzed at the exact moment Sixten opened the door. He gave nothing away. Just asked the usual questions runners ask: about speed, how it had felt, clothing versus temperature. I answered briefly but comprehensively as he led me down through the tunnel system, back to the Test Rooms. Our safe haven.

Ingrid was sitting in front of her screen as usual, only looking up quickly to note my return. I sat down next to her on the bunk and stared into the map of the world. All these triangles, crosses and lines.

"I've been thinking," I said.

Ingrid turned to me: that long, absorbing look.

"Yes, my treasure?"

"Sixten . . . what do you actually know about him nowadays?"

"More than I need to. Why do you ask?"

"Oh, I was only wondering about him when I was out just now. A fascinating person, imperturbable and yet sensitive. There must be a lot beneath the surface."

"There's no surface, only depth. Sixten is all solid."

"But can he handle the pressure?"

"It just makes him even harder, tough as a diamond."

"And temptations?"

"If you mean women, my treasure, they've of course always flocked around him. But trust me: Sixten can withstand anything and anybody. There's no-one I would sooner trust with our lives."

2.13

One week later, on October 23, it was time for what Sixten called Aina's "jubilee". In other words, her seventieth birthday.

As we were helped up through the hatch, Ingrid first and Jesús María last, I heard a strange sound, some sort of distorted music. I looked around the laundry room. The next time I caught it, on the half-flight of stairs on the way up to the hallway, I recognized it very well: like an echo from another time. The cheerful theme tune from "Dallas" the T.V. series in the late '70s—and it seemed to be pouring out of the hybrid.

Nobody had ever called my cell phone. Its only function had been as a transmitter and receiver of encrypted messages between Alpha and me, while it had lain hidden in the ruins of the hut for half a year. Yet the tune could not be coming from anywhere else.

The others were a step or two ahead of me in the hallway, on their way into the living room. Yet they did not seem to hear the ring tone at all. It was the first time Sixten and Aina would be meeting the third person in our company, and we had now been kicking our heels 328 feet under their house for more than six weeks so everybody's attention was probably focused on this awkward encounter. The mood was charged. Festive, however. All of them—but neither Jesús María nor myself—were laughing too loudly.

We had also arrived extremely late, since the preparations had taken much longer than expected. We had been given a selection of Aina's old clothes, from the time when she had been a lot thinner, and Jesús María was given permission to unstitch and redo them as she wished. Out of these she had managed to make a tight mauve dress which fitted her paradoxical shape—everything that was artificial: a wasp waist, enormous breasts, and something that looked like a hump on her back—as well as a bottle green party dress for Ingrid. I had been lent a dinner jacket by Sixten.

Jesús María had also equipped us with disguises. We had decided to play it safe, even though Sixten insisted that we would be the only guests and that the blackout curtains would make the house look empty and unlit from the outside. As if Sixten had taken Aina out for a surprise birthday dinner, which was apparently what the neighbors had been told.

So I was blond and curly, with hair to my shoulders. Besides that, I was wearing ice-blue lenses in roughly the same shade as Ingrid's—or rather, as she had been wearing earlier, before becoming a brunette with a neat bob and chocolate-colored eyes. Jesús María had a thick red wig and intense green lenses.

Best-looking was Aina herself. She must have devoted hours to her make-up. The sort of discreet elegance that first has to be chiseled out with great care and then filed down again just as scrupulously. The diamond ring had been taken out in honor of the day and sparkled alongside her slightly too-broad smile. She was wearing a black pleated skirt, a pigeon-blue angora sweater and matching high heels.

Aina really deserved more guests, I thought: a much larger gathering. But she had had to accommodate herself to *the cause*, as she and Sixten called it, because our paths happened to cross around the month of her seventieth birthday.

At about the same time as my ring tone started up again—whoever was calling must have been keen to get hold of me—Ingrid leaned forward.

"Forgive me, dearest Aina. But your pearls seem to have got tangled up in your chignon, just there at the back of your neck. You can't see it yourself. Let's step in here for a second. Can you help out, Jesús María?"

And the next moment all three of them were gone, vanished into the bathroom. Then came a short vibration from inside the hybrid: definitely audible in the silence around me.

"Is there another bathroom?" I asked Sixten.

"Of course. There on the other side of the passage," he said.

"And take it easy. I can wait a bit with the champagne. A few seconds at least."

I managed to get the cell phone out. The display showed five missed calls from *No caller I.D.*—one this morning, which must have been when I was in the shower, and four in the past hour—as well as two voice messages and a text. I sat on the toilet lid and listened to the first message. Did not dare to stand in case it was going to knock me off my feet.

It was not Amba and the children, which I had hoped as much as dreaded. Rather the opposite.

"Erasmus, my little lost lamb . . ."

I switched off the message, cutting into Edelweiss' gentle voice, stared straight ahead. Then I played it again, my eyes closed: pressed the cell phone tighter to my ear so that no sound could escape.

". . . as you well know, I've always had a particularly soft spot for you. Even worried about you, in many ways looked on you as a son, ever since you came to us.

"And now I really do have reason to be concerned. Because news has reached us that you've taken yourself off the formation, and what's more with the briefcase in active mode. Which shouldn't even be possible."

He smacked his lips, gave a heavy, audible sigh. It was hard for Edelweiss to speak for so long at a time.

"All of this is serious enough, although it could still be put right. But we've also found out, through the same reliable sources, that you're now in a group together with Ingrid Oskarsson: our former Alpha.

"And I'm aware that you know her from before, Erasmus. Better than most of us, apart from myself perhaps. That you think you're pretty well acquainted with her.

"But what really troubles me is that however much you know about her, or you may think you know, she will always know more about *you*. Which means that she's going to exert a strong influence over you. Very strong.

176

"Since we also know about Oskarsson's plans, which presuppose your own participation because of our rigorous security measures—the impossibility from a pure technical point of view of doing anything like that on one's own—I'd advise you to call me as soon as you hear this. Help us to render this woman harmless."

The first message ended. I played the second.

"I've already tried to call you a number of times, Erasmus, now that we've received definite confirmation of what we previously only suspected. Maybe you're still asleep. But as soon as you wake up, I would ask you from the bottom of my heart, with all of your and my care for the world—everything we've fought so hard for together—to get back in touch with me. We do not have a minute to lose."

He must have exerted himself to get out the last bit, before he would have had to drink, rest, breathe.

"Because I can guarantee you that a nuclear explosion of the sort Oskarsson is planning would not only extinguish all life in those parts of the globe where the bases lie. The consequences would also be that the ozone layer disappears for ever, for all time, in the same way as over Mars once upon a time; permanent drops in temperature of twenty to thirty degrees worldwide, before the U.V. rays burn up the entire surface of the earth once and for all. Only a fully fledged apocalypticist would do something like that.

"But you know all of this—at least in theory. So call me, Erasmus, my dear friend, that's all I'm asking. A brief moment of cool, calm reflection: I'm giving you ten hours with effect from now."

When the message ended, I just sat there with the cell phone in my hand and my head between my knees in an effort to get some blood back to my brain. Then I filled the basin with cold water and dunked my head, as if I were being waterboarded, five times up and down. Then I dried my face and hair with their pink towel and sat down on the toilet lid again, steeled myself. Opened the little envelope on the cell-phone display.

It was not an S.M.S., as I had thought, but a media message. I did not even know it was possible to receive something like an image on such an old cell phone. The picture was also hard to make out, due to the low resolution. The only thing I could see was a large white surface in the foreground, some sort of long stick with a darker top and a blurry figure in the background.

The image was incomprehensible—until I suddenly realized what it must have represented.

Although my head was still cold from the water, I felt the heat rise up over my hair as if I were already in flames. The content of the picture was simple, almost stylized, like the message. A plastic jerry can in the foreground, a matchbox beside it. And Zafirah in the background. She who was always sent into the thick of things.

I clicked on the timing information. The picture, the almost over-explicit message saying, "WE ALL BURN SO FAST AND FOR SUCH A SHORT TIME", was received at 17.33—when Edelweiss' ultimatum of ten hours from the day before, when he recorded the messages, ran out. And immediately after, he had tried to call me four times: as I was making my way through the secret hatch under the floor drain up to the hallway.

Without even having to check, I also knew that his first call and the picture message must have been sent at precisely the times of sunrise and sunset in Sweden at this time of year. That Edelweiss, like Ingrid, favored *symbolic time*, as he called it.

I checked the actual time: my watch showed 18.16. Only then did I hear sounds from the hallway. The three women coming out of the bathroom opposite, Ingrid chatting away as she moved toward the living room—"Now just knock back the whole glass, Aina, you really need it!"—and Jesús María saying nothing. They had been taking their time in there too.

I managed to get to my feet, my body seemingly moving on its own. As soon as I came into the living room, Sixten forced a champagne glass into my hand.

"At long last, Erasmus. I have to admit I was wondering what on earth you were all up to in there, in your various bathrooms. But it'll have been worth waiting for . . ."

Aina interrupted, her smile even broader than Sixten's if that were possible.

"Long hair really suits you, Erasmus."

"Yes, you should have seen him when he was a student, in his first year . . ." Ingrid said—before she and Aina started giggling like schoolgirls.

I was trying to get a grip on the situation, my expression giving nothing away. The champagne must have gone straight to Aina's head. She who never drank a drop.

While I took a careful mouthful of the alcohol, I let my eyes travel across the walls, the marine paintings, the mustard-yellow curtain arrangement: all this intense normality. Trying to find the ways which Zafirah and perhaps Kurt-or-John would get in. As well as the hidden emergency exits through which we would soon have to escape.

Sixten emptied the champagne bottle into our glasses, cleared his throat and began his speech.

"O.K., everybody, it's time. The moment I never thought would arrive. When Aina at last becomes older than me!"

Small roses flushed Aina's cheeks, Ingrid gave her a sisterly hug. I looked around for the potted plant, had to stay sober. Sixten cleared his throat again before going on.

"Be all that as it may . . . as it may . . ."

When he looked down at the floor, a little too long for it to have been merely for effect, I thought I could see tears in his eyes.

". . . for our many long years together, my darling Aina . . . for the fact that Providence brought us together. *Skål* to you—and to us!"

"Amen to that!" Jesús María said.

An awkward silence followed: this may well have been the Nurse's first utterance in this group. I noted that she too had emptied her glass. Everyone except Jesús María then turned their gaze toward me. It was my turn next.

"To Aina!" I said.

Ingrid awaited her turn, a practiced speaker. Then she too raised her glass and caught everyone's attention. Let her look slowly and theatrically move between Sixten, Aina and me.

"*Für Elise!*" she said at last.

I jumped as if hit by a shock wave, could not stop myself. Ingrid's two small words had confirmed my hypothesis. It was Beethoven's best known piano sonata, the one which Lise Meitner used to play as a four-handed piece with her nephew and fellow researcher Otto Robert Frisch. Maybe not least because Lise's real first name was none other than Elise.

Besides which, the first letters in the name of the sonata were the same as on the key Sixten had given me: "F.E."

My thoughts swirled chaotically. What I simply could not understand was what Aina could have to do with any of this. Until Ingrid addressed the birthday girl, now all of a sudden pale.

"It was in many ways Lise, or Elise, who shaped even your destiny. Made my and Sixten's relationship impossible—and at the same time allowed you two to live your wonderful lives together. In one magical instant. Almost exactly forty-five years ago, on October 25, 1968, just after 4.00 p.m."

The silence became like a vacuum: we were all gasping for breath.

"And not even I, with my galloping imagination, thought that I would ever get to see either of you again."

A new artificial pause, and I stole a look at Jesús María. Even she was staring at her feet.

"But in the end, that's how it turned out: at your home in Ursvik, of all places. And at long last I want to take this opportunity to thank you for the fact that you too, in turn, have made it possible for me to be standing here today. That you have indirectly played your part in what we are now on the way to accomplishing.

180

So *skål* and a hugely happy birthday, dearest Aina! Your place in history is secure."

Sixten refilled our glasses once more before we clinked them in toast and were about to take our places at the table. I picked up my hybrid again and fingered the key in the right-hand trouser pocket of my dinner jacket. Held back a little as we made our way to the kitchen.

"Yet there's not a single word in my dissertation about any underground laboratory," I said, as quietly as possible.

Ingrid leaned closer. Her breath carried the fruity aroma of vintage champagne.

"No, I promised Lise that, my treasure. That she could take the secret to the grave with her."

Then she put her mouth to my ear: her warmth burned on my skin.

"But in practice it makes no difference, since the key has been lost without trace for decades. So no-one other than the angels knows what's under that trap-door."

2.14

It was impossible to concentrate. However much Aina asked, however hard she pushed me. Because I was thinking about the key, the trap-door, the laboratory, what Ingrid had said. And the two messages to my cell phone. Edelweiss' gentle voice. The photograph of Zafirah with the jerry can.

So there I sat, looking for alternatives, emergency exits, while Sixten placed the first course and then the main course on the table. Toast Skagen with fresh shrimp and Kalix bleak roe, filet of beef with Hasselback potatoes and morel sauce.

But Aina would not give up. From somewhere far away—although she was only on the other side of the table—she kept questioning me in her strong Swedish accent. She had a firm grasp of English terminology, all the technical terms: seemed to know most of what there was to know about even our own nuclear weapons. The whole expansion which the rest of the world had long since interpreted as disarmament. All of those damned speeches.

It was more reminiscent of an interrogation training session than a conversation. Aina's sharp look, her fiery, or maybe implacable, side. Her narrowed eyes which could surely see through anybody. The rest of the company—the birthday dinner party—slowly but surely faded away around us.

And in the end I could not resist. Talking as ever on a general level, no classified information, but still, I told Aina that our so-called "Revitalization" would cost us at least 350 billion dollars in the coming decade. And that the total cost for the world's nuclear weapons arsenals at the moment was estimated to amount to a trillion dollars per decade.

Because those in the humanities are often mathematically illiterate, I felt I had to clarify the amount. A one and twelve noughts. One million million. This before the vast world-wide rearmament, phase two, which would be the secondary result of our own efforts, I said.

Aina nodded eagerly. She reminded me so much of my mother before she vanished into herself: the same warm acuity. I gave her more to nibble on. Details of how much we were spending on nuclear weapons research right now, without the media bothering very much about it—at the same time as we were using all our negotiation skills and rhetoric to stop more countries from starting their own little Doomsday kits.

I took a deep breath and rattled off information. Told her that in the last financial year 433 nuclear weapons projects had been carried out at the Sandia National Laboratory, with a total budget of 2.5 billion dollars. Los Alamos had 293 projects costing 2 billion, Lawrence Livermore 159 projects for just over 1.5 billion, Y-12 seventy-six projects for 800 million, Kansas City 102 projects for 600 million, Nevada forty projects for 400 million, Pantex nineteen projects for half a billion and Savannah River ten projects for 150 million dollars.

"It's so incredibly difficult to take you seriously," Aina said.

I did not answer—because I did not know if Aina was being dismissive about us here now, our wounded little team, or about the entire nation.

"And yet we have to. Every second."

I said nothing. Listened for sounds from outside, any sign from the attackers, somewhere beneath Sixten and Ingrid's restrained conversation about the old times. Jesús María was not there at all, she must have gone to the bathroom.

"How do you mean, Aina?"

"Where to begin? Perhaps with your sporting talk: about the nuclear football, or the 'baseball' cards?"

Then she began questioning me about the briefcase and the cards, which reminded her of the collectors' cards from childhood. On the front there was a photograph of the possible terrorist. On the back, succinct facts: name, home town, relationships, suspected crimes, the basic necessities for those who ordered our drones into Pakistan, Syria or Afghanistan. So as to be able to lock the sight on that specific person's cell phone—regardless of who might be holding it at the moment of impact.

"What we're talking about is a death sentence which is completely unjustifiable from any legal point of view," Aina said.

Then she went on about how vulnerable the system was. The fact that around one thousand of our warheads, and about the same number of Russian ones, are incessantly online, fully primed to be launched at any moment.

"Isn't it strange, Erasmus, that everybody talks about this as if it were in the past, in the imperfect tense: joking about the Cold War—without realizing that the situation is unchanged today. And, with extinction, there are no nuances. Even if the number of warheads ready to be fired off during the worst years was perhaps three times as high as now, it's still more than enough. The combined explosive force of the American missiles alone can wipe out mankind—and make the globe uninhabitable for all time. In addition to disturbing the equilibrium of the universe, what with the effect of the sun through all those dust clouds rising high into the atmosphere and the cold emanating from the then desolate Tellus, well, you know . . ."

Aina emptied her glass, and kept on talking to me as if I had no role in the current events.

"And imagine if, or rather when, all of this is hacked. It is after all more than twenty years since Kevin Mitnick was said to be able to start a nuclear war simply by whistling into a pay phone . . ."

I naturally said nothing about the fact that, at that moment, our entire nuclear weapons system appeared to have been both hacked and encrypted by a lone individual. Out of the corner of my eye I saw how precisely that woman was leaning further and further over the table, ever closer to Sixten. As if lost in their common history.

Aina did not spare either of them a look.

"Recently I also heard a lecture on what are called autonomous weapons systems: war launched without us being involved. The academic said that man is more and more being regarded as the weak link in the chain. That we will soon find ourselves outside the 'decision loop', as she put it."

A scent wafted from the other side of the table, so distant and yet so familiar. Chanel No. 5, the most classic of perfumes. My mother's party perfume. I thought about remarking that Aina and she used the same fragrance. But I could not get a word in edgeways.

"And it's certainly not only you, Erasmus. The lunacy is spreading all over the world again. North Korea, Iran, this appalling Islamic State which could get its hands on a warhead, and Russia obviously. Did you know that the Russians practiced offensive nuclear weapons attacks on us as recently as last Easter, on Good Friday, as if nothing were sacred? The targets were in part the National Defense Radio Establishment on Lovön island, which would have destroyed our early-warning system, and the air base at Haghult. I assume you picked it up on your screens."

I gestured palms up, non-committally, so many incidents had occurred and I had no idea how much Aina knew—since Sixten had said that she expressly asked not to be kept informed of what we were doing. In case she got to hear anything at all about Ingrid's crazy plan.

"And do you know what really annoys me, Erasmus?"

I shook my head. Felt Aina's warmth, that paradoxically intense energy from this prim and proper person.

"That you Americans think you're pretty special. As if the U.S. could never go the same way as so many other dominant powers in history, often when they've been spouting about freedom of expression and human rights or have been culturally the most prominent. France under Robespierre, the Soviet Union after the Revolution. I suppose I don't have to say anything about Germany.

She reached for water.

"And if the worse comes to the worst, it won't need much in your case either. One single mad ruler—for example that billionaire clown who the other day threatened to run in the next presidential elections. Imagine someone like that with his finger on the button."

I held my hand over my glass to stop Aina from giving me a refill.

"Yet we can never know if a dangerous president represents a bigger risk that missiles will be fired off, if it couldn't just as easily happen with the most reasonable ruler. Because the nuclear weapons system is a kind of regime in itself. Lives its own life, with or without safety measures, calculations."

She paused, gave me an enquiring look. "You're very quiet, Erasmus . . . don't you agree?"

I met Aina's eyes. How could I remind her that that was precisely why I now found myself here in her home in Ursvik—and not with my own family, on the other side of the Atlantic. But my direct look must have been enough.

"But of course you do, my God, how silly of me."

Aina got up to start tidying things away, to make room for dessert. But Sixten gently ushered her back to her chair. Laid out side plates and cups, put the presents on the table in front of her, placed the princess cake in the middle of the tableau.

At that moment I clearly detected the smell of burning, perhaps even of gasoline, but thought it came from the candles which Sixten was lighting on the cake. Seventy of them neatly arranged in the green marzipan. The whole ritual took a while. First to light them, one at a time, with the elegant lighter which Sixten produced from the waistcoat of his dinner jacket. Then to let Aina have a total of five goes before she blew them all out.

Only after the applause died down did I hear the noise. The crackling sounded cozy, as if it came from a log fire—except that there was no fireplace in the house. It quickly grew to a roar, before the stench of fuel and smoke really hit us. When we came into the living room the blackout curtains were already in a burning heap on the floor, the discarded jerry can lying among them.

It took only a few seconds before the heat and the smoke became explosive. The modular construction of the house was as if designed for a pyromaniac: the flames spread through the rooms with lightning speed. I hoisted the hybrid onto my shoulders and drew my weapon. The Nurse came rushing out of the smaller bathroom as Sixten, with Aina tightly clutching his hand, led us through the smoke-filled hallway, where our outdoor gear was kept at the ready, toward the laundry room. More gasoline-soaked blackout curtains formed a ring of fire around the dryer and the drain in the floor. Effectively sealing off our only emergency escape route, down underground.

There was only one other way. Sixten rushed ahead up the stairs, the flames beginning to lick up the walls and the ceiling, in the direction of their bedroom. Unlatched the security locks, flung the window wide open and threw out the burning curtains— before jumping out with Aina held tight within his arms.

Then we threw ourselves after them. Straight out into the night.

3

FIRST DOWN

October—December 2013
Kiruna, Sweden

3.01

It seemed as though the atomic winter had started just north of Gävle. The branches in the never-ending pine forest were weighed down to the ground with the constant snow, a fine powder which fell like radioactivity but was its exact opposite. The picture of innocent, virginal white.

So far from what fell over the Japanese fishermen after the tests at Bikini Atoll in 1954, covering both them and the catch in their nets. Just days later the disintegration of their organisms was in full progress. Bleeding from mouths and stomachs, then their hair fell out, long strips of skin came off their backs.

We passed Bollnäs, Ljusdal, kept heading north. At regular intervals I carefully raised the roller blind and looked out. It had stopped snowing, but the drifts were piled up against the platforms like solidified ocean waves, frozen and bewitched in mid-movement. Ånge at around midnight seemed enclosed in ice. The birches around the station looked silver-dipped, stiff with hoarfrost. We were being transported through a tunnel of deep winter. I tried in vain to sleep, that typical yellow station light filtering in under the blind. The squealing of the carriages as they were laboriously connected to or uncoupled from the train.

It could have been peaceful, graceful. As magical as the endless night trains of my childhood to my grandmother's. My mother trying to teach me about the history of art, I her about cryptography. The aroma from her unconventional picnic, often some sort of Indian lentil stew with cumin and ginger, spread its way through the corridors where we spent the nights sitting on small fold-out seats, since neither of us wanted to or could sleep.

That is what it could have felt like now: momentary compassion, some sort of respite. If the feeling had not been the very opposite.

The memories were seething in my mind. How we had rushed

through the darkened surroundings of the houses, the street lights cut off. Yet the light from the massive blaze behind us—explosive as in war-time, napalm, fire bombs—allowed me to lead us to the bottom of the yard as the heat from the fire burned like a blow-dryer on the back of my neck. Along the paths of the wooded area beyond, our three silhouettes cast distorted shadows that chased with us between the trees.

I had tried hard not to look into the windows of the other houses, with all those families. Especially not the ones with teddy bears and little lamps shining all night long. Where I knew that children would be lying in deep and trusting sleep. Yet images of my own children flickered for a moment, from when they were very small.

Our youngest, Trinity, so cheeky from birth, insisting on sleeping in her own bed even as a toddler. Duality, our middle child, a gifted boy, anxious and a little lost: a copy of his father. Had never been able to fall asleep before I had read three stories to him or precisely fourteen pages of his book, always so deliberate. And then our daughter Unity, the oldest, first born and cherished, who in typical big sister fashion demonstratively blocked her ears as the stories were being told over and over again to her small brother in the same room.

Amba too flashed through in my consciousness, forcing herself up through layers of suppressed memories. Of her standing there in the doorway—invisible to the children—and later just shaking her head at my concessions to them, how I pandered to their every whim. And how she herself then, on some other evening, could do exactly the same thing while I stood there invisible to her. Engrossed in her own very special way.

With an effort I managed to close down each of the images again, almost one by one, calling on all my willpower. As I had trained myself to do before leaving, before my escape, after I realized that there would be no possibility for me to bring along Amba and the children. I extinguished the recollections as I rushed through the woodland—until my mind was black and nothing was left but flight, the smell of the fire behind us somewhere, the very intense present. Which was still much easier to bear than the buried images which had seeped up.

Then Ingrid picked up the path to Stockholms Centralstation. Since she no longer knew if the tunnel system was safe or accessible, we had to take the external route, above ground, under the cover of the dense trees next to the motorway. For once, Jesús María was last in our column. But in spite of her heavy medical pack, and the fact that according to Ingrid she had been largely inactive for more than a month, she had no difficulty in keeping up with us.

I knew nothing of Sixten and Aina's fate. I tried to picture in my mind's eye whether or not they had got to their feet again on the lawn, like two burning torches, but had no memory of it.

I lifted the blind again, made a note of the temperature on some advertising display alongside the tracks. Seven degrees, and it was only the end of October—and as far south as this, relatively speaking. Ingrid had said that there were record low temperatures this fall and that it was certain to become worse further north. As the train sped on, I kept writing in my notebook: described all of these events, from when we emerged through the hatch to celebrate Aina's birthday.

My pen made a soft scraping noise in the notebook, Ingrid sat and clicked away at her computer in the top couchette. In the mirror I could see her face in the bluish light from the screen: that new look I still could not get used to. Jesús María, unhappy with the middle couchette between Ingrid and me, was somewhere in the corridor, outside our locked door. The conductor had already passed by—clipped our tickets, looked at the false passports which Sixten had organized through some acquaintance at the relevant authority, without passing any comment—and would probably not return during the night.

To judge from the silence, there were not many others in our carriage. I turned off the light and paused until Ingrid too had switched off her computer, lying there under the matted gray woollen blanket: waited for the false sense of familiarity that darkness brings. Then I started to ask my questions, my voice low enough not to be heard beyond the door.

"Was it Sixten that gave us away? Offered up both himself and Aina, so that we would burn in hell?"

"Is that a serious question, my treasure?"

The silence that followed, Ingrid's surprise, felt genuine.

"Sixten was devastated when he rang. As usual he was mostly worrying about us, about others," she said.

"So he survived, miraculously?"

"Sixten has at least nine lives. Aina made it, according to the message he sent, also with quite bad burns."

The corridor outside was quiet. No sign that Jesús María might be trying to hear what was being said, not the least movement beyond the door.

"I saw him with another woman when I was out running the other evening," I said.

"Sixten?"

An exhalation in the dark.

"Let me guess: tall, blond pageboy cut, very fit. Figure to die for. At least twenty years younger than him."

"I wasn't looking that carefully."

"It was his daughter, Lisa."

"Daughter?"

"She should of course have been at Aina's party—had apparently come home for the first time in a long while—but that's where I drew the line. I've after all only seen a picture of her, didn't dare to allow any more people into our circle."

I lay quietly, calculating.

"O.K. . . . so that leaves Jesús María. Who was still in the bathroom when the attack came."

"She's my blood sister, Erasmus. Besides, she'll never betray us. She hates Kurt and John more than she hates you."

194

I tried to imagine the Team's bodyguards in front of me. So very distant and yet at the same time imprinted in our minds for ever.

"Kurt and John . . . they're animals, in every way. But why does she hate them more than me—even though I used her as a sledgehammer when we were escaping?"

"Because they did things to her that she will never forget."

Ingrid's voice floated through the sleeper compartment. Melodious even at low volume.

"Then she did things to them, in turn. So that they shouldn't forget her either. And since both Kurt and John were equally guilty, identical in their rotten souls, she made them identical on the outside too. A grim and bitter-sweet little joke. Very much in Jesús María's spirit."

I heard coughing in the corridor outside. Maybe the smoke from the roll-up, the drug, had caught in her throat. Ingrid lowered her voice once more.

"This was long before you yourself got so deeply involved, Erasmus. Actually a routine although relatively comprehensive piece of surgery, advanced camouflage in preparation for a major covert operation. One of our two guards—I can no longer remember which—was dark and good looking, brown eyes, and the other blond and with a much slimmer face, without that dimple in his chin. I think five or six interventions were needed before Jesús María was satisfied. Edelweiss let her have her way. Since then she has just reinforced the likeness with each new surgery, down to the smallest birth mark, until no-one can distinguish them any longer. I wonder if even Jesús María knows. Certainly not Kurt or John themselves."

Another cough outside the door. In my mind's eye I could see the conductor doing his night rounds, smelling Jesús María's cigarette, making a quick call. How the police would then board the train before it had left the platform and arrest us all. There were mass murderers who had been caught because they happened to drop a piece of chewing gum in the street—but that woman in the corridor simply had to test all boundaries.

"So it was Aina who reported us?"

"Mmmm. Or why not you, my treasure?"

The yellow station light leaked in over Ingrid's duvet cover. But her face was still in darkness: there was no way of seeing her expression.

"Me?" I said.

Once Ingrid had fallen asleep, I took the hybrid and opened the sliding door to the compartment as carefully as possible. Had to make what Edelweiss called an "Unreality Check": even in surreal situations some things are still more real than others. Jesús María was sitting pressed against the window, her eyes closed to the beautiful dawn, hardly seeming to notice me—until she took a powerful grip on my arm.

"Got tired of the Witch's tales, Erasmo?"

"She said it was you who turned Kurt and John into twins."

"And you trust any shit she comes out with?"

Jesús María took a last drag on her cigarette and quickly squeezed it out, between finger and thumb, showing no sign of pain. Then she started writing with her sooty finger in the condensation on the train window.

It took me only a few seconds to decipher the sequence D19 N19 15R 212 319 N5N 316 121 NG, with the help of my key sentence. The one which for most of my life I was convinced nobody else knew about—apart from me and my mother. Before first Ingrid and now Jesús María proved me wrong.

Clearly it said: "DO NOT RELY ON ANYTHING."

3.02

The sun is the strongest thing we know. The warmth which brings life to earth through constant nuclear explosions, fusions. Here even the sun had no chance.

As we slid into Kiruna station, the thermometer showed negative 26.7 at 11.00 a.m. when the sun should have taken the edge off the worst of the cold. There was still some time to go before it disappeared completely below the horizon. A month and a half, according to the calendar.

Ingrid led us alongside the railway tracks, in the direction the train had been traveling in, and then turned off onto a road. There were no people walking in front of us or behind, even though there seemed to be no other way into town. It felt as if the temporary station—more like a barracks building—had been lowered into the wrong place by a crane, left in the middle of nowhere.

Since we all needed to get some fresh air, we decided not to take the bus downtown. The snow creaked under our boots, the cold made the balaclavas from our combat packs stick to our mouths. The road was so narrow, without any sidewalk, that it required full concentration to keep out of the way of the traffic. When the biggest trucks drove by, we had to press ourselves against the snow walls.

"The mine," Ingrid said, continuing enigmatically, "it giveth and it taketh away."

Neither Jesús María nor I said anything in reply, we just walked on through the razor-sharp cold. It was almost a quarter of an hour before we approached something approximating a town center. I mouthed my way silently through the names on the direction signs, memorizing them for a possible exit route. Ingrid gestured toward the enormous square, containing more parked cars than people. The only movement came from the occasional solitary businessman on his way into or out of the Hotell Ferrum.

"O.K., co-ordinates . . . 125 miles north of the Arctic Circle. The world's largest town measured by surface area, at least on the basis of the old municipal system. And beneath us is the abyss. We're moving on the thinnest of ice—central Kiruna is cracking up, bit by bit, being swallowed whole by the mine. The treasure chest of iron ore which financed our great leap, from primitive farming economy to leading industrial and welfare nation. Most of the Swedish social and economic model."

Ingrid pointed toward the mighty black silhouette, covering most of the horizon.

"I've called it Mount Doom ever since I first read *Lord of the Rings*."

I squinted into the sun, tried to grasp the scale of the mine: the monster which Ingrid said was consuming itself. In the other direction lay the idyllic old parts of town, which were soon going to be torn down—like a movie set—when the town center would be forced to move a mile east. Demolished, I thought, like the fake towns which we had put up in inaccessible places. For the sole purpose of bombing the hell out of them during our nuclear weapons tests.

Ingrid turned toward me. You could see the breath from her mouth, even though it was covered by her balaclava, seeping out like gas.

"Do you recognize where you are, Erasmus?"

I shook my head.

"Look over toward the mountain, beyond the mine. You've been there a number of times. Been flown in at night to train, clearing up operations after a simulated drone attack at N.E.A.T., the 'North European Aerospace Test Range', by far the largest above-ground military training terrain in Europe. Nine thousand two hundred fifty square miles, as big as Belgium, just sixty-two miles straight out into the countryside from here. Belongs to Kiruna Municipality, technically speaking. But is nowadays managed by the Swedish Defense Materiel Administration and Swedish Space Corporation together."

Suddenly I could see everything. The constant darkness, the same above ground as below, crawling and slithering through inhumanly narrow tunnels, occasional glowing points, winter warfare. How we had been kept in the dark about the co-ordinates, had no clue as to our whereabouts, training to operate in this ignorance. We called it "No-Man's-Land".

Now we left the square behind us, kept to the edge of the soon-to-be former town center, passed charming wooden houses from the early twentieth century, which according to Ingrid—doubling as guide—dated from when the town was founded. The engineer's dream which led to the pioneer town being established so far from everything other than the raw material itself. Then we came into a residential area which seemed already to have been abandoned, with boards as makeshift cover for broken windows. Continued onward to the destination which was still a mystery to me. I had no idea what we were going to do here in Kiruna, had not asked: was trained not to do so.

So I kept on memorizing street names, Lars Janssonsgatan, Konduktörsgatan, Gruvvägen, noted every last detail. After some steep downhill stretches with snow packed hard underfoot, Ingrid pointed up to the left, in the direction of the hill: the area showed bare white among the low trees.

"Luossa Ski Hill. Created when the mine on this side of the mountain began to peter out, just a few years ago. So I've never actually skied there," she said.

After a brief pause, while Ingrid gazed up at the pistes, mesmerized, we kept moving forward for several hundred feet until we stopped in front of the substantial wooden building on the final slope down toward the mine.

Even here the windows had been boarded up, the facade had peeled making the plain wood visible in places, icicles three feet in length hung from the roof like needle-sharp weapons. You could

only just make out the text on the frosty signboard: HOTELL
SNÖFLINGA.

"Hotel Snowflake. The perfect hiding place. Officially closed
many years back, already sacrificed to the powers of the underworld," Ingrid said—before the barred door suddenly opened.

"Inko, my dearest friend . . . you seem hardly a day older than
when we finished secondary school, even with your new look.
Come in so I can lock up behind you!"

Ingrid and the large woman, probably of the same age as her,
but youthful and cool, with shocking pink hair and tattoos over
her bare arms, gave each other a warm embrace. Then the woman
solemnly turned her attention to the rest of us, switching into
English, somewhere between Sixten's and Aina's.

"Erasmus . . . Jesús María . . . wonderful to meet you. But you're
several weeks earlier than I was expecting, Inko."

"Yes, well, it was hard to be more precise."

"And I guess you still don't want to say what you're up to here."

"No, I'm sorry, Bettan. But as I told you, it's an extremely good
cause."

"I like those, Inko. You know that."

I looked around the eerie darkness inside: not one sliver of
light found its way through the blocked-up windows. From the
crystal chandelier in the lobby one could tell that this must once
have been a fine hotel. With the help of the man-high, cracked
rococo mirror I started to map out escape routes, hiding places,
the likelihood of a surprise attack from various directions.

Bettan laid three heavy metal knobs on the counter. A big key
for the room and two smaller ones for the padlocks on the front
door.

"I should say that it's pretty much safe for you to move around
in this neighborhood, even in daylight. And nobody will recognize
you anyway, Inko."

Although the whole hotel seemed to have been abandoned, I
noticed that there were no other sets of keys on the hooks.

200

"In here it's probably mostly the ghosts you'll notice. There's sometimes a hell of a lot of squeaking at nights, as if furniture were being moved around up on the old conference floor, or somewhere in the middle of the sauna. Even though it's nearly three years since we had our last group booking."

"And the Girls?"

"Oh, they're used to keeping out of the way. It's doubtful you'll see any sign of them."

Then more quick embraces—before we started up the stairs, Ingrid first, Jesús María last, before Bettan warned us about one more thing.

"By the way, there's blasting in the mine every night. At exactly 1.30 a.m.—to give time for the gas to disperse before the morning shift clocks on. It makes the beds shake, trust me. Pretty much all of the town trembles like my old grandmother's aspic."

It was hard to climb the creaking stairs without making a sound. Not even I—with all my practice, even as a child—managed it. Just above the staircase was a faded lounge. Worn-out Chesterfield armchairs in oxblood leather, heavy red curtains in front of the high, boarded-up windows, a bulky old T.V. on a rickety stand by the southern wall. Above the seemingly preserved bar—which still had an impressive range of alcohol—hung a yellowing sign which I had no problem in understanding. "The Ice Queen. Always open, honor system in operation."

We followed Ingrid into her room, which she said had the best view. She pulled open the curtains and removed one of the boards from the window.

Then we just stood there in silence, observing the remarkable organism of the mine. It seemed to be breathing, hissing and belching smoke, coloring the snow at the top a threatening iron-ore black. From there on down to the very bottom, the rock sides had been layered like farming terraces. At ground level, the mine then continued on down in a confusion of railway tracks, overhead wires, lamps, winches, relays.

After a certain time—maybe five minutes? ten?—Ingrid replaced the board with care, closed the window and pulled the curtains shut again.

"Not that it's necessary. But belt and suspenders, as they say."

On our way from the station, Ingrid had insisted that we would be safest here, nearest to the mine. Locally, the area was only ever known as the "Valley of Death". The hotel and surrounding buildings would be the first to be dragged down into the depths: so they had been declared uninhabitable some years ago, sealed up, and had become an excellent haunt for people who, for different reasons, wanted to go underground. Here, nobody would ask— and absolutely no-one would answer.

"Dearest Jesús María, would you mind leaving us alone for a little while? Perhaps make yourself at home in your room, change for dinner?"

"Sure, I can do that. I'll pull out my fucking *quinceañera* dress."

As soon as Jesús María had left the room, Ingrid took out her portable command terminal, left the set of keys in the lock, barricaded the door with a chair pushed under the handle. Sat down on the squeaky four-poster bed and gestured for me to install myself next to her. There was a faint smell of skin and soap about her.

Soon the map of the world could be seen on the screen, the *correspondences*. I let my eyes run from east to west, between our nuclear weapons bases on home soil. Followed the solid red lines between yellow triangles, then switched my look to the corresponding installations on the European continent.

"In case you're wondering what we're doing up here, my treasure."

She zoomed in on northern Europe, over Sweden, toward the little cross on the map. It could not be too many miles away. Step by step she clicked her way in on Kiruna, the old city center, and put a marker on Hotell Snöflinga. The distance from here to the destination was given on the screen as twenty-six miles. Estimated time to get there on foot: 8 hours, 32 minutes.

"You know about Esrange Space Center, the rocket range—but hardly its full extent. Not many do. Or are aware that Sweden has actually got something of universally strategic value. At least as important as the iron ore in Narvik during the war, or the heavy water in Rjukan. A good enough reason in itself to occupy this whole country."

On the screen, the security gates looked as neutral as at any space center or nuclear weapons facility. The basic rule was, the more valuable, the more low-key. When Ingrid tried to zoom in further, everything became pixelated: the global digital security setting for top secret installations.

"This, Erasmus, is the world's leading connections center for the enormous mass of information streaming down from all satellites at any moment. The hub itself, the main exchange. To begin with, the rocket center was mostly focused on weather forecasts and other innocuous things. Then they started getting orders for navigational data, concrete geopolitical mapping, more and more specific with each year. Nowadays our drones could not get too far without Esrange."

She zoomed out again. Moved along the dotted blue lines leading from the cross here in the northernmost part of Europe, back and forth over the map of the world.

"And I think this might interest you, my treasure."

The screen image now traveled over the Atlantic and on toward the missile base at Minot in North Dakota. I had recognized it without having to check on the map. Could distinguish this particular anonymity from all the other anonymities since decades back.

When we had zoomed in sufficiently, the display split as usual into smaller split-screen images. One showed the missile itself: its grayish matte surface, like a mighty underground whale. Two others depicted the above-ground exterior. Forested terrain, mountain scenery in the background, a light haze. The largest image was in the middle of the screen and showed the command

203

center itself. The control console, the panels, the forced stillness.

Routinely I checked the co-ordinates at the foot of the screen. Time, temperature, other weather conditions, the pressure inside the missile. All the metrics which the command center needed, including the alert level. And only then did I notice that the launch counter was rapidly spinning down.

The green numbers first turned yellow and then red, before starting to flash frenetically. The command center sent out calls, fully in accordance with regulations—but still nothing stopped. The launch phase too seemed to go according to plan. The smoke and heat development were immense: even the most distant trees on the exterior images had started to burn. I stared at the counter furthest down to the right, what was called the "Body Count". Was rooted to the spot. Could do nothing at all about it, stop the process, overpower Ingrid.

And it was, of course, already too late. Once everything has gone this far, the security system is designed to ensure that the process is *not* interrupted, stopping the missile from falling on populated areas in friendly territory instead.

"More or less like that," Ingrid said.

With a click on the control console she got the entire operation to stop—before it was rapidly rewound. The counter spun back to the beginning with equal speed, the alert level returned to yellow then green. In the end she clicked away the images from the base, as well as the world map, and closed the lid of the command terminal.

An ice-cold drop of sweat ran down my forehead.

"Isn't it amazing? Most of the conceivable scenarios are already on my computer, from our intensive training exercises around the world. And after our unofficial field trip out there to Esrange, the Magic Mirror will be complete: then I will be able to use this little gizmo to connect to the image streams from each one of the satellites and after that tinker with them to my heart's desire. From that point on I can simulate any course of events I want, wherever I want. Our pursuers will no longer have the slightest idea what is happening. Or whether they can even believe their own eyes."

When the drop of sweat ran down the ridge of my nose, I finally flicked it away. Tried to get up from the sunken four-poster bed, which was squealing and creaking, like a drowning cat. Ingrid waited until it was quiet again in the room.

"And above all, my treasure, after that you and I can burn out our entire global nuclear weapons system, from the inside—without anything untoward appearing on the monitors. Guaranteed not one trace. However hard you look."

3.03

That night I dreamed, not for the first time, that I was the little Japanese girl at an international conference for survivors.

Bashfully I told them how I had been in a tram and saw something like a flash of silver and threw myself onto the ground. Everything became black as ink, so dark that people were running into each other everywhere, like the blind rats which I had seen in the cage at the home of my friend.

When it grew fractionally lighter, I began to walk through the town, by now strange to me. I met a woman with bleeding eyes and a girl who must have been about the same age as me and who was shouting out the same thing all the time: "Help me, help!" Her back was burned to shreds, just ashes and soot, was still glowing like dying embers, the skin hanging down on her hips in strips. Crowds of people were making their way along the river bank. Jumped in and were immediately scalded to death by the boiling hot water.

I met an older woman, ancient, who was crying in the same way as the girl I had seen: also calling out for her mother—though she must have been dead for many years. It was so strange, I told the conference. But the only answer she got was: "Everybody else is in just as much pain as you. Try to put up with it."

In the end I found my own mother, but hardly recognized her swollen face and her closed eyes. The skin on both her hands was hanging loose, like rubber gloves. She died before the end of the war, I said in my account, and I never saw my father again.

After I had finished—"My thanks to you, I'm called Yukiko and I'm seven years old!"—everybody broke into long applause and then it was time for lunch. Reconvening at 13.15, the conference chairman, the American, said.

On the way out, just as the American had moved to try to

hug me, I pulled him down and thumped his head hard into the floor.

Then I ripped out his tear-filled eyes: first one, then the other. Because in any event he could never see what I had seen.

3.04

I worked on it all, on the situation I found myself in, in the only way I knew. The first mornings, short intervals: five reps of 10×150 yard sprints just behind the hotel, on the small path where the snow had been cleared to make way for the garbage truck. A resting walk back between sprints and a minute's recovery between reps. The extreme cold crackled in my nose as I breathed in. Negative twenty-two before the sun rose. Then mid-intensity strength training in my room and an ice-cold shower.

Slowly but surely I also dared to venture further afield, so early that few others had reason to be about. The third morning my wrist-watch showed 04.45 as I unlocked the front door. Warmed up with a few relaxed strides: 5×85 yards in the tracks left by the garbage truck. Then I followed the unlit ski track straight in-between the gnarled dwarf birches, silvery with frost, small shining ghostly figures twisted in pain and dread. The snow made my headlamp superfluous. After a few hundred yards my eyes had adjusted. My spikes also held perfectly on the icy surface, my steps unexpectedly light. Despite the cold I was able to maintain 6.9 minutes per mile without too much effort.

The track followed the edge of town, even further down into the sink-hole, in the direction of the mine. Yet I resisted the temptation to try to penetrate further into the area. Didn't dare to allow myself to be sucked in, dragged down. After three laps—my watch showed just over seven and a half miles—I adjusted the straps on the hybrid and increased my speed to six and a half minutes per mile. It was my benchmark. The indicator that I was at last back in fighting shape after the surgery in Ursvik.

I took the hotel stairs to the conference level in four big steps. The meeting room had been built as a kitschy Lapp hut with low lighting, and it backed onto the sauna and a small gym which time had forgotten. I turned on the aged treadmill and ran another seven and a half miles, at fast distance pace, before I finished off with a hard set of strength intervals.

Only then did I start to approach that state of white exhaustion, dizziness, the absolute limit. The near-unconsciousness which had been my elixir of life for so long. Which had made me able to endure.

Because sooner or later we all become addicted to something in this world. Soldiers in wartime have always been stoned: on drugs, political rhetoric, religious fanaticism. But research showed that even in peacetime a quarter of all military personnel in the U.S. regularly took drugs, not just hash but also cocaine and L.S.D. On a number of occasions hundreds of people had even been arrested after crackdowns at our nuclear bases.

In the sauna I let the key lie in the palm of my hand, burning me. Wondered about showing it to Ingrid after all. Telling her that I was given it by Sixten: that the key to Meitner's secret underground laboratory had not after all disappeared. And that he had given it to me—not to her.

But I did not, for that very reason. That it was me and not her he seemed to trust.

So the days went by in their curious way, even here. Between meals Ingrid mostly stayed in her room, barricaded behind her locked door. Claimed to need every waking hour—and that was a long time, she told us, most of the day—to complete the process. Connecting all our nuclear weapons around the world.

Jesús María I never even glimpsed. The first days after we came here, to this strange hotel with its meandering corridors and stairs which somehow never seemed to connect, I had on a few occasions tried to find her. Knocked on her door during both day-time and night to ask her how she could know my "Key Sentence". The basis for my most secret book cipher, which I had shown only to my mother, there by the kitchen table as a prematurely adult thirteen-year-old.

But Jesús María was never in her room—and it took me more than a week to trace her. She had joined the so-called "Girls", a number of young women without residence permits whom Bettan had taken pity on. One early morning, on my way from the sauna, I caught sight of one of them walking down the next staircase to prepare breakfast in the kitchen area. So I followed the trail to Jesús María, and found her in their midst, as busy as the rest.

That also helped me to solve the mystery of the food. How for breakfast alone they could serve cold poached salmon, reindeer sausage, potato salad with thick home-made mayonnaise, scrambled eggs, Kalix bleak roe and fresh-baked rusks with cloudberry jam. The lunches and dinners were even more lavish: as if they had been meant for many more than just Ingrid, Bettan and me. Which they obviously were.

And soon we found ourselves in November. The passing time was measured by the blasting: at 1.30 a.m. each night everything shook. I had to carry out my checks—even though the briefcase, according to our technicians, was constructed to withstand a direct hit. Take it out of the hybrid, open the lid, continue the ritual up to the point where the electronic eye, the iris recognition, appeared. Then I started closing the case again. Carried out all these complicated commands, pressed long three-letter sequences on the keyboard, in the exact opposite order.

That was my routine, identical in every way, by the light of a single candle which was meant to neutralize the bluish glow from the screen in case anything seeped out through the boards covering the window. In case somebody was keeping me under observation. I ran an eye over the apparatus, looked to see that everything seemed in order after the blasting, and in some way it looked back at me. Everything exactly the same way—until November 2, 2013.

Just before closing the case that night, noticing the timer showing 02.07, I saw a terrifying reflection in the screen. Despite the fact that I had as ever locked the door, with the set of keys still in place, wedged the chair under the door handle, someone had

210

managed to steal up behind my back. Pin my arms and bend my head sharply backward.

Then I felt the warm little kiss on my throat.

"I obviously came in the nick of time, my treasure. On the way to taking matters into our own hands, were we? Completely lost patience?"

There was a smile on Ingrid's grotesque skeletal face: a mixture of war-paint and Halloween makeup, as if she had been playing around in front of the mirror. But her voice sounded purposeful and crystal clear.

"It's All Saint's Day here in Sweden. Yours, Erasmus, and everybody else's."

She took out her costume make-up, and in the reflection on the screen I could see how my face was quickly being transformed into a devil's mask. How her eyes pierced right into me as I slowly answered:

"Yes, Ingrid . . . I was starting to think there would never be any action up here."

Then it did not take many minutes before we were out on the main road, taking the narrowest streets through the sleeping town. Not a soul anywhere, not the smallest light in any of the cottages. Just snow, the drifts, the thick forest reasserting its mastery as soon as we left the enchanting little wooden quarter behind. The mountain of doom which hung brooding over the area. Through the silence of the night I thought I could hear the town cracking up inch by inch.

The mine gave and the mine took away, as Ingrid had said. In many ways it was the only thing capable of supporting life up here. Yet she said that there were also many who had high hopes for Esrange. For space tourism, Virgin Galactic, Spaceport Sweden. During weekends and holidays, the Swedish Space Bureau's megaphones blared about free ice cream and movies in Folkets Hus, the People's House.

The freezing air fizzed in my nose, which I kept free of my

balaclava so I could breathe more easily. The extreme cold had returned after a brief pause: a thermometer decorated with neon reindeer on the front of a house showed closer to negative forty, even though the Arctic nights were more than a month away. On December 10, the sun would disappear below the horizon for three endless weeks.

The computer had shown the distance to be almost exactly the length of a marathon, just under 26 miles. We kept up a suitable speed, about seven minutes per mile, despite the hybrid slowing me down by about 10 per cent. It meant that we ought to be at Esrange at 05.30 at the latest, before the night shift finished, according to Ingrid's information—and with strength remaining for the assignment itself. We could then reasonably be back at the hotel before they cleared away breakfast.

Ingrid ran with a free and springy step, kept up her pace, hips straight and upright, all the way until we stopped a mile or so from the installation. Saw the characteristic light in the sky: the reflection of the searchlights was always at least as revealing as the satellite dishes. At that point we turned off straight east into the forest. The snow was lying feet deep, Ingrid measured the weight of her steps exactly right, not breaking through the frozen crust.

Although we had never once trained together, every one of our movements was synchronized. Ingrid must have carried out similar assignments for decades before my own training began. We stole forward toward the seemingly unmanned north-east gate, the moon remaining behind the clouds. It would not be easy for anyone to spot us through this barely half-open terrain. When we reached the gates, I memorized the co-ordinates: E.S.-1219-V. While Ingrid got to work on the code lock, the security system itself, I stood in the dead angle of the surveillance cameras and kept watch, my weapon drawn under my non-reflective black running jacket.

The seconds passed extremely slowly, as they do at times like this—before there was a click from the lock. The upper red lamp lit up for a moment, but by the time we ran through the gates Ingrid had managed to short-circuit the security system. It was silent and excruciatingly cold all around. Our slip-on boot spikes were light-weight and flexible, designed not to betray our steps, no matter what the surface.

And it is hard for an outsider to understand how easy it is to break into an installation, even if it is guarded around the clock. How quickly human psychology falls victim to routine.

Even after years of training, long theoretical rehearsals of security measures, it is different in practice. Card games get in the way, or intense discussions in the middle of the night while sitting in front of screens—about money for the children's education, the latest baseball games, maybe an imminent divorce, sicknesses and deaths. The inevitable result is brief periods of inattention.

After lengthy searches through his enormous database, Edelweiss had concluded that those periods were generally between 8 and 29 seconds long. "One never has more than half a minute," he said. "But with the right training, that's oceans of time."

Which is why we now moved in quick intervals, randomly interspaced, before finding a new camera shadow and waiting for a few minutes. All the while I expected us to be discovered. Because there is no way of knowing when the periods of inattention occur: at any moment we could run into a couple of sleepy guards. Or maybe some super-professionals called in from N.E.A.T., the world's largest military training ground, just minutes away by car, in response to an alarm being triggered.

And it had been so long since the adrenaline last pumped through my body in this way. I enjoyed that feeling of being on edge, the watchfulness even while moving at top speed. How this natural drug made me reckless and incredibly strong.

Ingrid was in the lead, I followed her light steps. We passed through some interior doors with unexpected ease. Despite the strategic importance of the center—the other evening, Ingrid had said, Swedish television news revealed that Esrange had made possible our latest spy satellite over the Middle East—the security personnel here too seemed to be neglecting some of their routines. After all these years without incident it was so easy to ignore, or simply forget, to seal all doors fully in accordance with regulations.

Edelweiss had compared it to brushing one's teeth: if you begin to neglect one single ritual, others will soon follow. He would therefore sometimes ask us to breathe on him, even in the most tense situations. In his book bad breath justified as hard a punishment as more concrete breaches of regulations.

Most surveillance centers were also wrongly built from the start, something one only noticed if one thought offensively—like an attacker, not a defender. The guards would look out into the night, toward the gates, up into space, at all their screens. But rarely right behind their backs.

"I'm ready," Ingrid whispered only a few feet from the control board. Her skeletal face turning toward my devil's mask and the guards still with their backs to us.

"Are you, Erasmus?"

I nodded—and in the next moment she dashed toward the hard discs, the storage center for all the launch footage the satellites sent streaming down, while I took care of both guards more or less at the same time. I pressed lightly on the soft spots behind the ears of the first one and his chin immediately sunk onto his chest, as if he had fallen asleep at his post. The second one just had time to defend himself. As he raised his hands to his head, to protect against direct blows from behind, I pinned them together and thumped his head lightly onto the control board. It does not take much to knock somebody out.

After a few minutes, Ingrid stuck the U.S.B. into her jacket and we set off at top speed in the direction we had come. When other guards appeared with drawn weapons from a sliding door in the wall, we both stopped in mid-movement. It was Ingrid they wanted: they hardly looked at me. I stood stock-still, registering the scene around me. The flashing bright red lights, two heavily armed special guards, the alarm pumping straight into my brain.

Edelweiss had preached that no human being can know exactly how he will react in the most critical situations. An entire life of training can't make us absolutely sure of ourselves. "Not even you, Erasmus," he had said. "Not even me."

Yet it did not take many seconds before I knew. The guards who just before had seemed so invincible, beasts straight up from the underworld with their automatic weapons pointed at Ingrid's temples, were now more like two pitiful small beings in a terrifying medieval painting out of one of her lectures. It could have been Caravaggio, Bosch, or maybe Bruegel's eternal struggle between heaven and hell.

It was a moment of white fury, violence which was both uncontrolled and fully focused. First one, then the other. And I managed to tie both their arms together behind their backs, creating an impossible creature, a kind of physical paradox, so it was not clear where the one began and the other ended. It must have been a torture for them, their screams cut through my head like knives, until I managed to close the heavy and thick protective door behind us. Silence once more as we rushed out onto the enormous asphalt area, heading toward the gates.

"You didn't have to take them down in that way, Erasmus. Their cries alone must have activated every guard post in Norrbotten County. There was no need for an alarm," Ingrid said when we got back into the cover of the pine trees beside the main road.

I both nodded and shook my head. Out here you could not hear a sound from the installation, no flashing red lights could be seen, nothing to interrupt the serenity. The alarm had only gone off behind the scenes. After one mouthful of drink each, Ingrid led us a much more remote way back. One could already make out the first signs of dawn. Gradually we got our speed down to under 7 minutes per mile so as to be back in good time.

It did not take long before the nausea washed over me. After vomiting twice in quick succession, and covering the result with snow like a dog, things improved: the ultra-violence cleared from my mind. We were back at the Snowflake by 08.43. I had time to take an ice-cold shower, rinse away the last few mental images, before we went down separately to the dining room for breakfast.

3.05

The day passed without any reference on the local news, either radio or T.V., to an incident at Esrange. Which was only to be expected.

This type of break-in at a highly classified site rarely became public. Neither intruder nor those in authority had any interest in spreading information about it. Those who were called "Our new principals" on Esrange's homepage, and who had already put a stop to the Tourist Office's guided tours at the base, definitely did not want that.

Come evening there was still no leak, even on encrypted specialist blogs. During dinner Ingrid said that we should celebrate.

"With whom were you thinking?"

I looked around the spacious dining room, at the crystal chandeliers and the murals with local motifs. As usual only she and I were sitting at the table; the Girls and Jesús María presumably came only when we had left.

"Bettan must have gone to bed. She's an early bird: says that the blast at 1.30 a.m. is her alarm clock. But I'm going to fetch a special guest," she said.

We were still standing in the Ice Queen, when Jesús María came in, like a reluctant teenager. Without a word she went behind the bar and started to mix margaritas.

"And what are we celebrating?" she said.

"Go on, Erasmus, tell her! Excuse me, I have to make a call," Ingrid said and disappeared.

Yet again: I'd been trained in all sorts of mind games, since decades back. But I still could not see through Ingrid's strategies. I assumed that even this was some kind of test. That she would later learn from Jesús María what I had said, how much I revealed.

If I really was someone worth holding by the hand as the world was ending.

"It's my birthday today. Fifty-one."

"Sorry, my poor Erasmo. You'll have to contain yourself a few months more before celebrating. To be precise . . . 104 days, isn't that right?"

Jesús María must have known pretty much everything about me even before our escape. Now the two of us were alone together for the first time since she had written her message in the condensation on the train window, more than a week ago. She crunched on an ice cube from her glass, raised her eyes from her drink and looked me straight in the eye.

"Feel nice to be able to fight a bit? This morning?"

I kept quiet, followed my usual tactic. Let the opponent lead. Show their cards.

"What else has the Witch said about me?"

"Not much . . . that you have terrible memories from home."

"That I have a forked tongue?"

"As distinct from Ingrid?"

"No, seriously, Erasmo, I'll show you."

As Jesús María put out her tongue, I looked down into my glass—but still managed to catch sight of a deep groove: full of glitter that might have been diamonds, but more likely cheap bling. Then I emptied my drink and put the question.

"How come you knew my key sentence?"

Now it was her turn to wait, to divert.

"Did you know that some researchers see weaving as the first binary system, nine thousand goddam years ago?" she said at last.

"That the weft thread which goes over and under the warp threads, up and down, can quite easily be transformed into digital stuff, you know: on and off, one and zero? And that's why the loom was so perfect for industrialization—punch cards could easily communicate with them. And why machines can knit but not crochet."

"So what you're saying is that even someone like you could master coding and decryption."

"Exactly. And even someone like you."

She looked at me, long enough for it to begin to mean something.

"But no-one can escape, Erasmo, however fast one runs. Neither you nor me. Not even Ingrid."

She took a piece of paper and the weed—or whatever it was—out of her pocket, put her glass down, started to roll a cigarette.

"Ingrid's and my paths crossed, our *destinies* as she would say, at an Army base on the Mexican border. There was only one other woman there at the time, in the late '60s. Damaged goods, just as I was. Had to sew her up from inside out."

I looked at this strange little figure, with her cloven tongue, who could not possibly have turned forty.

"But you can't have been at the base at that time. You'd be at least sixty-five by now."

"Didn't the Witch tell you what a good craftswoman I am?" Jesús María said as she walked out, leaving me alone in the Ice Queen.

It must have taken at least half an hour, maybe more, before I made my way to Ingrid's room. Knocked three times, short pause, then twice more—and finally one loud knock. The usual signal. Yet Ingrid still only opened when I whispered her name, pressed tightly to the door.

"What did Sixten say?" I said.

Ingrid went back to the bed and her computer, kept tapping away at the keyboard, did not seem surprised by my question.

"They have been harassing him since our operation out at Esrange. Poor Aina too. Even Lisa."

Ingrid still had her eyes fixed on the screen.

"So they're on their way here now."

"Sixten and Aina?"

"No, the others, those who are after us."

The bed squeaked as she got up and crossed the floor toward me, still standing just inside the door. Looked me straight in the eye.

"Sixten is also on his way. He's finally been given permission by Aina to become more directly involved in *the cause*. He'll be here as soon as he can."

Perhaps I did put up some resistance when Ingrid then gently lifted the hybrid from my shoulders, took out the briefcase, laid it with the lid open on the bed next to her computer and made all the necessary preparations. Perhaps not. In any case the images appeared on the screen again: the same as when Ingrid showed me the trick a few weeks ago. Exterior and interior scenes from our intercontinental missile base at Minot. Four smaller scenes from the surveillance cameras—and one larger one in the middle, from inside the command center itself.

Everything seemed to be normal, according to the indications at the bottom of the screen. Pressure inside the missile, humidity, alert level.

"So now it's our move, my treasure."

When Ingrid began to enter commands on her keyboard, I fell in with her rhythm, like a musician. At the same time I keyed 122 129 on the keyboard in my briefcase: the code which I had shown my mother there at the kitchen table, at the dawn of time. Which clearly became "HELP" by way of my strange key sentence.

Our little four-hands piece had immediate effect. The green markings quickly turned to yellow, then red, as they had before. Everything felt at the same time terribly heavy and unbearably light. A soft murmuring in the deepest recesses of my mind, as if from something electric, a fan perhaps, a humming refrigerator. The launch counter was quickly spinning down to zero. The exterior images showed the wide expanses to the north, west and south of the base beginning to vibrate as the hatches in the ground opened up revealing our silos with the hundreds of ageing Minuteman-3 missiles, dinosaurs from the Cold War; as if a minor earthquake had struck. The ground shook, smoke from the ignition engines billowed over the surface.

And despite the indicators blinking with apparent anger, the desperate warning cries which could be heard crackling through the base's loudspeaker system, this time the events just continued to unfold. The missiles really were launched—even if they all then exploded still deeply embedded in their silos.

The smoke spread all the same, the gas and flames quickly broadening out through the support tunnels. The missile operators in Global Strike Command ran for their lives. The body count in the screen's bottom right-hand corner had risen to eighteen in less than a minute.

Then Ingrid closed down the image on her portable terminal, all with a single command, which made the same happen on the screen in the lid of my briefcase. I felt her watching me—and turned to meet her gaze: that ice-gray challenge.

"I don't think we can cope with seeing more for now. Forgive me, my treasure. But it was in the heat of the moment."

3.06

There was a painting. I had never seen it. And yet I *had* seen it, before my own eyes, day and night. Always carried the reproduction hidden in my combat pack.

I had never been able to experience the original, at the Prado Museum in Madrid, because it had been to all intents and purposes impossible for me to get security clearance for private visits overseas. I knew that it was a relatively small painting—like so many other truly great works of art: not more than four feet by five and a half. Yet he had managed to include so many terrifying details in it.

I brought it out again, the night after Ingrid's simulated attack on Minot, to comfort me or mark my despair. There were no nuclear wars at the time of Pieter Bruegel the Elder in the middle of the sixteenth century, we must assume, so he may have had second sight. The painting showed exactly what the aftermath of the big bang would look like. Scorched earth and bare trees, the feeling that nothing at all had survived, could survive, wandering skeletons milking the soul out of the few things remaining to be plundered, driving around a cart full of skulls, piles of dead bodies. Everything moreover steeped in a sickly yellow-brown tone. This was what Bruegel called "The Triumph of Death".

But the strangest things of all were in the painting's bottom right-hand corner. The terror-struck people, the few still living, who together with phantoms and corpses seemed to be being herded—or themselves fleeing—into what looked very much like a railway cattle truck. And outside the open door one could see something resembling an iron cross.

Bruegel's painting was truly prophetic. And not just about nuclear war—also the Holocaust, the transports to the concentration camps, the killing toward the end of the Second World War.

222

You must understand. But you won't.

Just as we had never understood, before it was too late.

On September 3, 1949, one of the American W.B.-29s
patrolling the airspace beyond the Kamchatka
Peninsula recorded unusual readings on its
sensors. Some sort of radioactive debris had been
picked up, three hundred times stronger than the
established maximum safety level. Further testing
determined that the radiation was caused by
nuclear fission. Ten days later U.S. military
experts assigned this military event the code
name "Joe 1", from Stalin's nickname "Joe". The
Soviet Union had detonated an atom bomb.

Barely three weeks after the radioactivity
had been registered near Kamchatka, the news
reached the committee of researchers and
industrialists who were to decide on next steps.

From then on it was not only a question of
whether the U.S. should try to develop a weapon
with perhaps one million times the explosive power
of the atom bomb: with a realistic possibility of
wiping out mankind. But also whether the Soviet
Union would soon acquire a weapon with the same
potential.

In reply to a question about the effectiveness
of this new weapon, the hydrogen bomb, General
James McCormack gave this answer:

"If all of the theory turned out to be
true, you can have it any size up to the sun or
thereabouts if you wanted . . . one million times
more powerful than the atomic bomb."

True, there were theoretical problems to be
overcome. Many of the scientists had not only

223

technical but also strong ethical doubts over the development of the hydrogen bomb.

Hans Bethe was one of those scientists, another of the prominent nuclear physicists among the intellectual diaspora gathered in the U.S. to work on the atom bomb. In 1933 he lost his research post in Germany because of his Jewish heritage, and during the war became the head of the theoretical division at Los Alamos. In due course he also became an active participant in the development of what was called the thermonuclear weapon, the hydrogen bomb: what was at first only referred to in conversation as "Super".

Bethe went into the project with a secret hope that the technology would turn out never to function. During the intensive ethical discussions in the fall of 1949, he went for a long walk with his Austrian colleague Victor Weisskopf, across the campus of Princeton, trying to imagine the effects of a full-scale thermo-nuclear war. Much later he revealed what they had concluded:

"We both had to agree that, after such a war, even if we were to win it, the world would not be like the world we want to preserve. We would lose the thing we were fighting for."

The General Advisory Report, which in 1949 eventually resulted from the intensive discussions of American researchers and industrialists on the subject of the hydrogen bomb, was also unambiguous. Thermonuclear weapons should never be developed. The atom bombs already in the U.S.'s arsenal were more than sufficient, it said, to counter even a large Soviet attack.

"In determining not to proceed to develop

the super bomb," it said, "we see a unique
opportunity to provide by example some limitations
on the totality of war and thus to limit the fear
and to arouse the hope of mankind."

The continuation, in the minority report,
is a classic example of applied scientific ethics:

"Necessarily such a weapon goes far beyond
any military objective and enters the range of
very great natural catastrophes. By its very
nature it cannot be confined to a military
objective but becomes a weapon which in practical
effect is almost one of genocide. It is clear that
the use of such a weapon cannot be justified on
any ethical ground which gives a human being a
certain individuality and dignity even if he
happens to be a resident of an enemy country."

And further:

"The fact that no limits exist to the
destructiveness of this weapon makes its very
existence and the knowledge of its construction a
danger to humanity as a whole. It is necessarily
an evil thing considered in any light."

And it is these evil things—thermonuclear
weapons, hydrogen bombs—which even to this day
stand proudly in position across the surface of
the earth. Each and every one of the upward of
twenty thousand individual warheads has an
explosive force which is at least ten, and in some
cases a thousand, times greater than the only
nuclear weapons which have ever been used. The
atom bombs dropped over first Hiroshima, and then
Nagasaki.

3.07

For the weeks that followed, I remained convinced that the incident at Minot must have been simulated. Digital conjuring with the help of the footage Ingrid had managed to take away with her from Esrange, manipulated images streamed from the satellites. Another test of my determination and loyalty.

I never asked her directly—since things never became any clearer when I did. And there was no sign from our pursuers, not even now. No reaction, no counter-move.

Until Edelweiss called.

I knew it had to be him as soon as I heard the ring tone—at 4.00 a.m.

In Edelweiss' universe, nothing happened by chance. The time of his call fell precisely in the middle of the hour of the wolf on my side of the Atlantic. When we had learned that all people with a normal daily rhythm were at their most vulnerable, the body's activity level, temperature, blood pressure at its lowest—and the melatonin at its highest. That is why attacks just before dawn had become so popular, since our military researchers discovered the effects of melatonin. Especially because our night-combat technology was so superior to that of the impoverished states which we invaded: Grenada, Iraq, Afghanistan, Iraq again.

But I had been awake for a while. Had not been able to fall asleep again this time either, after the night's blasting in the heart of the mine, once I had completed my check of the status of the briefcase. I lay there listening to the ghost furniture squeaking against the floor on the conference level above me. Stared at the spiders finding ways in everywhere, in spite of the cold that should have frozen them all solid before they came in.

Yet I let the ring tone cut through the room: the "Dallas"

theme tune. Four, five, six times . . . Then I just did it. Pressed the green button, waited out Edelweiss' heavy breathing.

"Ah, Erasmus . . . did I wake you? Sorry, one really should hang up after the phone has rung more than four times. But my mind must have wandered for a moment. No doubt feeling a bit lost in spacetime."

I did not manage to get a word out. It was such a long time since I had last heard Edelweiss speaking live. The voice of that person who awakened in me such strong and confused feelings: intense hatred and something bordering on admiration. Not warmth certainly, but heat.

"Perhaps you've felt the same way lately, my dear friend. Ever since the incident at Minot? That reality has shifted a tiny bit, sunk out of sight, like a sand dune. Have you seen a six-eyed sand spider try to climb out of a deep pit in the desert? How it struggles, fights for its life, even though it's made for just this biotope."

I did not want to follow him to any of the strange places where our dialogue often wandered.

"You know that the missile attack wasn't real." I said.

"Not *real*?"

I gave nothing away, wasn't going to fall into the trap. Just let him continue in his gentle voice.

"I would guess that the relatives of those who died at Minot do see it as perfectly real, not to mention the fourteen seriously injured, and their relatives, to the extent that we humans can determine that. On average twenty-one dead makes about eighty-four nearest and dearest. On top of that the same number again of not so close relatives, like rings spreading in the water: brothers and sisters, cousins, grandparents, stepchildren maybe. I'd say you're talking about three hundred people more or less directly affected. We do of course try to stress the importance of their not disclosing anything about what happened, because that would prejudice the longer-term possibilities, both for us and for you. And that doesn't come cheaply. But if we were also to pretend that it was all just one big

227

fiction, even their dead relatives . . . I don't think that even our whole military budget would be enough to pay all of them off. People are extremely sensitive about the genuineness of their sensory impressions, as you know, my dear friend. Can take it pretty badly if that's questioned."

He fell silent, let me dangle in the uncertainty. Which of these two less than wholly credible people was the more believable. Ingrid or Edelweiss. The devil or the deep blue sea.

"But I understand exactly how you feel, Erasmus. How one can evolve after a long time in the vicinity of that woman. I know what you've been through earlier, many years ago—but not in a situation like this, as quarry on the run, with all the psychological pressure. And there's a lot I could tell you about Oskarsson."

Then, in that very moment, I began to speak.

First he listened, but eventually a conversation of sorts unfurled. Some kind of dialogue. A transaction took shape. Time vanished, as it so often did with Edelweiss. When he hung up at last, it was 6.00 a.m., November 20. And nothing had become easier. Rather, very much harder.

I pulled the curtains aside, removed one of the boards, observed the mine in the yellowish artificial light. There were still three hours and nineteen minutes to go until sunrise. Three weeks until the Polar Night, beginning December 10. The day when the sun sank beneath the horizon here in Kiruna—not to reappear until the New Year.

I knew that that ought to be the signal. The one symbolic point in time, the starting pistol for our move away from here: to the next stop after our apparently successful intervention out at Esrange.

So the days went by in the same nerve-racking stillness. Jesús María usually behind the scenes with Bettan and the Girls. Ingrid less and less with her computer in her room and increasingly often in front of the T.V. or in the Ice Queen—which in itself was a sign that she would soon have finished her business here. Often practicing advanced yoga while watching the game shows she seemed

228

passionate about: the more mindless, the better. Extended her body out of the Chesterfield armchair, in whichever direction, at times straight up into the air with no apparent support.

I tried to keep some sort of control. Training, showering, suppressing doubts, anxieties, dreams. Going through that technical-occult ceremony of the briefcase day and night. Counting the number of hairy spiders as they made their way into my room, every night trying to convince myself that their sheer number indicated they could not be real.

And the person we were waiting for was Sixten. For whatever it was that he could add to Ingrid's lunatic project: this ex-engineer from Sweden's former nuclear weapons program. But once you had met him—experienced his reserved warmth, how calmly he gave and received confidence—you were no longer sure you could manage without him.

By lunchtime on December 10, the first day of the Polar Night, he had still not come. I was passing the time with Ingrid in front of the T.V. After yet another game show, she switched channels to a midday re-run of a documentary about a presumed Swedish mass-murderer who, after years in a psychiatric hospital, had turned out to be entirely innocent.

I could not stop myself, was sucked right into the story. This man had seemingly been influenced by his therapist into confessing to actions he had never carried out, by recovering his own "repressed memories". Guided into a world of mirrors in which he himself could determine the rules and show the investigators evidence which had already been written about in the media. In this way the man was able to dupe the Swedish judicial system, the police force and a number of the country's best lawyers.

From my dissertation work, with all the Swedish source material, I had learned enough of the language to be able to follow what was going on in this documentary. Large parts consisted of a sub-titled interview with an American psychologist. Her theories about "false memory" had become the film-makers' key to understanding

229

what had happened. The historic breakthrough for the theories had come when the psychologist managed to get several subjects in an experiment in the '90s to recall, in exactly the same way, having been lost in a shopping mall as children, something which had never happened to any of them. During the interview the psychologist called this process "implantation". Fictitious memories which are deliberately implanted deep within an individual's mind.

We did not say a word to each other while the documentary was playing. Only when the credits started to roll did Ingrid turn to me.

"She looked much younger with her new hairstyle."

"Who do you mean?"

"The psychologist, of course. She became my best friend during those first fragile years of study, at Columbia, when I was starting to build up my own double life: in the same way as you yourself some decades later, my treasure. She and I were studying two quite different subjects, but in the academic world there's a lot of important stuff that crosses over between them, bridges over dark waters."

At that moment—when I was presented with an unsought opportunity to ask follow-up questions, to try to make some sense of Ingrid's life story, logistically as well as chronologically—she suddenly got up from the sofa.

"It's time, Erasmus. A little over two hours before he's due to collect us. Less than an hour till sundown."

3.08

Then Ingrid led the three of us, with full packs, in among the low line of trees and up toward Luossa Hill. She had managed to track down Jesús María in the hotel. Now she was in front of me and I could hear her breathing. Not because there was anything wrong with her fitness—far from it—but she sounded like a predator out for the hunt.

Once we reached the slope we saw that there was an impressive Saturday crush, low-level chaos. But Ingrid did not hesitate and made her way through the line. Seemed to trust entirely in her new face, confident that no-one would recognize her even here.

"These are my last rentals, ma'am . . . but everything looks about right for you." The young blond man in the rental store tested the length of the skis against Ingrid's height, assessed the bindings. She inverted the poles, placed her hands in the baskets and measured their height in line with her forearm and elbow. "Just to warn you, the lifts close as soon as the sun has gone down, that's our tradition for the day, for the Polar Night après-ski. The party goes on until midnight . . ." Ingrid paid him no attention, looked through the window at the mountain. "You'll have half an hour at the most on the slope, barely ten minutes without sun and twenty with. At 11.45 a.m. it'll be gone for the year."

"That will be more than enough," she said.

"And these two won't be skiing?" he said, gesturing to me and Jesús María.

"Oh, they're just my fans."

"O.K. Got it." The young man smiled in our direction. "Have you been here before?"

"On top of the hill centuries ago, my friend. But I've never skied the slope."

"So, in that case you won't have experienced our sun ritual

either. It was meant to be a bit of fun when we opened a couple of years ago, on Polar Night, to try to get people in. It turned out to be such a success that we've kept it going. It's our third year now. And the same clear sky as before."

"What's this ritual about, then?"

"I think you should wait and see, ma'am. It's pretty cool, even if I say so myself."

The young man went out and closed the door while Ingrid put on the boots. I leaned forward and whispered to her:

"Seriously? Ski here, now, among all these people?"

"Have you ever known me not serious, my treasure? I simply can't leave without trying the piste, can I? And Bettan said that this would be the best day of all. We've got enough time before we're due to be picked up, just after lunch. Only a few runs, before the lifts close."

As she got into the lift line—she had given me her large backpack but kept her small one—Ingrid fired off her most irresistible smile.

"Besides, I just wanted to show off a bit of my former magic for you, from the good old days. If you just spread out a bit and keep an eye open, I'll feel completely safe here. This is my natural element, I'm almost on my home turf. And the bigger the crowds, the lower the risk."

Without further discussion—about who should stand where out of the two of us, any strategic considerations—Jesús María started to half-run up the steep lower part of the slope, stopping just below the tree line. I remained where I was, by the side of the lift line, with not only the large hybrid but also Ingrid's pack at my feet, which limited my ability to move and intervene. Yet my reflexes kicked in as I began to survey the crowd. Any suspicious-looking individuals or groups, conceivable threats, potential escape routes.

But for the most part it all seemed peaceful. Among the other skiers some, especially the teenagers, appeared to have stolen a march on the ski hut's planned après-ski party. Their shouts to their friends waiting in line were loud and shrill, but at least the group was preoccupied. Nobody seemed to be taking any notice of Jesús María, who now stood a few hundred feet above me, looking out over the masses. Nor of Ingrid.

Except for me. I could not take my eyes off her. How she let her seventy-year-old body dance and play, dominating the whole piste, at once relaxed and theatrical.

As she took the lift up again, having slid to an elegant stop at the tail of the lift line, my eyes resumed their scan across the people who filled most of the piste. Using the usual profiling. One possible risk group was four men in their fifties. Most of the skiers were in pairs, except for one bunch of six young people. Eight pairs were single-sex—five only men and three only women, who all seemed much younger—and six were mixed.

It was not easy to identify any particular characteristics among them: not when they were all wearing helmets and goggles, with their faces protected against the extreme cold by balaclavas, and the same sort of clothes. They were more or less indistinguishable from each other, except for their height. Even Jesús María and myself.

Only three sets of skiers stood out. The first was a couple who seemed to be absorbed in each other further up the slope and not far from Jesús María. Even at a distance one could see the intensity of their embrace. The woman almost disappeared within the man's frame.

The next was of course Ingrid, who cut through the swarm of people with the ease of a razor blade. She made a number of turns on her way down, with an expertise which showed us that she could have done as many more or less as she would have liked. She appeared spellbound by the snow and the sun and the skiing, unaware of what was going on around her, buried deep within herself.

When the third conspicuous skier, an enormous man on his own, swung in to the lift line again, I thought I should watch him closely—which was becoming more difficult because an increasing number of people poured in by the minute, some coming up from below. Non-skiers, they stepped off the T-bar, about half-way up. The skiers coming from higher on the slope also stopped at the same point. Within moments it had become nearly impossible to make one's way through the mass of people just below the point where Jesús María was standing. Two snowcats, each towing a refrigerator, braked suddenly in the crowd—whereupon the drivers jumped off and started to hand out bottles of beer.

At that precise moment the sun rose above the hill opposite us, at an angle which allowed the lowest of its rays to fall just where the people were all gathered. From where I was, suddenly alone at the bottom of the lift—which was still running but was now not being used by anybody—I saw the faces in the crowd all turned toward the light, gazing at the pale disc of the sun. I could not help thinking about our early nuclear weapons tests. How the spectators had been sitting in rows, some with sunglasses, some without, admiring the ball of fire as it hovered half up in the sky, before the throng here raised their bottles and shouted *"Skål!"* to each other and to the now so distant star.

Then the music began to boom through enormous speakers at the base area, while people who seemed to be total strangers hugged and kissed, as if on New Year's Eve. I looked at my watch: 11.21.

So this was the sun ritual—which instantly made the security situation much more fluid, so much harder to calculate. Ingrid was now almost the only person still skiing, and she had a clear view to both sides of the slope. But to navigate the crowd of people in the middle of the piste she needed to carve a sharp turn far out to the right, about where Jesús María seemed to have hidden herself away in the trees. Then she descended, carving giant turns around the lift pylons.

Only one other person could be seen on the piste. The solitary giant of a man, who became, in an instant, so recognizable. That terrifying pattern of movement, conspicuous even on skis.

When he took the lift up again just three seats ahead of Ingrid, who was gesticulating at me with her index finger to indicate that she wanted only one more descent, I started running up the hill as fast as I could with the hybrid on my back and her pack on my front. I noticed the amorous couple to the right of the festive crowd, just near to the point where Ingrid would be passing in a minute or two, but I was still too far away to be able to shout a warning—even if she were able to hear anything at all through the music and the buzz of the throng.

So Ingrid would soon be caught in their ingenious trap, with me as nothing more than spectator.

When the young man from the rental store looked at the clock and began the countdown—from sixty, second by second, as "The Final Countdown" blasted from the loudspeakers—I managed to get a reasonably clear line of sight through all the people as they stood there with eyes screwed tight shut against the disappearing sun, shouting out the numbers in unison. Was able, as I struggled to make my way through them, to follow what was happening behind their backs.

I watched as the pair of lovers, that is to say Zafirah and Kurt-or-John, first swept up Ingrid in what from a distance looked like an awkward embrace. And how something—or rather someone— then derailed their entire plan.

The binding on one of Kurt-or-John's skis released as Jesús María threw herself at him—and in so doing set Ingrid free to ski downhill at speed. Zafirah melted into the crowd as if her presence had been an illusion, the passing of a shadow, while the other one of Kurt-or-John let himself be carried within the shifting mass of people, beyond reach.

Only Ingrid can have seen the rest of the events unfold, while the numbers approached zero and the volume of "The Final Countdown" continued to rise, drowning out the primal roar which must have followed.

I was too far away to be able to get involved. Just watched, like

Ingrid, who had swung in among the trees on the other side of the piste, as Jesús María grabbed the ski which Kurt-or-John had lost, and with it hit him across the face. He staggered, fell backward from the force of all the pent-up rage, while the blood started to gush from his forehead, nose and mouth, effectively blinding him.

Jesús María raised the ski again. Held it like a giant scalpel, standing over Kurt-or-John's prone figure.

The steel edge of the ski was drawn straight across his abdomen, slicing it with as much fury as precision. Yet Kurt-or-John did not come apart—since there was still bone there, the skeleton itself.

The rapidly growing pool of blood glistened, as it pumped out of the body rhythmically and the year's last rays of sunshine was reflected in it, before it began to be absorbed into the snow. I gazed at the red on the white, that remarkably beautiful contrast. And the human remains lying there, Kurt-or-John like a slaughtered animal, steadily drained of blood, or a reindeer dragged down by a wolf on the hillside. Mused for a moment over the rate at which a human body can empty.

The countdown was completed. As the crowd yelled "THREE . . . TWO . . . ONE . . . ZERO—goodbye, thank you for another year!" I had to turn around quickly to see the sun sink behind the hill and leave a thin yellow-red line on the horizon. I checked my wrist-watch: 11.45, just as the young man had said. Saw the crowd start skiing down to the base so as not to miss the start of Polar Night après-ski, still not noticing anything of what had happened right behind their backs.

When the sight up the slope was clear, I stared at the last of the blood, not gushing but slowly seeping over the snow—before Jesús María dragged what was left of Kurt-or-John into the trees.

3.09

Back at the hotel, Ingrid took a quick shower while Jesús María disappeared off to the service area, down to the Girls. Probably to say her goodbyes. Bettan had laid out a magnificent farewell lunch, but had not herself appeared for it. None of us ate very much, either. Not even Ingrid.

Jesús María eventually appeared at the table.

"You were a godsend," Ingrid said. "It seems they knew a bit too much about us: someone must have been indiscreet. That was a close call. Thank you."

"*Igualmente*," was Jesús María's answer.

Before I had time to ask any questions, trying once again to understand the relationship between these women, not least that last reply, Bettan came into the dining room.

"He's here now," she said.

I noticed that Ingrid did not give Bettan a farewell hug before we vanished into the Kiruna afternoon, by now pitch-dark. Small snowflakes whirled in the air, stars could no longer be seen in the sky, the wind whistled through the low birches.

The man in the snowmobile suit gave Ingrid a clumsy embrace, before reaching out his mighty right glove, first toward me and then to Jesús María.

"Niklas. 'The Magnificent'. Was it you who ordered the sight-seeing?"

"Yes, thank you, my love. I'm so grateful. Bob and Mercedes will love it," Ingrid said, back to her playful self with incredible speed after the incident on the slope. Jesús María sat in complete silence. Did not react at all, seemed still to be up there on the mountain, with Kurt-or-John's remains fresh in her mind. I held back too. Tried to work out what role I should be playing now.

"No problem, Inko. But I have to admit I had no damned clue that you had cousins over there."

"I'm glad I've managed to keep some secrets from you. And I suddenly had the idea of showing my only American relatives our little world. Before it's too late—and the whole lot sinks into the deep."

"Mmm, I know: like Atlantis."

As he steered his pick-up truck out of the neighborhood, surprisingly slowly, Ingrid turned to us in the back seat.

"Niklas will always be very close to my heart. And not only because he was my first tragic love. He and I also took care of a large construction venture in the old days, massively complex, before I decided to try my luck in the U.S. using the project as an example of my work. That's when we began to call him 'The Magnificent'."

"I think you were probably alone in that, Inko. But thanks anyway."

I stole a glance at Jesús María, who even now made no effort to join in the banter. Sat there in a sulk while Ingrid played her charades. Niklas pointed at the analog thermometer on the *Norrbottens-Kuriren* newspaper building. Held the steering wheel in one hand, his giant glove still on.

"At least minus 37 Celsius, isn't it?"

"36.8 at the most," I said.

He peered at me in the rearview mirror. It was always easy to win people's confidence, to begin to build trust.

"Wish I had your eyesight, Bob. But where should we start, Inko?"

"Take the church. God's work."

Once we were in the church, she began to explain. That the exterior had been painted in Falun red and the roof covered in shingle; that the influences from Sami cots could be seen in the construction of the roof beam; how the light fell.

And it was so strange to hear Ingrid lecture again, the whole enchantment. Then we went out to the divine little park, with snow as thick as cream lying on the branches of the trees. That strange feeling of grace. At least there and then, in this particular moment.

Ingrid also told us that Kiruna Church was voted the most popular twentieth-century Swedish building in a national poll. And that this particular masterpiece would be spared destruction, since a gigantically complicated process was planned to move it in its entirety to another site in town.

"But Kiruna Town Hall is a tragedy. This will be the first and last time that you see it," she said.

While Niklas drove us there—it was a lot safer for us in the truck than out in the streets during business hours—I tried to understand why Ingrid let us do this in the first place. Whether our sight-seeing might have some specific purpose, some connection to our assignment. Or if it was just designed, on the spur of the moment, to break the torment of our inactivity while waiting for Sixten.

But as soon as I stepped into the enormous entrance hall, feeling my eyes rise all the way up to the ceiling—I had to catch my breath at the sheer size of the space—I no longer cared which it was. I climbed reverentially up the broad stairs—and then stood there on the upper floor and slowly ran my hand over the por-phyry railings. A few feet away from me, Jesús María was doing the same. Closed her eyes, sighed, opened them again. Seemed, like me, hardly able to take in the idea. Of demolishing something like this, in peacetime, as if it had been an enemy military target.

I then went down into the basement and tried to interpret the local authority's sketches of what was called the "Kiruna City Transformation". Nothing really seemed to hang together. Not the dimensions, nor the scale, the size of the vast area which was to be moved in comparison with the small new center being built.

When we took the guided tour into the mine, just before it closed to the public for the day, I had the same feeling. At the Visitor Center a third of a mile down, we jostled with a group of American tourists, their cries of "Oh my God!", "Unbelievable!", "Fantastic!", "Awesome!" ricocheted off the rock. I stood before the sketches in silence. Still trying to get my head around the "City Transformation", until it was time for the tour bus to return to the surface. But despite the detailed diagrams showing how the vein ran—a one-mile tunnel of magnetite—and all these precise aerial photographs, I still did not understand why such a large part of town had to move.

I could not help thinking of Edelweiss' "scenarios", his false trails, diversions. Or the model communities which we threw up somewhere in the desert, only then to be able to bomb the hell out of them.

Back in Niklas' truck we snaked our way up the mountain, increasingly on smaller tracks rather than roads, right into darkness. Until we saw the shining skulls in the trees. Heard—and felt—the music vibrating through the car.

Niklas' camp turned out to be a crackpot hippie collective with death metal as its distinguishing characteristic. Violent music pumped out over the mountain. End of days lurked everywhere. Skulls, bones, garish posters saying "The Town of Death" or "#kirunaisdyingfight" with English text draped over the Swedish original, maybe for our sake, grotesque plastic heads stuck on poles, maybe hinting at those at the Inner Station in "Apocalypse Now". Ingrid whispered that they represented the members of the Kiruna local government council.

We changed into jumpsuits like the one Niklas was wearing, before he led us out to the sleds. One could hardly hear the dogs' furious barking over the music, their urge to start pulling. And soon the drift snow started whining across the camp. Through the combined din Niklas had to shout to us—even though we were standing next to him.

Jesús María helped Niklas to harness the twelve dogs, before taking her place nearest to them. I myself sat immediately behind her as we wrestled my hybrid and her medical pack down between us. Finally Niklas climbed up onto the runners at the back with Ingrid, still wearing her pack, next to him.

The dogs yelped madly before we got off to a start, uncontrolled, directionless. The back of my seat banged painfully against my vertebrae as the sled slid and bumped down the first steep hill below the camp. But after about a minute the barking had died away. The dogs forged ahead, twelve animals and one human conductor perfectly choreographed, each one with their exact place in the rigid hierarchy.

We were moving much faster than I had expected, despite the thickening snowfall. I had no idea where we were heading, was also under no illusion that I would be told if I asked. But at least we would not make ourselves visible in this open mountain terrain. "The worse, the better," Edelweiss used to say about the correlation between weather and combat: there was no better camouflage than a sandstorm, thick fog or heavy driving snow, and Ingrid had taken this into account.

The snow lashed continuously against our covered faces, onto the balaclavas, goggles, headlamps. What little we could make out of the landscape was like sea bed rather than mountainside. The ice-tortured dwarf birches reminded me most of all of coral. Jesús María sat silently in front of me, observing the identical rhythm of the dogs, their co-ordinated instinct to run.

I closed my eyes and concentrated on trying to pick up some of Ingrid and Niklas' conversation, in Swedish and through the howling wind. Wiggled my toes inside my boots to thaw out my right foot. Not even our winter equipment could deal with hours of sitting in what must have been negative twenty-two degrees, even though the temperature always rises when snow begins to fall.

"And are you sure you want to go all the whole way out there, Inko, in this nightmarish weather?" Niklas said.

"Absolutely. Now that we've come all the way across the Atlantic. It's an adventure for us, after all, and we're outdoors people just like you. It's probably still your fault that I never choose the easiest way."

"Yup, we got around, were pretty off-piste. But that was pre-history, forty-five years ago in October. I'd never have recognized you if you hadn't called first. But I recognized the voice, naturally, same as ever."

Niklas was quiet for only a moment. Then his curiosity got the better of him.

"And that guy Sixten . . . still in touch with him?"

"Not a peep since I left for the States. Ages ago."

"Well, you were as different from each other as could be, Yin and bloody Yang. It would never have lasted."

Suddenly the dogs turned in toward the edge of the trees and stopped at Niklas' low command. The hut had appeared like a mirage out of the snow: even thirty feet away we had seen nothing of it.

It was not much to look at, either. As I scoped the building, I saw that the roof had collapsed toward the northern gable, where plastic had been riveted—although that too had started to tear due to the weather conditions. Not one window retained both panes of glass. But the doors appeared to be largely intact, so it ought to be possible to shut out the worst of the cold by stuffing extra clothing from our packs into the gaps. When I returned to the group, Niklas glanced at our packs as Jesús María and I lifted them from the sled.

"I assume I don't need to ask if you've got proper gear with you. Bob's pack is after all bloody gigantic. You can also keep the jumpsuits until you come back to the camp."

"Awesome, thank you. And so long as you come and get us again tomorrow morning, everything will be just fine," Ingrid said.

He turned the team of dogs around, said a coaxing "O.K.", their simple command. A few seconds later they had vanished into the darkness and driving snow. Ingrid led the way to the hut, managed to open the warped door without too much of a problem. Let us go past her, closed the door again and stopped a few paces in, looking around dreamily.

"We used to sit in here and kiss before we could even read. Niklas' mother had been involved in 'Operation Sepals' during the war, one of the most important cogs in the wheel from what I understood: the Germans let the Sami roam free as reindeer over the border, perfect couriers. Then the Tourist Association never bothered to reclaim the hut. The mineral vein runs just under here, you see, so when the company stopped its open-cast work and went underground, there was probably nobody who wanted to sit here rattling as the whole of Mount Doom was blown apart. Except me and Niklas—and eventually just me. Here you can do whatever you want without being watched, in case you're wondering."

Jesús María had not said a word. I waited for Ingrid to explain what we were doing out here in the wilderness. But she looked at her watch.

"We certainly wouldn't need to keep anything from Niklas. You've seen what the camp looks like, right? He would never report us to any authority, not a Swedish one and even less an American one, and absolutely no way to the military."

When Ingrid checked her watch again—no more than five minutes later, still standing over by the door—I did the same. 21.52, December 10. The beginning of the Polar Night and the date of the Nobel Peace Prize ceremonies: all this symbolism. And our crumbling little cottage would be a perfect hiding place when the police started questioning everybody in the immediate vicinity of the slope tomorrow morning, like Bettan for instance.

"But by now Niklas will have stopped thinking about turning around and coming back to fetch us out of this rat-hole, he'll have gone too far already. And once he's back at camp, my informants tell me that nowadays it doesn't take more than a thimbleful before he's out for the night."

Then she turned and opened the door, letting in the ice-cold wind and driving snow.

"So it's time to get to the real meeting place."

3.10

Ingrid led us, packs on our backs, headlamps lit, straight into the storm. We crouched before the wind, carefully balancing our weight so that we did not break through the snow crust. The cold stung in our nostrils with each breath. The snow kept falling— which should make it nearly impossible for anybody to spot us.

The only thing I could make out was that we were surrounded by thick forest. The dog team must have turned off sharply and headed down the mountainside, before dropping us below the tree line again. Ingrid followed a trail further and further in among the trees. The heavy snow made the branches sag: if necessary we could use the space under them as escape tunnels.

As the storm grew heavier and denser, Ingrid was several times forced to stop and retrace her steps. Counted her paces back and forth, double-checking, stopped by a tree and ran her hand up and down the bark, as if looking for some kind of markings. We kept close behind, so as not to lose sight of her.

After a few minutes she signaled us to halt in what seemed to be a more open place. She wandered here and there with her eyes fixed on the snow—before suddenly sitting down and starting to dig vigorously with her hands, like a child. Jesús María and I did the same. Our winter gloves were clumsy, but there was no doubt a reason why Ingrid chose not to use the collapsible shovel in her combat pack.

Under the snow there was at first nothing but pieces of granite, and then increasingly black composites, laden with magnetite. Only after removing the deep layer of stones on top of the bed-rock could we glimpse the control box in the light of our headlamps. That was why Ingrid had avoided using the shovel, preferred the sensitivity of her hands.

With great concentration she then set about prising open the box with some sort of tool, laying bare the control buttons. The panel was large enough to allow one to key in the code—and, as ever, small enough that one's hand would cover the movement of the fingers, making it impossible for someone else to read. A dark hole opened up in the snow.

Against the howling wind, Ingrid had to gesture to us to lead the way down. I could see out of the corner of my eye how she erased our trail: stretching one hand up out of the hole to scrabble back in place as much as she could of the natural camouflage, small piles of gravel and diluted iron ore, while the entrance to the tunnel closed above us.

So Jesús María took the lead through the steep, unlit passage, the narrow bore allowing us to place our feet on either side of the fall line even here, almost climbing down the rock wall, like Spiderman. I shivered, pulled myself together. By the time we reached the finished tunnel floor, Ingrid had managed to catch us up. We pulled off our balaclavas and continued in double-quick time along the vehicle track which twisted steeply through the bed-rock. The stalactites hung from the roof like age-old objets d'art. According to my watch it took almost a quarter of an hour for us to reach the lock gates, the depth meter showed dizzying and steadily increasing co-ordinates. Negative 500 feet, 650, 800 . . .

Here too the gates conformed to regulations in every way. Three red steel doors, two for the shock waves and one a gas barrier with a pressure relief valve. Ingrid slipped past Jesús María. I leaned out from our little line to see her take a few deep breaths, shut her eyes. Then she quickly pressed the code on the control box hidden in the rock wall, hurried through the decontamination rooms, past the oxygen cylinders, the changing rooms, hardly sparing them a glance. Once we reached the rest area she turned on the light, switched off her lamp and sank into the circular, flame-colored sofas from the '70s.

I looked again at my watch. 23.03—and the depth, 1,132 feet.

Almost a quarter of a mile. Far deeper than any military installation I had visited.

"Welcome to Pluto. Mount Doom's hidden core," Ingrid said.

With some effort she removed her boots and put her feet up on the sofa. Wiggled her toes to get the circulation going again as she started to speak.

"We thought of calling it Uranus, after the God of the Heavens. But then we thought Pluto would be better. The direct opposite: the Romans' equivalent to Hades, the ruler of the underworld, the kingdom of the dead. And the one who gave his name to plutonium."

Ingrid paused and began to massage her feet. I watched her breath: puffs of human warmth. The temperature was more comfortable here than outdoors, but it hovered barely above freezing. The dank underground cavern felt so familiar to me, mold and high technology, must with a note of electricity.

"We transported a lot of plutonium here, and also uranium, which at the time was collectively known as 'atomic ash'. Every little trace of our early experiments within the program. And in due course other sorts of things—the residue from our Second and Third Tier development work. Using the same transport route as when we moved the mining engineers and blasting specialists from here in Kiruna to Ursvik, at night-time over a number of years. All those who built the Inner Circle."

We had learned to interpret all imaginable signs, whatever information was available at any given moment. So when Ingrid broke off in order to take three crunch cookies out of her combat pack and drink three mouthfuls of liquid—which made me and Jesús María do the same thing—she simultaneously gave away the fact that we would not be staying here for very long. A few days at most, hardly a week, since we were consuming so much of our provisions in one go. Then we would in all likelihood return to some sort of civilization, at least for a short while to get real nourishment into our bodies.

"Almost no-one had the faintest idea about any of this," she went on. "Not even our most senior commanders, politicians, ministers. It was entirely my idea: nobody else should have to take responsibility for this, come Judgment Day. When I was sucked into the program at the beginning of the '60s—still a teenager, fresh and clear, like a mountain lake—I read Sir Claude Gibbs' theories on how best to store nuclear waste. According to him, old coal mines, which one should then cement shut, would be safer than the bottom of the North Sea."

Ingrid finished off her third crunch cookie, for once showing signs of needing food and liquid. Jesús María and I did the same.

"And I had after all recently been sitting in the hut up there and literally felt in my body how the open-cast mining finished and the work penetrated deeper and deeper into the bed-rock. So I thought the atomic ash could slowly but surely be covered by the debris falling down from the higher levels, all this granite and magnetite. If, that is, we were able to blast open a secret connection sideways into the lowest part of the workings: synchronizing our efforts with the work of establishing the new main level at a quarter of a mile down. And everything went to plan. We imagined that this would eventually become a really big storage space for the waste from the program. Not only plutonium and uranium, but also for everything else we would have to hide. For the whole of 'Lise Meitner's secret.'"

Her choice of words made me start.

"But the story took another turn, of course, as so often happens. After October 1968, for certain reasons, no more waste was freighted up here. The others involved were all much older than us, began to die off, and there was nothing recorded on paper. So Pluto became as forgotten as Pompeii had been for a thousand years, until the archaeologists started to dig it up. In the end even Sixten stopped coming here once a year to measure the values."

Ingrid got up and led us through a long tunnel toward the red steel door. On the wall before it were gauges for humidity and the radiation level. They looked as if they had stopped functioning decades earlier.

"It's lying in there, still: the dragon's treasure. We began with the waste which already existed—the product of Meitner and Sigvard Eklund's very first experiments in the mid-'50s, which officially came from experimental reactor R.1 under Kungliga Tekniska Högskolan in Stockholm. Mostly metallic uranium sealed up in aluminum, and unfortunately the aluminum turned out to react on contact with water. Then we simply filled in with what we ourselves produced. Layer upon layer, year after year, in this top secret chamber beneath the gigantic volumes of debris from the construction of the new base level."

We returned to the rest area and Ingrid stretched out on a sofa while Jesús María and I sat opposite her. Her voice was just as engaging, even in that position. I closed my eyes and listened. Could not help but enjoy her fairy tales.

"And we really did manage to pull it off. It wasn't until 2007, when Nya Ursvik was to be developed and the last of the radioactive material had to be removed from there, that the so-called 'historic waste' began to receive any attention in the Swedish media. Then Greenpeace received a tip-off and had the good fortune to find the truck on the E4 motorway."

I opened my eyes again, saw that Jesús María was about to say something—and then held back so as to listen to more.

"But the very last of the waste from our Swedish nuclear weapons program was sent away to the States as late as last year, on March 27. Just over six and a half pounds of weapons-grade plutonium, nearly twenty pounds of naturally depleted uranium and a few other things in a top secret maneuver which had been planned for decades. As professional as if I'd done it myself—as indeed I had. But now from the other side of the Atlantic."

Ingrid seemed to hesitate before she went on. Swallowed heavily.

"In any case . . . with the question of the waste having been raised in the media, in 2007 Sixten came up here for the first time in years to measure the levels: was reminded that everything was still lying in here. And what he discovered was that the situation was not as serious as he had feared—rather it was a good deal worse. The waste from the later phases of the program turned out to be more toxic than we could ever have imagined. In addition, the radioactivity had spread far out into the ground-water."

Ingrid took another few deep drafts of liquid, cleared her throat.

"Yet we had a stroke of luck. The mine is of course owned by L.K.A.B., which in turn is owned by the Swedish state, so the connection between the nuclear weapons program and the mine could be hushed up. The vital part of Kiruna did have to be moved. But we could also bundle up our nuclear waste issue within the gigantic process which goes under the heading of "City Transformation".

At last Jesús María reacted.

"You mean all of that crap, Bettan's fucking tears because the hotel is having to close after being run by three generations of the same family, the fact that the town hall has to be blown all to hell, is just fake? That this is about plutonium and shit—and not the iron ore in the mountain!"

"That's not what I'm saying, Jesús María. I don't think anyone of woman born can work out exactly what's what anymore. These processes have for so long been wrapped up in each other, like concentric circles, boxes within boxes."

Ingrid took a Geiger counter out of her combat pack, our latest model, hardly bigger than a matchbox. It rattled more than ticked. Like a rattlesnake.

"So I promised Sixten to make an assessment of the radiation, since we were in this neck of the woods anyway. And as you can probably tell from your Geiger counter, we ought not to stay in here for long. I should say exactly thirty-nine minutes . . . until he finally comes."

I stole a glance at my watch, which of course showed 23.21.

Thirty-nine minutes until midnight: the constant chronological symbolism. Then I asked the question, even though I knew the mussel might snap shut for ever.

"You talk about your Second and Third Tier development work . . . Can you tell us more about it, Ingrid?"

"The short answer is 'No', my treasure, and we haven't got time for the longer answer. But I can say that our dreams of an atom bomb were only the beginning. The very first circle of hell."

3.11

When I woke up—and felt to see if the security strap of the brief-case was still lying over my wrist—Jesús María was sitting close to Ingrid on the sofa opposite. The sweetish smell and the stubs on the '70s oval teak table revealed their tale: Jesús María had already smoked too much. Ingrid looked pale and worn.

"You could set the stars by Sixten, the entire universe, the course of the world . . . " she muttered.

00.51. As it turned 01.00, Ingrid straightened her face, became our Alpha again.

"O.K. Improvisation," she said tonelessly and lifted her pack onto her back. "It's not safe to stay here any longer."

We moved up to the surface in silence. Everything in reverse, although it was much tougher going in this direction: up the steep tunnel, the layers of stones over the hatch. But we were soon above ground and heading into driving snow. By 02.14 we were back at the ramshackle hut.

The night passed relatively painlessly, despite the cold. Our sleeping bags were meant to be able to cope with negative thirteen, according to military regulations—and after burning a fire for about an hour in the open fireplace, the temperature at the hut's southern gable had risen to approximately that. When I finished my shift keeping an eye on the fire, I fell into a deep and dreamless sleep, as if drugged.

At 08.30 Ingrid tapped my shoulder. Still pale, resolute, controlled.

"Niklas should be here soon. We said *at dawn*, whatever that may mean in this weather and on the first day of twenty-four hour darkness. But I didn't think it was so important to agree an exact time. The plan was for Sixten to take us away from here, by snow-mobile, before Niklas returned."

Half an hour later the dogs and Niklas came into view through the cracked windows. They were at most thirty feet away, the visibility cannot have been much more than that.

"Wonderful night?" Niklas said once he had managed to force open the frozen door and the rolled-up fabric Jesús María had used to seal cracks.

"Divine. Definitely one for the memories," Ingrid said.

"Yes, it's been fantastic to experience the northern Scandinavian climate like this, full on," I said.

Niklas just shook his head as he led us to the dogs. And even their impatient barking had not been enough for me to find them on my own: it was brutally hard to manage the driving snow, despite all our winter training. The special goggles had no chance against these extreme conditions, which seemed to have got heavier rather than moved on.

"And you said Jukkas . . . are you absolutely sure, Inko? You know that I won't set foot inside that pile of colonial kitsch," Niklas said somewhere in front of me in the white-out.

"You can drop us off wherever you want within walking distance, Niklas. But Bob and Mercedes would never forgive me if I didn't give them the chance to stay at the Ice Hotel."

We took up the same positions in the sled. Niklas and Ingrid back on the runners, Jesús María closest to the dogs and me behind her. Despite the dogs' silence once they were allowed to start pulling—how willingly they heaved and hauled at the harness, just like me—the wind stopped me from hearing a word of what Niklas and Ingrid were saying. Whatever lies she was telling him now.

The snow covered our tracks, both sled and dogs. The landscape was like one enormous blanket. Some kind of light nevertheless seeped through low on the horizon, the world went from gray-white to white-gray while "dawn" broke and the Polar Night approached its brightest moment.

When the main road was a few feet away—and we were level with yet another wooden church which we could make out on the other side, still in the shelter of the trees—Niklas stopped the sled.

"And you don't want us to go in there first, Inko? The priest is normally around until lunchtime. Just get it done?"

Ingrid fell silent for a moment, for once had no ready answer.

"Another time," she said.

"O.K., give me a call when . . . But it should have been us, right?"

Ingrid got out of the sled, put the pack on her back and gave him a quick peck on the cheek.

"Yes, Niklas. It should have been us."

Then both he and the sled and dogs were swallowed whole by the whirling snow, while we labored toward the Ice Hotel. Even though it was only a regular weekday, just before lunch on Wednesday, December 11, 2013, long lines straggled to the reception desk. Ingrid still managed to find a way to the front—getting hold of the last three tickets to the daily showing.

Edelweiss used to say that there were only two ways in which to hide away effectively. Either in isolation: underground, alone on an island, in the middle of the desert. Or right in the middle of the throng.

It was for that reason that Ingrid and Sixten had chosen this commotion as an alternate meeting place. When the guide arrived, fifteen minutes after the specified time, there was hardly any elbow-room left in the hotel lobby. The tourists were glaring in irritation at our enormous packs that Ingrid had secured, against the odds, permission for us to bring them in.

Even the guide cast a troubled look at the backpacks—before deciding that this group was so large, and he was himself already so late, that it was hardly worthwhile sending us to the left luggage area.

And one would think that in our current situation, nothing else would matter. Just the escape, the briefcase in the hybrid, the assignment. That the rest of our existence would fall away. But instead I was hyper-sensitive, keyed up to the maximum. Every word from our guide registered with me, everything I saw. The

Main Hall reminded me of the most beautiful and terrifying stories of my childhood—the Grimm Brothers' fairy tales, *Narnia*, *The Lord of the Rings*. And later the Harry Potter stories, which I had read one after the other with the kids.

At the same time I tried to keep an eye on the other two. Ingrid seemed above all to be awaiting the signal from Sixten: usually looking in a different direction from the one the guide was pointing in. Jesús María had already left the group and begun to wander around on her own. When she thought that nobody was looking, she ran her hand over the wishing well of ice in the middle of the hall, furtively dropping a coin into the water.

Then she moved on to the mighty unicorn which dominated the far end of the hall, at least ten feet long from head to tail. When the rest of the group arrived at the sculpture—and Jesús María had already walked some distance away—the guide explained that it was made of *snice*. A specially balanced mixture of snow and ice for creating frozen works of art.

I came to think of the remarkable Gobelin tapestry which Ingrid devoted one of her many thought-provoking lectures to. One of the most enigmatic masterpieces of the Middle Ages, she had said, clicking slowly forward, slide after slide. Through the series which showed in the harshest detail how the unicorn was first lured and then killed. The blood flowing from its wounds, all the spears in one single body, the wild looks of the huntsmen: that beautiful white creature being sacrificed like Christ himself.

After a number of historic twists and turns, the tapestry—seven mysterious pictures in the most precious textiles—ended up at the Cloisters in New York, where my mother and I used to end our long walks.

How we then used to sit in their wonderful café under the arches, my mother with her black coffee and I with an enormous cup of hot chocolate with so much whipped cream so that it spilled over: she always insisted that it should be *too much*. Spoke to me animatedly about those strange paintings—with their depictions of primitive bloodthirstiness, the white unicorn being hunted and speared like any bull in an arena—ever since I had been far too young.

The final and most complex scene was called "The Unicorn in Captivity". Which was also the title of this mighty *snice* statue, here in Jukkasjärvi's Ice Hotel.

Before the Ice Bar opened, we were allowed to walk around on our own in the hotel rooms and the artistically decorated ice suites, which all had English names for the benefit of the tourists. Everything appeared frightening and incomprehensible to me, put me on edge. In the "Narcissus" suite a gigantic head of ice and snow was reflected in a huge frosty mirror. "Future Ancestors" was a labyrinth of allusions to religious rites which had not yet found their shape.

Then it got really unpleasant. I would not be able to get many minutes of sleep in "Solid Flow/Time Warps", "It's Alive" or "Before the Big Bang". But the worst of all, Suite 325 in the western gable, was called "The Martyrdom of Christ". Just a double bed—made completely of ice, like everything else—and a gigantic shining crucifix, on which a man-sized Christ figure was writhing in agony.

I kept close to Ingrid, even more so after the incident on the Luossa slope, watching everywhere for signs of Zafirah and the surviving Kurt-or-John. But there was just one other person in this terrible place: Jesús María stood stock-still and admired the work.

"I'd like to live here," she said.

We left her in front of her namesake and went out to the Ice Bar, which was packed full of people even though only three minutes had passed since its opening at 4.00 p.m. Ingrid somehow found a place at the bar and immediately ordered a vodka cranberry. I took a Virgin Mary and as we drank slowly, I sensed a feverish energy rising in her as we waited. The wall clock of *snice* struck 5.00 p.m. and she stared at it, then at her cell phone.

The noise level in the bar became more oppressive with each passing minute, a strangely lustful bellowing, Sodom and Gomorrah

125 miles north of the Arctic Circle. People crowded in on all sides around our bulky packs. Played and lost crazy sums at the roulette table, cut directly from the ice of the Torne river: every time the ice ball came to a stop, there was an ear-shattering cacophony of rejoicing and dismay.

Eventually Ingrid's cell phone did ring. Or at least it must have done—I heard nothing at all through the din. Just saw that she started, as if shot.

"Suite 325," she then shouted in my ear with the cell phone still in her hand. Her breath was heavy with vodka cranberry.

"He's waiting for us there. Glory be to God on high."

When we got to the suite, there was no sign of Jesús María. On the door Sixten had put his own handwritten piece of paper over the suite's name. It now read "ERASMUS' MARTYRDOM".

All these games. Sixten's cool temperament, even in a situation like this.

I could not help but smile, recalling our first late-night dinner at Ursvik. How he, as part of his conversational performance piece, had discussed Poussin's interpretation of the myth surrounding the saint who bore my name. How Sixten himself had apparently once hovered around "The Martyrdom of St Erasmus" at the Vatican Museum. Finally he walked away, but not being able to forget it, went back that same day. Then repeated this ritual several times during his week's holiday. The savagery of it had made a deep impression on him. How Saint Erasmus just lay there on a bare bench while his intestines, according to the myth, were wound out of his stomach by a windlass.

Sixten was now sitting in Suite 325, in splendid solitude, facing away from us on the double bed of ice, in the darkest part of the room. He continued to play his games. Pretended to be reading a book, not even to notice our arrival.

"Ah, so there's my knight in shining armor!" Ingrid exclaimed.

I hurried forward to take the book from his hand and gain his attention, without first studying the situation. Only close up could

I make out the title: *The Soft Spots*. The textbook to which our instructor in extreme close combat always referred.

Then everything went haywire. People were pulling and tearing at me from different directions. Blurred contours, imprecise movements, insufficiently synchronized pressure against the spots on my temples. Confusion, some form of combat perhaps. Zafirah's face inches above my own, the black of her eyes, without life, reflected nothing. I froze. A sharp stab to my neck as the needle pierced the vein. Slowly I started to lose consciousness, felt how the hybrid was lifted off me and my back was pressed directly onto the bare ice of the bed. I heard shouts, agitated voices, ultra-violence. Right there and yet somehow far off. As if I were under the surface, sensing everything through a tiny hole in the ice.

It took some moments before the initial numb feeling from the cold began to fade and my brain registered the pain. Just before I experienced the sensation of skin against ice, heat rather than cold, I gave Sixten another appreciative little smile. At how precisely he had managed to recreate Poussin's painting—as a living tableau.

My own terrible martyrdom.

4

SECOND DOWN

December 2013
Peer, Belgium

4.01

That night was one long stream of visions, hallucinations, images. Lucid dreams. Beyond reality.

I was waterboarded five times in succession in the water of the wishing well, a fraction above freezing. Then I was skewered by the unicorn's three-foot-long horn of ice—before my innards were slowly rolled up on it.

The experience of having died, if only temporarily, made the dreams worse than ever.

Not even Edelweiss had allowed us to take our practice sessions all the way. We could after all not be totally sure that the resuscitation exercises would be as effective as the killing methods. "And once you're dead you'll never be the same again," he had proclaimed without a trace of a smile.

As I regained consciousness, I dreamed that I was our most lauded president and was making a speech at a top-level meeting about nuclear weapons during the early years of the Cold War.

"Today, every inhabitant of this planet must contemplate the day when this planet may no longer be habitable," I began.

"Every man, woman and child lives under a nuclear sword of Damocles, hanging by the slenderest of threads, capable of being cut at any moment by accident or miscalculation or by madness. The weapons of war must be abolished before they abolish us. The mere existence of modern weapons—ten million times more powerful than any that the world has ever seen, and only minutes away from any target on earth—is a source of horror, and discord and distrust.

"I speak of peace because of the new face of war. If only one thermonuclear bomb were to be dropped on any American, Russian, or any other city, whether it was launched by accident or design, by a madman or by an enemy, by a large nation or by a small one, from any corner of the world, that one bomb could release more destructive power on the inhabitants of that one helpless city than all the bombs dropped in the Second World War.

"A full-scale nuclear exchange, lasting less than sixty minutes, with the weapons now in existence, could wipe out more than three hundred million Americans, Europeans, and Russians, as well as untold numbers elsewhere. And the survivors, as Chairman Khrushchev warned the Communist Chinese, 'the survivors would envy the dead'. For they would inherit a world so devastated by explosions and poison and fire that today we cannot even conceive of its horrors.

"In an age when both sides have come to possess enough nuclear power to destroy the human race several times over, the world of communism and the world of free choice have been caught up in a vicious circle of conflicting ideologies and interests. World order will be secured only when the whole world has laid down these weapons which seem to offer us present security but threaten the future survival of the human race.

"So let us turn the world away from war. Let us make the most of this opportunity, and every opportunity, to reduce tension, to slow down the perilous nuclear arms race, and to check the world's slide toward annihilation."

The applause which greeted the end of my speech would not die down. I bowed, gestured to the president of the other superpower, my opponent and new partner in the dreams of disarmament.

When the congenial formal dinner was over, I met the military advisors in my room for a final polishing of our plans for a full-scale and irreversible nuclear weapons attack on the other superpower.

I took one last close look at the calculations for the devastation. Felt a warmth through my body, like endorphins after a run.

4.02

And that was my frame of mind as finally I woke up, with a smile on my lips.

It did not take too many seconds before my mouth stiffened into a grimace and the warmth in my body was replaced by freezing cold. The lit-up ice figure of Jesus on the cross was staring me in the face, paralyzed with agony, just like me.

I tried to lift my naked back. But just the first inch of movement gave an indication of how bad the pain would be when my body tried to free itself from the bluish block of ice. Although I would be largely anesthetized by the cold.

The smell of Zafirah's heavily spiced scent—enough to provoke headaches even under normal conditions—was still hanging in the air, or maybe just in my memory. The steel-gray short wig, as well as Sixten's turquoise shell jacket, lay discarded beside the ice bed. As dysfunctional as my brain was, this made me realize that he had probably never been here.

I managed to get up after a number of unsuccessful attempts. It was like tearing off a Band-Aid. Except that it covered my entire back—and that it was my own efforts which were ripping open the wound.

I staggered around among the objects which had been spread across the suite. The hybrid was still there, but without the briefcase. My weapon, field knife, and the medical pack containing the treasured anesthetics and things far worse which could bring an end to everything at once, were also gone. As well as my notebook, the crunch cookies, the cell phone from the playground, my watch: everything that could keep me oriented. And the key which Sixten had given me.

But they had left most of the contents of the pack, including my field glasses, latest passport, currency, the matching credit cards in one of the hybrid's secret pockets. Probably hoping to keep me under electronic surveillance, waiting to see where the tracks would lead. Or they had simply been in a hurry.

My sweater and down vest lay just inside the hybrid's upper lid. I put my clothes on incredibly slowly, a few inches at a time, adding layer after layer with infinite care as if I were made of cracked glass. With some effort I also managed to get my winter boots on as well as the black snowmobile suit with the words "THE INNER STATION. Niklas' Adventures" on the breast pocket. I strapped on the noticeably lighter hybrid as loosely as I could, opened the unlocked door to Suite 325, "The Martyrdom of Christ", and went down into the sparse night lighting of the Ice Lobby. Scanning the area, I looked for some sign of either Ingrid or Jesús María. When the receptionist informed me they had checked out, I thanked her, turned, and—without a backward glance—made for the cover of the Polar night.

Our psychologists had told us that nobody could really explain how our will to live functions. Why it could suddenly stop. Or why it did not.

So I walked away from the hotel, reflexively, instinctively, although I could have headed down into the river instead. The clock outside the souvenir store showed 05.01, December 12, 2013. Everything was crystal clear and unreal. The area surrounding the hotel in power-save mode, the transfer buses like giant bugs sleeping along the main road.

But the vast restaurant on the other side, scaled to accommodate mass tourist assault, was still open at this time of night: for the most part as a gesture to a few individual truckers who had slept in their vehicles. One of them was sitting at a table inside, finishing his breakfast.

"Are you headed near Kiruna station?" I said.

"Certainly am, but I'm leaving right now."

"Do you have any alcohol in the truck? I can pay you for it." I showed him money. He nodded, got slowly to his feet and I followed him out to the biggest eighteen-wheeler on the road.

When I jumped down at the station he handed me a small, transparent, plastic bottle without a label. It could just as easily have been home-distilled spirit or face cleanser—an impression which downing the bottle in the bathroom on the train did nothing to dispel. But it did to some extent deaden the pain, and the effect of feeling frozen solid began to wear off.

I removed the jumpsuit and pulled on the neutral, black gear which I had taken out of the combat pack in the hybrid. I stared at the face in the mirror, still strange to me. The new lips, the fleshy nose: Jesús María's attempt to make me look like General Shubin. The face in the mirror looked back at me, searching for some trace of the man before the martyr. I saw the wreckage of a person—not only after the trials of the night, my temporary death. But also the psychological warfare.

By the time we arrived at Luleå, after not many hours' journey, the locomotive succumbed to the cold. While we were waiting, I went to the station store and bought a ballpoint pen and a notebook. Then eventually I sat down in the restaurant car of the new train, put the hybrid under the table and ordered an inedible Pyttipanna with cream sauce, sliced beetroot and two fried eggs. Carefully noted down in the new notebook everything that had happened since we left the Snowflake, barely two days ago.

When I was finished, my left temple started to burn with pain, as well as much of my back—I needed something else to concentrate on. I began a comprehensive analysis of the situation in my new notebook.

I made the basic assumption that the core team was now up and running. If not immediately after the launch at Minot, then in any case since the Ice Hotel. Apart from Zafirah and Kurt-or-John—together or separately—Edelweiss was presumably as ever at headquarters in Washington. On top of that, elements of the President's own forces had presumably been assigned to take us down. But in accordance with the directives, few, if any others at all, would be informed: not even the Vice President.

The remaining authorities, all of our jumble of more or less rival agencies, would probably have no idea either. Likely not the C.I.A. Presumably neither the F.B.I. nor the N.S.A. Almost certainly not the Secret Service either—or the S.S., as Edelweiss sometimes used to label them, the meaning hidden yet clear. They would only be thinking that NUCLEUS were away on yet another top secret training maneuver somewhere around the globe.

Even I was no longer aware of much more than pieces of the puzzle. I had no idea who had my briefcase or Ingrid's portable command terminal. Who were the hunters, who the hunted.

So I wrote down the names of the people in chronological order, without specifying their respective roles. In order of appearance during our flight: first Jesús María, then Ingrid, Sixten, Aina, Lisa, Bettan, Niklas. After that I added my ageing senile mother, as well as Amba and the children.

Then I put a cross underneath those who might be dead. That made at least half, maybe all of them. Eliminated in silence, as always during our classified assignments overseas. Later there would be talk of accidents and illnesses, chance fateful encounters: only we would know the whole picture, had sufficient numbers of paid informants.

Finally I added our nuclear weapons bases, both at home and in Europe, as well as other strategic targets—and began to sketch in the connections. Solid arrows between the squares represented movements which had already taken place, ones with dashed lines meant upcoming ones, double lines between people indicated that they trusted each other while single lines suggested fundamental uncertainty. And soon it all became one solid cloud of ink.

But come Stockholm, I had abandoned the analysis. There was only one way to clarify the situation, and that was empirically. At one particular place, and one only, on just one particular date. It was a guess. But an educated one.

After purchasing a night-train ticket costing an arm and a leg, I got some headache pills, water and a copy of the *New York Times* from a kiosk. There was still a quarter of an hour before departure, so I sat down among the businessmen who were smoking on the bench furthest along the platform, beyond the glow of the light. The newspaper was a day old: from December 11. I found what I was looking for, even though it had only been given one small square at the very bottom of the front page—so I leafed to the foreign pages and read on. The award of the Peace Prize in Oslo seemed once again to have passed without incident. And the views expressed about the Organization for Prohibition of Chemical Weapons were as effusive as ever.

Mobilizing public opinion against chemical weapons had been much more successful than in the case of nuclear weapons, since they never represented any direct threat to our own military power. Nerve gas had therefore already been banned long ago, even in wartime.

I laid the newspaper on the bench in order to take a few painkillers and rinse them down with the water. Only then did I catch sight of the article.

The entire top left-hand corner of the first page was covered with General Falconetti's picture. Edelweiss' most important play-mate, in dress uniform, with a chest full of shining medals. A small column on the first page of the home news section listed all of Falconetti's areas of responsibility: full operational charge of our nuclear weapons submarines, aircraft and land-based launch ramps. Highest supervisory authority over the military space program, as well as the entire digital war effort.

I pinched my arm and closed my eyes. But the article was still there when I opened them.

The most senior person responsible for the nuclear weapons system—at least officially, outside the Team, and therefore our nearest colleague—had been caught red-handed manipulating digital one-armed bandits.

A background article listed all the other incidents which had apparently come to light in the American nuclear weapons system during this fall alone. An entire unit of missile operators at the Malmstrom base had been failed during a security spot check, and the joint commander of two other unnamed nuclear weapons bases had recently been dismissed after similar controls.

In the article the Commander-in-chief talked of moral failings among personnel who had constantly to be at full readiness without ever being "deployed", as he put it. A psychoanalyst agreed in an interview that people who are "deprived of purpose" in the end also lose their judgment.

At the foot of the page there was a timeline of the revelations. As I read it, I was stunned. Because it was not now—as news of this unthinkable incident was becoming public—that General Falconetti had been dismissed from the military.

It had happened on October 24. The day after Aina turned seventy, the attack during her birthday celebration, our escape from the window of the burning house. It could be a coincidence—but probably not.

4.03

I had been to Bruxelles-Central only once before. During an exercise in the heart of the city, simulating a terror attack, the President's stand-in had taken shelter in the grand old station awaiting orders for evacuation. I had stood right next to him.

After sitting around in painful idleness, he had suggested we see who could be the quickest at counting the number of panes in the enormous barred windows running all the way from the doors of the front entrance up to the roof. I nodded: a stand-in should be obeyed in the same way as the President himself.

"231!" he said eagerly, after only about a second. He had obviously already counted them. "Simple mathematics. Seven sections times eleven rows times three panes in each!" he went on.

"Exactly," I answered. "Less the two missing panes at 3:7:2 and 5:2:1. So: 229 in total."

It was because of those sorts of things that I had become the Carrier and he was still a stand-in. Because I—and not he—understood that the picture always consists of millions of pixels, that it is the details which define the whole rather than the other way around, his military career would always be stuck in amateur dramatics and party tricks.

Otherwise we usually arrived in Brussels directly with the helicopter, Marine One. Only Kurt-or-John and I, together with the President, and a few select members of his own security detail in a separate little group sitting furthest forward. We would land on the roof of the grayish and anonymous N.A.T.O. headquarters building, far enough away from the center along the motorway, then go straight into the office of the Supreme Allied Commander Europe while the guards gave even me subservient nods.

The latest Admiral was amiable and relaxed. Had taken up his post at the same time as the President and was about the same age—which meant they had more in common than just their jobs: they could loosen up with some banter before the agenda for the day took hold, about acquaintances shared, someone's old girlfriend at university, the sports results. Occasionally about the nuclear football. Sometimes the President made as if to pass it to the Admiral, to take it out of my left hand and throw it across.

I had not moved a muscle, hardly even blinked. Through all these years.

During exercises we would instead land at and depart from the closed-off parts of Zaventem airport, called "Terminal X". Enormous, fully armed columns for the regular joint maneuvers with our European allies. One of many full dress rehearsals, physical and psychological preparations for the unthinkable, with or without nuclear weapons.

But now I had come here to Belgium, a man without a briefcase or a weapon. I got onto a local train, picked a seat in the center of an empty carriage and took out the newspaper I had bought at the station kiosk. The clock at the first stop, Leuven, said 14.12. That vague time after lunch on a regular working day. A perfect moment to strike—or to be anonymous.

And there was at least as much in the *Washington Post* as there had been in the *New York Times* the day before, an entire spread. The headline read AMERICAN NUCLEAR WEAPONS SCANDAL, the layout unusually brash for the newspaper.

According to its so-called defense policy expert, astonishing new revelations were continuing to emerge from the nuclear weapons program. For example, the majority of the operative personnel at yet another of our most important missile bases— Minot—had been suspended for security reasons.

But the expert wrote that this was still small beer in comparison with the latest, as yet unconfirmed, rumor. That another of the three most senior officers responsible for the whole of the American nuclear weapons system had been suspended pending the outcome of an investigation. The main reason was said to be that he had behaved inappropriately at an international nuclear weapons conference, had become intoxicated and bragged about how he saves the world from destruction every day, each second, just by not pushing the button. He had also, in the course of the conference, ended up at the homes of a number of women with doubtful security status. "Like in a James Bond movie!", the military political expert wrote.

I was not surprised: sooner or later our true personalities have a habit of emerging. And I had never had any time for General Goldsmith.

And yet—all this synchronicity. Everything coming out at once.

I stared out the window, trying to gather my thoughts Sat bolt upright, so as not to let the raw parts of my back touch the seat.

Flanders rolled by like a newsreel from the First World War. The same special clay which made the unusually deep and durable trenches possible, the deadlock, the same unceasing rain. It spattered ever harder against the window as the train took me further into this featureless part of the world, as if made to house in the greatest secrecy one of our key nuclear weapons bases in Europe. The sort of thing that we never confirmed, however strong the indications were.

I ticked off the names of all the artistically decorated station buildings on the Post-it note the woman in the ticket office at Bruxelles-Central had given me. *Tienen, Landen, Sint-Truiden, Alken* . . . And oddly enough there was a taxi available outside the station in Hasselt. Despite the rain, on this day of all days.

"Spotters' Day?" the driver asked. "To the base?"

"No," I said, "first a good night's sleep at the hotel. I'll take the risk of waiting till tomorrow to get myself there."

The driver hardly spared a glance at the kitschy decals on my enormous black backpack, which I lifted into the car with me. He spoke English as well as most people do around our overseas bases, knew that it was worth making that little effort. And that he should not ask any more questions than necessary.

So it was mostly him telling me. About what was obviously the reason Ingrid had been expecting Sixten on that particular day in Kiruna, so as to have enough time to come down here for this very occasion. The moment when everybody would be gazing in the wrong direction. "Misdirection", as magicians call it. When aircraft enthusiasts from the entire town, country, continent would be gathered for the one time in the year when one can see the airplanes in action at really close quarters. Our propaganda machinery in full swing.

"And it'll be especially spectacular this year, as you know! The whole area is super excited that this time they'll not only be allowed into the N.A.T.O. base, but the real one, right inside, so that the Americans can show everybody there are no nuclear weapons there. People are also speculating that something completely new is going to be demonstrated. The spotters have been standing in line for days—and the activists for even longer. Even though the gates won't be opened until seven tomorrow evening."

I glanced at the clock on the taxi dashboard: almost 4.00 p.m., the day before. Immediately before the first sign, *VLIEGBAS*, I began to recognize where I was, even as a car passenger. To kill some time I asked the driver to take a swing around the base. The area by the placard which read *Kiezel Kleine Brogel Spotters Corner* was for once totally empty. The enthusiasts who normally stood there for most of the day, gazing into the sky, since our fighters' take-off and landing times were classified even during training, must have moved over to the base itself.

Through the taxi window I looked at the encampment outside the gates. The rain had stopped, and enormous pools of water lay mirror-like. The tents of the demonstrators and enthusiasts stood not too far apart, united by a common interest. In the calm before the storm.

Then I let my eyes travel further: across the sentry box; the

272

high walls; the razor-wire fence which had been developed for Guantanamo and continually refined for our nuclear weapons bases around the world. I had been here so often, very recently, in another life. The Kleine Brogel nuclear weapons base was one of our central locations in Europe for exercises. As well as one of the keys to our complex intercontinental system of attack and counter-attack, in case events turned real. What went by the name "Global Strike" in our current war plan.

When I felt that I had reconnoitered enough, I asked the driver to take a detour past the fighter plane on the roundabout on the way to Peer. Our old F-16, one of our longest-lasting models, part of the classic old weapons system which was gradually going to be replaced as part of the "Revitalization". According to current plans, with effect from 2023.

As we approached the hotel, I had a hollow feeling in the pit of my stomach: even I was not immune to it. There was no way of knowing what would be waiting for me there. If Ingrid and Jesús María could have survived the attack in Suite 325. Whether I had been spared just to act as what we call a "spool of thread". Somebody one allows to run free, under constant surveillance, to see where the leads run and how many people are involved. How deep it all goes. How high up, so that everyone is identified—even myself.

"Will you fetch me tomorrow late afternoon, at 6.30 p.m.?" I asked the driver.

"Of course, sir."

The facade of the hotel was the same as ever, a piece of cultural history, military memorial, frozen time. The neon sign said "1815", the name of the hotel honoring the battle at Waterloo—one hour from here by the main road. Where even Napoleon was defeated.

The woman in reception looked the same too. Her name badge identified her as Valeria—in our military way we had called her Valkyria behind her back, because of her long blond hair and luxuriant figure—and she had clearly had some more work done to her face since I last saw her.

Yet when I handed over my passport she hardly looked up. Maybe because she simply did not recognize me after my own surgery. Or because she had a lot on her hands.

The lobby was packed with spotters. In many ways hard to distinguish from the various sorts of spies, not least our own, who always turned up when bases around the world opened their gates.

But in one respect the two groups differed markedly. The enthusiasts' binoculars were enormous, and stuck out of their backpacks, a status symbol of sorts: the bigger, the better. This was in stark contrast to the spies' smaller models, chosen in order not to arouse attention.

In some ways therefore I blended in among the enthusiasts with my large black hybrid, even my kitschy tourist decals had their equivalent on some backpacks—but in one decisive respect I did not at all. Valeria pounced on this like a hawk when she finally looked up from her computer.

"But where are your binoculars, Herr Gustafsson?"

"Oh, I was robbed on the way here, unfortunately. In my sleeping compartment. But I'll able to borrow from a friend. He's been here for a few days already, to get a good place in line because of the rumors about something spectacular tomorrow evening."

"And you think you'll be able to find each other among all the people waiting to get in?"

"It usually works out, with a bit of ingenuity. It's not our first time."

She gave me a searching look, could very well have been paid by our military command, to keep an eye on things. Then she gave me my room key.

4.04

I checked out just after 9.00 a.m., before having breakfast. Valeria still showed no sign of seeing through my new face, just nodded and hummed into the computer. The dining room was empty, all the spotters up with the dawn to stand in line at the base. There was a chance that Ingrid might be among them. If, that is, she was still alive. I picked up a couple of newspapers and loaded my plate with sausage, bacon and potato pancakes, knew I needed the nourishment since I had not had a proper meal for more than twenty-four hours.

I left the plate half empty, or half full. When the tourist bureau next to the hotel opened, I showed them my passport and in return was given my own key to the Bruegelhuis and a bulky black audio guide.

"So you like Bruegel, Herr Gustafsson?" the young girl at the counter asked in a broad Flemish accent.

"Actually not. He scares the living daylights out of me."

The girl stiffened. She did not know how she should handle this response, what to do with herself in her traditional outfit from this province, Limburg: the strange white kerchief and appliqué fabric flowers, the black blouse and lilac striped skirt with orange fabric sewn onto it. With her studied politeness, her language skills, her training in tourism at the local university.

Before leaving I bought a box of Bruegel pastilles, some post-cards of his most gloomy works, and I reached for a magic Bruegel cube, with which one could switch between ten or so famous paintings: for example change the tranquil "Hunters in the Snow" into the macabre and violent "The Fall of the Rebel Angels". As I walked out I could hear the young girl sigh with relief.

The rain fell heavily again, cascaded over the medieval square like a great flood. As I stepped through the entrance to the

Bruegelhuis, Peer's exhibition dedicated to its most famous son, the drops from my rain suit streamed onto the creaking floorboards. My legs felt shaky and unreliable on the dizzyingly steep stairs. Not only because I had wanted to come here for so long, the place where, according to the experts, Pieter Bruegel the Elder was born. Apart from the base, it seemed to be the only thing which justified Peer's existence. And I had always thought of getting away for a free hour during one of our training visits, although the opportunity had never arisen.

Once I got into the exhibition upstairs at the Bruegelhuis, I was alone. This would be the obvious rendezvous in Ingrid's mind. She had been fascinated by him first. Started her opening lecture to us with "The Triumph of Death"—and concluded our final dissertation session with "The 'Little' Tower of Babel".

It was in the immediate aftermath of 9/11, 2001, our world had been turned upside down. Ingrid did not seem to want to talk about my dissertation at all. Instead she showed me the viral images on the net, with Bin Laden or the Evil One's face in the cloud of smoke caused by the aircraft crashing into the World Trade Center. Then she opened an image of "The 'Little' Tower of Babel" on her computer. Clicked to zoom closer and closer in, highlighting how the black clouds in the top right-hand corner of Bruegel's painting really seemed to be coming out of the building: in the form of smoke or soot. As if something had crashed into that work too, from the side, before exploding against Babel's tower.

Here in front of the reproduction of that painting I switched on the audio guide. But the meditative voice did not say a single word about it, hardly referred to the strange black clouds.

I moved on and found myself standing there, my legs trembling under the weight of my body. Somewhere behind the thick velvet curtains I could sense the sounds from the square, life at lunchtime on St Lucia's day, Friday the 13th, in this small Belgian village with Bruegel and a nuclear weapons base as its claims to fame. I put the headphones back on. "*Pling*. Number 23. 'The Triumph of Death'. Bruegel's prophetic masterpiece . . ." Stood stock-still in the dark room, just let myself be sucked in. For one minute, three, maybe longer.

When I surfaced again and switched off the audio guide, I heard an unmistakable creaking from the flooring in the next room. Somebody was there, keeping more or less exact pace with me: a few times I tried suddenly stopping in front of one of Bruegel's paintings and the footsteps would continue for just a second or two too long. I breathed calmly through my nose. Almost inaudibly, as we had been trained.

But the person shadowing me, or at least keeping me under observation, always from one of the adjoining eerily dark rooms in the Bruegelhuis, seemed to be well trained. So nobody gave themselves away—and neither did I. It could just as easily be Zafirah, Ingrid or Jesús María.

Then I heard a soft, for most people imperceptible, click from the entrance door lock on the ground floor. The careful tread up the stairs revealed neither the person's gender nor their weight. Could have been a compact little woman with perfect control over her center of gravity or a large man. What I knew was that this was someone who had been trained to move with stealth in tight situations: presumably at the same school as me.

Back at the tourist bureau, after triple-locking the door to the Bruegelhuis—neither the hunter nor the hunted revealing their play—I asked the young woman:

"Are there more sets of keys to the house?"

"Of course, sir, why do ask?"

"Who was it who picked up the other ones? Sex, age, any distinguishing marks? Could I possibly see a copy of their passport?"

She stared at me, terrified, as if this were a police interrogation.

"Nobody's been here. Not a living soul since you. Not in this weather!"

She managed a little smile.

"Maybe it was our house ghost you heard. We call him 'the Spirit of Bruegel.'"

I gave her a long look, this naïve young woman, hardly more than a teenager, in her Limburger folk dress. I knew that everyone could be bought—or threatened.

"I can believe that," I said.

4.05

After a long and late lunch—I tried to get through a gigantic entrecôte cut from a Belgian Blue—and then a tedious wait after that, in and out of shops, the taxi came and collected me outside the hotel.

The rain was once again beating against the windows of the taxi, and only got worse as we approached the base. I stared out at the volumes of water biblically drenching the sidewalks along the roadway. Focused, meditated, with the key sentence as my dark mantra. "I love you . . . just as senselessly as my pretty weird and hellish father, for the time being and onward into eternity, Amen."

The driver got an excessive tip just for not asking any more questions, even though I was arriving later than almost everyone else. Once he had driven off, I put on a wig, mustache and beard in the shelter of the crowd. Despite the heavy rain there were more people outside the base than I had ever seen at similar events: tens of thousands, perhaps even reaching the dream target of one hundred thousand. Ordinary families with balloons twisted into the shape of F.16s with the words "SPOTTERS' DAY. Kleine Brogel 2013" on the wings. Enthusiasts and spies equipped with similar rainwear and tall rubber boots.

The activists, on the other hand, rarely had any equipment apart from their signs and streamers. So far they were being allowed to do much as they wanted. Even scribble all over the posters for the event on the perimeter fencing: "BOMB Spotters' Day", "NUCLEAR Spotters' Day".

Any signage relating to nuclear weapons had been tidied away prior to the event. By granting the public and the media access to the American base for the very first time, our military administration would meet two objectives: "proving" that there were no nuclear warheads on the base while keeping the activists one additional barrier away—the entrance had been set up by the outer gates, where anyone without a ticket would be stopped. According to the information signs, security procedures would be more stringent than at a civilian airport. Scanning and body search for everybody, no exceptions.

I stood still in the pelting rain, tugged the hood over my head while the lines wound their way forward, and pondered how I was going to make my way past the guards. Even the morass of activists were closer to the fence. A bizarre set piece, as necessary as it was mad, began to unfold.

The P.R. balance was delicate. Public opinion was usually our best friend—especially for the last ten years or so during which time the media hardly reported anything about the ongoing nuclear escalation, our new generation of weapons and carriers, the "Revitalization". But at any time the balance could tip the other way, as happened during the Vietnam War.

The guards could have bundled up this many activists in a few short minutes, and without for using anything heavier than batons. "But there is also a balance between common sense and sensibility," Edelweiss used to preach. A quick move against the idealistic youth around the perimeter fence, many of them still teenagers, would result in too much negative publicity. Destroy the P.R. value of the event in one go.

The instructions were therefore almost certainly that the guard force should refrain from escalation. Stand in their rows with automatic weapons at the ready. Let themselves be taunted by the songs and the chants, the obscene gestures, without batting an eyelid—until the activists moved first and tried to storm the base.

Somewhere on or around the base Ingrid and Jesús María could be waiting for the same decisive moment. A ripple through the crowd—disorder, ideally some violent scenes—would create the best opening for the mission, whatever it might be, because chaos is the best camouflage. An opportunity, in one way or another, to obtain root access to the base's servers which Ingrid needed in order to connect Kleine Brogel to the Nuclear Family: our network of warheads around the world. One of the final pieces in the jigsaw of her demented plan.

And it seemed possible that Ingrid might specifically have chosen this occasion. Spotters' Day. Friday, December 13. St Lucia's day, the Sicilian martyr she had told me they celebrated in such a big way in Sweden.

I scanned the crowds, but saw no sign of anybody who might be Ingrid or Jesús María. Nor of our main pursuers: the compact Zafirah or the vast Kurt-or-John, whichever had survived. None of those who had been keeping track of me—or maybe of each other—at the Bruegelhuis before lunch.

So once all those in line had finally passed through the check-points and the clock by the entrance to the base—the illuminated atomic clock which was yet another of our propaganda weapons—had whirred over to 19.30.00.00, I started to walk toward the sentry box.

It was going to be almost impossible to get in. The sort of task which was routine for me.

"Are there any tickets left?" I asked with a marked Swedish accent.

The guard in the box gave me a long look, without saying a word. I was so hard to place, with my wig and the trim false beard—somewhere along the continuum of spotter, spy, hipster—the enormous backpack covered in decals, the absence of conspicuous binoculars. He had often seen me here before and could not disguise the effort of the search through his memory. But he was not able to identify my new face.

"Would you be so good as to show me your passport, first, sir," he said at last.

I was ready to leap into action. Had already worked out my next step and the one after that, depending on what ensued: the positions of the guards relative to each other, the time needed to make my way through the outer and then the inner gate. But my passport only elicited a friendly *peep* from the computer. Both scanning and body search rendered unnecessary.

"A warm welcome, Herr Gustafsson. Here is your ticket!"

At our own base, like a pocket within the surrounding N.A.T.O. compound, everything was organized for Spotters' Day. Ministers and military commanders in the control tower, together with members of the media. Attachés and other authorized observers formed the innermost ring, interspersed among them were a few lucky enthusiasts who had won a V.I.P. package by ballot. Then increasing numbers of people in concentric circles, each marked out by yellow lines in the asphalt. The outermost, at least three hundred feet wide, contained thousands of people.

I had been given a ticket at the center of the action. And it seemed that everyone was waiting for me.

Because just when the guards had escorted me to my place—a few enthusiasts having to move a fraction to the right before the mass of people flowed together again like liquid—three F.16s took off with a terrible roar. I had said no thanks to the earplugs offered to me on the way across the base, yet another detail which distinguished observers from enthusiasts.

Through my field glasses I saw the F.16s perform a "barrel roll" in close formation and then a neat "co-ordinated roll". When the engines were at enough of a distance, the aircraft lights forming luminous bars against the black storm clouds, one could hear the exhilarated cheering of the fans in our inner base. With a few seconds' delay came the response of the activists outside the gates, catcalls and howls.

This was only the warm-up. Although the show continued with "cartwheels" and "split 'S's", impressive in themselves, everybody seemed to be waiting with impatience and even trepidation for "The New Trick". According to the taxi driver it had been the subject of speculation for weeks, even months. Something which had never before been shown anywhere.

I glanced at an official's watch next to me: 8.10 p.m. Some people were no doubt beginning to think, like me, that the rumors had been a way to try to match the world record for spectator numbers. The legendary Miramar Air Show in California usually attracted about seven hundred thousand visitors during the course of three days. Here they must have let in a hundred thousand people—for a single hour of flying stunts.

And that's when it happened.

The spectators were herded outward by the guards, everybody, starting with us right in the middle out to the widest of the concentric circles. Then the ground opened up right where we had just been standing, in the middle of the asphalt. Two luminous circles became visible a couple of yards below the surface. The one on the left had a diameter of about eighty feet, the right-hand one at most thirty.

I knew that marketing was becoming an ever more important part of the military machinery. That the cost of everything was growing, requiring more and more external financing since our Federal military budget was no longer sufficient—even though it was now 50 per cent bigger than before 9/11. That even the astronomical cost of our new generation of nuclear weapons was presumably again a gross underestimate. And that all of our current primary investors were gathered around me in the V.I.P. circle here at Kleine Brogel—as well as media and military dignitaries in the padded spectator seats in the warmth of the control tower.

That, of course, was why the opportunity was being taken to demonstrate our new guidance system: the advantages must have been calculated to outweigh the disadvantages. But with the enormous number of people gathered, it was as big a P.R. risk as an opportunity. Especially bearing in mind that the system had never before been tested outside strictly controlled conditions.

Conventional weaponry was more precise than nuclear warheads and missiles, which usually needed to be no more than approximately on target, because of their enormous explosive force. But during recent decades the accuracy of nuclear weapons had improved.

And soon the new B.61-12 bomb would be operational. Our most expensive nuclear weapon to date.

The bomb was not going to be more powerful than other nuclear weapons currently in existence—rather significantly *less* so: no more than three times the force of the Hiroshima bomb. Yet most external commentators agreed that this would be the most dangerous weapon man had invented.

By using the unique radar-based guidance system, it was thought that the margin of error for the B.61-12 would be reduced from on average three hundred feet for nuclear bombs to at most one hundred. The technicians had as usual been even more optimistic. Not more than sixty-five feet in acceptable weather conditions, perhaps fewer than thirty if operated with special skill, so they said. In this way, according to the rhetoric, we would be able to reduce the number of civilian casualties.

The critics saw this differently. With the B.61-12, they claimed, we found ourselves back in the 1960s, at a period in our history when the evolution of mankind appeared to have halted for good. With Cold War-era dreams of tactical nuclear weaponry so compact that it might be carried in one's pocket.

According to reports, which remained unconfirmed, the Russians had at the time developed a small pistol with californium for nuclear ammunition. Officially, we never got further than our experimental "Davy Crockett", a rifle with nuclear capacity.

So as the F.16s banked sharply over Kleine Brogel and flew back in our direction, they brought with them the moment of hidden truth. Even though there would be no official comment after the event, however much the peace researchers might blog about the fact that we had demonstrated the guidance system for our future and much-debated nuclear bomb.

I was therefore not surprised when the General jumped down and took his place in the left-hand red circle. I knew what efforts were needed nowadays to get the P.R. machinery humming, the aces that we had to throw into the game.

Hughes was the only one remaining of our three most senior official nuclear weapons commanders—since both Falconetti and Goldsmith had been dismissed. The man in the right-hand circle was also immediately recognizable. R.R. Maine, the hurried replacement for Falconetti, seemed to have put on hardly two pounds since his time as an American football superstar when I was young. The article in the *Washington Post* had not wasted the opportunity to joke about it: that the nuclear football too was now within his field of responsibility.

I suddenly realized what Ingrid might have in mind. There could be no better opportunity than here and now to allow a live nuclear charge to detonate. The result would not only be upward of a hundred thousand civilian deaths, together with two more of our most senior military officers, ministers, observers and crucial financiers. But also the worst possible publicity for the entire nuclear weapons system.

I tried to extricate myself from the crowd, but did not get very far. The voice of the American commentator crackled excitedly through the loudspeakers. "Ladies and gentlemen, children, guests of honor, ten seconds to bomb release. Nine, eight, seven, six, five, four, three, two, one . . . zero!" Through my field glasses I saw the bomb in free fall for a moment before the Kevlar parachute opened and swung to and fro as it sank toward its target. Despite the night-vision capability of my field glasses, it was impossible to tell whether this was a dummy or a real bomb—and if so, a nuclear one.

The cheers were raucous, time both running out and endless. Thoughts raced through my mind. To what the debater and former missile operator Bruce Blair had said during a visit to NUCLEUS, when asked what would be needed to carry out a successful attack at a nuclear base from the inside. By swapping a dummy bomb for a real charge, for example.

He did not have to think for long.

"I would say two to three people, given today's security system. Obviously harder the more people you have to involve," he had said.

General Hughes moved back and forth in the larger, left-hand circle, kept staring up at the falling object through the pelting rain. He too could not hide his excitement, or perhaps the slight concern one always feels during really complex maneuvers.

Then the bomb exploded—and an enormous bouquet of flowers cascaded across the sky and showered down on him. A phenomenal firework display, it must have cost a fortune.

General Hughes played it up a little. Looked skyward, shook his head and opened out his arms, before firing off a broad white smile for the benefit of the propaganda movies which would be sent out from here. And the message was unmistakable: that our military endeavors were all for the good of mankind. Bombs with flowers. "War is peace", as George Orwell expressed it.

Then came the last and unbeatable escalation in the propaganda warfare. When General Hughes gestured toward the smaller, red circle to the right.

With the roar of the crowd growing by the second, Falconetti's replacement stepped forward, theatrically placed on his head a burgundy Washington Redskins helmet from the old days, enjoying the moment to the full. When he closed the yellow visor over his face it took the commentator nearly a minute to make himself heard over the crowd.

"O.K., I know he needs no introduction, so I'm just going to say R.R. . . ."

"Maine!" the crowd chimed in.

". . . right, the man himself, one of America's all-time famous athletes. Now responsible for all our nuclear missile submarines, aircraft and land-based launch sites. Highest supervisory authority over the military space program. Our whole digital war effort. Ladies and gentlemen, a true American hero!"

A short pause over the loudspeakers. The crackle of static.

"Now he's ready for the decisive moment. Right, General?"

The man in the helmet nodded, gave a double thumbs up, like a pilot himself.

"And, ladies and gentlemen, children, guests of honor—are you ready too? Because here comes something that's never been done before: a trick of the absolutely highest degree of difficulty. The first demonstration of our new guidance system for precision bombs, which minimizes the risk of human casualty in humanitarian conflicts. I just want you to notice that General Maine's circle has a twenty-five-foot diameter and that the dummy bomb is going to be released from an altitude of almost thirty-three thousand feet. So cross your fingers, everyone."

When the only aircraft still airborne banked steeply and headed back toward us, I could clearly see through the maximum zoom on my field glasses the three, small, stylized triangles just under one of the fins of the warhead. Our own interpretation of the international nuclear symbol. The sign indicating that there really was a live nuclear charge in there.

I looked around in desperation—and saw no-one making an effort to interrupt the demonstration, prevent the catastrophe. Maybe no-one else had noticed the tell-tale markings on the warhead. One often only sees what one wants to see, after all: seldom what one cannot even imagine.

The F.16 climbed rapidly to 31,500 feet, to drop the dummy which was in fact a bomb, accompanied by the commentator's steady countdown. "Five, four, three, two, one . . . Bomb release! Watch carefully now, ladies and gentlemen, children, guests of honor . . . because today we're writing military history!"

I stood there as the nuclear charge fell, slow and dream-like through the atmosphere under its neat little parachute. Expected that it would be detonated at the same altitude as the Hiroshima bomb, 1,978 feet, as a sort of homage. Thought about Ingrid's dark allure; how infernal the elegance of her preparation of this pacifist mass murder. Letting somebody switch out the dummy—or perhaps she had done it herself—in order to turn world opinion against nuclear weapons once and for all.

The preaching over the loudspeakers rose to the level of an ecstatic evangelist: "Friday, December 13, 2013, the American base at Kleine Brogel, Belgium. You were here! This was not your unlucky day—but the luckiest day of your lives! To be part of something like this! 3,000 feet, 2,750 . . . 2,500 . . . Are you ready, R.R.?"

Our two-star general, the folk hero, gave the commentator in the control tower another thumbs up. Straightened his helmet, again pulled the visor over his face. I shut my eyes for some reason, put my fingers in my ears.

But I could still hear the explosion. A low, dull rumble, loud enough to be heard, but not enough to disturb.

Confused, I opened my eyes and saw that everything was still standing. Looked over at the small red circle where R.R. performed his carefully rehearsed trick, a perfect touchdown which proved that he really had stayed in good shape. Nimbly, he rolled a half turn to absorb the impact—before he touched the dummy bomb to the ground in the exact center of the ring.

Then I turned my field glasses toward the landing strips, the aircraft, the fuel depots. The area from where the blast came. That old-fashioned, low-tech explosion, the very opposite of a nuclear charge. Thick, roiling black smoke rose toward the sky in the north-east corner of the base. As far away as one could get from the circle where R.R. Maine was now getting to his feet, after the successful demonstration of the world's most advanced radar-based guidance system for bombs.

Maybe he had not even noticed the attack, been so absorbed in his own bubble of adrenaline and euphoria. Before he realized that the applause would not come, the sirens had started to howl across the base, the lights to flash. The voice of the commentator was replaced by a recorded loop: "All visitors are requested to vacate the area immediately and to follow the instructions of the guards. This is not a drill! We repeat: this is not a drill!"

I tried to control my breathing, assess the situation. Kept away from the guards who were beginning to direct all the guests of honor down through the evacuation exits which had been opened under the luminous red circles and that led into the network of culverts, then up onto the abandoned fields on the other side of the main road.

Instead I waited until the activists were let in. Because those in charge of the outer gate had been forced to avoid even worse consequences—maybe some people suffocated, a few civilian deaths—when, after the explosion, the demonstrators tried to climb the fences to see what had happened inside the base. Simultaneously, the security forces stormed in to stop the protesters from getting any closer; to our sealed-off but possibly still revealing storage site for the live nuclear warheads, from which the smoke was now billowing. Soon everybody else found themselves trapped. Children, old enthusiasts, families.

And when the chaos was at its height, I made my way out of the base. Above ground, amid the throngs of people: first through the inner gate, then the outer gate. I had been training for this kind of thing for most of my adult life. Navigating even in the most difficult terrain.

So I was able to follow the tall woman and her short companion through the chaos when I caught sight of their familiar movements about a hundred feet ahead of me. I stuck to them, my eyes on their backpacks—new black ones, I noticed—as they made their way along the side of the autoroute. Until we reached the taxi which was waiting in a clearing.

"What the hell happened?" the driver said.

"Can you skip Hasselt and take us straight to Zaventem, to the airport?" Jesús María said.

"How dangerous is it going to be for me, Madame?"

"Who knows, but you'll probably be O.K., you'll see. Either way, you'll get a shit load of money, you know that."

The driver scanned our motley crew in his rearview mirror:

Ingrid, propped up between us, more or less lifeless, sinking fast, and still giving off a distinct smell of burning even though her protective clothing had been fully extinguished. I remained, despite my disguise, vaguely familiar. The ever-baffling Jesús María. When he heard the sirens from the emergency vehicles approaching from the opposite direction, he drove off along the winding forest roads.

When we got to the airport we found a remote corner. Half-dragging Ingrid inside, Jesús María gave her an injection—pain-killer, sedative, God knows what else—and looked at me. She seemed almost to be smiling, maybe at my rudimentary disguise with wig, beard and mustache.

"O.K. Erasmo, where to now?"

I stared at her.

"Hasn't Ingrid said anything?"

"Zip, nada. You know her."

Jesús María saw my hesitation, or maybe it was horror, glanced at Ingrid and shrugged.

"So. Make a decision, Erasmo. Rise to the occasion."

I walked thirty or so feet away from her, from the café and the people, from the television screens showing the breaking news from the airbase—mostly material damage, no lives lost but some injuries among the fire fighters. This would make the Nuclear Weapons Scandal stories even harder for our military authorities to contain. I went into the telephone booth. Glanced at the huge clock on the wall outside: 21.12. Closed my eyes, went through the options, made up my mind—or perhaps followed my instincts.

"Erasmus, good Lord, you're alive!" Sixten said.

"Yes . . ." I said, and immediately pressed the red button, without really knowing why.

For a few moments more I pondered—it felt like minutes but could well have been seconds—looking over toward the two women there in the dark corner of the airport. If anybody else saw them they would not understand what was going on. Two women with bulky packs: even bigger than before, with yet one more large black bag which Ingrid must have been carrying over her shoulder. One of them awake, the other in a deep sleep, just beyond one of the airport cafés outside the security zone, next to the cleaners' storage area. A brief rest stop before the next stage on a long journey. Nobody who noticed us would begin to comprehend anything of the context.

A large hairy spider dashed across the floor. I knew it could not really be here, at a modern European airport, not that kind of species—yet my arachnophobia now seemed like the only real thing in my life. Not until the spider crept up my wrist, the artery, did I shudder: had to fight to control myself to not try to brush it off or even shout out loud inside the booth. In a cold sweat I looked around. None of the other travelers seemed to be in the least bit interested in us. Ingrid was still unconscious, her head against the wall, and even Jesús María had closed her eyes.

I took the phone, put in a few coins and dialed the number I had memorized, along with everything else.

"We're coming in. She's completely under, probably won't wake up before we reach you," I said.

Edelweiss breathed deeply at the other end of the line. I must have woken him in the middle of his obligatory 3.00 p.m. power nap.

"So you no longer believe Oskarsson's stories? That she's going to short-circuit the whole system," Edelweiss said.

I heard him pant through the trans-Atlantic static. Calculating, analyzing, weighing his alternatives without exactly knowing what his opponent's were. The art of war.

"And how can we know, my friend, that you're telling the truth now? Will keep your own little side of our bargain?" he said.

"How can I know that *you* will?" I said.

He held back, waited for my next move—which followed:

"Shall I try to get Jesús María to come in too?"

"Yes, do that. That would be good. Seats will be arranged for you on the night flight."

Silence once more, before his final remark.

"Posterity will be forever grateful to you, Erasmus. And you won't forget to bring the briefcase, will you?"

"Don't you have it?" I said, hanging up without waiting for an answer.

When I sat down again, with the anesthetized Ingrid as a barrier between me and Jesús María, she could not contain herself for long.

"So what's going on, Erasmo?"

I waited, deep in thought, before her next question provided me with an opening: "What did Sixten say?"

"That Washington is the next step," I said.

Now it was Jesús María's turn to sit quietly. Her move.

"Why's that?" she said.

Games of bluff are like chess, or any game of strategy actually: they depend as much on the opponent's imagination as one's own.

"He didn't want to say. But we'll get the information when we're there, from Sixten—unless Ingrid wakes up before then."

"O.K. . . ." Jesús María drew out her answer. "And who's going to be there, Erasmo?"

"Edelweiss, for sure. Probably Zafirah. Presumably Kurt-or-John."

She drummed her fingers against the edge of the bench, desperate for a cigarette or driven by those inner demons of hers.

"To hell with it . . . I'm in. When's the flight?"

5

SUBSTITUTION

December 2013
Dulles International Airport, Washington D.C.

5.01

She had been drugged to the eyeballs. It was surprisingly easy for us to make our way, with Ingrid in the borrowed wheelchair, through Zaventem airport, where Edelweiss had been pulling strings. The key word was "narcolepsy", that strange epidemic throughout Sweden which Ingrid had mentioned. According to some, the side effect of the mass vaccinations against swine flu some years ago.

Those who were curious and knew what the word meant needed no further explanation gave me a compassionate look, some succinct words of advice, a medical tip or two. Those who did not, did not need one either. They avoided Ingrid's ghost-like sleeping figure: assumed a case of substance abuse.

That was of course Jesús María's specialty. But on the way to Zaventem, and so far as I could tell during the subsequent flight, she did not smoke a single cigarette. Made not the slightest attempt to break the rules, no quick puff in the restrooms, no risk of everything for the sake of the drug's temporary solace. So for her, too, the stakes appeared to have been raised dramatically.

For my own part, I was suffering from existential vertigo, the floor swayed, my worlds were colliding. I had made a pact with the Evil One. I was playing for high stakes with the grand master himself—and even kidded myself I could win. Or at least that he would keep to the rules, let me and my family loose in the way we had agreed.

That after they had been given their freedom again, or whatever situation they found themselves in—I hardly dared to think about it—I should be granted safe conduct to the destination of my choosing, and might sink deep under the continental ice. Quite simply let the world of nuclear weapons take its course. Allow you to pass your judgments, should you ever get the chance.

Edelweiss had worked quickly after my call, set up the necessary logistics. When the staff at the check-in desk for the night flight to Washington saw my passport, we were immediately shown to the last counter in Terminal D. From there further underground to Terminal X, that secret domain where we were given first-class tickets and new identity documents, each set within its own padded envelope.

According to my new passport I was now Desmond Kern. Yet another witticism from the grand master. He had so often spoken about this during our strategy classes: that we should always identify the main character in the intelligence tangle we were to unravel. Only when all the roles had been assigned would we be able to choose an effective strategy. You have to identify *the core of the poodle*, he said over and over again.

And the name on my new passport left no room for doubt. What Edelweiss was saying, in coded form, was that Ingrid no longer had the lead role in the complex drama that had been playing out since our escape—rather that it was me. Out on the street Desmond Kern was Des Kern. But it came from the German expression *des Pudels Kern*, The Core of the Poodle. From Goethe's "Faust".

Once our flight had taken off, Jesús María ordered three shots of tequila straight up, no ice, no lime. We had yet to reach cruising altitude. Here in first class nothing seemed impossible. I did the same, hoping to be able to sleep a while, disappear for an hour or two, not have to think. A momentary escape.

Ingrid continued to sleep as deeply as before, and according to Jesús María her pulse would not start to climb until we were closer to landing. So it was the perfect opportunity for Jesús María and myself to rest, stretch our legs in the space the first row afforded—or for me to ask questions.

"What actually happened at Kleine Brogel?" I began.

"Well, whatever it was, it sure as hell wasn't what Ingrid said. For a while I felt like leaving her stuck down in there, in the collapsed store room: let the Witch burn on her pyre . . . but then I changed my mind. I've got some unfinished business. It'd be fucking hard to do it without her."

Jesús María fell silent, took another mouthful to finish her first shot.

"Twisted, all the same," she said.

I looked across at her, this opaque woman with a burn on her forehead, now that I looked, as I took my first sip. We had put Ingrid in the window seat, leaning her against the wall—and the cabin crew seemed sufficiently well informed not to ask questions.

"I always thought I'd take John out first. But that's not how it turned out."

"How can you be sure of that?"

"That it was Kurt on the slope there? For real, Erasmo? Don't you think I've known who was who, ever since this whole shit started, however hard I tried to make them look the same? Seen their birthmarks there before me last thing at night and first thing in the morning. All fucking night long. Each and every day."

As she paused I glanced at Ingrid's watch. A little more than seven hours until landing. So I had time to wait.

"Can you imagine, Erasmo, that it was Kurt's mentor who once saved my life?"

I think I shook my head.

"He killed my boyfriend Enrique in the most grotesque way you can imagine, I swear to you."

She took a big gulp from her second shot.

"That man was the very best security guard at the base, outstanding and brutal. Then he took two gifted young men under his wing and turned them into something even better, or worse, than himself, their mentor. They stepped into his shoes completely when he retired."

Silence again while she emptied the glass and started on the third.

"Including the handling of me. Did fucking everything that

297

their mentor had done, just as Enrique once had. Only better—and worse. Even hell has its nuances."

I stared at her.

"That's an awful story," I said.

Jesús María stared back.

"Don't pity me, Erasmo. Don't ever do that."

I shook my head, or did I nod? Waited for the rest—and then it came, almost in one long breath.

"My first job was in some shithole beauty salon at the back of nowhere. The worst kind you can imagine: eyebrows and cuticles, verrucas, the pits. Then a friend from school joined me and used her inheritance to buy the woman out. We shifted the direction of the whole damn business, changed all the signs and the interior, started offering body modification. My friend had been a textile artist too, gifted as hell. So we knew how to sew—and skin was no more difficult than leather or canvas. We were young and pretentious, massively inspired by ORLAN, that French artist. Money came in from people who started to travel to our little place to redo themselves: rich suckers wanting to look like movie stars. We exploited them so we could work at the other end of the scale. Stitch together those who were already in pieces, who'd been blown inside out, I swear to you, Erasmo . . ."

Jesús María gave me a searching look, considering my new blond beard. Trying to gauge if I believed a word.

"Then Enrique got wind of what we were doing. I had to leave my friend there, run for my life. Finally managed to get over the border to the army base—just as they dumped Ingrid there, ripped up after her violent delivery. So I fixed her. Did about the same thing I had always done: mended torn women. After that, Ingrid wanted to become my fucking blood sister and they couldn't very well let me go. Someone who was so useful to have around, in such a number of different ways. But I had to stay behind the scenes even at the base. Enrique could still sniff me out anywhere. He's a bastard, I swear to you, Erasmo."

She knocked back her third tequila, I kept sipping on my first.

"All of that medical crap I had to learn afterward. Which gave me the chance to do a ton of different things, anesthetic optional, but in the end someone always managed to get in the way. A whole posse by the operating table just to stop me from doing what we all actually wanted. Even when I put the chip into Kurt, so we could keep track of John too since they always moved in pairs, Ingrid was standing there cheering me on—but she never let me go any further. Went on about how she was saving me for some bigger assignment, that she didn't want to waste me in that way, always messing about with her witchery, you know. Erasmo, you know, don't you, all those fucking mind games."

She looked at me again, seemed to be driving at something specific. I stared into my glass, downed my second shot while she pressed the button to summon the steward. Her story was almost finished. Only its climax remained.

"I stumbled in on her, Erasmo. As she was digging around in the medicine cabinet, to which only Ed and I were meant to have the key, the one with the really heavy stuff. She was probably thinking of doing the interventions herself. Just imagine: you two wouldn't have turned out very pretty. But now I made her promise me I could join the flight too. Take down John and Kurt, in that order, when the opportunity arose. Granted me that in the end, after half a fucking life—in return for my silence."

I sank my third tequila at this point too, so I could order more when the steward came.

"And that must have been why she went skiing on that mountain the other day, like she was offering herself so I could take down Kurt. For my fucking sake, Erasmo. To keep her promise."

Then she reached into her pocket and brought out the syringe that we always had in our packs: pre-loaded with whatever was necessary to stop us from ever revealing any secrets to the wrong people. With a practiced movement she gave herself a shot in the thigh.

I had no idea what it contained. If it was something instantly lethal or perhaps the opposite: for casual enjoyment or maybe longer-term escape from reality. Whatever it was, Jesús María fell asleep immediately. Leaving me with the rest of my questions.

About her, about Ingrid, Sixten, Lise Meitner. The whole story.

5.02

The established view is that Meitner's conscience
would not allow her to get involved in military
research. But a letter in the Stockholm archives
paints a slightly different picture.

It is dated January 1915, and is addressed
to her friend and colleague of many years, Otto
Hahn. When Hahn received the letter, he was working as a field researcher in the German war-gas
project. It appears to be a reply to an earlier
letter from Hahn, which available sources suggest
has been lost, in which he presumably expresses a
certain crisis of conscience about his work. This
is what Meitner writes:

"I think I know roughly what you are working
on and can very well understand your doubts. But
on this occasion I am sure you are right. One has
to be adaptable. In the first place, you were not
consulted. Secondly, if you don't do this, others
will. Above all, whatever helps to shorten this
dreadful war is an act of compassion."

I have had the letter analyzed by a
graphologist, to try to confirm Meitner as its
author, and he had no doubts. It seems to shed
new light on her: the only significant researcher
in the field who chose not to join the Manhattan
Project and contribute to the construction of
the atom bomb. But if Meitner could justify
Hahn's military research effort with this type
of argument, saying that it could "shorten this
dreadful war" or that other people would do it

if he did not, she may have seen the development
of the atom bomb in the same light.

What Hahn was working on during the First
World War was something that must be regarded as
the next worst weapon of mass destruction in
history. Namely, ingenious gas grenades with two
chemical components—in part a substance which
first forced its way through the gas mask and
impelled the soldier to tear it off in panic, and
also the deadly poison which was then free to
enter the lungs and tissue unhindered.

Yet Meitner wrote her letter to Hahn
relatively early: at the age of thirty-five.
With an enormous passion for science which in
her letters in the Stockholm archives often seems
to overshadow everything else. The same year,
1915, Meitner expressed herself thus to her
closest friend:

"I love physics, and have difficulty in
imagining it not being a part of my life. It is
an almost personal passion, as if for another
human being. And I am, despite the fact that I
otherwise have a strong moral sense, a woman
physicist without the least guilty conscience."

For a long time she and science seemed to be
made for each other. In 1905 Meitner had become
the second woman to defend her doctoral thesis in
physics at Vienna University. Then the first woman
to be allowed to attend Max Planck's lectures in
Berlin, after a few more years his assistant as
well, and in 1926 the first female professor in
Germany when appointed to that post in Berlin. Her
colleague in the field, Albert Einstein, used to
call her "our Madame Curie". In 1935 Meitner and

Hahn together became responsible for the prestigious Transuranium Project at the Kaiser Wilhelm Research Institute in Berlin.

After that, things started to go downhill. Some researchers have seen it more or less as classic treachery. It was, however, undoubtedly Hahn who got Meitner—who was of Jewish descent—to leave the research institute in Berlin in 1938, possibly after direct pressure from the German government. In addition, Hahn accepted the fact that he alone would receive the 1944 Nobel Prize for Chemistry, for the discovery and explanation of the process of nuclear fission, and not share it with Meitner.

Soon after the discovery of the neutron in 1934, Marie Curie died of the consequences of her experiments with radioactivity. Meitner became the only woman left on the Parnassus of nuclear physics.

At the time it was a position not without problems. For instance, she seems never to have been fully accepted in Sweden after her flight there: according to most interpretations, her colleagues in fact worked in direct opposition to her. Possibly because she was the only woman among all these men. Maybe even due to an element of anti-Semitism.

In any event even her own boss in Sweden, Manne Siegbahn—who had received the Nobel Prize in Physics as early as 1924—seems to have been anxious that Meitner should not be given a position senior to his own. Siegbahn also seems to have had a part in ensuring that she was not allowed to share the Nobel Prize with Hahn.

In the letters, Meitner's descriptions of her situation in Sweden during the war often have a melodramatic streak:

"Scientifically I am totally isolated, for months I have not spoken to anybody about physics. I sit in my room and try to keep myself active. You can't really call it 'work'."

But this does not seem to be the whole picture. One could view things in a more positive light: an Austrian top physicist succeeds in fleeing to Sweden via Holland in 1938 and there, placed at her disposal, were more than adequate resources. Siegbahn's brand new research institute "for the promotion of nuclear research and the facilitating of the production of medically usable radioactive nuclides", according to the specifications for the generous financial support offered by both the Nobel Foundation and the Wallenberg Foundation.

According to the guest book from the apartment at Brahevägen, close to her work at Tekniska Högskolan, Meitner's friends flocked to her home. The wife of Prime Minister Tage Erlander, Aina Erlander, was a close acquaintance. The guests' comments are often delighted exclamations about the delicious food and mention the deep discussions which had taken place about war and peace.

In the spring of 1946, Meitner was offered the post of visiting professor at Washington D.C.'s Catholic University and was still often referred to as "The Mother of the Atomic Bomb". During her time in the U.S. she received hundreds of letters from admirers, was chosen

304

as "Woman of the Year" by the National Press Club, gave seminars at Princeton and had intensive discussions with Einstein. But despite this triumphal procession, Meitner still chose to live in Sweden rather than in the U.S. Concluding her guest professorship, she therefore left her close friends in senior scientific circles, declined all of the grand proposals put to her by Einstein and others, and returned to Stockholm.

There her circumstances had improved after all the international attention paid to her. Half a year after the American journey she got a personal professorship and an experimental laboratory in her own name: the "Meitner Laboratory", only loosely connected to Tekniska Högskolan.

But the atomic bombs were obviously casting their shadow over Sweden. Not even this small country far from the world scene could ignore what might happen, whether it be the risk of being attacked with the new super-weapon or the possibility of constructing one. Prime Minister Erlander's diary note from September 1945 is telling:

"The construction of the atom bomb can no longer be kept a secret, but the purely technical conditions necessary for such a project are missing in all countries except the U.S. It will take at least five years before the Russians catch up with the Americans. These five years will be decisive for the fate of the world. If the Russians' isolation and mistrust can be broken, peace is possible. If not, we must prepare ourselves for catastrophe."

It is hard not to think of Meitner in this

305

context. That her friend Aina Erlander could simply have passed on an informal message to her husband, who then agreed to meet Meitner for a cup of tea somewhere. That such a prominent researcher—within this very field—might at least have been consulted in an initially non-committal discussion about the possibilities of, and difficulties in, creating a Swedish atom bomb.

But despite all my searches in the Stockholm archives, I have found no empirical support for such a hypothesis. Nor the least notation about a meeting with the Prime Minister, no suggestive line in a letter, which might point to Meitner having had a concrete involvement in the Swedish nuclear weapons program.

Yet the uncertainty remains. We have essentially no knowledge about Meitner's last eleven years in Sweden. The decade when the hydrogen bomb began to be both mass-produced and deployed, which created the global nuclear weapons system in its current form. The trail ends with her becoming a Swedish citizen in 1949. In those sources which are available, Meitner's activities are mostly summarized as having consisted of being active in the F.O.A. and Tekniska Högskolan, where she participated in the expansion of the country's first experimental reactor, R.1.

To repeat: for all of these paradoxes I have been unable to find any more precise a description than "Lise Meitner's Secret". In the final chapter of this dissertation I will revert to its deeper implications.

5.03

I was woken by voices very close to me. Not just Jesús María's—but also Ingrid's. She looked at me, rosy about the cheeks, miraculously restored as so often before.

"Erasmus, my treasure, wonder of wonders, you can't imagine how happy I am to see you! That you managed to survive, after everything you must have been through up in Jukkas . . . what happened? What did they do to you, my friend? You must tell me everything, in your own good time."

I stared at her: this superwoman with her ability to endure pretty much anything and then rise from the ashes. I looked around the plane. Glanced behind me, across the aisles, toward the sleeping passengers in the dimmed light of the cabin. Checked for the air stewards who could still appear at any moment. Looked at the clock, still a few hours to go before our scheduled arrival.

"Yes, in my own good time . . ." I said.

"Then I can also tell you what we've been through. How we managed to catch up with them there in the forest, the whole commotion, before Jesús María and I escaped and made our way to Kleine Brogel in time for Spotter's Day."

Ingrid must have seen my anxiety, how I was still looking over my shoulder toward the economy class section, and in front of me toward where the cabin crew would be coming from. Yet she just kept on going—having switched into Swedish and lowered her voice significantly but still not enough.

"And I must really thank you for all your care on the way here. I could scarcely have been in better hands."

On Ingrid's fold-out table, as on Jesús María's, stood an almost empty glass. It did not appear to be her first tequila either, which might explain the flush on her cheeks. The sudden recovery. The miracle cure.

"Jesús María has told me about your wild plan. To take out John as well, right there in the lion's den, play with the fire. Show Ed who has the upper hand: the finger on the button. How big the risks we're prepared to take, both for ourselves and for the world. And then to vanish again, like the wind."

I nodded cautiously, tried not to look at either of them.

"That's it. That's the idea."

"I'm impressed, my treasure."

She stood up, got her new black bag out of the overhead compartment, and laid it on the floor in front of me. Continued in little more than a whisper in Swedish. It came back to me, everything she had taught me of this too, the language, during our dissertation sessions. Jesús María was showing no interest at all—had fallen asleep again, now assisted by the alcohol as well as the effects of the injection—seemingly like everybody else within earshot. The stewards were still somewhere else, the whole plane dimmed and in night-flight mode.

Ingrid seemed wholly reliant on Edelweiss' arrangements. Was content for him to keep pulling the strings, making sure nobody stopped us from walking into his lair.

"By the way, you might like to have this back . . ."

She gave me a strangely amused look and nodded at the black bag—so I leaned down and opened the zipper half-way. Saw the briefcase lying there. At least from this distance it looked the same as it had when taken from me in Suite 325.

"It's still functional. Retrieving it was top priority. We caught up with them in the forest, after fighting them off in the room of your martyrdom, Erasmus, and we were persuasive in our methods that led to its surrender. But they escaped. Not only Zafirah, also John. And the poor hotel guide, their dupe for Sixten. Whatever they paid him, it was not enough, my treasure. We chased after them in the snow—he was tired, struggling—Zafirah was not kind to him in the end, our weaver of unicorn tales."

She bent and opened the bag a bit more. Just so I could see

308

more of its contents: my field knife, cell phone, watch, crunch cookies, notebook, medical pack and my weapon.

But no key. The one that Sixten had given me in Ursvik: to Meitner's laboratory under the red trap-door.

"You see, it's all here!" Ingrid said triumphantly.

I zipped the bag shut, let it stay there at my feet, under my watchful eye. Had another sip of the tequila. Took a deep breath— and asked yet another of my questions.

"So why did Sixten give us away?"

Ingrid looked at me first, then gazed out of the window, into that black void.

"Did he?" she said. For a second she did not move. "They had Lisa, his kryptonite. Evidently took her as some sort of hostage after our swoop at Estrange."

The answer was like so many others with Ingrid. Little more than something leading to new questions, new inadequate replies. I tried another tack.

"And what happens now?"

"You've no doubt seen the headlines, my treasure: THE NUCLEAR WEAPONS SCANDAL?"

She turned from the window, looked into my eyes. I nodded.

"So Ed's therefore been made harmless for the time being. I've instructed my informants to release what we know to the media bit by bit, only as much as is necessary at each stage so that heads will roll—as in a medieval painting. Today, for example, the Secretary for Defense is going to have to go. And Ed knows that we still hold the trump card. That the next step is to disclose the existence of NUCLEUS, his own role, the unbelievable secret of our hidden mandate."

Ingrid paused. Continued in English.

"And even after that we still have an ace up our sleeves. Because the day you and I go public, my treasure, not even the President will survive for long. That two individuals, the Carrier himself and somebody who calls herself Alpha, had the entire nuclear weapons system in the palms of their hands for so many years—and have now taken off with their finger still on the button. That the future of the world is literally in the balance."

Jesús María woke up again, yawned, while Ingrid kept whispering in my ear. Her warm voice right into my mind. Her deepest secrets. Whispering, but still in a melodic voice that someone close by could detect.

"Besides that, Ed now knows that I've planted everything necessary—codes, structure, instructions down to the tiniest detail on how to complete the arrangements with a normal computer—with one unknown person. In case something should unexpectedly happen to us. Chosen one single person out of the seven billion who still populate the earth. And Ed will never be able to find that one small person, my 'Needle in the Haystack'. I call it Plan B: our common insurance policy."

Jesús María gave me an odd smile.

"No need to worry, Erasmo. I'm not the Needle. Me you can kill whenever you want."

I stared at Ingrid.

"Yes, Jesús María is the only one who knows. She helped me with the practicalities, in Ursvik. Tattooed all of the information in coded form onto Aina's body, a place where nobody looks: not even somebody who loves you more than anyone. That was why it took us such a long time in the main bathroom, if you remember. And that was why Aina had to pour so much champagne into herself so quickly. To cope with the pain—and on her birthday too: she who never otherwise drinks a single drop! But she didn't hesitate for one second to sacrifice herself for the cause."

I was overrun by a cascade of bad memories. The messages from Edelweiss that I picked up while inside the smaller bathroom, that image of Zafirah with the jerry can, the fire, our escape.

"So we've got Jesús María to thank for that. And for what happened out at the base this evening. She had to play your part, in the heat of the moment."

310

"Yeah. Hot as hell it was," Jesús María said.

"Yes, I simply don't understand what went wrong. The assignment, nothing more complicated than a distraction, had been perfectly set up by my helpers—did you notice the nuclear symbol on the dummy bomb?—and Jesús María helped me to get everyone looking in completely the wrong direction for a moment. But with the pyrotechnics—"

"Oh, give me a break. We'll all be dead and buried soon anyway."

Jesús María cut off the discussion and the mood turned tense, stifling. So I broke the silence with another of my questions.

"And why did you sacrifice Falconetti first?"

Ingrid turned away, stared out of the window into space. As if looking back in time. Then leaned even closer to me and revealed everything in one long-whispered fairy-tale.

"For a long time he was my only playmate. Eventually the one who gave me the job of creating an entirely new security unit after 9/11, *free hands*. That was when I contacted your old teacher from West Point, Ed—who else?—and asked him to put together a tight little team which would be unlike anything under the sun. But the whole time it was Falconetti, our four-star general, the most senior operational commander of the nuclear weapons system, who was the missing link between the President and me.

"He was so inspired by General LeMay in the 1950s, you see, that whole Cold War mentality. For Falconetti too we were always on a war footing. He insisted that we had to be ready at all times both to strike and to strike back, in full scale, have the tools to hand.

"And to be honest it was Falconetti, not me, who first formulated the vision of being able to direct the whole nuclear weapons system even when Centcom and the Commander-in-chief had been knocked out. On the run, fully mobile. But also in a situation like that we had to follow the basic outlines of our rigorous security arrangements: "No Lone Zone". Insure ourselves against a single madman—so that no-one would ever be alone with the decision, the ceremony for launching our weapons."

Ingrid paused, perhaps for effect, and Jesús María got up and went to the bathroom, just a couple of feet from the front row. I could hear her violent vomiting, the result of the drug she had injected herself with, or the tequila or both. Then Ingrid said: "But for two madmen we left the field open."

I swallowed, felt the nausea welling up. Possibly from having heard the sounds from Jesús María in the bathroom. Or because of the situation we all found ourselves in.

"So when the time came I needed you, my treasure. And had to throw Falconetti to the wolves—as well as Goldsmith, who always defended him. A few well-placed calls and some leaked e-mails was all it took. I let it all trickle out after their attack in Ursvik, as a small revenge."

5.04

When at last I managed to fall asleep in my seat, after another straight tequila, both women sleeping in the seats on either side of me, I dreamed that I was the last survivor of the crew of the Enola Gay and had suffered a serious heart attack while on a holiday in Tokyo. Beside me in the little hospital room sat my very old doctor—a woman long past retirement age—and she wanted to tell me before it was too late how it had actually been. Because she did not give me many more days to live.

She began by saying that there was nothing special about her story. That she had seen that light like all the others, the silver flash, the ghostly glare. That she was in other words not one of the seventy thousand people who died on the spot, which she had regretted for the rest of her life, every minute, she said. Nor one of the same number who died from the secondary effects, which meant that half of the city's inhabitants were killed by the bomb.

Instead she became one of the many *hibakusha*, the tens of thousands of survivors who after the war had become invisible. "Most people can neither see nor hear us," she said. "Can you?" she asked with a serious look, curious and determined. As if she really did wonder.

I countered with my experience of the event. That as the plane's navigator I had been responsible for getting us to the exact place that was selected just prior to take-off, more or less by chance, one of several possible targets. The random choice prevented information from leaking out. The choice happened to fall on her city and her life.

I also told her that I could still remember how the plane lurched, and that special metallic click when the Bomb was released, and how the sky was then covered by the mushroom cloud. When the pillar of smoke eventually sank away we could see that the place

313

where the city had turned into a black, formless mass, like a caul-dron filled with boiling tar. A sight nobody had prepared us for.

The very old doctor sat totally still as I told her this, like a beautiful statue. Then she nodded and continued with her story. Said that it had been an unusually beautiful morning in the city below our aircraft, that she was lying out in the yard dressed only in her underwear, more or less knocked out after a long shift at the hospital. "One always recalls irrelevant details like that," she said, "with such precision." She had, for example, wondered if it really could be a spark from a passing tram which suddenly lit up that ornamental stone lantern with such magical light. An instant later all shadows in the yard vanished. The sun, which had been shining so strongly just a moment ago, could no longer be distinguished against the sharp white glare of the whole sky.

Gradually she became more and more consumed by her account, started to spin around on her stainless-steel stool, wave her arms about. Tried to convey how the air had been filled with smoke and dust in the same instant, that the only thing which she could see of their old house was a lone beam sticking up crooked and twisted from the ground a little way off. When she then looked down at her own body she saw that she was naked. Being a scientist, she began—"funnily enough," as she now expressed it—to muse over where her underwear might have gone, how it could have vanished without she herself being at all damaged. Then she felt her face and realized that her mouth was just an open hole. That her lower lip was hanging down in a long flap and a five-inch shard of glass was poking out of her shoulder.

With the same peculiar absent feeling, as if she had seen all this in a movie, she called out for her husband and children. After hearing no answer from them, she took her place in the long lines which led to the hospital, as if sleep-walking. Many were walking with their arms sticking out strangely from their bodies, making them look like human scarecrows, which also puzzled the medical student in her. Until she understood that they held them like that to avoid touching their own burned bodies.

But the most striking thing, she recounted, was how they had all walked along in silence. How nobody screamed in pain and anguish or yelled out for their lost lives. Just this ghostly, deathly silence—from that moment on, ever since.

I said to the very old doctor that I still regarded the Bomb with a certain relief, since it had in my opinion ended the war and in that way saved many hundreds of thousands of soldiers' lives, both American and Japanese. That I would soon be closing my eyes for ever certain that what we did was *merciful*.

She nodded again, otherwise as still as before. Then she got up and walked to my bunk. Kneeled, kissed my forehead lightly, said that she forgave me. That she had already forgiven us all.

At that I took hold of her head—so very like Amba's: even the shape of her skull—and smashed it against the bedhead. It split at once, spilled out over my pillow and bed linen. Like a soft-boiled egg.

5.05

At midnight we landed at Dulles, after circling for fifteen minutes before being given permission to descend. Edelweiss no doubt wanted to demonstrate his power. That he held everything in his hand. Our escort appeared just to the right of the line for passport and visa control: on his sign it said "MR KERN" in handwritten capital letters. As if we were just any business group.

And it all seemed illusory. Edelweiss had his operatives among both the personnel and passengers. In front of us and behind us, shoes and clothes had to be removed, demeaning rituals behind half-closed curtains, people taken aside for regulation body searches. But we did not even have to place our enormous luggage on the conveyor belt. Because we had made a pact with the grand master, the very inventor of the concept of "war games".

While Ingrid and Jesús María then went to the women's restroom together, to assume their new looks, I walked up to the man with the sign. His appearance was familiar even though I could no longer recall his name. There were so many, after all, so interchangeable. And this one was not the sharpest knife in the drawer. His age suggested that he belonged to the ranks of the unpromotable, but he was probably perfectly suited for this assignment. Sufficiently skilled not to mess it up. Sufficiently limited not to understand what was really happening.

He gave me a regulation powerful handshake, looked at the hybrid. He did not seem to recognize me through the disguise and my new look from the cosmetic surgery in Ursvik. Then I stood chatting with him for a while, waiting for the "ladies", as he put it. Touched on the obvious topics of conversation, weather, football, gossip. Everything but politics. Somewhere beneath the tense surface of the situation—I could not imagine the extent of it, that I might even get to see my family, for a moment at least, before they were all snatched away from me again—there was still my depth of experience and training. Everything we had done to ready ourselves for a moment like this. For all that could conceivably happen. And more—for the inconceivable.

When Ingrid and Jesús María emerged from the restroom, after an absurdly long time—Jesús María with an intensely red wig, Ingrid with silvery-gray hair and a darker face color, to cover the burn marks from Kleine Brogel—guards appeared from nowhere and asked them to follow along to the security check. The escort and I could only stand and watch. I knew that this was no more than another power move by Edelweiss, that he wanted to demonstrate that at any moment he could crush us like small spiders under his indescribable weight.

Yet my heart was in my mouth when the metal detector gave out a sound. A dull rhythmic buzzing which stabbed through the arrivals hall. Jesús María seemed uncomprehending, waved her arms about in her now exaggerated Irish way, tossing her curly red hair: according to her passport she was now called Scarlett O'Hara.

After some brief theatricals, the mistake was quickly and seamlessly put right and Jesús María was let through, with a cursory body search for the sake of appearances. But I still found it hard to get my pulse back under control. The moment was closing in on me. I had assumed that the entire exchange would take place in separate corridors, hidden passageways, without any of us noticing each other. Amba and the kids set free and Ingrid in custody at last. Me handing her over with the briefcase to Edelweiss—and in return getting his guarantee that they would never harass my family again. At the same time releasing me to the freedom of determining my own fate, deep down under the eternal ice.

But this too would no doubt play out entirely differently from what I could ever have imagined. No-one, except for Edelweiss—and maybe Ingrid herself—could foresee that.

When she approached our escort, whose expression had not altered one iota during the incident at the metal detector, the now much older woman with her silver-gray hair in a topknot shook his hand so strongly that she almost seemed to be making a point. Ingrid probably wanted to show both him and me that she had her strength back. Seemed to have hardly a trace left of either the heavy anesthesia or the incident in Belgium. My plan already felt weak and uncertain. I had an uncomfortable feeling that it was all an elaborate set-up by Edelweiss. That everything in some way revolved around me and not Ingrid. Desmond "Des" Kern, the Core of the Poodle.

After Jesús María had joined us, still gesticulating wildly over the slight to her as an unofficial guest—she too showed herself to be a reasonably good actor—we started moving. Our escort turned off in the direction of the visa line but, without drawing any attention to himself, led us surprisingly smoothly through the enormous mass of passengers who had just landed.

Then we were swallowed up into nothingness. Only the merest pencil-thin line in the wall betrayed where the opening was, before the hidden door closed soundlessly behind us. Once we were past the air lock, everything was silent and sterile, as if someone had switched off the chaos and the racket out in the arrivals hall. We were now in the sealed wing of the airport, named after John Foster Dulles, of all people. Our Secretary of State during one of the most intense phases of the Cold War, in the middle of the '50s when the hydrogen bomb went from prototype to usable weapon. And the man behind one of the most important concepts of nuclear war, "massive retaliation", as well as the systematic deployment of our intercontinental missiles.

We had trained in here so often, simulated questioning which became progressively rougher over time, starting at West Point and continuing to the Team's most realistic simulations of total terror attack with nuclear weapons. But there had been significant changes since then. The walls seemed thicker than I remembered, the doors half open to the empty interrogation rooms heavily fortified even since our escape three months earlier. Or maybe in preparation for our arrival, the forthcoming exchange. "The Prey" in return for "The Hostage".

Without a word our escort led us away down the long corridor, past one interview room after the next. I counted the doors in order to keep myself oriented in the otherwise nondescript row: nineteen, twenty, twenty-one . . . Felt the lightness of the hybrid on my shoulders, the whole apparatus swaying in its cradle. Tried not to look down at the optically bewildering wall-to-wall carpet with the pattern of the deconstructed American flag. I already knew where he would stop. Yet I continued to count, as a way of meditating, processing, keying myself up. Thirty-three, thirty-four, thirty-five, thirty-six . . .

At last we arrived at what officially went by the unremarkable name of the "Interview Room". Only used for our fiercest interrogation training sessions, with or without torture, and real life questioning of suspected global terrorists. Before they were then sent on in due course to Guantanamo or one of our top secret locations around the world.

We ourselves always called it "Fort Knox"—because the walls were said to be at least as thick. It was hermetically sealed, escape-proof, stifling. Even before the improvements.

With a small bow our escort opened the protective doors: I noted that they had acquired yet one more layer since I had last seen them, were now quadruple thick, before he closed them behind us from the outside. Left us alone with the one other person sitting in here. He was even larger than I remembered. More than 6.5 feet tall, at least 290 pounds of muscle, total control of his body when he finally got up to shake our hands with his enormous paw. Just him against the three of us. If we three had still been on the same team.

"Hi there. Welcome to my little den," John said.

Quickly he went to our packs, took out our liquids, knew exactly where to find them. Literally poured out our whole supply into the drain in the tiled floor. Paid no attention to our weapons, the apparatus inside the hybrid, anything else—and we let him do it. Because in that situation we had no choice at all.

Then John sat down on the bench again, turned in on himself, eyes on the floor and fingertips together. Waited for the surprise which then came.

I had believed Edelweiss capable of a lot. Of most things; essentially everything.

But honestly not this.

5.06

I have read that a spider hears the sound of the prey in its web as tones: that the taut threads function like the strings of a guitar. That the spider can sense what sort of quarry it has caught from the frequency of the signal.

So as we sat locked inside Edelweiss' lair, the Interview Room, in the spider's web, he could very well have heard our music on the screens in his office. A soft tone rising to an atonal chaos as our group of visitors was brought in. One after the other, at short intervals, by the same escort that had brought us here to the sealed wing.

I closed my eyes, kept them shut, listened to the abrupt movements in the room, the rustling of clothes, the determined protests. The sounds of Jesús María, Ingrid, me.

And that of my former family.

Slowly I opened my eyes. Glanced hesitantly at Amba, under the cover of my new face. Her heavy make-up did not disguise the deathly pallor. She looked dogged, you could see the wild struggle going on inside her, holding all too few of the keys she needed to unlock the situation. Ever since I had vanished she had probably tried, in her usual way, to "interpret" everything, to get some idea of what might have happened, to make sense of it all, without being able to understand even the first premise. That we never had been that perfect academic couple: she an art historian, a specialist in the detection of fake baroque paintings, I a moral philosopher with a particular focus on the dilemma of nuclear weapons. That I had been living two parallel lives since my first year at university— which was in no way to say that I had not put my heart and soul into them both.

It was a masterly performance on Edelweiss' part. Directed at me and me alone: a thrust straight into my heart. A sublimely fiendish way of reminding me of the range of his talents. That he would stop at nothing, had mastered all the arts. Of how high the stakes were. In case I might have doubted it, or forgotten.

And this was only the beginning.

Edelweiss' act of bringing me and my family together now—more than three months after my flight, when things might have been starting to settle—was only his first move. Ripping the wounds open again, the grief, the sense of loss, the stitches. Placing us directly opposite each other to maximize the drama. John with Amba and the children on one side of the room, on the bare bench which ran the length of the wall and had the word INTERVIEWER burned onto it. Myself, Ingrid and Jesús María on the opposite bench, marked INTERVIEWEE, with the hybrid and all our other packs tucked under the bench. And thin mirrors running at eye level from one end of the opposing walls to the other.

It had been in here, during the West Point advanced course, that Edelweiss for the first time used his expression "the Theater of the Body". Said that it was this and this alone which unfolded in the mirror facing the interviewee's bench. And that they just could not help watching themselves, hastening their breakdown.

I continued to observe Amba, since I could not bring myself to look at the kids—and since for a long time she hardly seemed to notice my eyes on her. She was formally dressed, as if going to a party, with yet another newly bought sari, bright red, the sparkling end of the cloth draped over her head. She could easily have come straight from some event, or maybe just the Friday gathering of our neighbors in the academics' housing complex where Volvos from the 1990s stood sloppily parked in front of the hawthorn hedges trimmed without care.

Her clothes nevertheless gave me some comfort, if one could talk at all of comfort in this situation. The sari did not look like prison clothing at least. Although Edelweiss could have dressed his pawns in whatever costumes he chose.

It was clear that her thoughts were racing. Soon she too, without ever letting the children out of her sight, watching closely for the slightest reaction beyond their strange calm—the apathy of deadly fear—looked back at us as we sat along the opposite bench. Our anonymous little delegation.

A very short woman with the red hair of the Irish and a pleated skirt. A tall woman with gray hair and a certain likeness to Greta Garbo. A super-fit man with a big blond beard.

I assumed that Amba probably saw us much as was intended: as criminals of sorts, perhaps spies, maybe even terrorists, with no connection to herself and the children other than that we had now been bundled together in the same room. That she hardly knew who was going to question or be questioned. She would get no further than that now, with so many unknowns. Not even she.

That woman who would otherwise always cut through layer after layer, find the exact deviation from standard pattern in art forgeries, seemed able to uncover everything except my own double life. Whose default setting was bloody-mindedness, especially in her dealings with authorities. Who loved to contest everything, from her perpetual parking tickets to the proposed construction of an activity center at the old playground, which was of some cultural-historical interest. And who had been the one to push for our children's names.

"Unity" was our first, little more than nine months after we had first met at the welcome party for new teachers at my small Catholic university. Amba was not a member of staff and came along as somebody else's guest—otherwise the absurd logistics of what I was trying to do would have been impossible: the lies, the excuses, the invented study trips or conferences requiring nights away. Instead, immediately after her exams, she got a job as a forgery expert at the American office of Christies. With Amba's obvious lack of interest in "talking shop"—because according to her there were so many more important things to talk about—she was also able to accept rapid changes to our plans, without delving too deeply into why. My sudden need at puzzlingly short notice to head out and fetch or drop off something. So long as in return

I would cover reasonably often for the unexpected changes in her own schedule. Because some old friend had got in touch, or just her constant overtime at the auction house.

After the invasions of Iraq and Afghanistan, my double life began to be less demanding, since we were no longer involved in what was referred to as "direct warfare". Instead it became increasingly *indirect* with each passing year. The state visits shorter, sometimes barely twenty-four hours, in this digital age when our physical presence was no longer such a priority. Edelweiss' extravagant maneuvers often took place during one single long day, in which the world could just as well succumb to nuclear weapons attacks as be saved at the last moment.

On coming home from those simulations I had thrown myself straight into bed, unable to relate to the real—or unreal—world, had hardly the strength to kiss the children goodnight. For Amba's benefit I blamed the fact that the students' constant moral-philosophical paradoxes during our evening seminars had taken it out of me. How they just loved to twist and turn everything, always challenging their poor teacher. In fact I had never had any students. But I knew that Amba would not check that: that she reserved her suspicion, her well-known ability to see through almost everything, for her professional life.

As Amba began to get closer to glancing at my face, circling steadily, as if she were trying to recall something long forgotten, I looked straight at Unity for the first time. She was sitting closest to Amba. Still seemed cheeky, but afraid. Never before had I seen such an expression in her eyes: the very opposite of a spark, something which had gone out forever.

She was unexpectedly pretty, in a red dress that must have been bought after my flight. And even though she was sitting hunched up, resigned but ready to hit back, she looked to have grown at least two inches since I saw the kids for what I thought would be the last time. When on the night of September 4, 2013 I had peered into each of their rooms, held their doors ajar, and whispered a simple "Bye!" at them. Seen Unity lying there covered in sweat, entangled in her sheets, with that strange inner warmth which would not have lessened now with the onset of puberty. I clearly distinguished the drops standing out on her forehead, with the temperature being turned up here in the Interview Room: we had called her the "Steam Engine" when she was really small and the center of attention. During the two years that she was our only child.

Then, suddenly, it all became crystal clear. Why my entire former family was so smartly dressed. And how quickly one can forget the most central of things.

I checked my wrist-watch. The time was 01.14 the night following December 21—the winter solstice as well as Unity's twelfth birthday. They had been celebrating that evening, in their finery, with the house full of people and only Daddy permanently absent. This is what they had so abruptly been pulled away from. Probably at the exact time when the cake was carried in, given Edelweiss' unfailing sense of the dramatic.

Once again the memories came welling back, even though they were the last thing I wanted now. The first birthday had been at least as trying as the delivery. Unity had just been given her name, having simply been called "Miracle" during her first year. A group of reasonably intimate friends came to celebrate. Close enough to be invited to our home for the first time, distant enough not to ask any questions which were too difficult. Neighbors, some few chosen colleagues of Amba's from the auction house, none from my murky existence as a researcher at the university. No family at all, whether mine or Amba's.

I felt the eyes in the back of my neck, from several of Amba's female colleagues. I must have puzzled them with my contradictory appearance: the hard-as-steel body and the post in moral philosophy, the lure of my faintly melancholy air. Things which seemed impossible to combine in one and the same person.

When the guests arrived, it felt like the introductory psychological tests I had undergone at West Point's sealed wing. A glass fell onto the floor, the crash must have been audible all the way out in the dining room, a cloud of small shards, fine splinters. But when I went to clear up there was no longer any trace of the accident. Amba called from the living room, wondered where I had disappeared to, when the drinks would be coming.

Then I saw the glasses. They were on the tray, lined up perfectly as if in an interior design magazine, full to the brim with crushed ice and decorated with garish plastic umbrellas. I put them out on the table and the guests applauded enthusiastically. "What a man," one of the women said, "might I be allowed to borrow him from time to time?"

The child herself, little Unity as the main character in her party best, the odd little dress which Amba had had made. Neither then nor later did we ever manage to arrange a party for any of our children which actually pleased them. When they were a bit older I tried with treasure hunts. Did my best to pitch them to the lowest possible level, but the games were still far above their heads: with the exception of Duality, the children immediately became whiny and impatient, started to bicker, gripe for ice cream. Then I had to give up organizing them because our friends and neighbors began to talk, the children's questions spreading to their parents. A father who was a moral philosopher—yet put together such advanced ciphers that not even the grown-ups could work out where the treasure lay buried . . .

Maybe it had all changed now, even the parties. Since I was no longer there.

Duality was wearing a nice blue suit and seemed as introspective as ever, with that sparkling talent which never quite found its way out. He who was able to solve the simpler cryptic crosswords long before he started school. Was unfailingly the first to find the hiding place during my increasingly complex treasure hunts, before I was forced to stop. Here, today, he was giving nothing away.

Trinity, our youngest, was the antithesis of Duality and was sitting closest to John in her new purple dress. Seemed totally unafraid, as ever, although of course tired and nonplussed about the situation. She had always been a little rash for her age; not many seven-year-olds were prepared to take the risks she did. I was struck by the fact that she kept her left hand stuffed into a pocket in her dress. I couldn't help wondering if she had hurt it in some way, and began to worry the way a parent does.

Amba had still allowed our youngest to sit closest to the enormous John, like some sort of shield. And surely nobody who saw all that innocence and naïvety, Trinity's childish belief that she would soon conquer the world, that everything lay open before her despite her father's disappearance, could touch a hair on her head. Or maybe one person after all.

That man was almost touching the seven-year-old's fair head with his swelling muscles, crammed into his tight white T-shirt, already transparent with sweat. John put me in mind more of a torturer than a bodyguard. Which of course was the intention.

Time passed, as oppressive as everything else. I tried to stop myself from looking at my watch, could not allow the repetition to drive me out of my mind. Edelweiss knew better than anyone how to exploit the fact that waiting can cause severe psychological damage in itself. That awareness that something is going to be done—but not what, not how, not by whom to whom, nor why.

At short intervals my family began to look up, one after the other, to fix their eyes on us on the opposite bench. Seemed to be gaining some sort of courage, or perhaps it was the reverse: a collective sense that it was already all too late. That resignation which, according to our psychologists, could travel from person to person in roughly the way yawning does. Between individuals, members of a social group, even in a room full of strangers, proof of how empathic human beings are. So we were trained not to yawn when others started. To be able to resist our empathic instinct.

In the mirror along the opposite wall I saw Jesús María, sitting to my right, staring straight ahead. At the group on the other side of the room—or rather at John, from the very first moment. With a dull hatred that could almost be heard vibrating in the room. Ingrid too looked right across the room, let her eyes travel back and forth across the group.

So in the end I had to do the same. So as not to stand out, reveal my identity in a way which could prove fatal: not only to myself, but more importantly to my former family. Because naturally I had no idea what John and Edelweiss now meant to do with them. Who was prey and who hostage—and who would be sacrificed on the altar.

Which was the next phase in Edelweiss' devilish piece of theater. The very fact that he had made the arrangements so overwhelmingly complex—that none of us knew who in the room was a prisoner and who some sort of witness. Whether we, or they, came here freely, or were on the run, or in custody. What was going to happen, even in the next few moments. Who knew what about whose arrangements.

That there was no possibility for me, or actually any of us here on this bench, to make our positions clear to the others with the necessary speed.

Because even if I suddenly decided to change course, to try to get myself and my family out of this escape-proof space, how could I make them trust me? Reveal both myself and my intentions swiftly, to make them want to follow me? Explain the intricacy of the situation, with my unknown face beneath its heavy disguise— before John or maybe Ingrid took down both me and my family, either together or one by one?

The only way to loosen the knot was through violence. I would even have to neutralize my family, temporarily, first Amba and then the kids, before I could get them out of here. And that would be way too complicated even for me.

This was nothing less than a live exam in Edelweiss' favorite game: "Everybody against everybody". The exact thing we had trained for in narrow tunnel systems deep below our nuclear bases or in desert landscapes, the sky black with smoke from fires and explosions, with no clear view in any direction.

It invariably ended in furious violence, since mankind had never yet been able to find any other solution to insoluble problems. That was why we did not need more than a single guard in here, although in this case it was John. Because mutinying prisoners seldom act together but usually kill each other first, like scorpions in a small glass jar. And because there was in any case no chance of getting out of "Fort Knox" alive.

Soon we found ourselves in the next phase, following the usual pattern, when the reality of the situation started to sink in for my ex-family as well. One after the other they came to realize that in all likelihood none of us would be able to get them away from here: that we who were sitting on the benches opposite were just as much prisoners as they themselves, maybe more so. So each of them gradually deflated, in roughly the same way. Finally even Amba, and little Trinity, until recently so rock hard.

It was still quiet in the room. I glanced at my watch again, despite myself, and with increasing frequency, not least to get some momentary relief from the unbearable sight of my former family breaking apart opposite us. One moment it might be 01.53 and the next—after what seemed like an eternity—only 01.58. Then barely three minutes passed before I found myself looking at my watch again. It was a classic psycho-physiological effect. Time passed increasingly slowly in the locked room. In the end it more or less stood still.

Having no alternative, I kept doing what Edelweiss had always recommended for situations one did not comprehend: waited for the next move. In the worsening heat—that too presumably part of the game—my intake of breath began to burn at the back of my throat. At 02.26 my wrist-watch told me the temperature in the room had risen to 102.7 degrees. My family's movements became ever slower. Unity and Duality were whimpering softly, Trinity kept on nodding off, in the almost drugged way of someone in an overheated bedroom.

Only Amba remained braced. Ready for the fight, still watchful. Sometimes she would stare right into my face. Again that look, as if searching for a name that was on the tip of her tongue, some celebrity she had no personal connection with. As if she had vaguely recognized me from a newspaper photograph, under the heading "Wanted".

When my watch showed 02.43 and 107.8 degrees, I felt the blessing of fatigue for the first time. The sounds of dozing throughout the silent, hot room—all three children had now fallen asleep—were hypnotic. Even Amba's eyelids were drooping. It was impossible not to follow, and in the mirror I thought I could see how Ingrid too was struggling to keep awake. Only Jesús María still stared straight ahead, unbending. At John, who was in the same position as earlier: stock still, eyes turned down, fingertips together. The only sound which could be heard, softly but with increasing frequency, was that of John's heavy drops of sweat landing on the tiled floor, like Chinese water torture.

My next glance at the watch showed 02.57. I became more and more convinced that there would be no initiative at all from Edelweiss. That he wanted to let us melt into one single piece, like a grotesquely deformed tin soldier, here in the hellish heat.

And just at that moment, of course, came his next move. Just on the stroke of 3.00 a.m.

That was also when I first realized why he had arranged for us to be placed just like this. Amba and the children on the bench with the word INTERVIEWER burned into the wood, we on the opposite bench with the word INTERVIEWEE. Because John slowly got to his feet. Turned his head toward my family, tapped the children on the shoulder until they had woken out of their deep sleep, broke the now nearly three-hour-long silence.

"Listen up, ladies and gentlemen, or rather: *lady, girls and boy.* You now have the chance to put your questions. To the only ones

330

who, based on our research, know anything about Erasmus Levine's disappearance. So I think you should take this opportunity, kids. You too of course, Mrs Levine."

They looked so terribly confused, all of them, Amba included. Probably just like all of us on the bench opposite. Me above all.

When Amba then looked straight at me in a different way, deep into my eyes: as she used to once upon a time, I fell over backward even though from the outside I remained sitting upright. Because her eyes beamed like X-rays at the disguise and my new face. Through successive layers, hidden strata, as sharp as few others in her increasingly frequent hunts for forgeries. That strangely penetrating gaze I had fallen for that very first evening.

She must have recognized me—but if she did, she gave nothing away. Seemed to be allowing me the chance to run free for a while longer, as much as she was in a position to do so. Then she turned to John with tired resolution.

"No, I don't think we have any questions, Mr . . . ?"

"Smith. Peter Smith," John said.

I breathed out for a second or two. Even though this probably wouldn't advance my cause by more than a fraction. Then another thunderbolt, as Amba continued. They say lightning doesn't strike twice—which is mere superstition, of course.

"And to be honest, Peter, I don't care. The explanation which that police inspector with the funny name—Edelweiss, I think—gave me seemed good enough . . . that Erasmus had just run off with his old academic supervisor. That she'd bewitched him. And you could tell it was going to happen from the way Erasmus used to go on about that woman: I always regarded her as our ghost from the past."

I sat very still, shut my eyes. Paralyzed by the power in the room. The charge from the thunderbolt. But what Amba said next may have come as a surprise even to Edelweiss, who would surely be following all this minutely via the monitor in his office.

"And anyhow we'd stopped relying on him a long time ago. All of us."

When I was able to open my eyes again I saw the children nod. Well-mannered but perhaps with a little melancholy.

Then I saw something glint by Trinity's pocket as she turned and the spotlights in the room fell on it. I realized immediately what she had been clutching throughout this whole unbearable session. The last part of the trinitite, the glassy residue left by the first nuclear weapons test—when the desert sand in New Mexico encountered the blast, destruction and creation—which became a kind of rarity among collectors. I had given her a small piece on each of her birthdays, fragments from what Edelweiss had once given me. When I fled, in that last goodbye, I left all that remained of it in a gift box under her bed.

I tried not to look into Trinity's eyes as my family got to their feet from the bench opposite, Amba and then the children, from youngest to oldest. Closed my eyes as I listened to the last I would ever hear of Amba's voice.

"So if you'll excuse us, Peter, we want to go now. Get on with our lives. We have a twelfth birthday party to finish. A cake to polish off, bowls of candies just for us, piles of potato chips left—isn't that right, kids?"

5.07

As they were led out of the room by two escorts, one in front and one behind, there was a change of scene. A number of other guards came in and stood just in front of us, by our bench. Six of them in that small room, "Fort Knox": two for each of us. A man and a woman in each pair. Staring us right in the eye, trained even to blink as little as was physically possible, not one movement in their faces.

I tried so hard not to wonder where they were taking Amba and the children. Whether back into some sort of custody, maybe worse—or really back out to the suburbs, home, free, in a normal civilian car, where they might resume Unity's party with as much enthusiasm as they could muster the next day.

Had Amba played her role perfectly? Or rather broken every imaginable rule, and improvised, thought for herself, usually a prisoner's worst offense. Or had she articulated their genuine feelings about me? Real, deep hatred following my sudden escape.

One by one, I managed to shut down my thoughts of Amba and the children. Put into practice all the things I had so long trained for, never dreaming that this ultimate challenge would be where I would make use of them most. Not in my worst nightmares.

I looked past the guards toward John, who had assumed the same position as before on the bench opposite us: eyes on the floor and fingertips together, as if meditating. I had never before seen him like this. While Kurt was alive they had been indistinguishable, rarely speaking with anybody except each other, as only they were sufficiently receptive to each other's brutal humor. As far from being meditative as it was possible to be.

But perhaps this was John's way of mourning his life-long partner. Or brooding, stock-still, over the next phase in his revenge.

As I leaned further to my right to be able to see the whole

of him, my two guards—cheap Secret Service types, pawns on Edelweiss' board—followed the movement and reached for their weapons. Then they swayed back into position, since this was not turning into any incident. I stayed in the same crooked and uncomfortable position, watching for John's next move.

His T-shirt was now so wet and rank from the heat in here that every ripple of his mighty chest and stomach muscles had become visible. After a few more minutes he started to carry out a certain movement with mechanical precision. Seemed preoccupied with the small pool of sweat which was forming in the crook of his elbow, just below his sculpted biceps, and he dried it at regular intervals with a tiny ball of cotton wool. On the other hand he appeared not to care at all about the floods of sweat which simply ran down his bald scalp, continuing like tears over his face, and then onto the floor with a soft plop.

The next time I permitted myself to look, when I could no longer stop myself, my wrist-watch showed 03.56 and 108.9 degrees. My brain was calculating slowly in this heat. We were ten people in this low, long and narrow room, about ten by twenty-five feet with barely seven feet of headroom, which meant little more than a twenty-one-square-foot area totaling 141 cubic feet of air per person—and that was gradually but surely being consumed by us all. And humans breathe in 21 per cent oxygen and 0.03 per cent carbon dioxide—but exhale 16 per cent oxygen and 4 per cent carbon dioxide. It's an equation which cannot hold for long. Not here in "Fort Knox".

I could feel it in my head, in my sluggish thinking, how the oxygen was beginning to run out. And slowly, so slowly, it dawned on me why Edelweiss had called the guards, the pawns, into the game. Probably none of them had the slightest idea who we were. How much we were wanted, how seriously and covertly pursued. And they were not meant to guard us in any real sense, because that was still not necessary, given all of our multiple and partly contradictory agendas.

334

Their only role was to consume the oxygen, drive up both the heat and the carbon dioxide content in the atmosphere. All of the pressure in the room.

Once again I pressed my heel back against the hybrid, needed to feel that the briefcase was still there: the most important object in the world, the ace up my sleeve. Everything else had slipped through my fingers. My mission, my family, my life. My only remaining role was to save the universe. In some way deliver Ingrid to Edelweiss, put an end to her crazy idea once and for all, both Plan A and Plan B. Then be given safe conduct to my next and final destination—hoping against all odds that he would keep his end of the bargain. Would tell my family, once all the cards had been played, the true story of my flight. How I had been duped all along by Ingrid.

But how this was all meant to happen, the endless complexity of the exchange, was something I could not calculate. That had to be Edelweiss' problem.

And still the other two kept their silence. The expressionless Ingrid to my right, and Jesús María on my left, still staring at John. Intent on translating Ingrid's agreement to take him down into an end as macabre as Kurt's.

I tried to remain vigilant, once again running the alternatives through my mind, focused, dazed, absent, when the alarm went off. At 04.54, just as the temperature was passing the 111 degree mark, my watch, and Ingrid's, emitted a faint synchronized buzzing. The warning signal that the heat had now risen to a level where movement and mental functions were being affected. In fifteen minutes the watch would signal again, to remind us that human operational capacity reduces by 1 per cent every quarter of an hour at such high temperatures.

This was the sort of refinement technicians loved, intended for the army at the time of the desert invasion in 1993: our first war in really unbearable heat. All those involved had disabled the function, regarded as not just superfluous but at times deadly dangerous. One single buzz from the watch could after all be the difference between being able to move forward unobserved or giving away one's position.

That was why Edelweiss had picked it up off the scrapheap of history and insisted that we should never switch off the signal function. Not because he thought it could be useful to know where the other members of the Team might be—but rather as yet one more challenge, another handicap, for us to cope with.

In order not to attract the attention of the guards and make them suspect that I was planning something, I turned off the watch's signal mode. Collected the saliva my glands were still producing, swallowed when there was a decent volume of it. Behaved just as we had been taught for desert environments. Limit all functions, keep movements to a bare minimum, think of cold. The blessings of the eternal ice.

The thirst was the worst part, now as ever. Sometimes humans too stretch out their tongues, like dogs, in an ancient reflex from the age of cavemen. Our psycho-physiologists said that this was the ultimate warning sign. If you see one of your unit doing that, they said, you have to give as much as possible of your own liquid to them.

Now I had no liquid, neither for myself or anyone else, nothing at all after John had emptied out all of our bottles. So I could only observe in the mirror how Jesús María opened her mouth and stretched out her cloven tongue, cautiously yet still visibly. The diamonds or bling glittered in her mouth. So it was she—who from earliest childhood must have been well accustomed to extreme heat, the baking temperatures of Mexico's interior—who was the first of us three to weaken.

But then I realized that showing the tip of her tongue had merely been a signal to John. And at that point Jesús María finally took action.

"Excuse me, sir . . . Mr Smith . . ." she said.

"Yes ma'am?" he said.

"I need to use the bathroom."

John got up heavily and theatrically, like a statue rousing itself from centuries-long immobility. Came a few steps closer to us and laid his enormous hand on the shoulder of one of the female guards.

"This here is Mrs Jones. And she would love to accompany you to the bathroom."

Jesús María looked first at her, then back at John.

"Honestly . . . and no offense, Mrs Jones, I would feel more comfortable if someone like you were to come with me, Mr Smith. In this situation."

It took a few seconds before John answered. I counted, one technique for surviving unbearable situations: *six, seven, eight* . . . Then John went in an instant from being a psychological riddle— that eerily silent creature—to an open book. In two short sentences.

"Well, now. Of course I'll come with you, if that's what you want, ma'am."

And then his predictable minor addition:

"What wouldn't one do for a lady in need?"

5.08

The asymmetry in asymmetrical warfare rarely represents anything specific. Mostly it is the fact that things do not follow patterns, regularity, norms. That is to say: the expression can cover more or less anything that one does not understand. The trick is to operate strategically even when everybody's motives—both on your own side and the enemy's—seem obscure or simply unreasonable.

So here we were, me and Ingrid, without both John and Jésus María. And a new female guard came into the room with food for us all.

I tried to re-interpret the situation according to its new unfathomable premises. The next step had to be the exchange: an attempt to deliver Ingrid to Edelweiss in some way. Despite the fact that the guards in the room, now numbering seven, would hardly be sympathetic to that, likely would not even understand what I was trying to achieve. So first I would have to overcome them and then "Fort Knox" itself. And then whatever else was waiting outside the four-inch-thick walls.

But I had no choice. Somewhere deep inside I still felt a basic moral sense, some sort of world conscience. Maybe it was for the sake of my former family, which only an hour ago had been sitting here opposite me; maybe for everybody else's sake too. Under layer upon layer of toughening and steeling myself, my conviction had grown that Ingrid's ideas would jeopardize mankind's future more than anything else throughout history. With the help of the one weapon which had been built, deliberately, for our own annihilation.

I watched her in the mirror opposite, peered between the guards to see her sphynx-like expression, totally blank. Perhaps she was not following our training. Or she was still affected by the drug, had not recovered as miraculously as I had first thought. Small drops of sweat had begun to trickle down her face too, as she began to eat the yellow-brown sludge which had come in on the female guard's trolley.

It was hard to make out if this was meant to be breakfast, lunch or dinner: or what it was at all. Whether the revolting smell of rancid fat was meant to add to the situation. To the heat and the tension.

Yet we needed the food, as well as the liquid contained in it. Ingrid had emptied her plate—as had all the guards apart from the woman who came with the trolley and knew what this mess really consisted of—before I had my first mouthful. This was why our physiologists had chosen the concentrated crunch cookies for our combat packs. Because everything else could, under certain conditions, be impossible to eat.

I managed in the end to down half of my portion, despite the smell from our plates, the heat, the unbearable atmosphere. My wrist-watch showed 06.01 and 115.4 degrees. Ten minutes since John had left with Jesús María. I awaited Ingrid's move, had to let her go first, assumed that she was not incapacitated by the drug.

The clock crawled forward while the temperature approached 122. The hypothesis that this was really all about me and not Ingrid seemed more credible by the minute. That I was in one way or another the Core of the Poodle and the entire situation had been set up so that I and not she would be handed over to Edelweiss.

That the arrangements from and including Jukkasjärvi, in all their complexity, had in fact been designed precisely to lure me back into his lair. That they did not see Ingrid as the main threat to the world's survival, mankind's fragile future, our whole civilization—but rather me, Erasmus. The Carrier and not Alpha. That it was Ingrid who had first sealed an alliance with the Master of Darkness, Edelweiss, long before my own pathetic little efforts.

I kept staring at the tallest of the female guards: tried to remember where I had seen her before, the set of her shoulders, that icy look. Then my recollections came to a sudden stop. When my wrist-watch showed 6.10, she spoke. After a slight reaction, as the message sounded in her earpiece:

"Director Edelweiss will receive you now. Follow me!"

There was not really anything else we could do. Before we left the room, one of the guards cuffed his right wrist to my left and my right to Ingrid's left—while one of the other guards was secured to Ingrid's right. It was the classic formation. Two prisoners in the middle, one guard on either side. To break free would require a very advanced maneuver, a veritable Houdini exploit, huge raw strength and sublime timing. And with the bulky packs once more on our backs.

There were of course solutions even to this problem. The easiest one we referred to during our training as "Croquet", where the two prisoners swung their respective guards in toward the middle. The most spectacular results came if their two heads crashed into each other.

But it was all made much more difficult by the fact that there were five other guards, the crew-cut female one in front of us and four behind, even if we managed to pull off the trick perfectly. And last but not least: each prisoner was no longer on the same side—certainly I was no longer on Ingrid's.

The corridor was empty and cool, it felt as if we were taking a dip in the ocean after the extreme heat in the packed Interview Room. I stole a look at Ingrid next to me, her face still expressionless and impenetrable, like a mask. The female guard in front of us walked with determined steps without ever turning around. Seemed to be relying blindly on the fact that the six guards behind her would be able to keep matters under control.

I listened in the direction of the bathrooms, straining for some sort of sound—literally any sign of life—from Jesús María. But nothing could be heard and with each foot we drew further away. The wall-to-wall carpeting swallowed our footsteps. Everything was deathly quiet and ominous. Focused on something indeterminable.

Entirely logical in all its lunacy. The pieces of the puzzle no longer fitted, the figures on the chessboard weren't the right ones, even the rules of the game made no sense.

When we had reached the office—a white door with no name on it, no outward sign at all—the female guard brought our formation to a halt.

"We're here now, Director!" she said into the minimal microphone, invisible to anyone not in the know.

There was a click from the lock and the heavy door swung open. I noted that it too had been strengthened since I was last here: seemed to have gone from a tolerance of 14.7 psi of overpressure, the only standard for the unthinkable that we had been able to imagine, to at least double that. Roughly speaking, a direct hit from a smaller nuclear weapon.

The four of us went in, Ingrid and myself chained to our escorts, while the rest of the guards—including the woman seemingly in charge—remained in the corridor. Edelweiss was sitting at his desk facing away from us, reinforcing the impact of his presence. Heavy and mysterious as a Buddha statue. And when he spun around on his chair, I could not help but catch my breath: it had been so long since I last saw him in the flesh.

His dark persona was accentuated by the surrounding whiteness. The entire office, even the floor, had been painted in the same almost floatingly light color as everything else in the sealed wing. The vast desk was made of graphite gray metal and cast in one piece. On its surface lay a single piece of paper, some sort of document, and a black fountain pen. Edelweiss spared no look for Ingrid. Just stared straight at me and the hybrid on my back, the apparatus inside. The world's most important object.

"Welcome, my dearest Erasmus," he said.

I did not answer. You could almost hear him licking his lips, his words slurred with saliva. The breathing as labored as ever.

Four metal chairs in the same graphite gray were lined up in front of the desk. To sit down, the four of us had to do so at exactly the same time. Yet we managed it relatively easily: we were trained to be adaptable, both as interviewers and interviewees. We were even able to put down our packs in front of the chairs, my launch mechanism and Ingrid's portable command terminal, the full Doomsday potential. The guards, who had taken the weapons out of our packs, now laid them on the desk, beyond our reach. That too was intended to be psychologically destabilizing. So near, and yet so far.

I glanced at Ingrid on my right. She seemed indifferent to the way Edelweiss, her long-standing brother-in-arms, was treating us. He in turn still took an interest only in me. Observed me intently, seemed to be awaiting something specific. I looked past him, at the clock over the desk. It would soon be half an hour since John had taken Jesús María to the bathroom.

Then I shut my eyes and went on rehearsing scenarios. The first assumed that Edelweiss was indeed relying on me to keep my side of the bargain, meaning that he too would do as he had promised. That my family would be released or at least no longer harassed, and that I would be given safe passage, once Ingrid had been delivered to him.

The other was similar, but the other way round. It ended with Ingrid getting safe passage—having delivered me in her place. It was based on their seeing me and not her as the main protagonist in this whole piece, the Core of the Poodle. On her having somehow laid the lion's share of the blame on my shoulders.

And the third scenario, which appeared to be the most likely, was that neither I nor Ingrid would emerge from here alive. That they would seize the opportunity to take down both of the special agents, who had so spectacularly fled from the Team and placed the future of mankind in jeopardy, at one go. Regardless of the short-term consequences. Even the President's resignation, if it came to that, once details of our top secret formation were revealed by the media. Or the rolling out of Ingrid's Plan B.—which could, after all, hardly be worse than her first alternative.

But all three scenarios suffered from the same weakness. None of them took sufficient account of Ingrid herself. The scope of her fantasy, her power of imagination and ability to improvise: at least equal to Edelweiss' own.

So I was keeping a close eye on her too—trying to be vigilant in all directions at once—when Edelweiss pushed the document over the desk toward me. To make it possible for me to sign, all four of us had to stand up, like a controlled chain reaction. And not before Edelweiss handed me the pen, and I leaned forward over the paper, could I distinguish the name "INGRID OSKARSSON" in capital letters. The document was a delivery order for Alpha.

Then I felt a movement from her, a soft pull at our shared cuffs. My whole field of vision narrowed as I heard her melodic voice.

"I'm ready."

Intense focus on the guards, the desk, our assignment, like sunlight concentrated through a magnifying glass. Moving without thinking, reflexively. I did not even need to look at Ingrid as she continued:

"Are you, Erasmus? Then let us pray."

She had chosen the second alternative, the one we called "Prayer". Quickly bent her guard's right arm behind his own head and pressed him to the corner of the desk. His face slammed against the sharp-edged metal, cracking like an egg. At the same time, perfectly synchronized, I did the same to my guard on the other corner of the desk.

In an instant the rest of the guard force burst in, five of them with heavy weapons drawn, having obviously seen everything on the surveillance footage. The piercing alarm cut through my brain. I vomited onto the floor, my lifelong reaction to ultra-violence, straight onto the immaculately polished shoes of one of the dead security guards. Instantly, Ingrid raised her right hand over her head, signaling that the game was over. And my left hand, bound by the cuffs, followed it. Edelweiss was sitting stock-still, watching us with a strangely amused look on his face.

He tossed three envelopes across the desk in my direction. Then, without a word, he took the pen back from me, leaned across and drove its needle-like tip straight up the nose of the guard nearest to the desk. The silver nib disappeared completely—and the Secret Service agent crumpled like a rag doll and fell to the floor.

Inside me, all was calm, even though the alarm must have continued to pulse. The scene was like a movie frozen on one frame. Edelweiss again immobile. And none of the remaining guards with the least idea, any more than us, of that man's ever-complex agenda: that he was letting us both run free.

We got going, wasted no time on questions. Managed with some contortions to fish in the dead guards' pockets for the keys to our handcuffs, and unlocked them, before retrieving our weapons and the envelopes from the desk and the bags from the floor where they had been left, again tantalizingly close. Edelweiss continued to sit there, Buddha-like, watching.

I felt his eyes burning in the back of my neck as we ran out through the security doors, down the corridor with the packs. In the stairwell we stopped and I tore open the envelopes from Edelweiss. The same passports—still the Core of the Poodle—our money and cards returned.

The courtesies of his web extended throughout the departure process, reeling us out through the checks at Dulles with the same ease with which he had reeled us in through Zaventem. The illusion of freedom spinning down the departures board. Blind eyes and broad smiles through to the gate. Even as we seated ourselves on the Paris flight.

"*Skål* to Ed! For never keeping to the rules of the game!" Ingrid said.

"So why on earth did he set us free?" I asked.

"God only knows. Maybe he just wanted to play a little longer. Or has flipped, to our side."

She closed her eyes. I noticed more sweat running down her face—until I realized that it wasn't sweat at all.

"Why are you crying?" I said.

Ingrid turned to me, opened her eyes, gave me a tearful look. Did not seem at all surprised that I'd addressed her in Swedish, using one of the many basic expressions she'd taught me during our long discussion sessions.

"I'm grieving for Jesús María," she said, now also in Swedish.

"How do you know she's dead?"

"She isn't, my treasure, not yet. But there can't be too much time."

"Why do you say that?"

"I was the one who fitted the apparatus inside her. In the women's restroom on arrival at Dulles."

"Apparatus?"

"A machine from hell. I did exactly as Jesús María said: followed her macabre instructions. Because I made her a promise, before our flight to Stockholm, that she could take them both down. But not herself, never herself . . ."

She fell silent, dried her tears with the back of her hand. I looked around the cabin.

Then she gave a half-smile, before a last sentence in Swedish:

"And John is the one who will set it off."

I felt ice throughout my veins, in the midst of all the heat, even though I could not fully comprehend what Ingrid meant. How the duel between Jesús María and John in the restroom would actually play out. Except that it would be a dance of death in which they would both perish.

I looked at her, tried to recall the sequence of events.

"And most of all skål to Jesús María! My blood sister, all the way to the bitter end . . ."

The cloud cover was still above us, like thick gray-white cotton wool, as opaque as everything else at the moment. Soon, though, the plane would break through it all and emerge into the heavenly sunshine. Penetrate the clouds and allow light to flood the cabin.

There was a sudden flash, like sunlight. But it seemed to be hitting us before we had ascended above the clouds.

And I realized that it could not be the sun—the silver-white light was coming from land, not from the ocean to the east. What had happened next I recognized from my worst nightmares. After the sharp white radiance there was the unmistakable mushroom shape, soon swallowed up by the cloud cover. Just before we lost sight of the ground, it seemed as if the entire airport was in flames far below.

Finally the pressure wave, making the aircraft rock violently, knocking the cabin crew onto the floor, and eliciting hysterical screams from the passengers.

"What the hell was all that?" I shouted at Ingrid through the chaos.

She did not look back at me. Just stared out the window, even though one could only make out a thick whitish haze. Muttered the same sentence over and over again:

"Yes… what in heaven's name was that, my treasure . . . What in heaven's name . . . ?"

6

THIRD DOWN

December 2013–February 2014
Sicily

6.01

The flight to Palermo was delayed, like all the others here at Charles de Gaulle, security checks having been stepped up ferociously at all airports after the incident at Dulles International Airport in Washington. Probably Code Orange, maybe even Red.

But in practice it had probably been LILAC, the highest level of alert, ever since Ingrid and I had fled from the Team at the start of September. "Large-scale nuclear attack with critical consequences for global security."

It was December 23—but there was little sense of Christmas in the air. Most passengers in transit were tensely following C.N.N.'s live transmission on the T.V. screens, trying to make sense of it all, as were we. Just standing here in the bar, staring.

About nine hours had passed since the gigantic explosion. Speculation in the studios swung between a massive fuel leak from storage tanks to a planned terrorist attack. Shots of the mushroom cloud, taken by several passengers on different departing or arriving flights, were played over and again in slow motion. Yet the commentators, the "terrorism experts", were dismissive and said that too much was being read into them: that they were just a trick of the eye. They compared them with the photographs posted across on conspiracy theory websites after 9/11, which seemed to represent the Evil One in a cloud of smoke and dust.

All the while the death toll on the news crawl at the foot of the screen—the body count—rose with merciless arithmetic. At 1.12 p.m. it was seventy-two dead and 412 injured. Fourteen minutes later seventy-five dead and 409 injured.

Then my cell phone rang. It buzzed deep inside the hybrid, and even though the ring tone must have sounded as many as ten times before I pulled it out, the caller had not rung off.

I stared at the display. Edelweiss.

Eventually I pressed the green button as if in a trance and, by way of greeting, said:

"You're still alive . . .?"

"So it would seem, my friend. I thought you might want to know that."

"But no-one survives something like that, within such a small radius . . . It was a nuclear explosion," I said.

"Let's just put it like this, Erasmus: you saw that we'd taken certain precautions here in the sealed wing since you started at West Point. After the eleventh of September, the invasion of Afghanistan, the war in Iraq . . . the logic of the suicide bomber has to be countered in some way. Elementary game theory basically, nothing remarkable, risks, opportunities, pluses and minuses. So both the Interview Room and the Office can now, after the latest renovations, withstand a shock wave of 220 psi and a direct hit of up to 44 psi. And this explosion wasn't actually that powerful, in absolute terms—although it was certainly impressive for a microcharge. Unparalleled, I'd say. We certainly felt it!"

I listened, waited.

"On the other hand, it did knock out most of the rest of the airport. The whole international departure hall, just after you'd passed through it, I assume, parts of arrivals, duty free, the food court. In that sense the force of the blast was a scientific mystery. Which was explained—and at the same time increased exponentially—after we had the results of our first quick analyses. But I thought that you could perhaps shed some light on all of this for us."

I didn't give an inch, managing to hide my own curiosity. Let him keep going in his own good time.

"Because there were traces of californium both inside the restroom and in the fallout. Not only the usual microscopic residue you'd find after a nuclear explosion, but significant amounts. As if the entire charge had consisted of isotope Cf-251 or perhaps even Cf-252."

"Californium?" I said out loud.

350

Ingrid started.

"*Californium?*" she repeated.

I looked around at all the other passengers standing among the bar tables, to see whether any of them had overheard what we had said, that word. None of them had reacted at all. Edelweiss waited before continuing. Maybe he had heard Ingrid in the background, was waiting to hear if she would have anything more to say.

Then he swallowed audibly, that curious gurgling sound, and took up the thread:

"Otherwise it's relatively clear to us what happened. The surveillance cameras inside the restrooms have a form of black box which makes it possible for us to reconstruct the course of events, second by second, freezing the picture and spooling backward and forward, taking advantage of the blessings of modern technology—and that's what we had to do to get a better understanding. At first it seemed like some kind of complex mating ritual. In the end, though, there was not much left of either of them. I think you can probably imagine it all, broadly speaking, my dearest Erasmus."

I shut my eyes, pushed away the thoughts. For all those years Zafirah had tried to convince me of the blessings of ultra-violence, get me to discover its special power and cleansing effect, the catharsis of brutality. Said that it was her only relief after her mother had simply left them in their little village in Bahrain to join the mujahideen fighting the Russians in Afghanistan. She would sit there as a little girl with her father all night, watching boxing galas on some foreign television channel, leaning toward him in their wordless grief.

But still I never succumbed to the temptation: had always regarded brute force as a means and not an end. So I said nothing. Just waited for the last piece of information, even though I already knew.

"But finally they managed to consummate the act, the thing which mankind is, after all, created to do. And this resulted in his last little futility triggering the mighty apparatus she was carrying.

351

A neat little piece of construction, I have to say, evidently with the world's most expensive element as its active substance. The going rate for a gram of californium is upward of $80 million. I had to check that with our experts."

A short pause.

"But as one of them added: 'However one's supposed to get a hold of that much!'"

6.02

On the flight to Palermo I once again took my dissertation out of the pocket of my combat pants. I found the part dealing with californium straight away. Here too my style was peculiarly essayistic, light years from what was current in academic circles. I still could not quite fathom how it had managed to pass the Bulgarian examiner's sullen filtering.

The heading to Chapter Three was "THE ELUSIVE TRAIL OF THE TRANSURANIC ELEMENTS". I began to read, was drawn in, pulled back in time.

People had been searching for them for such a long time, predicted their possible existence, the world of science buzzed with rumors.
In 1935 Meitner and Hahn had been given joint responsibility for the so-called "Transuranium Project" in Berlin.

From a theoretical point of view, "transuranic elements" is only a generic term for elements which are heavier than uranium, that is to say with more protons in their nucleus, and an atomic number higher than 92. But in practice they both were and are so much more than that. Trans-uranic elements are by nature unstable, seldom exist for more than fractions of a second and are also called "synthetic" elements because the only transuranium which exists naturally on earth—and what is more, in extremely small volumes—is pluto-nium. Other than in a laboratory environment, the others have only been encountered in nuclear reactors or after atmospheric tests of nuclear weapons.

What came to be called neptunium and plutonium carried also for a long time the mysterious designations Element 93 and Element 94 because of their estimated atomic numbers. In other words, it was known that they ought to exist—all theoretical calculations indicated as much—but under conditions prevailing at the time it was in practice still not possible to produce any of the transuranic elements.

With the war and in due course the Manhattan Project came both the possibility and the driving force. Only then was it possible to generate sufficient impetus, energy and motivation to produce the new elements, perform the whole "transmutation" from one element to another. Neptunium was created in 1940, followed soon after by plutonium. The substance which together with uranium made the atomic bomb possible.

Yet in the end it was not Meitner and Hahn who discovered plutonium, despite the fact that they had worked with transuranic elements for longer than most. Instead that honor fell to the Swedish American Glenn Seaborg. And not only for plutonium, a substance which Seaborg was later responsible for enriching to weapons grade at Los Alamos, but also a number of other new elements, in close and fateful succession.

Curium and americium were created in 1944 and 1945, although without practical implications for the outcome of the war. With the arrival of peace, the short window between hot and cold war, Seaborg became professor of chemistry at the University of California, Berkeley. At the start of the 1950s his team there produced no fewer than five different transuranic elements in as many years. First berkelium and californium—named after their place of creation—and after that einsteinium, fermium and mendelevium.

The photograph on the facing page (Ill. 13) is a facsimile copy of an historic special issue of "Chemical & Engineering News". There we see Seaborg and his collaborator Stanley Thompson beaming at a test tube filled with a glittering pale substance against a dark background. The caption underscores the significance of the discovery: "MAGICIANS. Scientists Thompson and Seaborg pose like ancient alchemists in 1948, just before the discovery of californium."

In the pages of illustrations in the center of my dissertation there is another photograph of californium (Ill. 36). It shows a petri dish full to the brim with a silver substance. The original caption states that the container has a diameter of barely one millimeter. Not surprising, considering that californium is often seen as the world's most expensive material. At the time of writing, its price is approximately $60 million per gramme.

In the following section (Chapter Six) I will consider more closely californium and its different uses. Not only as a "neutron cannon" for starting up nuclear reactors or creating further new elements, but also, for instance, in the treatment of cancer or to search for gold or oil.

In the same section I will also look in greater detail at certain of the more speculative theories about californium as an active component in a number of very small nuclear weapons. From backpack-sized atomic bombs to the much talked about, but never fully confirmed, nuclear pistol with bullets filled with californium.

But let me dwell a little longer here on researcher and Nobel Prize winner, Seaborg. In the pages which follow, there are more photographs of him. The first one (Ill. 14) shows Seaborg as if in motion, slightly out of focus, surrounded by students on his way into a lecture hall, on one of his many visits to Sweden. He came often to his beloved second homeland, as guest of honor at gatherings for Swedish Americans or to lecture on his area of expertise. It was certainly no disadvantage that this also allowed him to keep up his contacts with the Nobel committee. In 1951 he was awarded the prize, jointly with his colleague Edwin McMillan, for "their discoveries within the chemistry of the transuranic elements".

On the facing page (Ill. 15) you will also see Seaborg and Meitner together during the Nobel dinner in Stockholm. He is smiling proudly at the camera, she characteristically shy next to him. One side of her face is looking happier, as ever. The other paler, almost sickly. It looks like two different people, if one covers up one side at a time.

This is the source of the working title for this dissertation, "The Two Faces of Lise Meitner". Before my supervisor and I decided instead to use the title, "Lise Meitner's Secret".

Her strangely ambiguous face can be seen in other photographs in these pages. For example in (Ill. 41), the only known picture of Lise Meitner with Edward Teller, the Father of the Hydrogen

356

Bomb. Enrico Fermi, who was central to the development of the atom bomb in Los Alamos, also appears in the photograph. On the reverse is written: "Meeting, Chicago, June 1946". That is to say, toward the very end of Meitner's guest professorship at the Catholic University of America in Washington, D.C.

But there is no reference to what the meeting might have been about. In her diary, Meitner says only that it was surrounded by "stifling security arrangements". And then adds: "It felt more like being a member of a secret society than participating in a scientific discussion."

Opposite this mysterious photograph is another much later one (Ill. 42). It shows Seaborg at Meitner's home in Oxford in 1966. He had gone there to present to her in person the prestigious Enrico Fermi Prize, for her "extensive experimental studies leading to the discovery of fission". A belated consolation for having been denied the Nobel Prize and all the other distinctions which Meitner was never awarded. When the honor was announced, Meitner stated that she did not want to travel across the Atlantic to receive the prize, which was interpreted to mean that she still did not wish to be associated with the bomb. But when Seaborg then offered to travel to her home in Oxford instead, she accepted immediately—and is said to have received him with joy and pride.

The photograph shows Meitner, now close to ninety, looking with apparent delight at a small, black case which Seaborg is handing to her. It cannot have been the medal itself in the case, because that is already lying in a velvet box on her lap together with the plastic-covered diploma.

What the case really contained I have been unable to discover, despite extensive researches in the context of this dissertation. In my concluding section (Chapter 10) I nevertheless describe some of my hypotheses—and what their significance might be for how we should view the woman, and the mystery, that is Lise Meitner.

6.03

I closed my dissertation, tried to get some sleep for the first time in more than a day, just as Ingrid was doing in the seat next to me.

But the questions would not stop buzzing around in my head. Why had Ingrid agreed to return to D.C.? Why had Edelweiss let us run free? What had actually happened in the restroom at Dulles, causing that massive explosion? Who had won and who lost? What was the relevance of californium in it all?

And still I did not think of putting any of the questions to Ingrid—since she so rarely answered them in a way which made sense to me.

When finally I started to fall asleep, I kept being woken by a series of flash-like dreams of the mushroom cloud outside the airplane window. That unfathomable power, billowing outward slowly and mercilessly like a colossal thunderstorm. Something so far beyond human scale and yet so near. I felt totally drained, depressed and bewitched, like a drug addict after his first kick.

It may well sound particular to me, personal, perverse. But this longing for the forbidden, the worst thing imaginable in human history, was a universal symptom. To the extent that our psychologists even had a name for it, a diagnosis: the "Doomsday syndrome".

Yet what I had experienced was such a tiny part of what would happen in the actual moment. Edelweiss had done his best to make us understand how high the stakes were. The weight and importance of our assignment. The enormous difference between the atomic and the hydrogen bomb, fission and fusion, nuclear and thermonuclear weapons. That the first ever hydrogen bomb, on just its first test, had an explosive force of 10.4 megatons: one thousand times more than the atom bomb over Hiroshima.

He kept reading out the stories in his frighteningly gentle voice, from my very first time at West Point, the attempts at descriptions, the eyewitness accounts.

"I could have sworn that the entire world stood in flames. The heat rays burned my back even though our ship was thirty miles from ground zero. The blinding ball of fire had a three-mile diameter, seemed to hover motionlessly before slowly rising toward the heavens, like a gigantic gas balloon, a foreign planet, another sun".

This from a marine, a former Harvard literature student, in a letter home after his first experience of a hydrogen bomb test.

Edelweiss then turned to actual footage and simulations in the Team's headquarters. Hour-long sessions four storeys below ground, the lecture hall's lights dimmed as the giant screen lowered softly from the ceiling. Always starting with what it would have looked like if the "Bikini Baker" atom bomb, with an explosive force equivalent to the bomb dropped on Nagasaki, had exploded directly above Manhattan.

The cloud spread out gradually, as if in slow motion, with a final width of a few hundred yards hanging over our slender island. When the shock wave came, the soundless picture just trembled fractionally, before the fires and destruction. Soon the simulation faded out and the room fell into total darkness. Leaving us in suffocating silence.

Then the Manhattan skyline once again came hovering out of the darkness. The clock in the bottom corner of the image was counting in thousands of seconds. But now the heavens above the skyscrapers were entirely, blindingly white. The ball of fire covered Manhattan's width. Then came the devastation itself, whole skyscrapers being snapped off like matches.

The first time none of us had said a word, we were just trying to fathom what we had seen. After a minute or so of absolute silence, Edelweiss explained—still through loudspeakers with the lights down and not making the slightest effort to create any comfort zone—that this was the clearest way to illustrate the difference between an atom bomb and a hydrogen bomb.

The first simulation, he went on, showed an old atomic bomb; the second represented the scenario for an early model of the hydrogen bomb, the first ever tested, codenamed "Mike". Even that would have wiped out the whole of New York's downtown in one single moment. The greater part of the city.

Then came all the secondary effects: the fires, the asphalt bubbling on the streets, melting together with the human masses into some sort of new organic composition. The water starting to boil in New York harbor. The unimaginable levels of radiation.

What Edelweiss was doing, as I now see it, was to imprint the whole situation visually onto us. How vulnerable the world had become with effect from the first test of the first atomic bomb— when the technology showed itself, against all odds, to be possible. How very much more so with the hydrogen bomb.

And that there was always a small human being sitting deep within the system, carrying out the rituals or even pushing the button. The last link in the chain. So susceptible to temptation, the whole scope of his own humanity.

Out of the loudspeakers in the jet-black lecture hall, Edelweiss then proclaimed that the "Balance of Terror" was no longer a question of states, military alliances or political or religious ideas. That in peacetime it lay more within each individual person who came sufficiently close to nuclear weapons. That those of us who are furthest within the system first and foremost have to stand up to ourselves. At any given moment.

Then he had started to run the actual footage. First with "DOG, 81 kilotons, Enewetak atoll, April 1951". Still not a thermonuclear weapon, but the final test of what came to be called the Mark 6 atomic bomb, which was kept in storage for almost a decade longer. In the foreground about thirty V.I.P. visitors were lined up in white deckchairs on the Officers' Beach Club on some small Tahitian island paradise, just outside the security zone. In accordance with regulations they were all wearing their dark protective spectacles as they watched the ball of fire light up the sky, like at an outdoor cinema.

After that came the hydrogen bomb tests. "ERIE, 15 kilotons, Enewetak atoll, May 1956": Edelweiss used to freeze the picture at the exact moment when the group turned away to protect their eyes. "STOKES, 19 kilotons, Nevada desert, August 1957", like a jelly-fish with tentacles of sand and fire stretching all the way down toward the dunes. "OAK . . .", in the same constantly blown-apart atoll, ". . . 8.9 megatons, May 1958": the soldiers sitting like schoolchildren at a picnic on the edge of a cliff, just far enough away according to the safety regulations of the time. And on he went, onward through the history of nuclear tests—right up to the comprehensive ban in 1996.

So we really did try to understand, each time Edelweiss showed us these scenes, at least once a week during my almost twelve years in NUCLEUS. All these shifting yet very similar expressions of our most unimaginable invention. The thermonuclear weapon which could not just split the nucleus of atoms but get them to melt together. Manipulate nature itself, simulate the sun's inner processes, the very pre-condition for life—and from now on also for extinction.

To comprehend the incomprehensible.

6.04

By the time we landed in Palermo, Ingrid had also woken. As elegantly evasive as ever, she answered my hushed questions, again in Swedish and for safety's sake on our way out through the arrivals hall, in the buzz of the crowd. Kept side-stepping until once again I gave up.

But so far as I could understand we were now meant to be in the very final phase of her Plan A., likely on the way to the resolution itself. The moment when I and this deranged woman would so literally be holding the fate of the world in our hands. The inhuman weight on our shoulders alone as the circle—the *correspondences*, the Nuclear Family, all these imperfect metaphors— came to be closed. When the picture on her screen was finally complete, all those triangles and crosses were joined up once and for all. Our entire global nuclear weapons system either short-circuited or launched.

For some reason I had followed her all the way here, to this very last stop. Maybe so that I could prevent something from happening. Maybe only, as in a movie, because I had to see how it all ended.

I followed her like a dog on a leash, or a puppet his master. Nothing that Ingrid did was ever predictable. So instead of the airport train we took the bus in from Falcone-Borsellino, named after the two lawyers who fell victim to the Mafia in the early 1990s, blown sky high and at the same time becoming secular martyrs.

Again we chose to hide in plain sight, among crowds of people. Standing up, in a packed bus, in the firing line, where anyone at all could have picked us off through the windows. And what's more on the way into the heart of the city, in infernal traffic, right at the start of the *riposo*.

I assumed that Ingrid too had counted on us being watched, in

363

one way or another. That one or more people would have followed us—were waiting for us here. That the only possible reason why Edelweiss had let us go was that we were both now to be "spools of thread". That they would wait, possibly until the resolution itself, to see how far up and how deeply the conspiracy had penetrated. The work which, according to Ingrid, she had been pursuing across the world for decades.

I looked at her as she stood pressed tightly against me with the bulky pack between her feet. Looked at her new face: more Garbo than Ingrid Bergman. The woman who had been my guide and mentor throughout my adult life. First spell-binding lecturer, then supervisor for my dissertation, eventually Alpha for both me and the whole Team. After that some sort of cicerone. Someone who did not lead you out of things, but rather only further inside. Deep into myself, the heart of the entire system. *We two against the world.*

She did not look back, kept staring out through the window: hungry, inquisitive, like a charter tourist. I soon took my eyes off her and did the same. I had been here so many times before, had landed directly at Sigonella in the south-eastern region, take-off point for not only our bombers but also the unmanned drones heading for the Middle East. Our fort facing the Muslims.

I had never before taken the airport bus, and had this ground-level view of the island. It all now became both more and less frightening. From miles up in the air, or on the screen simulations, there were no people to be seen—no-one to be defended or exterminated. Here they were everywhere. On the bus and outside, swarming, sweating, yelling, sounding their horns. The human factor.

When we got off at Palermo Centrale, Ingrid chose the first person we came across, in an Italian which sounded flawless. It seemed that it was not far from the station to the Palazzo Abatellis she was trying to find. But there was a strangely hot wind blowing through the alleys as we hurried with our heavy bags and, even though there were fewer than forty-eight hours until Christmas Day, I soon found myself sweating. The Mediterranean lay glittering at the end of a few streets, a picture-postcard scene.

I did not realize where we were going—until we stopped outside a brown-walled building, the Palazzo Abatellis, housing the regional art museum. I had not been there before, but now knew exactly where we were. She had given me a reproduction of that painting on one of my uneven birthdays, a very good miniature to hang in my office next to Bruegel's better-known version. The one which I had taken out of its frame and hidden away in my combat pack before the flight.

"16.48. We've got twelve minutes, my treasure," Ingrid said.

We cut across the breathtakingly beautiful courtyard and walked straight into Hall Two. And there it was. Mighty, imposing, overwhelming.

Even though I had studied most of what there was to be read about the twenty by twenty-foot fresco, which had to be split into four sections so that it could be moved from the Palazzo Sclafani during the war, and thought that I was prepared for it, it took my breath away. The immense power in this burlesque vision of Doomsday from the mid-fifteenth century. One of many models for Bruegel's own version, inspired by the Black Death which started to run rampant in Europe during the fourteenth century and, according to the sign next to it, painted by an unknown artist.

What this version of "The Triumph of Death" was missing was the Fleming's strangely nuclear sense of doom, the sickly yellowish background, everything burned out and bare. Instead, the skies were full of small out-of-place flowers—and none of the people depicted around the edges were being loaded into what could be seen as railway carriages or other modern death transports, as in Bruegel's masterpiece.

On the other hand, the fresco which now filled our vision had an even stronger focus. You could not take your eyes off the skeleton riding in the center of the painting, or avoid being drawn in by its maniacal smile. Not least because it was precisely the central part of the image which had been the most damaged by its hasty transport during the indiscriminate bombing of the city. It really looked as if someone had set out to destroy its central portion— with some kind of acid.

"Isn't this insanely beautiful?" Ingrid said, her hand on my shoulder.

"Yes, insanely," I said.

Then, after some time—impossible for me to assess or even comprehend—she led me across the courtyard again. All the way back to the station, just in time to buy tickets and board before our train pulled out, heading south.

And it was not until we were approaching Sigonella, some hours later, that I woke up properly again. After sunset the darkness had quickly become like a wall outside our window. Since the moon was hidden behind the clouds, not even the contours of all our radar installations up on the mountain ridges were visible.

Officially we had never had to admit that there were any American military bases at all on Italian soil, not even here at Sigonella, since here too all of the garrisons lay within the walls of the N.A.T.O. bases. But according to Edelweiss' strategic presentations, in Italy alone we had sixty-four of our own installations. In total more than ten thousand American soldiers, upward of a hundred nuclear warheads.

What is more, the dream of perfect synchronization of all of our combat forces, not just in Italy but throughout the world, was to be fulfilled after the last step here in Sicily.

The objective was that nobody should be able to hide from us any longer—and the key to it all was a new creation by the name of M.U.O.S., "Mobile User Objective System". Not many people knew what its exact function was. Why we spent such huge sums on the gigantic parabolic antennae, which demonstrably caused high levels of harmful electro-magnetic radiation inside the security zone, throughout more or less the whole of Sicily. Or devoted such extravagant efforts to suppressing local opposition to them.

The system was to consist of five satellites and four enormous ground installations to house the antennae. Soon the last satellite would be ready to be launched from Cape Canaveral—and sometime soon, at the beginning of 2014, the fourth and last base was to be formally inaugurated here in Sicily. The last point on the line around the globe from Western Australia, via Virginia and Hawaii.

Nowhere had the dishes encountered such protests as in Sicily. In and around the small town of Niscemi, thirty-seven miles south of Sigonella. For that reason we had not even been told the date for the opening of this last M.U.O.S. base.

So we passed through Sigonella and it was in Niscemi itself that we stepped out onto the platform. The evening breeze was still warm, my wrist-watch showed 68.4 degrees, at 19.39, December 23, 2013.

The final countdown had begun.

6.05

There are levels of believing and knowing. The only thing I believed was that I could never know. Not even what it would occur to Ingrid to do in the very next moment.

This time she led us hurriedly across the square outside the station. It was filled with festive decorations. We passed a blue neon-lit Christmas tree and went into a supermarket. Homed in on the meat counter. She asked for the pre-ordered turkey in her perfect Italian—and then let the boy manning the vegetable section load the trimmings into the shopping cart. Potatoes, fresh Brussels sprouts, ordinary yellow onions and small white globe ones. Then she picked up some kind of preserve that could have passed for cranberry, butter and flour, onion and seasoning for the gravy, white bread and dried sage for the stuffing. I recognized it all so vividly from my mother's Christmas arrangements. Also one box of panettone from the huge piles of them, filled with pistachio nuts and chocolate chips, and a few bottles of matured grappa.

"For our first few week or so," she muttered half to herself, "so we don't have to show our faces outside any more this year. Just until the Jesús María business has blown over."

Well after closing time, with a sullen young girl in a Santa Claus outfit letting the last customers out, we crossed the square again with an even heavier load. Most people did not spare us a look— despite our voluminous backpacks—as Ingrid took us further into the poorer quarters around the via Dante Alighieri. Our disguise seemed good enough: the son with most of the Christmas shopping. Plodding along with all that weight in his hands, a few steps behind, while his mother scurried along in front with her significantly lighter carrier bag.

Even though Ingrid was not only taller than me, but at least four inches taller than anyone else we came across. The short

Sicilian men in their made-to-measure suits, on the square, on their way home after the stores had closed or maybe after a round or two with colleagues at their bar after work had finished for the Christmas break. The old ladies inside the stores—who were buying things before the weekend in a frenzy—but not to be seen in the street. As if swallowed up by the darkness.

Step by step Niscemi closed in, drew down the shutters, doused the lights across whole neighborhoods. The Christmas decorations grew scarcer, the presence of neon trees more sporadic.

But banners remained hanging from balconies in tight succession, as they had been all the way from the square, rainbow-colored, saying "NO M.U.O.S.". As I put down the grocery bags to rest my arms and check the time, 8.42 p.m., I could see the first aerosol graffiti on the crumbling facades: "MAFIOSO + U.S.A. = M.U.O.S." Then another message a few feet further on: A SINGLE SPARK CAN IGNITE A REVOLT AS BIG AS A BLUE WHALE, as Ingrid translated it, in the same ominously dripping blood red. Followed by an ever-increasing number of dark messages along the steep via Dante Alighieri.

Since a couple of years earlier, direct confrontations between the demonstrators and our own security forces had become the rule rather than the exception. After arousing mostly local media interest, the issue then spread to the national media and from there onto the radar of certain strategic military commands—and for the first time NUCLEUS became aware of the local resistance.

The activists naturally knew how to achieve the greatest impact. In addition to the sprayed slogans on the walls and the banners hanging from the balconies, the well-known graffiti artist Blu had come here, to the small mountain town of Niscemi in this remote corner of the world, and created two enormous murals.

Ingrid now stopped in front of one of them. It had rapidly become a signature piece, not just for the opposition here but also for the whole carnival-like and escalating peace movement. Amba had a reproduction on one of her tote bags.

The painting was confrontational, exaggerated for effect. A grinning Death, playing the M.U.O.S. system as if it were a xylophone, with the bars sending off missiles instead of tones. It was General LeMay's Cold War dream—and seemingly also Ingrid's and maybe Falconetti's too. To be able to control all these separate command centers as if they were one instrument. Fire off, or short-circuit, all of our nuclear weapons in one historic moment.

Even senior military figures had speculated aloud as to the exact purpose of the M.U.O.S. system. What could lie behind these vast investments? Why our reaction to the young anarchists' opposition had been so extreme, almost personal. It was not only the so-called "defense analysts" in trade journals who had concerned themselves with the question, but also editorials in the mainstream media who would normally have left us alone. Even within the military apparatus itself there seemed to be a surprising number who had little more than basic information.

What seemed clear to most people was that M.U.O.S. would in due course replace G.P.S. as the world-encompassing communications network. That this new system would, as with so many other day-to-day technological functions, start as a high-tech military application and then be made available to the public. G.P.S. had, after all, been developed by our defense authorities during the '70s, even if it was not brought into operation until 1994. That network was therefore twenty years old—and still we found it as ridiculously hard as ever to communicate with our most dangerous units.

Because the entire nuclear weapons system was, behind the scenes, a patchwork of barely functioning connections, even nowadays controlled by floppy discs and other out-of-date technology, often without any backup whatsoever. Our heavily armed submarines were the worst example, something which was regularly raised by analysts and commentators as justification for their diametrically opposed opinions: an argument for comprehensive disarmament or for a much needed arms build-up.

These modern sea monsters, U.S.S. *Rhode Island* and our

seventeen other "Ohio Class" atomic submarines invisible deep beneath the world's oceans, now rarely rose to the surface. Each had the capacity to wipe out whole continents. But if we needed to communicate with them when they were cruising at depth in stealth mode, their stand-by position at times of high alert, it could take up to fifteen minutes to transmit three encrypted letters from sender to recipient, with the help of antennae at two eighteen-acre communications bases in Michigan and Wisconsin.

What is more, there was no technical possibility for the commander on board the submarine to acknowledge receipt, confirm whether he had understood the message correctly: whether for example he should surface—or fire off all his warheads.

These defects were used to justify the new communications solution. Certain training exercises in both the Arctic and the Antarctic had indicated that M.U.O.S. ought to be able to take care of these problems, using the new system's spectacular ability to establish contact with areas which had previously been unreachable. Not only beneath the world's oceans, but also below the pack ice at both poles, which in itself would permit a new colonization of these regions.

Yet as usual they were missing the crucial point. Certainly, M.U.O.S. would replace G.P.S., give rise to new communications possibilities, dramatically greater operational capacity. But the inner meaning of the system was, according to Edelweiss, something more important.

Everything is very obvious once you know. How perfectly this system fitted into our nuclear build-up, the "Revitalization". Edelweiss had compared it to our superior night-combat technology, developed in time for the first Iraq war. He said that M.U.O.S. would be the same sort of game-changer. Allow us to exploit the advantages of the coming generation of nuclear weapons, synchronizing all these minor miracles with each other, justifying the trillion-dollar investment. The radar-guided B.61-12 hydrogen bomb. Our new generation of nuclear weapons submarines, with a dramatically improved striking power and precision. Missiles with previously unthinkable levels of performance.

So here we were. At the place for the fulfilment of this world-wide system, in a godforsaken town next to our last M.U.O.S. base: the missing link. Marching up the steep streets with the groceries and our luggage filled with Doomsday potential—and the graffiti along the way like whispering reproaches, pointing fingers, an almost audible murmur.

At a deserted square, in what seemed to be the town's outer edge up on the mountain ridge, Ingrid led me off on a small path to the right of a baroque church. In the shelter of a pine tree she took out her torch and shone it onto the laminated map which somebody had mounted on a gatepost: a calculation of how far the radiofrequency radiation from the system's mighty antennae would extend. The red area covered most of Sicily.

This was one branch of the opinion ranged against the installations. When the army doctor at the M.U.O.S. base died of leukemia, a fact which only emerged because activists and the local media began informally to exchange information, the protests against the health risks of the system began to attract support from international doctors' associations and humanitarian groups. Mothers of soldiers serving at the base soon joined forces with them.

The other branch of the protests was opposition to war in general—not least this type of military communications system, which more effectively facilitated warfare. Which in turn created a link between the protests here in Niscemi and the worldwide peace movement.

So Ingrid would presumably wait for just the sort of massive uproar which the graffiti promised, the moment itself: a revolt as big as a blue whale. She would synchronize our move with the inauguration of the last M.U.O.S. base, just as with the protests at Kleine Brogel. When everybody was paying maximum attention in the wrong direction.

The problem was that none of us in the Team, not even our own

Alpha, had been able to find out precisely when the formal opening was to take place. The date had been shrouded in impenetrable secrecy for several years. Maybe there was nobody who knew yet. Maybe even the person responsible, whether it was Edelweiss or the President himself, was waiting for a purely random date. Simply improvising. To keep the anarchists at bay.

After several minutes immobile in front of the map, no doubt reflecting on the scale of the radiation's red zone, Ingrid hurried us on again. Led the way up into what was to become our rudimentary safe house.

Instinctively I mapped out escape paths, red and green zones. Not one strip of light seeped out through the building complex's drawn blinds, even though it was no later than half past nine. The dirty yellow facade was full of cracks, covered in graffiti. Only one set of entrance stairs had functioning lights—and it was not ours. Once inside the stairwell, Ingrid dared to light her torch again, since all of the doors on the landings seemed to be closed.

And even if one door were to be opened, against all the odds, it would hardly make any difference. These were places where you did not ask questions. Where neighbors would at best stare silently at strangers like us—soldiers, plainclothes policemen, American agents?—from their darkened hallways.

Up in the corner apartment itself, everything was very much to type. The first stifling smell of mold, two mattresses nibbled by bugs, or possibly mice, lying directly on the floor in the one large room, an open kitchen which in true Mediterranean style had been half moved out when the entire process must have been interrupted. Oven and refrigerator were functioning, even if the latter was buzzing like an engine on the point of breakdown, while one half of the sink had simply been removed. An ancient black-and-white T.V. stood next to the mattresses on the floor—with another on top of it. One with a functioning image, one with sound.

In short, here was the bare minimum needed for an assignment.

Walls and ceiling, remote location, views in three directions.

That view through the broken windows made me catch my breath. The barely distinguishable contours of the mountains against the black of the sky, single lights along winding streets leading down to the sea, the stars blinking like coded messages to us, the long path of the moon across the water. The world over which the final battle was soon to be fought. The only one we had.

Again I considered whether to escape, run hard in one single burst to the sea, travel north to the eternal ice and the rendezvous with my conscience—but I did nothing. Perhaps because I wanted to see how everything would play out. Perhaps because I could still prevent something from happening, play a part.

Ingrid put the turkey in the refrigerator and turned on the T.V., the volume low.

C.N.N. was reporting ninety-seven confirmed deaths and about the same number again of serious injuries from the explosion at Dulles, which according to the commission of enquiry had been caused by a leak in the airport's fuel storage facility. Heads had begun to roll among those responsible. Two of the most senior members of staff had been forced to resign. An expert in the studio was saying that the head of the airport itself could not remain in his job much longer.

The fact that other people had reported feeling seriously unwell after the accident had found an easy explanation. Members of the inquiry team were quoted as saying that aircraft fuel exploding in such large volumes could cause those sorts of unpleasant, but nevertheless temporary, secondary effects.

Such, then, was the situation just before Christmas. Everything hidden, artificial, distorted: awaiting some kind of resolution. Both heavy and light, suspended, unpredictable, yet in some way predestined.

6.06

On the evening of Christmas Day—after we had spent two days checking the hybrid, the portable command terminal and the news, and I had updated my notes, all of it some kind of paradoxical peace—Ingrid poured herself some more grappa by the oven and said that the turkey was ready.

"Just go and wash your hands, my treasure."

I went into the bathroom, bolted the door as well as I could, let water run into the basin. Looked at my wrist-watch. 21.29 here in southern Europe, high time for the turkey to be ready even at home—or whatever I was to call it—on the other side of the Atlantic. I keyed in Amba's number. Waited, hesitated, before pressing the green button.

Then I hung up after just two ring tones. I had promised myself. Never again listen to Amba's voice, not even her voicemail.

Instead I went ahead with the other call. The woman who answered was very friendly, knew at once who I wanted to speak to, and went to fetch her. When she came to the telephone her voice was as upset as it was every year.

"Hello? Is it you?"

"Who else would it be, Mom? It's that time of year. A really Happy Christmas to you! And in case you were wondering, I've won again this year."

I heard her hesitate, some unspecified fear, anticipating something terrible.

"Won our bet! I was the first to call this Christmas too, Mom."

If I had not heard her breathe, I would not have known she was still there. The silence was dense and seemed almost brittle.

"We're just about to eat the turkey, your great recipe as always. The simplest possible stuffing, you know: sage, onion and breadcrumbs."

"The turkey . . . ?" she said slowly, before that irrational rage surfaced: "I never made turkey, Erasmus. I hated poultry!"

I let her anger subside. As well as that eerie feeling I always got when she spoke about herself in the past tense.

"I've got to go now, finish things off here, Mom. But a really Happy Christmas to you."

She had fallen silent. Probably wondering which of her stock of standard expressions she should now use. Phrases from the past.

"I understand . . . And the same to you, my darling. Look after yourself and the whole of your wonderful family," she said.

"Absolutely. They send their warmest Christmas greetings to you too. We'll speak again soon, Mom."

"Of course we will, Erasmus. And don't forget now, give everyone my love."

I pressed the red button, filled the sink with ice-cold water and took as much oxygen into my lungs as I could. Then I dunked my head in the water. Counted to myself—thirty seconds, forty, fifty, sixty—before coming up for air, flushing the toilet as I bawled out my pain.

As I came out of the bathroom, Ingrid put down her cell phone by the oven.

"I took the opportunity to make a call, since you were in there for a while."

Her movements were strangely heavy. Maybe it was the grappa. Maybe more than that.

"Sixten sends his Christmas greetings to you too, Erasmus."

"Sixten?"

"He said he'll be coming here when it's time. For real, he said, no alias this time. He's got Aina's full approval to join in the final battle between good and evil. Perhaps get himself crucified, become a martyr along with us, my treasure. That is what he told me. Aina will stay at home. That pure little angel."

"And Lisa? Is she safe?" I said.

She did not answer, but bent to take the turkey out of the

376

oven: at least seven pounds just for us. Said nothing, focusing on getting it onto the table—and then disaster struck. First she swayed, her balance failing her, which in turn caused the fat to drip from the oven tray. Then she slipped on the greasy floor. The turkey flew in a gradual arc, as if in slow motion, bounced a few times on the floor and came to rest with its legs sticking up in the air.

I would probably have started to roar with laughter, for the first time since our flight in September, if Ingrid had not begun to cry. Like a little girl, shaking and trembling.

I went to her, tried to put my arms around her, console her. She just shook her head violently and shut her eyes tight. When she opened them, they were blurred from the alcohol and some sort of sorrow, like a misty mirror.

"I'm sorry . . . " she managed to say.

"For what?"

She did not answer, just squatted down and tried to pick up the slippery bird, dropping it on the floor once more. Only when she had managed to put the plate with the turkey on the table did she turn to me.

"For spoiling our Christmas dinner."

She kept fiddling about with the plates, straightening the cutlery. Seemed to take a deep breath before asking:

"But could you possibly bring yourself to eat the turkey anyway?"

I nodded slowly. "Why ever not?"

She sat down, poured water into one of our glasses and drained it in one go, blinked, opened her eyes again. The tears still covered her retinas like a layer of glass.

"Thank you, my treasure."

I sat down opposite her, while she began to carve the bird as if she were carrying out a medical dissection.

"But to answer your question . . . Lisa is free and safe again, thank heavens. But she's not coming here. Even though Sixten said she desperately wants revenge on the people who took her hostage."

"So why isn't she coming?"

Ingrid got to her feet again, went to one of the kitchen cupboards, opened the door and stared at its contents. Maybe to hide her expression when at length she answered:

"Sixten promised me that I would never have to see her again."

6.07

She took the wine bottle out of the kitchen cupboard, moved the plate with the turkey aside and put the bottle in the center of the table with a certain emphasis.

"Château Latour. Already seven years old when I bought it in the '60s, recommended by a woman in a small specialist store in Oxford. These days it's one of the more expensive ones at auctions. Would you like a glass?"

I did not have time to raise my hand to stop her: had planned not to drink a drop until our move on the M.U.O.S. base, and I still did not know if it was to take place this evening or in one year's time. She filled my cracked wine glass to the brim. It looked like a magic potion. Dark red, dense.

"My idea was to give it to Sixten. But it never happened."

She poured at least as much into her own glass, raised it with a slight smile.

"I think we should try it right away. Skål, Erasmus! To the irony and deadly earnest of history."

I raised my glass. The liquid ran thickly across the roof of my mouth. It was a divine wine—and exceptionally ill-suited to the situation we were in. Our miserable little safe house, the dreadful assignment, my state of dependence. On just this woman.

Then she began to pile the turkey and trimmings onto my plate. I just let it happen. Both white and brown meat, stuffing heavy with the smell of sage, potatoes, cooked small onions, Brussels sprouts and finally the cranberry preserve and the gravy, shiny with the turkey fat.

Ingrid treated every dish with equal precision and care. Because she wanted to dwell on the importance of each one to the whole. Handled them all like the most delicate crystal, even the potatoes which had been over-cooked in an eerily familiar way.

I took a mouthful, then more. Vanished into Christmas memories.

"Is it O.K.?" she said.

"Absolutely. Congratulations. Exactly like my mother's!"

"Yes, you told me all about it, my treasure, every little detail. That's why I let the potatoes cook a few minutes longer."

When her glass was empty, Ingrid reached for the bottle to refill it. Stopped short, studied the label, leaned forward and read the text. I did the same. *Grand Vin de Château Latour, Premier Grand Cru Classé . . . 1961.*

"You see: not a scratch on the label. Even though the bottle has been through a lot, I can tell you. But there's usually been something to hand to wrap it in. I've carried it round the world, through the gates of hell, close to my heart. Almost as I would a child, Erasmus."

She emptied half of her next glass in one mouthful, but I continued to sip the wine. Stayed on my toes, fully in touch with my senses. Realized that this was the moment of truth.

"I always thought that I would give the bottle to him, when it was the right time, for some reason or another. Kept it hidden away for ages. For almost half a century, I almost forgot it. I didn't drink a drop of alcohol from March 2, 1970 until this fall. Right up until I met Sixten again, and Aina, up there in Ursvik."

As she paused, I could make out sounds from the apartment below, for the first time since we had arrived. Some sort of muttered prayer, music, a choir: a repeat T.V. transmission of Midnight Mass from the evening before, I hoped. Unless it was my own demons.

"But there was never really the opportunity to give it to him in Ursvik, either. So I thought that the two of us could crack open the bottle this evening. Together. I've always seen you as my divine son, Erasmus. The treasure sent by heaven."

I looked down at my plate, trying to think of something to say, in response to her tipsy little melodrama. But I could not think of anything.

"We were so young, you see. I wasn't more than seventeen when I first saw Sixten, in the tunnels which became our secret meeting places, and he only two years older. Each of us as consumed by the vision as the other. From day one we had a plan ready, taking in the whole of our lives—not just for ourselves but for the country, the continent, the world. Until the end of time."

I glanced at her. She did not look back, but she took a small piece of turkey from the otherwise almost untouched plate. Chewed pensively, concentrating on what she was saying, trying hard to remember it all.

"And you must understand, Erasmus: the post-war period was indescribable, trumpet blasts and Doomsday fanfares everywhere. You've read most of what there is to read about it, but you still wouldn't understand. All these persistent dreams about things man was never meant for. And when Sweden's nuclear weapons program was assembled at the end of the 1940s, the thought was of course that we in Sweden should also build an atomic bomb—following the development, not leading it. Create the same sort of fission weapon that both the U.S. and the Soviet Union already had."

She was looking past me. As if telling her story directly to my notebook, for posterity rather than for me. Then followed a monologue lasting many minutes, as spell-binding as ever.

"But we had Meitner. Our most secret weapon. Sixten actually met her once, deep in the bed-rock, while installing those red-light-emitting diodes we'd been given as prototypes. His very first assignment in the Swedish program, nineteen years old and a newly minted senior high school engineer, still wet behind the ears. Lise was then in the process of leaving Sweden and her underground laboratory. So at that important moment in history—at the start of the '60s—they more or less ran into each other, right there by the red trap-door.

"Sixten has always described it as a short meeting, fifteen minutes at the most, but intense. Just the two of them, alone in the roughest part of the bed-rock. But Lise nevertheless had time to describe everything to him in broad outline. Probably wanted to offload it all before fleeing to Oxford.

"So Lise told him that she had been corresponding intensively with her world-famous colleagues ever since that triumphal tour of the U.S. in the spring of 1946, as the 'Mother of the Atomic Bomb'. All those letters you and I never found, however hard I looked in the Swedish archives. To and from her nephew Otto Robert Frisch, of course—as well as Hahn, Fermi, Teller, Seaborg, even Oppenheimer himself.

"And no-one had understood what she was working on. Nearly all of those most closely involved thought it really was to do with the atomic bomb project. That that was the secret which needed to be protected from the public, even from certain government ministers. And in fact it all stayed secret for thirty-five long years— until some technology magazine fancied that it had *exposed* the Swedish nuclear weapons program in the mid '80s.

"But that was just a red herring, my treasure. Because according to Sixten that was what Lise told the people who arranged it all for her, this top secret, fully resourced laboratory under one of the deepest tunnel links in the bed-rock. That we in Sweden could simply skip the fission weapon, the atomic bomb, and move straight to the second step and fusion technology.

"So when America detonated its first hydrogen bomb in 1952, there was apparently dismay in the Inner Circle. That anyone else had managed to get there first! But even the hydrogen bomb had been a red herring, because Lise was way beyond that. Her hidden research under the red trap-door in Ursvik was not about the hydrogen bomb either, not about fusion techniques—but rather transuranic elements. The third and maybe final step. The field she had started to look into with Otto Hahn in Berlin, already in the mid '30s, long before the war broke out."

Then Ingrid went on to talk about things I had known for decades: details, dates, scientific struggles. I recalled from our dissertation sessions that strange sleepwalking feeling. The next time I stole a look at my watch it was 22.49. It took more than an hour of historical circumstances before she was back with her own story.

"... but just before I myself came into the Swedish program, in 1960, Lise all of a sudden moved to Oxford. The Inner Circle suspected that it was because she had failed in her research. That this super-brain simply could not handle the shame."

She paused momentarily, met my look for the first time.

"But in actual fact it was the precise opposite. As Lise confirmed to me when she and I met for the first and only time, many years later. She fled not because the experiments had failed—but because they had succeeded.

"Because it had indeed shown itself to be possible to create the ultimate weapon, with the help of transuranic elements. And because she did not want that fact ever to come to the world's attention. So Lise's thought was to take herself and her findings off to her relatives in Oxford and bury them there for all time, without any other living person hearing a peep about it."

She kept her eyes pinned on me, as if she were talking about me rather than them.

"That was why Sixten and I devoted almost all of our time together in the program to trying to understand what we called 'Lise Meitner's secret'. To following in the footsteps of her work, since she never responded to our efforts to get in touch with her. With the help of a small group of researchers, old enough to be likely to die within a few decades, if we did not succeed.

"So we too worked on a sort of Kinder egg: three secrets, one inside the next. Within what Sixten and I called the First Tier development activities—which essentially all of those involved were engaged with, the dream of producing a Swedish atomic bomb— there was a tight little group to whom we had given the impression that we were in fact planning a Swedish hydrogen bomb, what we referred to as Second Tier work. We told them that Lise had been doing just this, and that was the reason we were so desperately trying to follow her tracks.

"But in actual fact Sixten and I, like Lise, were devoting all of our efforts to a Third Tier development project. The ultimate weapon. As we saw it, transuranic elements were going to bring Sweden to a new era as a superpower. The first since the death of Karl XII at the beginning of the eighteenth century.

"That was why the tunnel system became so peculiar and so extensive: because we needed to hide it as it was being built. New emergency exits were forever required. Secret spaces like the fallout shelter where we met up after our flight, my treasure, strange little play areas where Sixten and I let our chosen few scientists test the short- and long-term effects of those elusive transuranic elements. Like the Test Room."

A moment's silence, a faint smile. Then she noticed my empty plate.

"Would you like some more?"

I nodded, had my plate filled up again. Began to eat. Alert as she continued.

"One day we just came to a standstill. Our huge appropriations via hidden accounts, which had made all of this development work possible, boxes inside boxes, together with this meandering tunnel system designed to conceal the left hand from the right, all the night-time bus loads of explosives experts and mining engineers to and from Kiruna, the massive logistics, slowly but surely started to run dry because our secretive little group never managed to produce concrete results. Not just the coded transfers from the Swedish state, where those arranging the money movements were under the impression that we were still working on the fission weapon: the atomic bomb, the First Tier development project. But also the largest part of our funding—which came directly to Sixten's bank account. From a mysterious financier with the signature J.E.

"Once I had met that peculiar Edelweiss a few times, after a couple of years in the U.S., he revealed that he had been the name behind the initials. That most of the support for the research Sixten and I were organizing had in other words come from the American nuclear weapons program. Via him, of all people, as a front.

"Eventually Edelweiss explained to me that Sixten's and my Swedish development project had been a relatively large expense even by their standards. And that the Americans too had been wondering what a super-brain like Meitner might have been up to over there in Sweden during all those years, why she had always turned down their invitations. And since they never got to the bottom of it at the time—despite what was apparently a major espionage effort, Stockholm's addresses crawling with agents, even at Tekniska Högskolan—they felt they needed to find out what she had actually achieved. Before anybody else did.

"So Meitner's name was all it took to justify these magnificent allocations from the U.S. to Sixten's account, a number of heavily encrypted transfers among many others, right across the globe."

She paused and I looked up from my plate, which was empty again. She must have sensed some sort of doubt.

"You must understand, Erasmus, that nearly a decade had passed since the invention of the hydrogen bomb by the time Sixten and I came into the program at the beginning of the '60s. So both superpowers were thirsting for yet another Doomsday weapon, to keep up the pace: as few as seven years had passed between the birth of the atom bomb and the hydrogen bomb, from 1945 to 1952. So the transuranic elements had to be the next step. Both sides did whatever it took to get to the apocalypse first. Cared nothing about either the financial or the ideological burden, every layer in the process had only to demonstrate to the one above that it was actually doing something.

"And Edelweiss himself was one of those most actively involved in the search for 'Lise Meitner's secret'. That man was to become my direct boss for thirty-three long years—before our roles were reversed and I became his superior, as Alpha in our newly created Team. But he never found out that I was the one in that position. Until our magnificent flight from NUCLEUS, my treasure."

I took a deep breath. I had come into the story, been addressed, given perhaps the biggest supporting role. She looked past me, into the darkness, out through the window. As if back in time.

"Be that as it may . . . at the same time as our funds were drying up came the news that Lise was dying at her home in Oxford. So this was in October 1968, as you know. Sixten therefore asked me to go there before it was too late and try to get the missing piece of the jigsaw, The Holy Grail. The Philosopher's Stone. Whatever was needed to allow us to create the third generation of nuclear weapons. He was convinced that Lise still had the secret with her, perhaps just in her head, and that I was the only one capable of getting it out of her. That I had the gift. To persuade and manipulate, the sort of thing I'd mastered since my childhood."

She began to waggle her foot, I heard the soft rustling of her best mufti trousers under the table. Not even Ingrid could keep the mask in place as she approached the seat of her pain.

"In fact I did not want to travel abroad at the time. I was already five months pregnant—filled with dreams and terror, in equal proportions—even though I was hardly showing. You know I have always been good at hiding things. I was almost as slim as normal in the middle of my pregnancy, didn't say a word about my condition to Sixten. But I've never been able to say no to him. So I took myself off to Lise, all the way to her sickbed, introduced myself as one of her students from the guest lectures at K.T.H. A real admirer.

"And it took its time, it really did, a whole day and night of meandering discussions. But in the end I managed to persuade her that I was just as much for the cause as she was, that peace was mankind's natural state. So finally Lise sat up, reached in under her pillow and gave me two objects. First, the key to her underground laboratory. Secondly, the tiny black case which Seaborg handed over to her, together with the diploma and the Fermi medal, when he visited her home in 1966.

"I recognized the case at once, from the photograph I had seen in the newspapers: the one which we put into your dissertation many decades later. But it was significantly heavier than I had supposed. Just an inch or so wide, at most two inches long—and weighing as much as lead or refined gold.

"Lise gave me both the key and the case on the condition that I should not ask any questions and as soon as possible destroy both objects for all time. The significance of the key escaped me, however. Until Sixten told me when we met again up in Ursvik, for the first time in nearly forty-five years. So I told her about Mount Doom. Promised that I was going to throw them both down there, among the mass of debris from the excavation of the new 1,770-foot level, back home in Kiruna. Right inside what we in the end started to call Pluto."

I could feel the heat in my face, my temples were pounding—reactions which one could never really control, however much one trained. The theater of the body.

"And it was those objects which sealed my fate. The case and the key, in that order. Brought to an end that phase of my life. The program and Sweden. Sixten. Love and death."

She gazed at the label on the wine bottle again. Intact after all years.

"I bought this so we could celebrate when I got home. One wasn't quite so careful in those days, people both drank and smoked all the way up to delivery, just kept going as if nothing had changed. And the woman in the wine store assured me that it was the best there was. Could be stored essentially for as long as one wanted. Although that in itself was less important: Sixten and I were going to crack it open as soon as we had the chance."

Maybe I nodded, before I stole a look at my watch. Nearly midnight. I emptied my glass, waited for the finale. And after a long pause it unfurled.

"I was stopped at customs at Arlanda airport, my treasure. Even though I had hidden the objects as thoroughly as always—in a

secret compartment in my suitcase which I had designed myself—
the officers went straight for them. Pulled out first the case and
then the key."

She stopped again, waited, appeared physically to be wrestling
with her memories. I counted the seconds to myself. *Twenty-five,
thirty, thirty-five* . . . before she felt she could continue. Edelweiss'
trick for both keeping a semblance of control and holding out,
giving yourself something else to think about in certain situations.

"So I found myself facing a military tribunal. I realized that
all was lost. Our lives together, mine and Sixten's. Our common
dreams about the Doomsday weapon, our love child.

"I confessed to everything straight away, every element, with
some significant variations. Told them that I had stolen unimaginable volumes of the material—californium, already by then the
world's most valuable—from Professor Meitner. What else could
I say? It was there in the case, all the evidence they needed. That I
had in addition taken the key to her secret laboratory over there
in Oxford, where I claimed the material was produced according
to principles of which I had absolutely no idea. To protect Lise I
said nothing at all in my own defense,my so-called lawyer hardly
needed to begin playing his part.

"In return I was spared military prison—and was instead effectively exiled. They had organized it all smoothly. In the car on the
way out to the airport they told me my activities could be considered part of Sweden's contribution in kind for the ability to shelter
under the U.S.'s nuclear umbrella going forward. That I would
become some sort of asset to the American program instead. Which
was flattering in a way, a kind of recognition of my celestial talents.

"But I've always wondered what would have happened if there
had been a different judge, someone other than Aina, at the military tribunal that day, October 25, 1968. If they might then simply
have erased me without trace: that sort of thing does happen even
in civilized countries. So for this I thanked her when I finally had
the opportunity to do so. In Ursvik, almost forty-five years after the

event, on her seventieth birthday. For sentencing me to exile rather than oblivion."

When she had to rest for a moment, she just stared at me with her ice-blue eyes. I felt a shiver deep inside.

"But it wasn't hard for me to shake off my guards, even in those days. They lost me right where we stopped at the airport. I headed straight down into the underworld, the furthest extremities of the Inner Circle, our link to the construction of the new motorway all the way out to Arlanda. Which was in practice being built for use by the fuel tankers for the American bombers which were to be permitted to land there from then on. Another of Sweden's services in return for having the protection of the U.S.'s nuclear weapons in case of war.

"For weeks, months, after that I lived like an animal inside the peripheral parts of the tunnel system. But I had an incredible stroke of luck. Met a woman, Sireen, a refugee from Jordan after the Six Day War in 1967. She had a job cleaning the construction workers' huts in the forest and brought me food from there early each morning. Kept me alive, literally, until it was time."

She shut her eyes, seemed to be seeing everything before her. Her eyelids fluttered, as if she were having a nightmare.

"It was a terrible delivery. Almost everything tore inside me. Sireen had helped out in the field during that lightning war, knew roughly what to do when I was in the most acute phase. After that I had no choice, you see. Was basically unconscious, torn and broken, no way out. So I left my little girl with Sireen. Begged her to do whatever she could to get the baby to someone called Bo Sixten Lundberg at the F.O.A. in Ursvik.

"Ever since my visit to Oxford I had thought that the baby should be called Lise if she was a girl. Then I began to think that it would be too obvious, too likely to arouse suspicions, I probably became a bit paranoid down there in the solitude of the tunnels. So I wrote 'LISA' on a label and tied it round her little throat and left her with Sireen.

"Hours later they managed to find my hiding place, far inside the most remote connecting tunnel, to which I had crawled with my remaining strength in order to die, and they took me by ambulance plane across the Atlantic and straight to the base. Jesús María had to sew me together then and there, that fallen angel, my blood sister. Restored me like a work of art. Her first ever assignment in the military."

I took a last look at my wrist-watch. 00.37 on December 26, 2013, 65.8 degrees in our room. The co-ordinates I needed to hold on to.

"So that was the only condition I imposed, when Sixten asked me if we wanted to use Ursvik as our safe haven, after our flight. That I did not under any circumstances want to meet Lisa. That I should never see her as a grown woman."

She got to her feet and tidied away our plates. Moved to the sink, half turned away from me, and began to unpack the dessert. The panettone with diced oranges and raisins.

"So one could understand Sixten's actions, my treasure. Why he did as he did once they had taken Lisa."

The last sentence also came as she had her back to me, facing straight into the kitchen cupboards, after a pause of about twelve seconds.

"And she's my kryptonite too, you see."

6.08

The next day I felt I was wrung dry, had no strength left. As if I had emptied the bottle of wine on my own. Anxiety coursed and tore through my body. Doubt. Hesitation.

When Ingrid went to take a shower, toward evening, pallid from the previous day, the alcohol and the emotional storm, I called Edelweiss. Not wasting a second.

"Did Ingrid have a child with someone called Bo Sixten Lundberg, in the spring of 1969?"

"A child? Ingrid Oskarsson?" he said.

I hung up right away, more uncertain than ever. The apartment was swaying. When Ingrid had finally finished—she must have been practicing her yoga in the bathroom, on the tile floor, for certain the "Destroyer of the Universe" once again—I had to ask. She sat there showered, fragrant, in her long underwear and holding an impossible yoga *asana*, tapping away on her portable command terminal.

"Don't you ever have doubts?" I said.

"About what, my treasure?"

I so wanted to be able to give a sincere answer: that I had been full of doubts and still remained so, caught between trust and dread. But I could not say anything.

"Do you?" she asked me back, as I stood there silently.

"Always," I managed to say. "From the moment I wake up until I eventually fall asleep. Which is when the nightmares start."

She took my hand, pulled me gently down into a sitting position. I would hardly have been able to resist, even had I wanted to.

"I feel so sorry for you, my treasure."

As soon as I was beside her, right next to her on the mattress, she changed the image on her portable command terminal. I tried to look at it rather than at her.

"And for me it's the same," she said. "Every single second."

The map of the world came up on the screen, with its yellow triangles joined by solid red lines. Our seven home nuclear bases. Those initials which I knew by heart ran like a reflex through my reptile brain, three-letter sequences from east to west: SJN CWM BLM NDW WMM KW. Seymour-Johnson in North Carolina, Whiteman in Missouri, Barksdale in Louisiana, Minot in North Dakota, Warren in Wyoming, Malmstrom in Montana and Kitsap in Washington.

Then over to our eight European nuclear weapons bases, the sequence ITG TIA IRG BGK BBV NLE, from east to west. Incirlik in Turkey, Ghedi Torre in Italy, Aviano in Italy, Ramstein in Germany, Büchel in Germany, Kleine Brogel in Belgium, Volkel in the Netherlands and Lakenheath in England. The first thing I noticed was that the red lines to and from Kleine Brogel were no longer dotted but solid. That what we did there must have been successful, despite or maybe because of Ingrid almost having been burned up.

Even one part of the previously dotted blue connection from Esrange in Kiruna all the way down to what I now knew to be Niscemi in Sicily, a wide arc over a large part of the world, had become solid. But the other arc in the circle, from Niscemi back up to Kiruna, was still dotted and incomplete. This was no doubt what we had come to fill in. The end of the story.

Ingrid zoomed in on the black cross on Sicily—and a square popped up on the screen, emerging from the place itself. Exactly the same scene I had watched many times during the past year, ever since my fiftieth birthday in February, when I received the D.V.D. anonymously at my office at the university. The one in which Greta Garbo as Mata Hari tries to take the telephone receiver from Lionel Barrymore as General Shubin. The two enemies who Jesús María had later tried to change us into with her surgeries, either for fun or in deadly earnest.

Ingrid started to play the scene. A new code surfaced in my

subconscious: itching, nagging, a feeling one cannot fully describe. Twenty-four digits and three letters swirled through my brain. Nine sequences of three each, like the nuclear weapons codes. 151 221 621 11R 211 612 21C 19D 216.

I deciphered the message. Once again used the strange key sentence from the darkest days of my childhood. *I love you just as senselessly as my pretty weird and hellish father, for the time being and onward into eternity, Amen.*

And the clear text turned out to be simple, much more straightforward than I had been expecting, without any of Ingrid's usual cryptographical refinement. "THESE ARE THE CODES" was all it said. No more, no less.

Yet I listened to Ingrid's proud tones, like those of a child, without once looking at her. Just gazed straight ahead at the screen.

"Elegant, don't you think, my treasure? Antiquity's most secret art wrapped up in our most modern systems, a technological span of about 2,500 years. It took time to perfect it all. But you can't get any more secure than this, with the R.S.A. cryptosystem likely to be cracked soon, when all our digital security will have crumbled."

She clicked on the keyboard and the image dissolved into pixels. The code had been contained in one single frame. The sequences which had been implanted in me using subliminal techniques, in a split second, and furthermore hidden inside a classic old movie.

I was impressed, as always, but not convinced.

"You know that sooner or later even this type of advanced steganographic file will be opened up."

"But of course, my treasure. I've therefore made some other arrangements. Belt and suspenders, as they say."

Ingrid fast-forwarded, basically through the whole movie, all the way to the ending. In the very last scene, that strange feeling came back to me—as if something was itching in the furthest recesses of my mind: just as Mata Hari is being taken out to face the firing squad. Ingrid rewound, and then played the movie forward again, extremely slowly, frame by frame.

I noted yet again the strange fact that in the movie Greta Garbo never delivered the line "I am ready" to her guards. The perfect last words which the real life Mata Hari is said to have spoken when she was fetched for her execution in France on October 15, 1917, at the height of the First World War. Sentenced to death as a German spy even though she was in fact working for the French.

Then Ingrid froze the movie at the precise moment when Garbo steps out of her prison cell. I checked the figures on the single frame onto which they had been written against that same key sentence from my childhood—but got nowhere. However I tried to read the sequences, I could make no sense of them. Ingrid laid paper and pen before me on the floor and I wrote down the numbers and letters, exactly as they occurred to me in my unconscious. 111 319 172 015 151 65K 101 117 10C O31 018 412 P10 R24 151 2O1 24.

I felt the heat of her stare from beside me. My cheek began to glow, as if it were about to catch fire.

"Use your imagination, Erasmus. Your wonderful memory. Our common history. Because what was it that you wrote to me when you signed the dissertation? You must recall, surely? That sentence on the front cover which I tore out and immediately burned, just to be on the safe side, but will still remember for the rest of my long life."

Reflexes are a funny thing, the way memory works. Suddenly I started simply to speak the sentence out loud, even though I had devoted hardly any conscious thought to it for more than a decade. *To my dear supervisor and friend, who helped me enjoy the unrelenting hunt for Lise Meitner's half-century-old secret—although I never managed to find it.*

I did not even have to wait for Ingrid's reaction, since I already knew the answer was right. I started to decrypt the code with the aid of the new key sentence. The first letter of the first or maybe eleventh of its words, in both cases a "T". Then the first letter in the first or thirteenth word in the key sentence, again a "T" or an "H". I scribbled down the letters and the words, rapidly found my way through to possible and less likely alternatives. What the clear text soon revealed was not actually a message on its own—it was just meant to be hooked onto the earlier one.

I read it out aloud for Ingrid, as if in class.

"THESE ARE THE CODES—THAT WILL MAKE THE CODES SUPERFLUOUS".

Ingrid nodded calmly. Then, in a gentle, matter-of-fact tone, almost hypnotically:

"An entirely new program, my treasure. The file size doesn't alter when new information is added, which was of course other-wise the weak point in digital steganography, as you know."

"Yes, but what does it mean?" I said.

"Oh, I think that will become obvious when the time comes."

She closed the window showing the map of the world, as well as Greta Garbo surrounded by guards in the frozen "Mata Hari" scene. All the sequences of numbers hidden inside one single frame of the movie.

"So this is our insurance, yours and mine, in case neither of us can remember the code at the crucial moment. As we stand there with the weight of the world on our shoulders. Now you too have a chance to learn it. In one day, two, a week, maybe a month—until it's time for the final combat. The battle for our souls. For the future of mankind. Before then you have to know it by heart, my treasure."

Ingrid closed the lid of the portable command terminal, folded her body together softly. I still felt her gaze burning in from the side but I kept on staring straight ahead. Tried to control my nausea, the classic side-effect of subliminal tampering on my cere-bral cortex, the very depths.

"Because man thinks that it's he who controls the nuclear weapons system. But there's probably no need for me to remind you about computers, Erasmus, the 'war games' phenomenon, the entire space program, nuclear power which did not come into the picture until more than twenty years after nuclear weapons. Everything which we originally created for the sake of that system and not for ourselves. So it's not we who control the nuclear weapons. It's still they who control us."

Only then did I look at her, right into her eyes, perhaps because she took my arm and turned me carefully to face her.

"And yes, my treasure, I do doubt—that we will actually rise to the challenge, you and I. Every waking moment, all through the nights. That we really will be able to stand up to our own darkest sides. The entire Doomsday syndrome."

6.09

After that, we bided our time.

I recorded Ingrid's story in my notebook, detailed everything she had told me. I also continued my rock-hard training sessions on the mattress and took freezing showers, while Ingrid spread herself out more and more across the room with her yoga *asanas*, like a spider.

At other times I clicked away with my magical Bruegel cube from Peer. Changed "The Tower of Babel", with the cloud of smoke extending from the apertures in the building, through the other works all the way to "The Fall of the Rebel Angels" and back again. Checked the functionality of the hybrid twice each day. The keyboard's launch mechanisms, the safety procedures, the whole process. The age-old information with the President's options in case of a nuclear attack. "The biscuit". And in the late evenings I went for dogged runs outside when the whole building closed down at night, tasted freedom. Listened to the sounds from the apartments below us. The clinking and the music, the soft murmuring.

At night—before the dreams took over, those terrible images— I was convinced that they had to be the sound of prayers. A sort of plea for the future of mankind.

I also began to re-read my dissertation, from cover to cover. Looked at my reproduction of "The Triumph of Death", rolled up in my pack. Forever trying to find some sort of answer to it all: the enigma which I was facing.

And then there was the homework which Ingrid had given me. Together we watched the ending of "Mata Hari", over and over again. Recognized the subliminal effects of the steganographic message. "THESE ARE THE CODES—THAT WILL MAKE THE CODES SUPERFLUOUS". We let it wash over us both, in strange long sessions, as we had during our work on my dissertation. Systematically burned the codes into our synapses.

Ingrid hardly ever left her command terminal, never went out, barely ever got up from the mattress on the floor except to prepare food or go into the bathroom. When the leftovers from our Christmas dinner ran out—both the turkey and the panettone—there was the whole of the larder to get through. She made soup from lentils and beans, pasta dishes with no real taste: food for food's sake.

And then we stared through the window. I gazed far away into the distance, down toward the sea, the escape I could never really bring myself to make, however many opportunities my evening runs miles away from the apartment afforded me. Looked at the world as if each sight was going to be my last. She seemed to gaze in a more concrete way, examining, reconnoitering. Always fully on the look-out for our pursuers.

But eventually there was not much else to resort to except the T.V. As time passed we left C.N.N. on throughout the day, bellowing out the world's course, that theatrical chatter which was both comforting and threatening. Especially since it was increasingly about our issue in particular, our field. What Ingrid called her *arrangements*.

The evening programs began more and more often with the headline "THE NUCLEAR WEAPONS SCANDAL", white block letters against a black background. There were now two additional bullet points in the short summary:

April 2013:
    In an unprecedented move, an Air Force commander stripped 17 of his officers of their authority to control and launch nuclear missiles.
    The officers, based in Minot, North Dakota, did poorly in an inspection. They were ordered to undergo 60 to 90 days of intensive refresher training on how to do their jobs.

August 2013:

A missile unit at Malmstrom Air Force Base failed a safety and security inspection "after making tactical-level errors – not related to command and control of nuclear weapons," the Air Force Global Strike Command said.

The 341st Missile Wing operates about 150 of the 450 Minuteman III nuclear-tipped intercontinental ballistic missiles in the U.S. forces, according to an Air Force statement.

October 2013:

A military officer with high-level responsibility for the country's nuclear arsenal lost his job.

He was formally relieved of his duties as deputy chief of U.S. Strategic Command. A military official said his demotion was connected to allegations that he used counterfeit gambling chips at a casino.

October 2013:

Just days later, a U.S. general who oversaw nuclear weapons was relieved of his duties after he boozed, fraternized with "hot women" and disrespected his hosts during an official visit to Russia, Air Force officials said.

The General led the 20th Air Force, responsible for three nuclear wings.

According to an Air Force Inspector General report, he bragged loudly about his position as commander of a nuclear force during a layover in Switzerland, saying he "saves the world from war every day".

December 2013:

The Secretary of Defense is forced to resign—in the wake of what is now generally known as the Nuclear Weapons Scandal.

January 2014:

At the Montana base, 34 Air Force officers entrusted with maintaining nuclear missiles are accused of cheating or turning a blind eye to cheating on a competency test.

One evening toward the end of January 2014 there was also a feature which the news anchor delivered with a slight smile. She announced that the channel's special reporter had at last been given access to one of our large missile bases, after months of negotiation, although the reporter had promised not to reveal which base it was. But according to our sources, the news anchor continued, conditions are approximately the same everywhere. "And this is what our reporter saw. Look carefully: you will not believe your eyes!"

What followed was an almost satirical piece about the analog technology at the nuclear weapons bases. For the female reporter who had managed to get into the top security base, everything seemed as laughable as it was terrifying: the enormous missiles, the pointless round-the-clock state of readiness, the huge cracks in the facade.

She latched in particular onto the fact that the guidance system still used floppy discs to store the literally life-or-death information. That both the codes and the procedures existed only on what remained of this age-old technology, with no reasonable possibility of backup or synchronization with other systems. Her facial expressions heavy with meaning, the reporter also revealed that there was only one functioning adjustable spanner to tighten the nuts on the warheads of our 450 Minuteman III missiles. And that this spanner was couriered back and forth between our underground nuclear missile bases in North Dakota, Wyoming and Montana.

She could not say, nor even understand, that this was how we wanted it. That Edelweiss had in the end managed to persuade us in the Team of the increasing superiority of the low-technology approach. That the absence of an industrial standard and any recognizable structures made it much more difficult for anybody to penetrate our systems using high-tech methods. That our most senior commanders had started to take their critics seriously some years ago. Those who were sounding warnings that a system which was always "on-line" and in "stand-by mode", with several thousand nuclear missiles ready to destroy our civilization in just a few minutes, had to be the most attractive of targets for the world's most advanced hackers. Regardless of what their motives might be.

At the same time, an amorphous system like this made Ingrid's work in linking it all together even more complex. But, as she herself used to say in reply to the students' repeated complaints that everything was so endlessly complicated, all these links between different disciplines and centuries constituted the very historical framework of moral philosophy: "And who ever said that it was going to be simple?"

But there was still nothing on the news about our flight, hers or mine. About the briefcase itself having been removed from the system, together with one of the two portable command terminals. Not a word about the most fateful thing of all.

And that same evening I found the courage to ask Ingrid why. She turned her eyes away from the televisions. Explained it once more, as if to a child.

"Ed and we are still chained to each other, my treasure. He knows very well that I'll reveal everything as soon as he makes any serious attempt to capture us. And what's more that I've planted a Plan B. with some other person on this earth—without him having any idea who it is. Who might be the Needle in the Haystack, among the world's seven billion inhabitants. Who won't be able to cause as much damage as you and I, it's true, but with the help of some of my chosen supporters still enough to eliminate nuclear weapons as a military strategic tool for decades to come, if not longer."

"Was that why Edelweiss let us go at Dulles?" I said.

"Perhaps. Or else he wants to see where it all leads, follow the threads the whole way. Or maybe just give himself time to understand our irrational style of play. The fact that we were prepared to offer up Jesús María in exchange for John: a black knight for a pawn. Or maybe he's just turned."

Then she said nothing more—and I did not ask.

When C.N.N. at last changed topics, we switched to the local news. Ingrid no longer needed to translate the items about the M.U.O.S. base, very close to us here, 3.24 miles according to her computer. The pictures told their own story. The protests and incursions, the whole resistance, seemed to grow by the day. As did the violence of the reaction. The T.V. images showed another encounter between encroaching activists and the local authorities: that is to say a loose mixture of Sicilian policemen, N.A.T.O. forces and American security guards. Young women being beaten nearly unconscious with batons. A soldier stamping three times on an activist who already lay on the ground, trying to shield his head with his hands.

The next feature showed another eruption on Etna. We sat spellbound, watching that thick, glowing mass consuming everything in its path. A natural weapon that still nobody could protect themselves against. I could not help thinking of the parallel with our assignments, now and always. The merciless snail's pace, that slowly gnawing panic, terror, petrification or obliteration.

* * *

But when the signal finally came, toward the end of February, it was unmistakable. I knew it in the same instant that I saw the headlines on C.N.N. This would be Ingrid's starting point—as well as that of the military authorities at the M.U.O.S. base. The moment when everyone would be looking in another direction.

The fuzzy images in the darkness showed soldiers without uniforms. Quick, almost invisible movements in low resolution. Their clothes tight-fitting and jet-black, darker than the surrounding night, what was called "general combat wear". In theory they could have been any mercenaries. Yet all those in the know were very clear about where they came from. That the persistent rumors to the contrary were disinformation, cyberattacks, red herrings. Just the sort of hybrid warfare that we ourselves had been trained for—and against—throughout our adult lives.

There had been many warnings that Russia would occupy Ukraine, probably going in via Crimea, even from our own observers. Those who had long been obsessing about the traditional enemy. That it was Russia which would continue to be our main sparring partner, regardless of the fact that the headlines were talking about al-Qaeda or Iran or I.S. Whatever that alarming group now happened to call itself.

The C.N.N. commentators seemed almost relieved that the natural order of things had been re-established. That it was us versus them once more, west against east. One of the presenters already used the expression "Cold War 2.0".

And if Ukraine had not, after the fall of the Berlin Wall, handed over its nuclear weapons to Russia, in return for what was then called *protection*, the tension could rapidly have become apocalyptic. When the images shifted to Moscow—where soldiers were seen leaning out of train windows, their loved ones cheering and crying all at once, and men in bars were following the crisis on wide-screen T.V.s as if it were a sporting event—I came to think of the crowds on docks and station platforms waving soldiers off to the First World War. To what was meant to be a triumphal march, a walk in the park.

According to the experts in the studio, Russia had brought its new S.S.27 long-range missiles into service just a week or so earlier. And days after the Russians' gigantic training maneuvers on the theme "Simulated large-scale nuclear weapons attack", which they otherwise used to hold in the fall, our forces had replied with yet another comprehensive "Global Lightning" exercise. So the game was already in full swing.

In addition, what our security services had been warning us

about for many years had now been made public in the usually reliable magazine *Foreign Policy*. The C.N.N. anchor asked the experts for their views on what the Russians themselves simply called "Status-6". Their plans for a new underwater drone armed with a powerful thermonuclear weapon, causing especially high levels of radiation, designed, for example, to attack New York's harbor area. Making the city essentially uninhabitable for decades to come, through both its primary and secondary effects. Rather like Edelweiss' simulations: the hydrogen bomb over Manhattan slowly blossoming out on the screen.

Some of the experts in the studio pointed out another remote but natural association: between the continuing "Nuclear Weapons Scandal", with burned-out missile operators cheating on safety tests as a matter of routine, and the growing crisis in Crimea. That a cure for the missing sense of purpose they had felt was perhaps near at hand. And that "our boys", as he expressed it, might now have an objective in their minds following the Crimean crisis. Not just the underground missile forces, but also the men handling our nuclear missiles on submarines, or bombs from aircraft. That this would at least get them to pull themselves together.

I tried to read his facial expression. Whether he was being serious, or just trying to be amusing. In this situation.

The wind had been building up over the last few days; the first scirocco of the year was rattling the window panes. Even the indoor temperature rose by the hour in line with the strength of the wind. I put aside thoughts of going for a last run around the area, some sort of meaningless reconnaissance. Instead I went to bed at the same time as Ingrid turned off the T.V.s and returned to her terminal.

"It's confirmed," she said, "the inauguration of the M.U.O.S. base will be tomorrow."

6.10

I dreamed I was General Curtis LeMay, some time during 1954, the year which he had foretold as Ragnarök. When we were for the first time to confront the full military potential of the Soviet Union, following the introduction of nuclear weapons into the world.

We sat gathered together before an early form of computer, the whole potent little command group of S.A.C., Strategic Air Command. I had finally managed to plant at least the idea in their minds. Let our spy planes fly so close to the frontier that they could ratchet up Russian preparedness to the point where an attack against them might feel justified.

There is an historic moment, I said, breaking the silence, when we could win a nuclear conflict with Russia. That moment is now. Not earlier, not later. The Russians will need a month to deploy their 150 hydrogen and atomic bombs in total. Our 750 will need no more than a few hours.

The bulky computer helped me to illustrate the unthinkable, unfolding events step by step. With the help of an astonishing level of technology for the time, successive maps showed the evolution hour by hour, how the Soviet Union was being covered by ever thicker lines. Each line represented a separate flank in the attack. Everything pointed straight at the heart of Russia, Moscow, and on the way there the rest of the country was being wiped out as collateral.

The final image was not a map but a manipulated photograph. It represented the whole of enemy territory as one single smoking, radioactive, stony desert. Across the picture was a single line, in vivid yellow capital letters: "THE SOVIET UNION, 1917–54. R.I.P."

Then I pressed the button, transforming simulation into reality. A calm warmth spread through my body.

6.11

I was woken up by my cell phone. A Swedish number, one that I did not recognize. After a while I decided to answer—just as the caller rang off.

Waiting for a message to be left, I looked at my wrist-watch. Time 02.31, indoor temperature 82.2. The mattress was soaked with sweat in the stifling scirocco heat. I thought about opening a window, but there was no catch to hold it. The wind would immediately have smashed the cracked pane against the wall.

I listened, looked, and listened again, but no message came into my voicemail. Ingrid was sitting at the kitchen table, turned away from me, with the costume make-up spread out over the wax tablecloth. The light of the moon was so strong that she needed no lamp. Its bluish sheen tinged the whole apartment in a new tone, with the whining of the wind as an eerie backdrop of sound.

"Who was that?" she said, without turning around.

"I've no idea."

I got up from the mattress, showed her the cell phone, the numbers still on the display.

"That's Aina," she said.

"What would she want with me? And no message either . . ."

"Women of our generation don't like leaving them, you know. Or what was on her mind was something she didn't feel like recording. Why don't you call her, my treasure?"

When I pressed the green button, the recall function, I tried to picture Aina lying there alone on a February night in Ursvik. How Sixten might have just left her and started to make his way down here. Having heard the news from Crimea last night and understood the significance. How Aina might not have been able to get any sleep in his rare absence. Staring out of her window at the snowdrifts—before picking up the phone at last, and choosing me to call.

I called back, but pressed the red button before she answered. Did not pick up her next call, or the one after that. Could not really find room for Aina's anxiety too. For Sixten, for the world—and maybe for us.

Then I laid the cell phone aside, sat down on the other side of the kitchen table and looked at Ingrid's changing face. How it seemed older with each dab of costume make-up. How she was overtaking her real age, somewhere around seventy if I was to believe her stories. How she placed the Lucia crown on her head, tried it out, grimaced into her pocket mirror.

There is something about the scirocco. In Sicily it is said to be a mitigation for women who kill their husbands under its influence.

"A penny for your thoughts, Erasmus."

She turned to me in the pale blue-light of the moon, this suddenly aged woman. Or perhaps it was my own imagination which made her look different. It was as if I too were feeling the effects of the scirocco, its faintly occult power, the bewitching wind which ripped and tore at the shutters.

"None at all, Ingrid. Not a single one," I said.

She let her gaze dwell on me, waiting. Then filled my silence.

"I spotted you immediately, my treasure, already during that first lecture. Saw your full potential. And now it's time for your exam. We two against the world."

Ingrid got up, put on her pack. Passed the hybrid to me: I accepted it without a word. Looked at my wrist-watch. At 04.00, the witching hour, we left our safe house for the last time. Swapping some sort of security for a fundamental uncertainty. Not only for us, but for the whole of mankind.

Once we were outside, my watch showed 75 degrees, in the middle of the night, February 22. My cheeks began to glow as I followed Ingrid along a new path in the shelter of the mountains, below the ridge, hidden from the moon—much quicker than the calm miles during my evening runs. The weight of the hybrid was distributed equally between my back and stomach, thanks to Jesús María's genius. There was not a cloud in the sky and the light was magical. I looked up, into space, experienced the weight and lightness of the moment. Felt like a reed in the warm strong wind, a mere insect, a dwarf spider. Shivered again despite the temperature.

Once we had come some way into the ravine, Ingrid forked off due south, through a small cleft leading to the durum fields which ran gently down to the sea. It was of course only a diversion. The sort of thing that people like us did without even thinking, as synchronized now as in Kiruna. Then she found her way back to our original course, a classic zigzag, adapted to the natural obstacles of the mountain.

Soon our pace was down below 8.3 minutes per mile, even with the hot south-east wind directly in our faces. Ingrid was always in the lead, the "Destroyer of the Universe" coursing through the illuminated landscape. Since the full moon was like a spotlight, keeping close to the lee of the mountains, we sought out shadows.

In the hollow down near the M.U.O.S. base itself—where we could, for the first time, make out the enormous antennae, the topography having concealed them until then—we paused. Drank, ate one crunch cookie each, checked our surroundings from the shelter of the last small olive grove above the facility. Gazed at the anarchic mass of people and tents, which left very little open space on the vast, steppe-like slope below us.

This area alone must have been nearly four square miles in size, 2470 acres, the equivalent of almost two thousand football fields. It had of course been strategically correct to put the base here. So as not to risk being hemmed in by any form of attack, as could have been the case in a bowl between the mountains. It had allowed us to hold frequent joint maneuvers of air and ground forces on a larger scale. Have the space to really roll out the foot soldiers. Sometimes entire divisions with tens of thousands of infantrymen, rehearsing chaotic combat operations with drones hovering overhead.

But the enormous open space in front of the base also offered a perfect gathering place for activists. And even if half a million of them were to turn up here for the inauguration today, at this remote corner of the island, they would still have twenty-one square feet of ground apiece.

Not as many as that had come, at least not yet. But the distinctive noise of the mass—a roar of whistles, songs and chanted slogans, both in unison and dissonant—could be heard clearly all the way up in our olive grove, about a half a mile away, even though it was not yet 5.00 a.m. In all likelihood none of them would have slept that night. Just stayed awake and watchful, let the jungle drums sound out, after having picked up the same news that Ingrid received on her portable command terminal. That the inauguration would take place some time during the coming day. That the authorities believed the peace movement too would be focusing on Crimea, on "Cold War 2.0", and not this place. Which seemed a gross misjudgment given the number of activists who had gathered around the base.

The first activists must have been in place for days and nights, maybe even weeks. In the sharp light of the full moon we could see that the tent villages had a permanent look about them, seemed fully established, homely in a chaotic way, with swim-wear and towels hung out to dry, their dots slowly climbing up the surrounding slopes. At regular intervals, delighted little cries even penetrated the mass when the scirocco gusted across the slope before the base, making the camps in their entirety shiver, the costumes flutter.

When Edelweiss held his special presentations we had often expressed surprise at the tactical thinking—or rather the lack of it—of the peace activists. But he made it clear that it was not a matter of short-term tactics but rather of a long-term strategy. That for them it was at least as important just to be seen, to shape opinion and stimulate debate, as it was to make their way into the base unseen.

With the help of their different costumes, they could also bring together the conflicting objectives of the protesters in a light-hearted way: they attracted attention as well as offering camouflage. The way in which the activists dressed up had also developed in international demonstrations in recent years. Become a sort of pacifist *haute couture*, some kind of arms race of love. And here in Sicily the costumes really seemed to have become one with the age-old carnival traditions of the island.

After the sun had come up at 06.41, and dawn began to draw out the colors of the activists, Ingrid and I could just tick off the standing figures. All these complex anti-heroes borrowed from the dramas of antiquity. Ten or so Lysistratas and as many again Medeas. And in addition the authentic heroes: Mahatma Gandhi, Alva Myrdal, Eleanor Roosevelt, any number of each of them. Edelweiss had assured us that this too was a part of the activists' cold-blooded strategy. That a large number of entirely disparate individuals, ranging from real idealists to genuine terrorists, could wear exactly the same outfits. So that the powers-that-be should never know who lay behind which disguise.

Here too as at Kleine Brogel there were a number of examples of what he had, during his presentations on the threats posed by peace demonstrations, called the Love Dress. Pink wigs and glitter on cheeks, piercings everywhere, grotesquely large lips and breasts, false penises, much naked flesh on both women and men.

On top of that, figures out of the *Bhagavad Gita*. Often extreme allusions to what Robert Oppenheimer, with his interest in religions, is said to have thought during the first test of an atomic bomb in the New Mexico desert on July 16, 1945—code-named Trinity, like my youngest daughter. Only weeks before the invention was tested for real over Hiroshima.

The quote had spread around the world following a T.V. interview many years later, long after Oppenheimer himself had started

410

to argue against the proliferation and use of nuclear weapons. When he revealed that he had come to think of those precise words as it became clear that the atomic bomb would actually work: "Now I am become death, the destroyer of worlds." Vishnu's words in the Gita, as he assumes his four-armed shape to persuade the Prince to do his violent duty.

And then there were images of the enemy, skeletons, demons, zombies. Many of them clearly inspired by Death on Blu's huge mural in Niscemi, that macabre figure playing the whole nuclear weapons system like one single finely tuned instrument.

But despite all these spectacular costumes, most striking still was the sheer number of people around the M.U.O.S. base. If the number of activists gathered at Kleine Brogel had been more than one hundred thousand, here there already seemed to be twice as many. Despite the base's remote location—and the fact that there were still some hours to go before the formal inauguration.

But the peace activists had recently got fresh wind in their sails, all around the world. Alongside their reporting on the Nuclear Weapons Scandal, C.N.N. had been covering recent developments at the U.N. General Assembly. A joint proposal by a number of smaller states to launch negotiations on a treaty outlawing nuclear weapons had, against all expectations, been adopted.

The small states' logic was as simple as it was compelling. According to the resolution there were only two alternatives. Either nuclear weapons were not a means of combat sanctioned by the laws of war, in which case they should be forbidden under international conventions, or they should be regarded as a legitimate weapon. Which in turn meant that all states should be permitted to acquire their own nuclear weapons, on the basis that it was not for the U.N. to prescribe a fundamentally unequal world order.

None of the experts in the studio had thought that the resolution had any chance of success, despite all of that. But that a proposal for negotiations was at least adopted was in itself a victory. The first public sign of life in years from the peace movement.

Not long after that there were huge demonstrations against Britain's proposed renewal of Trident, the new generation of nuclear weapons, its own revitalization. The seventy-five thousand who gathered in and around Trafalgar Square represented the largest nuclear weapons protest since three hundred thousand had gathered in Hyde Park more than thirty years before, in 1983, against the deployment of cruise missiles at Greenham Common.

The renewal of interest around the nuclear weapons question had persuaded even the largest American media companies to make the pilgrimage all the way to little Niscemi—and, after the ever-complicated choice between definitely appearing in a bad light sooner, or eventually doing so later, our administration seemed to have given way to pressure and approved the applications for accreditation. The sanctioned white press buses stood neatly lined up at a safe distance from the base, in fact at rather more than a safe distance.

Partly because the activists' camp now covered an area with a radius of about half a mile, maybe more. Partly because nobody really knew how far the effects of the possible confrontation would spread.

So the scene was set. The inauguration of the fourth and final global M.U.O.S. base, the completion of our new communications system with its enormous but partly hidden potential, would most likely be the lead story in the American T.V. stations' morning news programs, thanks to the time difference. Or rather: the violent clashes which would soon be taking place around the inauguration.

This was what Ingrid was expecting. The maximum possible focus, but in the wrong direction, that age-old magician's trick. So that the real drama could unfold elsewhere, probably in some place deep beneath the surface of the facility.

It was now 07.49, the temperature 77.5 degrees here in the shade of the olive grove. The sun was shining mercilessly on the activists in their costumes and the defenders in their tight uniforms. The force of guards still did not seem nearly strong enough to be able to stop the activists from storming the base, did not appear to have been reinforced in any significant way. Nor could I detect any of our pursuers. Not Zafirah, who preferred to operate alone in the heat of things, but was presumably now supported by some of the President's own most capable security staff. Not Edelweiss either—he would likely still be in Washington, directing the drama.

The pursuit had to be concluded in the same silence which had governed it for more than five months. Even those on our trail had to synchronize their actions with the movements of the crowd, as did we: both hunters and hunted, trying hard not to risk drawing the slightest attention from the media apparatus in curious attendance here, not to disclose the black hole at the heart of our organization. And thereby lend the headline "NUCLEAR WEAPONS SCANDAL" a new dimension.

Revealing that a very small group of people had so much operational power. The top secret war plan, for the most part still unapproved. The existence of an Alpha whose mandate in certain cases exceeded that of the President himself. The man with the briefcase, the nuclear football, like a pulsating red light at the very center of our group. And finally: that the two of us had been on the run together since September of the previous year.

Ingrid and I stared into the gigantic crowd, the absurd carnival. There was no sign of Sixten either. He had told her that he would not be joining us until the moment of the attack, when the tumult would start to build up. And she said that she did not want to risk arousing suspicion among those using drone images to analyze the internal structure of the mass, in case they began to follow our movements more closely, placing their digital markers on us.

She looked at her wrist-watch—and turned to me for the first time since we had arrived at the olive grove.

"You wouldn't like to call Aina again, my treasure?"

I took out the cell phone, saw that I had five missed calls from her number. Called my own number, let the engaged tone ring for a certain length of time.

"No answer and no voicemail," I said.

"Then it probably wasn't anything important, my treasure."

When eventually the sun fell on the olive grove she took the last of Jesús María's preparations out of her own combat pack. The final remnant of that woman's jet-black humor. Without a word I put on the full beard, the curly black wig and the torn brown shift made of homespun cloth. Realized what she was trying to get at—even though I knew that from the outside I would look no different from all the other martyrs around the perimeter of the base.

It was my mother who told me the whole story, long before I was old enough to understand the detail. She always emphasized that she had been thinking of Erasmus of Rotterdam when deciding on my name, the great European humanist, the symbol for an entirely new world: he who disputed the issue of free will with Martin Luther. But she also told me the colorful story of St Erasmus, who had been born in 240 and died in 303, one of the many victims of the Emperor Diocletian's persecution of Christians. And it was my mother who first told me that the saint's symbol was a windlass and that he was martyred by having his intestines slowly wound up on one. As time went on I became almost obsessed with the grim fate of the saint. And Jesús María had put his symbol onto my outfit, elegantly but discreetly. On the lower part of my top, level with my intestines, there was a small windlass embroidered in blood-red thread against the brown of the fabric.

Ingrid scrutinized me, my look yet again entirely new, as if she were trying to get to the bottom of something. I had to look away. At that she put on her own simple outfit, on top of her general combat gear. It looked exactly the same as in Belgium: a white nightshirt cut off above the knees so as not to inhibit movement, blond wig, crown of light in her hair which she would cast off before we went in. Allowed ourselves to be washed along in the big wave of activists, before moving off on our mission once inside the gates.

I could see almost thirty more Lucias along the base's perimeter fence, without even having to pick up my field glasses. In all probability the most common of all the ensembles being worn by the activists. So there was little risk that anybody would connect Ingrid to the incident inside Kleine Brogel, that inexplicable electrical fault, the sudden smoke at the base.

According to legend, St Lucia came from Syracuse—a hundred miles to the south-east from here, and died just one year after Saint Erasmus. After her torture, Lucia ended up as a prostitute in a brothel. In due course she too, according to the typically convoluted myth, had both boiling oil poured over her and a sword pierce her throat, surviving both. Only when somebody nevertheless gave her the last rites, was she able to be at peace and leave this mortal coil.

Ingrid picked up what looked like a normal lighter and lit the candles before placing the crown on her head, although it was hard to see the flames in the bright sunlight. There was a slight smell of crude rubber or oil. The candles did not blow out even when the wind gusted in the olive grove. They were probably made with some special agent, some chemical witch's brew.

Then she led us out from the treeline, traversing the slope down toward the installations. None of the security guards who had mingled with the activists made any move to obstruct our way as we took our place by the sign which said "MARTYRS FOR PEACE".

The crowd grew by the minute. Normal people, those who were curious, family members, full-blown idealists who had taken the day off from their jobs in the village or perhaps didn't have one in this depopulated area. Global peace activists from far away, with well-worn routines from scores of similar demonstrations. Thanks to the costumes it was as hard as ever to distinguish the professionals from the amateurs. Streamers with the "No M.U.O.S." message were hanging on the fence surrounding the establishment, like strings of white glue binding it all together, while none of the guards made any move, vastly outnumbered as they were. Gradually the activists inched forward. The mass' slow landslide.

I then heard a dull roar, first thinking that it must be thunder from some distance away, the normal climax of a scirocco. I looked up at the clear-blue sky—and saw that it was filled with drones from Sigonella.

After that the all-terrain buses arrived, together with the airborne convoy. The Marine One helicopter was escorted by about ten others from the H.M.X.1 squadron in Quantico, Virginia. The special forces troops streamed out of the buses, made straight for the gates, where they lined up in full readiness. The dark bellowing of thousands of soldiers with their adrenaline pumping, even before anything had started to happen. The lighter yelling from the protesters, by now surely closer to three hundred thousand.

Through the field glasses I saw the doors of Marine One opening and our new Secretary of Defense step out. If it really was him—and not just a double. Dropped into the ceremony to mark how important the installations were, the entire M.U.O.S. system, while the real Secretary stayed in Washington to plan our strategy for responding to the developing crisis in Crimea.

He had a Carrier at his side. A dummy, for the sake of appearances, as was the briefcase in the Carrier's hand. The apparatus which, according to Ingrid, would now have lost all meaning as it was decoupled from the system.

Then came another dull sound from all around us, of people rather than machines. The enormous mass divided, like the Red Sea, while a small figure in a devil's mask made his way slowly but determinedly toward the gates.

"Blu," Ingrid said.

I watched his progress: a Messiah being urged on by people thumping him enthusiastically on the back, lifting him up through

416

the crowds. Even twelve-year-old Unity knew about him, had talked about his work. How he made his breakthrough in the suburbs of Bologna and had then wandered all over the world like a ghost. Never more than one mural, or exhibition, at a time in any one place. Identity unknown, computer not connected to the internet, all the necessary measures taken to avoid being traced. His face always in different masks.

Yet he had painted two murals specifically here in Niscemi, in the same place, for the first time in his career. Once Blu had arrived at—or rather been led all the way to—the main gate, he turned around and shouted something which I could not hear. At that, a long line of women wearing black dresses and shawls started moving. They too were allowed to make their way through the crowds to the front line of activists. There they spread out along the wide expanse of the circle. Silence fell over the scene, a sort of collective gathering of breath.

Ingrid checked her watch and I did the same: time 12.51, temperature 96.4 degrees in the burning sun. The sweat was already itching under my clothes. She turned her eyes to me, still in her magical burning crown of light, with that look.

"Now it starts, St Erasmus," she said, with expectation in her voice.

As if we were at the movies. Or watching a classical tragedy.

6.12

It began with Blu climbing to the very top of the fence. Securing himself with his feet and starting to wave his arms. He was a master at parkour, a seasoned urban explorer, accustomed to finding his way in everywhere to access the perfect painting surface. Through my field glasses I observed the soldiers studying him, their bodies tensed and ready, trying to decide whether he was holding any form of weapon. But in the end they just let him sit there and wave in his devil mask: a bad strategic decision.

Because it looked as if what Blu was doing was conducting events—which turned out to be the case. With his long arms and eloquent hands he set the whole course of events in motion.

The dark humming rose from the women in black, who, maybe inspired by the Mothers of the Plaza de Mayo in Argentina, were perhaps campaigning for the health of their children and grand-children after the warnings about the risks posed by the parabolic antennae. The sound spread through the gathering, in a widening circle by the perimeter fence, dull and rhythmic like the chorus in a Greek drama. Only when it had reached all the way back to me and Ingrid, somewhere in the middle of the crowd, could I distinguish the two words. Even my Italian was good enough for that: I remembered the phrases from my mother's obsession with opera. The message could hardly be plainer.

"*Maledetto, Malefatto,*" the crowd chanted, over and again.

"A cursed and evil construction," Ingrid muttered to herself, or perhaps to me.

Yet the show had to go on: the Defense Secretary's speech, the inauguration, the authorities' own manifestation. At precisely 1300 hours the fireworks started, just to demonstrate that we had the ability to put on light shows which could be seen even when the sun was at its zenith here in Sicily. Then it was the turn of the

418

Secretary, just as the last car-shattering explosions were fading away, at exactly ten after.

He played his role perfectly, pretended not to notice the women's dull refrain now coursing rapidly throughout the immense crowd. The security troops stood still as the drones hovered above our heads.

The Secretary, or his double, said just what was expected of him. Played to his strengths. Empty phrases for the media about global security and addressing the terrorist threat. M.U.O.S. not only making it possible to co-ordinate global military forces, but also radically increasing each individual soldier's possibility of survival during complex operations.

This was not what the activists wanted to hear. The ability to wage war more easily, anywhere on the earth's surface. The new communications technology as the spearhead of something that nobody could yet oversee—and with the worrying side-effects of the powerful antennae.

Yet the answer from the crowd cannot have been what was expected. No furious booing, shrieks or howls, as at Kleine Brogel. Just that continuing dull, dark chant, the two words, four syllables each, rhythmic and foreboding. *Ma-le-de-tto . . . Ma-le-fa-tto . . . Ma-le-de-tto . . .*

Until the chorus suddenly stopped, at exactly the same time as the Secretary reached the end of his speech. That was the signal. And Blu jumping back down onto the ground outside the fence.

As he stood in front of the specially trained troops, our hardest-drilled forces, I did not need the field glasses to make out their fear, despite the machine guns at their chests and the high-tech armor covering them. You could tell from their postures, the theater of the body. How they recoiled before that little man with his only weapon a devil's mask. How the soldiers themselves put on their masks, folded down the riot helmet visors, assumed their roles.

And then everything let go. The collective energy of the

hundreds of thousands of activists was like a small nuclear charge. An ear-shattering roar of abuse and exaltation. A triumphant primal scream rising from the plain straight up toward the drones in the sky.

And if it had not been clear to me which strategy the military would be adopting when the time came, it became very obvious as soon as the special forces commanders stepped to one side—so that Blu could be the first of us all to get into the base.

Because a crowd of that size heading in one direction is a force of nature which cannot be resisted, unless one is prepared to use a level of violence which would be enough to turn public opinion very hostile. We had learned to measure the power of the crowd in terms of an equivalence with herds of buffalo, goods trains or steamrollers: calculating what Edelweiss called the Onslaught Effect.

As the front rows poured through the gates, thoughts of other historical processes from our times flashed through my mind. The fall of the Berlin Wall, perhaps the Orange Revolution in Ukraine, the Arab Spring. Events where the odds faced had been at least as high. Where one party had had such a hold on power, the arms were as unequally divided, the security forces both organized and strong. But where the undercurrents had been almost as impossible to foresee.

This nearly pacifist strategy was of course made all the easier for the military by the media's presence. The fact that all the journalists and photographers had dared to mingle with the activists, were rushing around with their cameras and notebooks, penetrating ever further into the burlesque chaos of fancy dress and heavily armed special forces. As at Kleine Brogel—but on an even larger scale here, with even more people in uncontrolled motion—there was quite simply no alternative but to admit us all. Despite the huge strategic importance of the installations.

Ingrid and I let ourselves be washed along in the wave. Ran quickly but carefully over a collapsed fence, giving the razor wire

420

a wide berth: it had already injured a number of people on the way in, cutting open clothes and flesh on any who were not aware of its multiple function, how it grabs onto things as well as slicing into them.

Blood from the activists' lacerated calves and thighs could be seen against the pale gray of the cement flooring inside the gates. But still the tide of people kept rolling forward. Surging, spreading out in all directions at once, like water or gas.

One might think that a mass like this is a single flood wave, streaming in a certain direction. And in this case there must have been tens of thousands moving from the gate all the way over to the gigantic parabolic antennae—soon to be made famous by the direct transmissions of the T.V. companies' morning reports

But Edelweiss used to stop the reels during his lectures on mass psychology, winding forward and backward to demonstrate that only rarely was there any collective movement. Many of those who were now here, dragged along without any clear idea of what they were doing, would certainly have liked to turn back had they been able, were not after all willing to risk so much for their ideological convictions. Some others had already been panicked by the crush. Yet more had specific objectives, such as picking up some trophy from within the base.

The secret lay not so much in understanding that a mass heading in a certain direction always contains people moving against the flow—but rather *how* they do so. And then to match one's own movements scrupulously to this pixelated pattern.

Ingrid showed herself to be a master of just this. We were therefore able to move both with and against the swarm toward the eastern periphery of the facility, while the main wave surged toward the western part, where the M.U.O.S. antennae stood brooding on their secrets. One Lucia among certainly hundreds, perhaps more. One bearded martyr lost in a crowd of them. Without anybody apparently taking any notice of us.

The sweat was now itching inside my beard and costume.

Not even Jesús María's perforated fabric wicked enough of the condensation in what must have been approaching 104 degrees in the boiling sun. I did not take the time even to glance at my wristwatch, only kept looking straight ahead, following Ingrid's sure course through the sea of people. The hot wind lifted us forward, until I caught sight of our objective a few hundred feet ahead, through the chaos of costumed people. Everything grew quiet around me. I felt the hybrid against my body. Saw the whole train of events like a simulation on a computer screen. The activists, the soldiers, the choices of route open to us.

But in the end there is a limit to what is achievable. Ingrid's strategy showed itself to be a classic—and yet it would prove impossible. To take the back way into the underground level, through the emergency exit, in the opposite direction to the built-in logic of all security systems. The protective doors at our facilities could only ever be opened in one direction: nobody was allowed to move against the flow. And that is therefore the very thing that we were now going to attempt.

The air-intakes were the sign. We had always pointed out that the small ventilators were still not small enough, and therefore not invisible enough, to deter the enemy. Our technicians had just shaken their heads and said that they could not be made any smaller. If we were wanting to house more people underground, often for even longer periods according to our increasingly opaque scenarios, the air-intakes had to be larger.

So we knew what our target should be. As did, to judge from their actions, the two female figures who blocked our path, one about thirty feet in front of the other.

Alva Myrdal, the leading figure of the Swedish U.N. disarmament committee from the '60s, came straight at me. In other words Zafirah in the guise of the venerable stateswoman. Her body compact and small, the center of gravity low. It seemed to me that she had become more solid since I had last seen her, even more terrifying. The Team's most committed ultra-violence specialist.

It all went extremely fast. Out of the corner of my eye I saw Ingrid moving toward the air-intakes—but also another masquerade figure moving even faster in the same direction. Yet one more Eleanor Roosevelt, tall and sinewy with her muscles clearly visible through the long sleeves of her dress. It could hardly be anyone other than our Close Combat instructor. A nameless, melancholy woman from Rwanda, with unconventional techniques honed during their civil war. The only one who could defeat Zafirah in training.

But I was forced to shift focus. As Zafirah came in for the attack she began screaming. I looked at the open mouth behind the Alva Myrdal outfit and make-up, saw it move in slow motion, but heard no more sound whatsoever. Just focused on sliding into the fight zone. Minimizing the chances of her getting me onto my back, as she usually did, putting pressure on my larynx until the air ran out.

Much more easily than I would have expected, like in a dream, I got in close. As I grabbed hold of Alva Myrdal's wavy hair and managed to twist her head, with the same crunching sound as when you break the neck of a pike, she seemed to be trying to say something to me. Her mouth was still wide open. I knocked her over backward with a powerful shove to her chest, and kept banging her head against the cement, and then there was no longer any question of her speaking.

All this took place in silence, as if the volume had been turned off. I registered a very specific smell. Familiar, yet impossible to place, under the thick stench of blood and brain tissue in the heat.

I left the lifeless woman behind me. Rushed up to the two surviving women by the air-intake, the protective doors. Saw Eleanor Roosevelt throwing herself headlong over St Lucia. Heard the Close Combat instructor's surprisingly deep bellow cut through the hum of the crowd when she got Ingrid down onto the ground.

But St Lucia had a weapon to fight back with. From flat on her back she raised her upper body, in a slight bow, as the instructor sat down on top of her—setting fire to Eleanor Roosevelt's wig with her chemical crown of candles.

Although our tough instructor fought with immense courage as the flames spread inexorably through the wig, she had no chance in the end. However much she tightened her grip on Ingrid, trying to drag her down to hell with her, set her alight too. Because this Lucia was wearing a nightshirt made from a special impregnated fabric of Jesús María's.

Then I was paralyzed, frozen in movement as if I had been shot.

Because just as I reached Ingrid, and the combat instructor ran screaming like a banshee away across the base, with the flames reaching her scalp, spreading fire to other victims around the facility, I was suddenly able to place the smell which had risen from Alva Myrdal's dead form.

It was a ladies' perfume, perhaps the best known of them all. But I had met only two women who actually used Chanel No. 5 as their signature fragrance. The first was my mother, who was now in secure accommodation in an idyllically located home for dementia sufferers in northern Connecticut.

And the other was Aina.

6.13

So it turned out to be a classical drama after all. A tragedy of mistaken identity.

I suppressed the thoughts of Aina as we moved on silently through the low, dark system of culverts, in the opposite direction to what was intended, from the emergency exit inward rather than the other way around. I did not even raise my eyebrows when Ingrid simply led us in by pressing eight symbols on the buttons on the concealed control box and the doors opened.

Both the alarm and the surveillance cameras appeared to have been knocked out already, as well as the emergency lighting. Ingrid's Lucia crown lit the way for us. The glow projected my shadow onto the wall, flickering jerkily, the smell of raw rubber and fuel nauseating in the stifling tunnels. Whatever was burning in the crown must have been napalm or some more modern pyrochemical substance.

We had only occasionally had the opportunity to rehearse a scenario like this. It was based on the assumption that a mole had prepared the way in the facility in question, one of our missile bases under the prairies of the Mid West. Ingrid must have done something similar here in Niscemi—as part of all her planning over so many years, decades according to her, that secret global folk movement. All aiming for just this moment.

I felt the weight of our mission growing heavier step by step. The hybrid seemed suddenly to be filled with lead. Every step required an effort, as if I were moving under water. After a few minutes we reached the door: marked with a simple "C.C." in neutral gray letters. Thoughts were racing through my mind. On the other side was the place where not just our fate would be decided—but also yours, the fate of all future generations.

Reflexively I readied myself for close combat with the guards inside the command center, no doubt reinforced for the inauguration. Tensed myself. Drew my weapon, in case there was going to be space enough.

But Ingrid stopped fifteen feet short of the door. Began to fumble at the ceiling, until she found the control box for the entrance. The light from her Lucia crown now fell in a way which let me see what she was keying in on the tiny set of buttons under the lid—not the symbols themselves, but the movement of her fingers. The code had been the same up in Ursvik: everything is easy once you know. When she keyed in her "LISA 1969", a sliding door opened soundlessly to the right in the metal wall.

I had to work hard to follow Ingrid as she ran at top speed down the spiral stairs on the other side of the door, turn after turn. So as not to lose the light from her crown but at the same time keep my dizziness under control, and the nausea from the pyro-chemical smell. I clung onto the handrail. The piercing alarm must have been a figment of my imagination, all the mental warning lights flashing red in my mind. Yet they no longer helped: I paid no heed to her, just flung myself after.

Once down on level ground I just had time to see Ingrid open one more invisible door, following the same ritual, with the same code. Here too the sliding door opened in silence. When it closed again, sealing us off from the world, Ingrid turned to me and made a sweeping gesture across the control console.

"*Ecco*. What I amused myself with while the M.U.O.S. began to be built over our heads—since I had to be in the vicinity but invisible, as Alpha. I had help from more or less the same construction team who were working up there on the surface, but at odd times. And also a number of others who were ideologically committed. Activists, moles, daredevils. People who signed up for the military only to deconstruct it. The sort whose silence one never has to buy."

In here too the lights were out, but Ingrid's napalm candles were more than enough. She pulled out one of the two chairs in front of the control console for me and sat down in the other.

I sank into my seat. Scrutinized every one of the controls, all the possible functions, repeated the exact sequences of this techno-logical-occult ritual for myself while Ingrid continued.

"The only thing we really needed to communicate to the local commanders was the huge importance of the installations. That even if the sky were to fall, the project had to go on. No details beyond that—only that nothing was to be obstructed, that the M.U.O.S. protests had to be suppressed at all costs. So I never had to make myself known. Could just hover around down here like an underworld spirit, an Alpha who gave her oracular orders digitally, everywhere and nowhere."

I laid the hybrid on the floor, unlocked the keyboard, made the whole apparatus operational. Shut my eyes and just listened to that melodic voice.

"Yet not one of our secret helpers understood what I was doing during all those years; they were just working on a single piece of the puzzle and sometimes hardly even that. So no-one other than I, not even Ed, knew that this installation represented something so much bigger than the completion of the M.U.O.S. system. That the key to the whole of our nuclear weapons system was to be found here, 138.13 feet below the upper command center."

She took out her computer, the portable command terminal, opened up the lid, started to key in the access sequences. I did the same, following the rhythm exactly. The cold-blue light of the screen blended with the warm glow from her crown of candles. My own shadow quivered on the steel wall to my left, like a ghost, an unholy spirit.

"The thought was that nobody other than Sixten and I would need the codes down here. My thought during all the years— the thing that honestly kept me sane, just enough, kept the pot simmering—was that it would be him and me sitting here now. Reunited in just this moment."

I said nothing, nor could I utter a sound, just kept clicking my way into the system. Completed the first complicated series.

Just what was necessary for the screen to be revealed in the lid, the simulated fabric screen slowly sliding away to the right, Alpha's increasingly mannered security rituals. The puzzle pieces in the map of the world softly slid together, step by step: the sign that every one of the sequences was correct.

Only once the whole map became visible did the yellow triangles appear, one after the other, each needing another correct sequence of at least twenty-one and up to twenty-nine symbols. First our nuclear bases in Europe, now joined together with solid red lines. Then the image zoomed out over the Atlantic, to the U.S., the home nuclear bases. The numbers flickered before my eyes. I heard Ingrid's words as a part of this whole ritual, everything seeming to flow together.

"Because it was important for me to keep to our regular security routines, just in case one of us might not be able to resist the temptation, the Doomsday syndrome. So there has to be two of us, we two, even in here: *No Lone Zone*. But it had to be you instead of him, my treasure, my best stand-in. Sixten should instead be standing guard at the bottom of the spiral staircase outside this door. That is what he and I agreed when we spoke on Christmas Day."

I hacked ever deeper into the system, heard the muted sound of her keyboard at the same pace as mine. Her portable command terminal and my nuclear football. The man with the briefcase, the Carrier, with his Alpha. It ended with the blue lines meeting all across the world—all the way from Esrange in Kiruna to the one here in Niscemi. The Nuclear Family was now complete, all these *correspondences* under and above ground. Man had at last gained control over his own Fall.

I watched in awe as Ingrid stood up and placed a U.S.B. stick into one of the ports on the desk. The control console came alive, all the different screens lit up in blue and green, the monitor started with the same image as was on her computer and the inside of the lid of my briefcase. The world map, the bases, the yellow triangles.

Then she moved her chair closer to mine. I looked across at her—and she glanced back, gave me that look, before she fixed her gaze on her keyboard. Waited for me like an old jazz pianist. Counted the rhythm for herself.

The scene from the movie, when Mata Hari begins to tug at General Shubin's arm to stop him from revealing her beloved Rosanoff as a spy, flickered past in my subconscious. Then I saw the clear text in my mind's eye, "THESE ARE THE CODES ..." I keyed in the sequences following exactly the same rhythm as Ingrid: 151 221 621 11R 211 612 21C 19D 216.

On all the screens—both hers and mine, as well as on the large round monitor on the control console—the red circle above the globe, between all of our nuclear weapons bases, started to blink rhythmically. The text "RED ALERT" soon covered the world map.

My whole field of vision grew small, seemed to be sucked in toward my brain with a strange fizzing sound, soon vanished almost completely. My hands became heavy and stiff. However hard I tried, I could not move them an inch in any direction.

Through my tiny hole to the world I could see how Ingrid was now looking right into the innermost part of me, as if I had neither skin nor skeleton. Once again she waited out my own rhythm, the next step in our mission, the message which *en clair* read "THAT WILL MAKE THE CODES SUPERFLUOUS". The life-critical sequences, so that she could synchronize her own movements and do the same.

But since I sat there immobile, doing absolutely nothing, the alert status soon switched over to "FIRING MODE". All of our warheads around the world were now linked and ready to be fired off.

The text which appeared next on the screen I had never seen before. Not during any of Edelweiss' most unthinkable scenarios, our very worst simulations, had I been able to imagine that any conceptual possibility like this was indeed built into the system. "WARNING: EXTINCTION MODE," it said.

Yet my hands still lay there, like pieces of dead meat. The circles above the world started to blink in a fuzzy lilac, almost fluorescent color. This was the beauty of the apocalypse. A gentle electronic chirping sounded around the room. It could have been a shrieking alarm, maybe at full volume—but if so then tempered by my enclosed being, receptive only through that little hole to and from the world.

The yellow triangles on the monitor penetrated in my eyes, luminous with all their inconceivable significance. Villages, remote areas, hardly even places as such, which for some reason had been chosen to host our nuclear weapons according to the strategy we called "sharing". Who were allocated their predetermined roles in this classical tragedy.

I heard a ghostly voice in the room. It took a moment to realize that it was I myself who was rattling off the names, like a medieval incantation: "Incirlik, Araxos, Aviano, Ghedi Torre, Ramstein, Büchel, Volkel, Kleine Brogel, Lakenheath, Kings Bay, Whiteman, Barksdale, Minot, Warren, Malmstrom, Kitsap. And then Niscemi . . . Niscemi . . . Niscemi." The key to the entire system. The secret of secrets.

Only when Ingrid grabbed my right hand in her left, with surprising roughness—like a strict piano teacher trying to help an obtuse pupil with fingering, once more teacher and pupil, mentor and novice—did my body recall the rest of the code.

Every time Ingrid pressed my right index finger against the keyboard, at exactly the same time as she typed out the same sequences with her own right index finger, an ever larger part of the code appeared in my mind. We sped through the sequences together: 111 319 172 015 151 65K 101 117 10C O31 018 412 P10 R24 151 2O1 24, Ingrid driven in pursuit of her goal, focused on not just me but also on her own keyboard and the control console monitor.

"EXTINCTION MODE ACTIVATED". The briefcase flashing, the command terminal flashing. The consoles around flashing in bright red.

She gripped my hand tight, pulled it away from the keyboard. The light from the screens flooding dark shadows across her face then blanketing her features in white—her eyes wild, glistening—close to my own. I tasted the sourness of her breath, the fumes of napalm from her crown.

"Erasmus, my treasure. We have control. Our lonely little moment," she said. And moved closer. "Yet maybe not so lonely."

Ingrid pulled my hand to her own terminal using my index finger to sequence an unfamiliar code. A new map flooded all the screens: Russia, China, Iran, a field of yellow triangles tangled by red lines in a web across the giant land mass of Eurasia.

"I have had a little help over the years, Erasmus. In small corners. Do you understand me, Erasmus? Are you ready?"

Then I could not take any more. I remember violent retching—my body writhing from within to escape from itself—eyes bursting from my skull. I fell into the black beneath the table. Ingrid bent with me, soothing, stroking my hair with her free hand, the thin bones of her left still entwined around my own.

And that explained why not even she noticed the two other costumed figures in the command center. Maybe the figures had already been standing in here when we arrived, biding their time behind us while our concentration was so focused to the front, getting hold of our code sequences. Maybe they had followed the threads all the way in. I myself, however, only became aware of them when the grip on my wrist tightened to such an extent that it could no longer be Ingrid who was holding it. Then I recognized Zafirah's spiced scent, for the first time since the Ice Hotel. Her concentrated power applied to the arteries in both of my wrists.

I had hardly enough strength even to turn. Just caught a glimpse of Zafirah's furious, made-up presence behind me, modeled on Death: the image from Blu's mighty mural in Niscemi.

When in the next instant she cut the hidden main fuse, the whole control console went dead. Then Sixten cut the power to both my briefcase and Ingrid's computer, including the reserve batteries, not hesitating, knowing exactly how to do it. Needing nothing more than a free hand and the light from Ingrid's Lucia crown.

Not pausing, he opened the protective doors—smoothly keying the code: LISA 1969—and led Ingrid toward the spiral staircase. They seemed to me like an abstract sculpture. The tall woman and the even taller man. The two lovers with the projects they had once had together: Doomsday and the child.

He had his weapon against her throat, in a stranglehold she was unable to break, he as trained as she. Both in their masquerade costumes. Mahatma Gandhi and St Lucia, entwined, joined for one last time. She so decisively betrayed in her cut-off Lucia nightgown and theatrical crown of lights.

Not one of us said anything. We simply went up the stairs together, all four figures, in two pairs. When we came out through the sliding door by the upper command center, the special forces stepped in: six fully armed soldiers around each one of us. Sixten —Mahatma Gandhi, the pacifist—halted and waved his pistol at Ingrid.

"This woman will face a military tribunal for grave breaches of security."

Then Sixten turned to me with his steel-blue eyes, for the first time since our meeting again here. I saw clearly that he was crying, his voice cracking.

"But this man is an altogether different case. He killed my life companion up there, a few minutes ago. She had been my heart and soul for forty-five enchanted years. And he did it in the most savage way imaginable."

7

FINAL QUARTER

February–March 2014
Niscemi, Italy

7.01

It was not an interrogation in the conventional sense. But in Edelweiss' sense. Began only after endless waiting.

"Well, here we all are. Together again!"

Edelweiss seemed to be overlooking the fact that while there were indeed as many of us in the lecture hall as had been in NUCLEUS, six including Alpha, two were new. Kurt and John's replacements were dramatically different from each other—one tall and dark, the other short and ruddy—but functionally they were the same. Animals with no great evolutionary finesse. Muscles and reflexes, the most rudimentary wiring, trained to react to the slightest stimuli.

They were two out of the ten special security agents who had taken us under guard from the depths of the M.U.O.S. base and off-site to a secure location. The bodyguards were standing behind me and Ingrid on our stainless-steel revolving stools fixed to the podium floor. To avoid any repetition of the incidents at Dulles airport, no guard was secured to us. We were chained instead to the stools, with our hands cuffed behind our backs: an arrangement as good as escape proof.

While waiting for the interrogation to begin, the guards at regular intervals spun us around on our stools. Not for any reason I could make out—just because they could. In this particular moment in time, they had the power and the possibility.

These people probably had names too, some sort of designation, real or invented. But since none of them had as yet been used, I had no means of knowing what they were. I just said "Kurt-or-John," if for example I needed to go to the bathroom to throw up after some particularly rapid revolutions on my stool. A meaningless bit of fuss, which probably did not even register with them. But it was the only thing I could do in this situation. Thrash around a little under the gallows.

Edelweiss had moved himself here from our headquarters in anticipation of events, pulling his strings. Was sitting in his special chair, in the center of the first row of the audience seating. In the armchair to his left was the briefcase in its original guise: black and anonymous. The security strap was attached to his left wrist, in accordance with regulations. Ingrid's black backpack containing the portable command terminal was propped up against the briefcase.

So everything remained under cover, hidden. Machines and men, brooding over their secrets.

Zafirah, the other surviving member of our original Team, was one seat beyond the briefcase and the backpack. To the left and right of her and Edelweiss were framed photographs. On the low podium in front of them, a candle was burning. The portrait to the left, as I looked at it, showed a dark young man with a pronounced dimple in his chin. The one to the right was similar but with sharper features and blond hair that was crew-cut in those days. Both Kurt and John—whichever was which—looked so expectant in those old portraits. Ravenously curious about the future.

And then there was one other person here. Not in the audience seating, but on the podium, between me and Ingrid. He was even more shrunken than we were: seemed to have given up all hope. But he had no chains holding him down onto his stool, nor any guard standing behind him.

He finally drew the first question from Edelweiss.

"Would you like to tell us about the events out in the courtyard, Sixten? Describe what really happened here? Even though I know it will be hellishly difficult for you."

Sixten said nothing for several moments, and out of the corner of my eye I noticed his quick glance at both Ingrid and me. Although he cleared his throat several times, his voice over the microphone remained thick.

"Yes, hellish is the right word, Joseph. Pretty much impossible, I'd say."

436

So we all sat buried deep in his silence, almost drowning: *ten seconds, twenty seconds, thirty seconds* . . . The pressure mounted down here in the stuffy air of the lecture hall. What emerged at last was Sixten's description of the events at Niscemi, detailed but accurate as ever, his grief over Aina's death a powerful minor tone coloring it all. People can sometimes do that. Handle mixed feelings, play the contrast like one single instrument, sometimes in one and the same sentence.

When at last the interrogation proper started, Sixten's role became clearer with each question. For example, the fact that he had waited so long for Ingrid to return to him. Ever since 4.03 p.m., October 23, 1988, as he said without a moment's hesitation.

That was the moment when Edelweiss had contacted Sixten, since Ingrid was on her way to visit Stockholm for the first time in connection with our joint work on the dissertation. And since Sixten still remained on Edelweiss' payroll.

It became clear that he had been Edelweiss' eyes and ears in Sweden for more than fifty years. Not only during the almost twenty years after Sixten saw Ingrid for what he too thought would be the last time: when she was stopped at customs at Arlanda with Meitner's californium—which, according to him, was also when Sweden's nuclear weapons program ended. But also long before that. During the whole period of time from when Sixten, just eighteen years old, came to F.O.A. in Ursvik and became America's clandestine tentacles in the worrying developments in Sweden, with Meitner as its priceless resource: the world's leading nuclear physicist outside of the Manhattan Project.

Edelweiss wondered—just out of curiosity, he said, or maybe it was to emphasize Sixten's loyalty for the rest of us listeners, who might not be as familiar with this distant spy's travails—how much of his time had been devoted to watching over Oskarsson during these last decades. From the time he had been contacted about her in 1988.

It was during the time when Sixten was closing down his

infiltration of the disarmament commissions as a member of the Swedish delegations, because Alva Myrdal and Inga Thorsson were no longer seen as opponents. When global détente was growing, leading in due course to the fall of the Wall and the spectacular collapse of the Soviet Union.

Sixten closed his eyes and counted. Then opened them again and formulated his answer.

"Well, my work relating to Oskarsson must have taken up roughly 40 per cent of my time, in total, over the last twenty-five years. Possibly as much as 45 per cent. Maybe even close to 50."

I could not help smiling at all this pointless accuracy. Edelweiss began to describe a circle with his right foot. But it took a while for Sixten to spot it, that unfailing sign of impatience, as he spelled out his assignment in detail for those of us who did not know.

"During the later part of that period, when your concerns regarding not only Meitner's activities but also Oskarsson's grew, I started to lay out bait on some activist and similar sites which Aina also frequented, so that I could be confident that it would be just us who Oskarsson would get in touch with—when at last she made her long-planned move. But most of my work involved keeping all of you on the other side of the Atlantic updated about Levine's and Oskarsson's work on the dissertation, trying to get a reasonable overview of the Swedish aspect: which archives she visited, the people and institutions she contacted and so on. At that time I think I was working more than full time on Oskarsson. I'd say about a 110–115 per cent, from the moment when she finally made contact with me on October 25, 2008, forty years to the day after we were separated. When she took the bait."

I looked at Sixten, tried hard to understand how far one might be prepared to go just to find relevance. Whether it had ever been out of some sort of conviction.

Zafirah took over the interrogation, cut straight to the point.

"And why did you sacrifice Aina?"

Sixten stared at her. Frozen. As if he had not understood.

"Sacrifice?" he repeated.

Then rolled the word around on his tongue a few more times, as if it were foreign to him. As if his English was less than perfect— as if he had never heard the expression before.

"I assumed it would be enough for me to slip a sleeping pill into her tea, lock her in the kitchen."

We sat in silence, interviewers and interviewees, on the podium as well as in the audience. Sixten leaned forward and drank from the plastic cup on the lectern in front of him. Again I was counting the seconds. *Twenty, twenty-one* . . . The pressure built, a whistling grew in my ears, before he continued.

"There were provisions there, stockpiles of both food and drink. And she could sleep on the kitchen sofa. I did not expect to be away for more than a few days, so Aina would still be in good shape when I got back. She would have had to find a way of dealing with her bathroom needs. But we don't in any case shower more than a few times a week, these days, either of us."

After a long, renewed silence—upward of a minute at least—it was Zafirah who spoke, glancing in the direction of Edelweiss, with a blunt follow-up question.

"I'm afraid I don't understand, Sixten. Enlighten us."

"Well . . . This isn't easy for me, you know."

"Try."

"So . . . the night before I was due to leave, there was this desire between us, for the first time in many years: as if Aina had sensed that this might be the last night . . . for me. It was then that I saw the tattoo on the inside of her left thigh. And bearing in mind what Ingrid had revealed to me, it wasn't that hard to put two and two together. To work out that my adored wife was the key to the whole of Plan B., what Ingrid had termed the 'Needle in the Haystack.'"

Ingrid cleared her throat. Just that—cleared her throat—and let Sixten continue.

"But I had to leave so early in the morning and couldn't think of any reasonable alternative. So I locked the door on her just after she had kept me company with a quick cup of tea. And I am pretty sure that there's only one key to the kitchen. And the window panes would not have been easy to break, with the type of protective glass I've had put in, not without special tools. Yet still she managed to get out of there. My stubborn little Aina."

The last part of what Sixten said was barely audible. One of the two new Kurt-or-Johns went to the very back of the enormous lecture hall and turned up the volume of the loudspeakers.

"And you know how it ended, of course . . . the dreadful thing that Levine did, which I was forced to witness just before you and I had to make our way down into the tunnel system, Zafirah. I recognized my beloved at first sight, even in that costume. My own Alva Myrdal . . ."

I stared straight ahead, felt Sixten's wordless fury and grief from the side. Knew so well that one can live both sides of a double life with equal passion.

Then it was Ingrid's turn to be questioned—and Edelweiss took over.

"First of all I would like to thank you, dearest Ingrid, for helping us start the reboot here in Niscemi. We can reverse your little plan, have the digital footprint of your code sequences, can find the patterns. I don't think it will take us too long to decipher them, put the weapons system back in place again. We may even disable the briefcase without your assistance. Although we would much rather have it—together with the names of your helpers around the world. So we can now once more defend ourselves with the ultimate means, if the same thing is used to attack us. God help us . . ."

If Ingrid had been at all derailed, perhaps to some extent devastated, by Sixten's account of how he had misled her for the whole of their lives together, it did not show. She just sat there ramrod straight, in the shadow of the gallows—still managing to seem untroubled.

"You will not get names—people—from me. You have your counterparts under stones unturned across the world, Ed. Let them do the work. And God help us."

The candle flickered in the warm draft that blew under the door into the lecture hall and she appeared transfixed in the flame for several moments. Then she began again. Said that what both Edelweiss and I had for so long been seeking, "Lise Meitner's secret", did not exist. Not in that sense. That it had been a mere illusion, an integral part of Ingrid's plans for decades.

Edelweiss took the bait right away.

"But Ingrid, this is so interesting . . . do you mean to tell us that the very strange happening at Dulles airport, a nuclear explosion with californium as active substance, did not in fact have anything to do with Meitner?"

"Let me put it like this: causal connections are rarely just causal. So yes, Lise had a lot of californium—relatively speaking—in her possession, a small black case, about two inches long, filled with the world's most valuable substance. She had received it from Glenn Seaborg when he visited her at her home in Oxford in 1966 to deliver the prize. And when I met Lise some years later, shortly before she died, she still did not know why Seaborg had given it to her. Whether he was hoping to hide his discovery from the world, or to give her some token of his affection, or even to pass over to her—the only person he considered his intellectual equal— the responsibility for taking this idea to the next level, before the Russians did. According to Lise, Seaborg had found a new way of producing californium and then keeping it stable with liquid ammonia and another highly secret compound, in a practical container of this sort. A small, copper-lined and battery-powered climate chamber which could maintain a very low temperature for several months. A real *Wunderkammer*, as she called it.

"But I'm guessing that this was a prototype for small nuclear ammunition. We may in other words have been well ahead of the Russians even then—it was only toward the end of the '70s that they managed to construct something similar for the bullets for their much talked about californium pistols. But the cooling device that they needed weighed more than 200 pounds, according to our reports. Which was one reason why the weapons never went into full service."

There was no outward sign that Ingrid was accused of any crime: her demeanor was of someone delivering a report. Except that she was chained to a stool made of stainless steel with a six-foot-five guard standing right behind her.

"But Lise could not test what Seaborg had given her, whether it was something which could have been taken further—assuming she wanted to do that. She would not even have been able to open the container without a substantial risk of exposure to lethal doses of radiation. So before I left her, I had to promise Lise that the case of californium would vanish from the face of the earth. She was adamant that transuranic elements could be used to create even more dangerous Doomsday weapons than we had ever been able to imagine—her own research suggested as much. Her anxiety was that people would never be able to resist the temptation to use them."

Once again she cleared her throat.

"This was the moment that sowed the seeds of pacifism in my mind. Lise demonstrated to me with a simple sketch how one could harness the world's nuclear weapons—and then re-route the network. It may have been no more than a passing fantasy, an impossible dream. But from that moment on I began to work on it. The whole project I called 'Lise Meitner's secret.'"

Silence, a dramatic pause. I could not help but smile at Ingrid's talents, even in a situation like this. Her absolute freedom when anything but free.

"I meant to take the case up to Pluto, leave it underground at the Kiruna mine, inside Mount Doom. Hide it there for eternity— together with the waste from all of our futile attempts to create new nuclear weapons based on transuranic elements. But you stopped

442

me at customs. Took both the case and the key to Lise's underground laboratory in Ursvik."

"Yes, we did have wonderful Sixten to thank for being able to have our people right there at Arlanda, just when you landed after your visit to Oxford," Edelweiss said with a smile.

Ingrid turned to Sixten, her features calm, open, as Edelweiss continued.

"I don't know if you realize this, Ingrid, but you Swedes have always been so flexible. As devoted to betraying secrets as to preserving them. To all this double-dealing. For example, first trying to create your own nuclear weapons and then working hard to prevent anyone else from having them—when things did not go as you had hoped. For you, an arms build-up and disarmament seem to be nothing more than two sides of the same coin, heads or tails, chance rather than destiny. For myself, I'd be very happy to have none but Swedes on my payroll!"

Sixten did not say a word. He just leaned forward and drank another mouthful of water. Maybe it was starting to warm up in here. I was no longer capable of judging, was freezing cold inside. But Ingrid still seemed unconcerned by Edelweiss' little outpouring: his attempt to twist the knife in the wound. She twisted it back.

"After that it was quite a long time before you suddenly asked me to take another look at californium, *Joseph*. And I realize that it might have appeared like a reasonable question at that time, in the mid '80s, when everything seemed possible. That this idea even came up—at the same moment in history, when in all seriousness we were pouring billions into Star Wars: imagining that we would wage nuclear war far out in space. So the thought of californium as an active substance in our new generation of nuclear weapons was indeed no crazier than many other things then. Or what do you say, Joseph?"

Edelweiss' heavy breathing, amplified by his microphone, was the only thing that could be heard in the silence. A hissing sound, as if from a respirator. When he did not answer, she kept going.

"But I soon discovered that the scientific basis wasn't solid, that it would hardly be possible to achieve anything like that on an operational scale within the foreseeable future. I started to fan the flames, however, because I noticed how that old vision still fascinated you all so much: the endless promise and threat of transuranic elements. The possibility of producing small nuclear weapons, pocket-sized but at the same time with unimaginable explosive power, the ultimate Cold War fantasy in modern form. Working on Erasmus' dissertation was also inspiring me with new ideas for disinformation. So I had you all looking the wrong way for decades. At the same time as I slowly but surely undermined the whole system, right under your own feet, you were just standing there staring up at the sky. Into the dust which I was throwing in your eyes."

"Yes, congratulations, Ingrid. I would guess there's only one person in the world who can really understand how you think, see into the remotest corners of your mind. And by a strange coincidence he's sitting there next to you," Edelweiss said.

Still Sixten showed no reaction. Neither did Ingrid. She kept on giving Edelweiss all the answers, since it was all too late in any case. Too late to remedy a lifetime of deceit.

"And of course Aina had that case of californium with her in Ursvik the whole time. In your own home, Sixten, for each of those forty-five years. Somewhere in your freezer, very simply, the first hiding place she could find—since she did not want to touch it ever again. Aina had managed to pocket it in a wonderfully intuitive moment, when she was supervising my hastily assembled preliminary hearing at Arlanda. Sixten, on the other hand, ended up with the key to Lise's laboratory, but he didn't find anything there that he could understand—which is why he was hoping to go down there again with you, Erasmus: the supposed expert on Meitner's secret. If Zafirah and Kurt hadn't fire-bombed the house in Ursvik, flushing us out before he got the opportunity. I imagine that's the only reason he helped you there, my treasure, showed us all the way to escape through the window. He needed you for later."

Ingrid paused, looked first at Sixten without getting any reaction. Then she turned to me, the same calm, open features.

"Imagine my surprise to find the key in your hybrid at the Ice Hotel, having returned there after retrieving the briefcase. We left you to your dreams, Jesús María and I. But I kept wondering, of course. What had my treasure been thinking?"

I could not meet her gaze. She continued before I could form the words to respond, or question—I was not sure which—and her attention returned to Edelweiss.

"Jesús María, my little dark angel, got hold of that small black case of californium during Aina's birthday party last fall. While we were tattooing the codes onto Aina in the bathroom she revealed that after taking the case at Arlanda, she had simply put it away at the back of her freezer, wrapped in some nondescript grease-proof paper, knowing that it needed to be stored at that temperature, and that Sixten would never think of looking there. Hiding it away in plain sight. Aina said she thought it was some kind of explosive charge, but was not much more specific than that. It had later made the move to Ursvik with them, and lain in the kitchen undisturbed until Jesús María grabbed it in the midst of the chaos during the attack on the house, thinking it might come in useful at some point. Then she eventually crafted some kind of device, maybe during our stay in Belgium. Combining the case with a simple detonator she must have stolen from my combat gear, then wrapping it all in Kevlar, with her textile talents."

Once again a pause, while we held our breath.

"So I had no idea what exactly the device was that I helped her insert inside herself in the bathroom at Dulles. Even my fertile imagination did not go that far. But I did think that it would be sufficiently powerful to kill John when he set it off, doing what he always did with Jesús María. I tried hard to dissuade her, but

445

having given her—my blood sister—a promise before our escape from NUCLEUS, I felt I had no argument. So neither I nor, I think, Jesús María, understood the terrifying force with which she was 'impregnated'. The third operational nuclear explosion in history. And one I am going to regret for the rest of my life."

There was then a break in which Ingrid and I were allowed to go to the bathroom in silence, closely guarded by Kurt-or-John, and to drink two plastic cups of water each. On the way back into the lecture hall, we encountered Sixten coming in the opposite direction. He and I looked away from each other, while out of the corner of my eye I saw Ingrid staring straight at him. The trace of a smile passed across her face.

When everybody had returned, the scene was all set again and it was my turn.

"Erasmus, my friend . . . could you give us your own perspective on all this?"

I observed Edelweiss' almost childish curiosity, the breathing which had his whole organism heaving and swaying. I inhaled as deeply as I was able with the chains across my chest—before taking it all from the beginning: in one flow, from the moment I was sucked into Ingrid's maelstrom.

I said that I had begun my university studies with the unusual combination of a major in medieval history and a minor in moral philosophy. When it appeared that I would have the same teacher for both of these very different subjects, it seemed strange at first, as if the college was not approaching this in a very serious way or was suffering from a staff shortage. But then that teacher had linked the topics together in such a spell-bindingly obvious way.

After that came the recruitment to West Point, which took place following my first lectures. I could not at first take the recruiters' quiet questions entirely seriously—I of all people, a drifting pacifist, a young seeker for something, as obsessed with cultural history as with encryption—but then I had fallen hook, line and sinker.

446

The spiral staircase up to the helipad at the university was the frontier between this fundamentally humanistic world and the fundamentally unhumanistic one in West Point's sealed wing. Then the wordless flight over the Hudson, the initiation rite.

I told them I was asked by "Ingrid Bergman" if I wanted to become her first doctoral candidate. That she had just vanished as soon as my dissertation was finished and accepted, against all the odds, her and my vague search for "Lise Meitner's secret" while I myself was stowed away at the Catholic University in Washington.

It was such an incongruous relief to spew it all up, right there, as a witness before my Team, the survivors of what Edelweiss had once called NUCLEUS: our top secret elite force against barbarity, terrorism, the darkness within. Because nothing mattered now. Because the system had in the end swallowed us all, was so much bigger than any one individual. Even an Ingrid Oskarsson, it would seem.

At first Edelweiss did not appear interested. He had after all heard my formal history so many times before, ever since he interviewed me at West Point, the episode that sealed my fate.

It was my private history he was after: what had driven me, attracted me. What it was that could get a person to diverge, head off in a diametrically different direction. So it was at about that point that he started to listen to my account in a different way, to wake up. Edelweiss moved his hand to his face. Passed it over his chins, the rolls of fat, that remarkable landscape of skin and folds, like a foreign planet.

"And at around that time you come into NUCLEUS, my dear lost sheep—only to bale out again later, regardless of the cost. Leaving everything of importance behind. Abandoning house and home. Your beloved wife, the little children with their strange names, who hadn't even reached their teens before you cast them adrift. As you did your country, your assignment, gambling with the fate of the world: placing such huge pressure on our civilisation. What is it that can drive a man to do that? Can you give us any clue, Erasmus?"

I stole a look at Ingrid, searched for words. And then they just came.

"Because I found my way back to the real me, slowly but surely, that lost pacifist who had once upon a time enrolled at university because he had a desperate need for some sort of moral compass. Because I was being hollowed out from inside, until all that was left was a thin shell. Because man doesn't get that many chances to rescue his own world."

The silence was deafening. Edelweiss regarded me with curiosity, more amused than worried, seemed to be waiting for more. I took a deep breath—but Ingrid got in ahead of me.

"I'm sorry, my treasure."

Silence once more, watching and waiting. I thought I caught a glimpse of Sixten giving her a quick glance.

"But those were never your words. They were mine," she said.

I turned, leaned forward to look past Sixten: looked right into Ingrid's blue-gray eyes. Met her gaze.

"I shifted you, Erasmus, hour by hour, month by month, year after year. It was I who sent the cuttings in the brown envelopes to your office. Worked on you with all the methods I had available, finally got you to take the step. To flee with the briefcase, leaving everything behind, your finger still on the trigger."

I stole a look at Edelweiss. Felt some sort of warmth inside. Ingrid was trying to defend me, to save at least one of us. So I just stared at the floor and did not interrupt. Listened to her melodious voice, as I so often had before.

"You had naturally been barred from getting into the missile forces, during your first officer training course, after that incident during the security regulations exam. Do you remember anything of that, my treasure?"

I shook my head, let her go on with her piece of theater. From the rest of the audience there came only the same silence.

"One of those in charge of your training, with whom I worked at the C.I.A.'s Project M.K.Ultra—their mind control project—called me afterward, deeply troubled. He saw your capabilities, of course. The strength, the aggression, the madness, but he had no idea how it could be tamed. So he asked me to try. Promised to cover up what had happened if I came to the conclusion that you could be of any use to us.

"And I had seen the potential already during the first lecture of the introductory course. All this brutality within you, scarcely concealed by an obsessive interest in doing something about it: in moral philosophy, medieval culture, magnificent paintings through the ages, humanity's most brilliant achievements. The very opposite of all this war and destruction. Your questions about 'The Triumph of Death', for example: how animatedly you looked at the painting, with fascination and fear in equal doses, like me. I thought we complemented each other wonderfully. So I decided that you would be the perfect hit man in disguise."

Ingrid waited, gathered her breath. I tried to do the same.

"I took you under my wing. Thought that you could turn out to be the chosen one, my comrade-in-arms to implement the plan which had begun to grow inside me when I met Lise in the '60s, right before Sixten vanished and with him our fantasies about a new Swedish golden age built around nuclear power. Become 'my treasure'.

"During all of our work—somewhat fictitious on my part—on the dissertation, only the two of us, I was free to practice my skills undisturbed. Inculcate you with some sort of pacifist conviction, without making you operationally unusable, take away all that dark energy. I had learned a lot at M.K. about how thoughts take root: what memory researchers came to call 'implants'. Gave you such a strong resistance to ultra-violence that you literally vomited—but only after you had carried out your assignment. All those appalling dreams you told me about during our sessions. And I succeeded in the end with the trigger command itself."

I stared at her, felt myself falling headlong, through layer after layer.

"M.K.'s program for mind control was probably like the bulk of our cutting-edge research from the Cold War. Most of it hocus pocus, pseudo-scientific crap—and some aspects astonishing even by today's standards. We had such endless resources, you see. Yet most of it was buried for fear of what later generations would think. As early as 1973, when I hadn't been in the project for more than three years, I was charged by the head of the C.I.A. with destroying every suspension file at M.K. Tens of thousands of documents, more or less speculative research reports about remote mind control and truth drugs, straight into the shredder, night after night.

"But I've always been a bit rogue, have taken my own decisions. So I kept some things which I thought might one day come in handy. After a few years working as supervisor of Erasmus' dissertation, while at the same time being the Woman with the Briefcase, I then got that question from on high: simply could not turn down the role of Alpha in this new team. All the opportunities which that would give Erasmus and me.

"And our chance came just when I thought we were both going to crack. When I managed to persuade our Administration to fill the gap after the canceled state visit to Russia with an official visit to Stockholm. I could at last contact you, Sixten, and take up your offer of safe harbor during our flight. Even though I knew it would reopen old wounds. Or maybe, to be honest, for precisely that reason."

Ingrid avoided all eye contact with those looking at her, that cross-fire: from Edelweiss and Sixten, Zafirah. Everybody—except me, staring, as much amazed as terrified.

Then Edelweiss cut in with the obvious question:

"You brain-washed your poor doctoral candidate?"

"I wouldn't put it quite like that, Joseph . . ."

She turned to me and I tried very hard not to look in her direction.

"My dear, poor Erasmus, I can understand if you see it that way. But if you do, please interpret it literally: as washing the brain. Getting you to see and think clearly. A terrible invasion of your psyche, that much is true, throughout all those years—but also critical to the cause, as cursed as it's blessed. And this is the only crime I'll confess to. Apart from that, I'll leave judgment and sentence for posterity."

The interrogation could have finished more or less there. But I was scrambling so desperately for a foothold: needed to know before we both vanished without trace. So I put the question, there and then, in front of the congregation, all the witnesses. The one that had been gnawing away at my mind ever since Alpha made contact via the D.V.D. with "Mata Hari", where it all started. Some sort of final "unreality check".

"So was that how you got hold of the key sentence, Ingrid, the whole code system? My main secret from childhood?"

She met my gaze. Took a deep breath, began to mumble, maybe only I could distinguish the words in the phrase.

"*I love you just as senselessly as my pretty weird and hellish father, for the time being and onward into eternity, Amen.*"

I think that everything became still. But inside my head there was a hissing, a roar, as Ingrid went on.

"Erasmus, I'm sorry . . . but I thought we needed something in common that neither of us would forget. Not even when confronted with the worst challenge any human being has ever faced: with Doomsday in the palm of our hand. So I burned my own code system into your subconscious as well. Tested you first with the arachnophobia. And when that was securely lodged I—and you—were ready for that abhorrent memory from childhood. The moment when a mother disappears within herself."

She hesitated for an instant—and then went on to clarify.

"So you have to understand. It wasn't you who made up the code. Not you who had a pathological fear of spiders. Not you who sat there at the kitchen table with your distraught mother, only thirteen years old and showing her the book cipher as some kind of distraction. Who had a dark enough imagination to come up with that peculiar key sentence.

"No, it was me, Erasmus. And my own poor little mother."

7.02

When you no longer understand anything, everything can be a clue.

Which is why, inside the solemn solitude of the isolation cell, I took out my dissertation and started to turn the pages again. From cover to cover, over and over. Trying to remember the exact circumstances in which each separate part had been written. What I had been thinking, what she had said. Who I might indeed have been at various stages.

They had also let me keep my notebook. Not out of kindness, but because they genuinely wanted to know, Edelweiss said. See the end of my chronicle. How I would describe even this unlikely ending. So I did as they—as Edelweiss—wanted, did not know what else to do. Was scrupulous not to change anything to fit the knowledge I now had. Or to judge what might have been real and what was not. In that way I kept the account pathetically innocent, or ignorant, up to and including our interrogation.

The question is, of course, what is credible in all of this: the whole tangle of mind control, multiple agendas and cosmetic transformations. Where the very existence of nuclear weapons, man's ingenious invention for exterminating himself, may in the end be the most unbelievable thing of all. The Doomsday conviction I tried to explore in my dissertation.

You must understand. But you won't.

How there was very nearly no further development, how it could all have been interrupted.

Most of it happened over a few months in 1949.
Robert Oppenheimer, the father of the atom bomb,
came to the conclusion during the fall's demanding
discussions within the General Advisory Committee

of scientists and industrialists. That the next step should under no circumstances be taken. That the hydrogen bomb—the thermo-nuclear weapon, the scientifically miraculous idea of trying to imitate the sun's fusion processes, not fission but fusion of the atomic nucleus, The Evil Thing—should never be either researched or developed.

During the committee's final meeting on October 29-30, 1949, the engineer and businessman Hartley Rowe made his classic remark: "We already built one Frankenstein." Some years later he developed his reasoning: "I may be an idealist, but I can't see how any people can go from one engine of destruction to another, each of them a thousand times greater in potential destruction, and still retain any normal perspective in regard to their relationships with other countries and also in relationship with peace."

The committee's conclusion in its final report to the decision makers could not be misinterpreted. The message was crystal clear. The atom bomb, fission technology, could not be compared with this thermo-nuclear weapon. The hydrogen bomb was something utterly different. Partly from a technological point of view, partly—and primarily—from a moral one.

In their report, the committee described the critical differences between a hydrogen bomb and an atomic bomb. Emphasized that a thermo-nuclear chain reaction of that sort, based on deuterium, heavy hydrogen, would have limitless potential: "This is because one can continue to add deuterium . . . to make larger and larger explosions."

454

But there were proponents. One of them was
Glenn Seaborg, named earlier. During these days
at the end of October 1949, when the committee
held its conclusive meeting, Seaborg was in Sweden
on a lecture tour. He had been invited by Manne
Siegbahn, Meitner's first Swedish scientific
contact. According to some of my sources, Meitner
and Seaborg met during this visit. What they
discussed is nowhere recorded—nor is there an
explanation for the fact that Meitner chose
exactly this moment to become a Swedish
citizen.

In earlier discussions, Seaborg too had been
doubtful about whether the hydrogen bomb should
be developed. But during the visit to Sweden he
wrote a letter to Oppenheimer, which he even
recommended him to show to the committee's other
members. In it, Seaborg strongly supported the
project's historic necessity: the need for a
speedy, full-scale development process. "Although
I deplore the prospects of our country putting
tremendous effort into this, I must confess that
I have been unable to come to the conclusion that
we should not."

Most researchers in the field emphasize
the historical background to Seaborg and others'
conversions. The situation at that point in
history, during and after the convulsions of
the war. Just as the American security services
produced evidence to show that Germany during the
war was one step ahead with the development of an
atomic bomb, the Soviet Union was now the issue.
The dreaded enemy no longer Adolf Hitler, but
Josef Stalin.

In this way, humanity once again found itself in what I call "reverse logic". The one thing that was absolutely unthinkable became the only thing that was absolutely thinkable. Something that required the greatest possible effort, gigantic investments, the depths of mankind's ingenuity, seemed, in the end, inevitable.

After an intensive debate around the turn of 1949–50, the U.S. political and military leadership decided to disregard the committee's almost pleading report recommending that the development work be shelved before it had even been begun in earnest. The arguments in favor of this new kind of nuclear weapon, at that time called the "super bomb", were mostly about being able to destroy the Soviet Union first. "There will be no second time", was a refrain of the advocates of the hydrogen bomb.

In the decision makers' written answers to the scientific committee in January 1950, however, the tone was different. Here there was nothing at all about mutual destruction. The rhetoric had been toned down, and even what remained was colored by the gravity of the moment: the irreversibility of the path toward an impending catastrophe of biblical dimensions. The feeling that even the atomic bomb was no longer deterrent enough.

The Joint Chiefs of Staff regarded it as "necessary to have within the arsenal of the United States a weapon of greatest capability, in this case the super bomb. Such a weapon would improve our defense in its broadest sense, as a potential offensive weapon, a possible deterrent to war, a potential retaliatory weapon, as well as a defensive weapon against enemy sources." The super bomb, they argued, "might be a decisive factor if properly used." They preferred "that such a possibility be at the will and control of the United States rather than that of the enemy."

It was an irony of fate that the man who came to lead the development work, eventually called the Father of the Hydrogen Bomb, was Edward Teller. The same man who, following the dropping of the bombs over Hiroshima and Nagasaki, maintained that a new internationalism was the only solution. The catchphrase for the then relatively comprehensive global movement was "One world or none".

In *Bulletin of the Atomic Scientists*, a magazine launched after the war to give worried scientists a forum within which to try to limit the growth of nuclear weapons technology, Teller had written: "Nothing that we can plan as a defense for the next generation is likely to be satisfactory: that is, nothing but world union."

Just a few years after this, in other words, Teller became responsible for the next historic step in the arms race. This weapon, the hydrogen bomb, was developed without even those most closely involved knowing very much about the consequences. In this case, about the nature of the thermo-nuclear reaction itself.

At first it was believed that the reaction could not be limited: the more deuterium, heavy hydrogen, that one added, the more powerful it would become. A violent process with endless power and duration.

Then Teller changed his mind about that too. There was indeed a limit to the purely destructive potential of the thermonuclear process. At about the 100 megaton level—in practice double that of the most powerful nuclear weapon ever devised, the "Tsar Bomb"—the atmosphere would disappear into space. However much one increased the charge beyond that, only the speed with which the earth's atmosphere would vanish into space would increase. Not the explosive force itself.

This was the type of calculation that set the course for the most advanced scientific project of its time, with by far the greatest budget and an entirely unknown potential. It reminds us of the fact that Nobel Prize winner Enrico Fermi more or less in earnest wanted to make a bet with his research colleagues about whether the atmosphere would catch fire or not, just before the first atom bomb test in New Mexico.

None of those engaged in the development of the thermonuclear weapon had any idea of its secondary effects. How long it would take for our entire civilisation to be obliterated—or if the greater part of our atmosphere would vanish into outer space.

Yet what the scientific committee in its report had called "an evil thing", had a racing start. Like a self-playing piano at top speed. For most of those involved in the development of the hydrogen bomb, everything must have been broken down into detail: thousands of challenging intellectual and practical problems needing to be solved—until the entirety became a fact. Once again, scientific curiosity took over.

Many of those involved have testified to the almost unbearable silence after the test of the first hydrogen bomb, "Mike", in November 1952, during the age of slow communications. The telegram from Teller to one of his key collaborators, Marshall Rosenbluth, therefore came as a great relief.

It contained just four words, in the typically low-key jargon of scientists. A confirmation that history's hitherto worst weapon of mass destruction had now been born without mishap.

"IT WAS A BOY," the message read. No more, no less.

7.03

The last night, I lived that nightmare again. Dreamed that I was back in the subterranean eternity of the facility, carrying out the Test. The missile itself was as ever only a few hundred feet away. Eerily silent in its specially constructed silo, like a gigantic chained beast, a chrysalis brooding day and night under temperature control and exact monitoring of levels and flows.

No detail could ever go wrong. Once a month each of us had to do the Test, to ensure that we still remembered the correct procedures—in case anything should happen, unlikely as it might seem.

Otherwise, here we were to sit all day long, throughout the year, decade after decade, deep underground, so the status quo could continue. Up on the surface the concluding phases of the Cold War would soon be over, the world would spin forward to the fall of the Wall, *détente*, eventually 9/11, our invasions, global terrorism as a kind of counter-attack, the President's fine words about a world free of nuclear weapons. But down here, time had stopped.

I often thought of it as the strangest assignment in the world. The enormous tension which never found its release: 100 per cent concentration on total inactivity. On nothing other than nothing ever happening. The fact that we had created a system all around the world which could never be used, on a scale that was larger than human life.

Equally often I wondered why we operators never received a fraction of the attention the missiles themselves did. Nobody ever checked our levels, flows, the temperature of our brains. So long as we passed the Test, all our lights showed green.

The first question this month was what we would do if the seismic alarm went off in gate L.04 after the obligatory L.F.F. test, the control routines for seeking out Launch Facility Faults. I read swiftly through the multiple choice answers.

(A) Sound the Security Alert.

(B) Contact F.S.C. (Flight Security).

(C) Contact the next gate, L.05, and obtain two confirmations from the E.M.T. team.

(D) Contact M.M.O.C. (Missile Maintenance Operations Control).

And then my mind went blank.

I tried to control my breathing. Knew after all that help was within reach: the crib that had been circulating among us without any fuss, with our commanders' approval, for many decades. That all I needed to do was to make that little sign behind my back to be told the secret, the one that in fact no longer needed to be kept secret from anybody, except during inspections. As was the case now.

The crib was our insurance. As well as that of our superiors, the whole system's.

Because the rigid and non-negotiable requirement from the nuclear weapons command, in other words our political establishment, was that we had to score 100 per cent on the long and demanding Test, each and every time. We were all playing to the gallery. No operator could achieve that. Not in this subterranean solitude, with the inhuman psychological pressure that we faced all day long, with only the mighty missile and its gently sighing premonition of Doomsday for company.

But all I ever needed to do was shape my fingers to make that sign behind my back. Discreetly enough so that only the necessary people would see it: the commander and the person with the crib within reach. My breathing was already back to normal, just the realization that the commander would soon be pushing that paper gently into my hand helped with that.

Which must have been why it took so long—a minute, maybe closer to two—before my pulse really started to race. When I realized that no-one was coming to my rescue this time.

I cast my eyes around the examination hall at Gate L11,

hardly bothering to hide my desperation, even from the inspector, the sullen gentleman furthest back along the wall. At last I caught sight of his smirk. It was the most recently arrived operator, a ginger kid from somewhere in the Mid West, and he was pointing discreetly at his knee under the desk. That is where he had put the crib.

There was a roaring in my temples, I felt the blood coursing in time with my pulse, rising with each second. My uniform jacket was becoming soaked with sweat, everything seeping through.

Desperately I tried to concentrate on the next question. What measures should be taken if "M.O.S.R. X." appeared on the screen in the control room.

The only thing I could recall was that the acronym stood for "Missile Operational Status Response X.". Again I looked over at the new recruit. His eyes were focused downward. Moving between the Test on the desk, and the crib on his knee. No glance in my direction.

I read through the choice of answers as slowly as I could. The acronyms flickered before my eyes. Panic at the thought that I would not be allowed to remain down here, in my blessed sealed-off refuge, poured through my body. That they would dismiss me right away. I heard myself breaking the soft rustling quiet of the examination hall, mumbling the different options:

(A) Begin with an L.F.F. to check whether the information on the computer screen really is correct.

(B) Contact Flight Security immediately.

(C) Call Team immediately using the separate S.I.N. telephone network.

(D) Order an immediate and total evacuation of the facility with the exceptional command Emergency Launch L.F.F. Evacuation.

When I caught up with the new arrival after the Test—just outside the hall, on the way into tunnel T24 heading toward the canteen, in full sight of all the inspectors—I just took him down. Before I smashed his head into the metal floor, not once but repeatedly, the answer suddenly occurred to me.

"Of course, answer 'D'," I said, looking straight into his terrified eyes—and went on: anything can happen when it's "Status Response 'X'!"

7.04

Before they came and fetched me, after a number of days or weeks in my isolation cell, and when I had told them that my chronicle for Edelweiss was complete, I was granted one last telephone call. Custom dictated that one should ring home. A pointless and heart-rending conversation, a repugnant punishment, certainly, for the soon-to-be-deceased, but maybe even more so for the dependents.

Yet I could not stop myself from putting Amba through it. She was now my only hope of hearing some form of truth before it was all too late. Who would recall what I had told her about my mother, maybe even that scene at the kitchen table when I was thirteen, or my spider phobia. Whether I had revealed things I should not have during our first night together, immediately after the welcome for new teachers at The Catholic University. When she and I had poured out our memories to each other: lifetimes in fast-forward. Perhaps said something about once having been a violent young man, which Ingrid had referred to during our interrogation, and not at all the pacifist, before she had started working on me. Or muttered something in my sleep.

If nothing else, I wanted to tell her everything, give her my own version. Try to get her and the children, if not to understand—how could anybody do that?—then in some way to forgive me. At least just say that, for form's sake. As my last rites.

But she did not answer: she never did with unknown numbers. There was only that voice, still teasing, still with the same message I could remember since so long ago. "Hi, it's Amba, I'm probably busy with something incredibly exciting. But leave your name and number and I'll call back as soon as I have nothing better to do."

For a moment I thought of leaving a message. But again . . .

what good would that have done? I pressed the red button, and they took the telephone away.

Then I brought out the reproduction. Bruegel's masterpiece from 1562, more than four centuries before the year of my birth. Almost time enough for his vision to become reality. I laid the picture on the bunk, using a couple of the door-stopper-sized nuclear weapons thrillers from the bookshelves in here to flatten it out. Studied all of its details for the last time. The arc from Bruegel's visions of Doomsday to our own. His yellowed, scorched landscape, the piles of dead, the entire, almost nuclear, apocalypse.

When the clock radio showed 17.00, I switched on the T.V. It was the guards who reminded me because I had lost all sense of time. As the camera swept over the auditorium of the World Forum of Nuclear Weapons Security at The Hague, I could still identify almost all of the ministers, doubles and agents. As well as the "Carriers" of all of the nuclear weapons nations—with their briefcases and professionally neutral expressions: the seven official states' holders of their secrets, codes and rituals.

The red wine was excellent, as was the beef filet, even if I had left the plate standing for an hour or so on the desk under the T.V. I ate slowly, chewed the meat thoroughly. Really tried to savor my last hour. Observed the new Carrier's motionless face a foot or so behind the President: the culmination of what had been the Team's "Revitalization".

Proof of the fact that they had achieved the improbable feat of persuading the decision makers, the very few who were sufficiently in the know, that it really was worth continuing with an asymmetrical little unit like this to carry out asymmetrical warfare. That it was precisely this that had saved mankind on this occasion— skillfully pursuing two defectors, following them all the way into the heart of the conspiracy that had being going on for decades, and which all the others had failed to uncover, all these cherished institutions like the C.I.A., the F.B.I., the N.S.A. and the Secret Service.

That unthinkable strategies could only be revealed by unthinkable structures. That the nuclear weapons system had to be defended with the same conceptual madness that created it.

After the President's formal speech—his constant assurances that a nuclear weapons-free world was the only conceivable solution—I rose to turn off the T.V. Knew that this was what they had wanted to demonstrate. How the show kept rolling on at the nuclear weapons summit, as if nothing at all had happened, while the rest of the world remained in ignorance of the flight and pursuit—as well as the capture. How not even Ingrid and I had been able to make any difference.

But up close to the T.V., I froze. Suddenly I recognized our new Carrier. The same woman I had seen with Sixten in Ursvik, briefly, but long enough for her image to linger. The same guard who took us to Edelweiss' office at Dulles airport. Her appraising ice-blue gaze in the Interview Room, her supple way of moving with the briefcase a couple of meters behind the President on their way out from the Nuclear Weapons Security Forum. It must be Lisa, Sixten's daughter. Ingrid's daughter.

I knocked back the rest of the wine. Thoughts whirled around in my mind. About who I was, about Ingrid, my mother, Lisa . . . This entire tapestry of deception. Who I might once have been. How I had then become somebody entirely different, if Ingrid was ever to be believed. With that lover and that daughter . . .

I tried once more to gather my memories, get them in some semblance of order. The scene at the breakfast table with my mother and the thirteen-year-old who might have been me, her despair, my way of trying to get her to think of something else, the book cipher as distraction, that strange key sentence which had welled up from the darkness inside me. Had this really happened? Could something so real simply never have existed? I tried as best I could to recall what had been said during my and Ingrid's endless sessions on the dissertation, images which were both seared into my mind and faded. My early days at university—how I had been picked up by the recruiters, chosen for special services or the missile forces, at the same time as I threw myself headlong into Ingrid Bergman's moral philosophy lectures.

I grimaced, frowned, scribbled fragments of recollections on the back of the last pages in my account for Edelweiss. My witness statement. Myself as example, held up as a warning to posterity.

Once Edelweiss had it, my report of what can happen when two sufficiently dedicated people make common cause, he would destroy it or bury it in some obscure military archive. And as soon as he was pensioned off, if not before, the next person in charge would look at this little notebook as some kind of refuse from the past. When a new special team would have been in existence for a long time, called NUCLEUS II or something of that sort, and the "Revitalization" would have left our nuclear weapons system bigger and more powerful than ever. Long after Ingrid and I had been erased.

When they opened the door, the line-up was as I had expected. Two groups of guards, four thugs in each. One outside my cell, one outside Ingrid's about fifteen feet away. Her group of guards led by Zafirah, mine by our close combat instructor from Rwanda: with the burns still as a macabre memento from the battle with Ingrid at the M.U.O.S. base. I got to my feet, pushed the note-book into the left-hand thigh pocket of my combat pants, to be delivered to Edelweiss as my last act. Walked through my cell door.

For a moment we stood there like that, both groups. I glanced back at Ingrid. The dark star that had guided me through so much of my life. As impossible to resist as to do her bidding. She who had deceived and transformed me, for good or ill, bewitched me until I no longer had any grasp on who was her and who me. Stately, broad-shouldered, proud and majestic, like Greta Garbo. Like Mata Hari in the movie, on her way to face the firing squad— with no regrets for what she had done.

I had wondered why the director had not used that quotation as a dramatic ending. If, that is, the Dutch dancer and double agent had in fact spoken those words when she was taken from her cell.

But Ingrid used it now.

"I am ready."

The guards did not react to what appeared to be a gesture of submission, a final acceptance. Their expressions remained blank, they stood immobile, waiting. Even our Close Combat instructor in front of me. Zafirah alone tensed her body, but did not make any move, waiting for orders through her earpiece from Edelweiss.

"Farewell, Ingrid. It always was we two against the world," I said.

She did not answer directly, but continued with the last part of the trigger command, apparently so harmless:

"Are you ready, Erasmus?"

8

END RUN

April 2014
Greenland

8.01

Of the ultra-violence which followed that trigger, I have only sporadic memory.

I know this: I would not have managed my escape without Ingrid. She attacked Zafirah without warning, a diversion so that my sister-in-arms from Afghanistan did not anticipate the stab—swift, sharp—into her eyes, my fingers through the orbital socket to the soft tissue of her brain. The shock of slaughter, of the Team's most violent fighter, before the killing had even begun, disarming the guards. Even the Rwandan combat instructor, who must not have recovered fully after the defeat at Niscemi. Between us, Ingrid and I erased or maimed—hard to know in the frenzy—them all. Broke out to the corridors and the two armed guards along the way, where—this I believe—Ingrid sacrificed herself as a parting gift to me. Distraction as art. Her action for my freedom. Her line of defense, drawing fire, permitting my exit into the surrounding streets.

Memory returns. I was hidden for some precious hours by local tradesmen, bitter opponents of the Niscemi base. Within their network, they organized my place on a fishing boat and away from Italy. From there, bound for Copenhagen, I hid on a large cargo vessel, then smaller boats, the last an icebreaker with only the most basic storage. Finding or stealing what I needed as I traveled north.

It was not difficult to bypass the checks in Thule harbor, under cover of the crowds that gather when the first ships arrive with packages and the mail after long winter months. All this yearning for home. People in environments for which they were not intended.

After a rapid march, in part a steady run, I completed the 150 miles over the ice to my goal. The temperature rose at first but then it fell, although never becoming unbearable. The moon shone from a clear sky and revealed traces of the facility, both upper and lower parts. The multi-layered secret—like Ingrid's and Sixten's work on what they called First, Second and Third Tier development, and from about the same era. The beginning of the 1960s. The time of promise, of lies and illusions, of Doomsday dreams.

A slight indentation in the glacier was the only sign. Small but decisive evidence of what could not remain hidden through the decades, although we had been convinced it would. The start of the way in, below. I crept and wormed my way through the metal ventilations shafts, instead of the usual entrance along much wider but already collapsed upper ice tunnels.

And now I sit down here, at my destination. Around me hangs the inner darkness of the continental ice. I let the headlamp I found in a storage room on the cargo vessel play over the walls, and gape, amazed at what mankind can create: cannot stop the tears. I have never seen anything so overwhelming, or so insane. This gigantic hall under the glacier, at least fifteen feet high and three hundred by three hundred in area, excavated and sculpted in the smallest detail, with fixed chairs, benches and work surfaces entirely made out of ice.

It is a little like the Jukkasjärvi Ice Hotel, but in deadly earnest, literally so. Edelweiss told us that ice was the chosen material even here in the command center, making everything as flexible as possible. So that this whole interior could be torn down and built back up again, in a few days at most.

The chair I am sitting on is broad and theatrical, like a frozen throne. Covered with Arctic fox fur, still in perfect condition, from the mammal with the best protection against extreme cold. One of the few which has really adapted to this environment. So we humans have just taken its equipment, put the chalk-white protective material on a number of the bare ice surfaces down here.

But the most remarkable thing stands in front of me: the enormous control panel. The only thing in here not made of ice. The very heart of this command center for the thousands of launch sites which were going to be built under the ice, where hundreds of climate-modified Minuteman missiles, called "Iceman", were to be aimed at Russia.

This whole construction was intended to be bigger even than the Inner Circle in Ursvik, under a surface area three times the size of Denmark, with a complex tunnel network for the missiles, 2,500 miles long.

So the code name "Project Iceworm" was perfectly apt. Edelweiss had called it an historical high point, never since exceeded, in double-dealing and underground engineering. Above the ceiling of the command center was the official part of the project, called "Camp Century". What we presented to the Danish authorities as an experimental station for cutting-edge research into how man should not only be able to survive but also thrive in an arctic environment, fully equipped with stores, library and chapel.

Now the control console is as defunct and abandoned as the rest of this masterpiece, both the official upper level and the lower top secret level. The system as a whole was powered by the world's first mobile nuclear reactor, which was removed before the facility was deserted in the mid '60s, after only a few years of operation, when the geologists established that Greenland's pack ice was not at all as stable as had at first been thought. That the elasticity in this natural material would cause the installation to break up, the missile tunnels and command center down here as well as the lodgings and low-temperature laboratories above.

So it was all left behind, in the greatest haste, like the Inner Circle. Was allowed to remain standing as it was—because the falling snow would cause the ice sheet to grow even thicker, burying the secrets under a blanket of eternity.

But then came the greenhouse effect. According to some calculations, it would not take more than a few decades before traces of these highly classified installations would literally surface. Radiation and nuclear fallout had already started to become an issue between our Administration and Denmark's, each of us N.A.T.O. partners, and soon the new revelations would make the relationship poisonous.

So I find myself sitting here, alternating between writing and just gazing. Everything feels as if in a movie: with the help of my headlamp I can change the scenes, from close-up on the pale bluish sheen on the desk in front of me to wide angle on the similar nuance of the walls. Light up the historic darkness of the Command Center, this palace of ice.

An exploration of my immediate surroundings has revealed much that is still well preserved down here, as if it were a museum of man's worst fantasies. Even some rudimentary food supplies are largely intact, freeze-dried, but there are also cans and some powdered soups. Some of the gas canisters are still functional. I could keep myself going down here for months more, far longer than I will need.

And when I also discovered the parchment, everything became clear to me. What I would have to do with all that is in my notebook, now that Edelweiss can no longer bury it.

Because the world of paper has been superseded by the digital age, and still nobody knows how long information recorded with either medium will last. All those war directives, indispensable instructions for everything from nuclear weapons to cipher systems, the bureaucracy of conflict. Turning to dust or vanishing into thin air. But parchment on the other hand has a track record. The Dead Sea Scrolls, for example, are still legible—two thousand years after they were written—having been stored in a cave.

Edelweiss had talked about it during one of his historical presentations on the subject of Camp Century and Project Iceworm at the beginning of the '60s. Said that among numerous scientific experiments on the effects of extreme cold performed in this location, there had been tests carried out in collaboration with the Library of Congress which showed that very low temperatures were effective in preserving parchment: it remained in the

474

same mysteriously natural state as early man and mammoths found buried in ice. This was interesting to us too, he said, now that the short, digital era appeared to be nearing its end. When the R.S.A. encryption had more or less been cracked—and no form of digital storage could promise data integrity for more than a century at most.

So I take one of the preserved rolls out of the half-century-old metal cupboards and unpack it. One can still make out the veins of the dead animal, the sheep from which the parchment came, a slight blue blemish within the writing surface. With a certain reverence I pick up one of the special pens which I find beside the packages.

Then I start to transcribe my testimony from the notebook to the parchment. Despite the damage it has suffered during the months of my flight, the damp and cold, blood and impact, the journey here, it is mostly legible. I keep adding things as well. Descriptions of nightmares, my inner musings, parts of my dissertation as I still recall them.

In short, the whole of this account as you have now found it and are reading it. You, posterity, whoever you may be. Somewhere in my future and your present. After a certain time—a week, two, more, it is no longer possible to measure time deep under the inland ice—it is finally ready. Now comes the conclusion.

My headlamp does not reach as far as the door at the opposite end of the hall. But the route is familiar to me. I have memorized the sketches ever since Edelweiss' historical lectures, regarded this as my ultimate goal long before Ingrid began sending her encrypted messages to the cell phone at the playground. When I realized that I would not be lowering the briefcase and myself under the so-called "eternal" ice, as I had dreamed and feared, but would instead meet Alpha somewhere 253.3 feet under the surface of Stockholm. And then proceed onward in her company, without having any idea where we were going.

I shiver—maybe because of the memories, the situation I find myself in, this monumental solitude—but hardly from the cold. The atmosphere down here is as mild as I had expected. Edelweiss told us about the mysterious hot springs found under the continental ice, like discoveries of gold, when work started on producing this ambiguous facility at the end of the '50s. That they were the reason why the temperature could be markedly higher in this hidden lower level than in the officially open higher one.

This too is where I shall now be going, lowering myself into eternity in the largest of those hot springs. Having hidden my chronicle so that any pursuers will never find it—but you will, when everything is revealed by the parchment. And because the whole installation will surely rise to the surface long before my chronicle is irreparably damaged.

This is the only way for you to get to know my story. Start to imagine all these unimaginable things. Realize that NUCLEUS, the Inner Circle and Project Iceworm, the nuclear weapons themselves, did once exist. Were an actual part of our reality.

Because you must understand.

And maybe you finally will.

I brace myself, tense my body, ready myself for the last short stage of all. Get up from the throne of ice, leave the command console, walk through the next, smaller hall, the last one. And there it is: a simple little cross on the door the only sign.

The chapel down here is modeled on the one up there, a part of the whole civilian community built as a *trompe l'oeil*. Scenery and mock-ups to hide the truth, one level down.

I open the door, which only offers a slight resistance after all these years. The feeling of reverence is almost paralyzing. I move at a snail's pace, as if sleep-walking. In here, too, everything is made of ice. On Edelweiss' photographs, the crucifix was reminiscent of the one in Jukkasjärvi.

Then he had also showed us pictures from after the abandonment of the installations. The crucifix had for some reason been the only thing, apart from the nuclear reactor, to have been removed. His theory was that it could well have been a group of curious urban explorers who visited and took this most significant souvenir with them.

I search the wall with the light from my lamp, soon find traces of the upper hole, just visible. Try with a screwdriver from the engine room on the icebreaker. At first I make no progress— but after long enough, with sufficient persistence, the tip finally penetrates the surface. Then I move the screwdriver around to enlarge the gap. The ice which surrounds it is significantly more solid, like cement, almost diamond hard.

The result is quite simply the perfect hiding place. When I push in the rolls of parchment, as I soon will, and then cover the hollow with ice which has fallen while I was digging away, nobody will be able to find it. Not before the walls melt, and the ceiling, this entire place is laid bare by the effects of climate change.

But before I complete my account for you in what I hope will still be some sort of posterity, I sink or perhaps fall on my knees here in the chapel. Clasp my hands and for the first time in many years say a prayer. For our nuclear weapons future. For you, for us, for myself. Whoever I might be.

Then I pick up the pen again, scratch the last lines into the parchment. Close my eyes, listen to the silence, feel the mild air of the eternal ice against my eyelids.

In just a few minutes it will definitely be over: when I have walked the four hundred feet or so from here to the hot spring and disappeared for ever.

After that, it will all be up to you.

EPILOGUE: OVERTIME

The woman stared at him, with the most intense gray eyes he had ever seen.

"Do you remember who Tomoya Kawakita was?"

The doctor shook his head, turned his back to the woman and ripped the sealed package of the syringe open, checked the fluid level, started the ritual.

He glanced through the glass pane at the broad outline of the single figure on the other side, from the light to the dark. The intention was obviously that he should not see who was standing out there.

The silence became oppressive.

"A baseball player, ma'am?" he finally said.

"Baseball player?"

"Yes, ma'am. You'd be surprised how many like to talk baseball in this situation."

It was casual chat, gallows small talk: the only strategy he found bearable. Some said that it helped the subject to cope.

"I see . . ." the woman said. "No, he was a Japanese American, the last one convicted by us of treason, 1948, just over half a century ago. Mistreated our prisoners in the camps during World War II."

Her voice was hypnotic, as in a lecture hall, or maybe a therapist's. The doctor had to master himself to continue his preparations. Turned without a word to the woman, rolled up the left sleeve of her tunic as she continued:

"But he was reprieved in 1953, by Eisenhower."

Still silent he tapped the point on her arm, a few times more than necessary. The vein was clear to see under the skin.

"Do you have any clue what I've done?"

The doctor had been here before.

"Of course you're totally innocent, ma'am, acted in good faith or self-defense. I expect you tried to save the world."

He gave her a smile. Of respect and of humility for his task.

"Something like that," the woman said.

She met his gaze, smiled back. The doctor felt the heat spreading through his body, as if he himself were being infused.

Then he looked away and raised the syringe.